POOR LITTLE DEAD GIRLS

Lizzie Friend

Merit Press

F+W Media, Inc.

Published by Merit Press
an imprint of F+W Media, Inc.
10151 Carver Road, Suite 200
Blue Ash, OH 45242. U.S.A.
www.meritpressbooks.com

Trade Paperback ISBN 10: 1-4405-8453-2
Trade Paperback ISBN 13: 978-1-4405-8453-4
Hardcover ISBN 10: 1-4405-6395-0
Hardcover ISBN 13: 978-1-4405-6395-9
eISBN 10: 1-4405-6396-9
eISBN 13: 978-1-4405-6396-6

Printed in the United States of America.

10 9 8 7 6 5 4 3 2 1

Cover design by Stephanie Hannus.
Cover image © 123RF.

This book is available at quantity discounts for bulk purchases.
For information, please call 1-800-289-0963.

Chapter 1

"Living here is going to kill me, Dad. Even the dogs look like snobs."

Sadie watched as a poodle in an argyle sweater pranced down the sidewalk outside the window of their old Camry. Its hair was shaved into a pattern of puffy snowballs—its body mostly bare—and the puffs on each ear were dyed the same shade of pink as its owner's crisp polo shirt. She groaned and looked over at her dad in the driver's seat. "I mean, seriously. I'm not even sure that lady's an actual human and not some Stepford robot engineered to look rich and smug."

He stifled a laugh. "Just remember what a great opportunity this is. If an athletic scholarship to UVA or Northwestern means spending a few years eating tea sandwiches with WASPs who like to humiliate their canines, then so be it." He grinned, and she couldn't help but laugh.

"And don't be so judgmental," he added. "It makes you sound like some hick from Oregon who doesn't know how to use the right fork during the salad course."

She rolled her eyes.

"It's the small one, by the way. That will probably be on a test at some point, so you're welcome."

She turned back to the window. When the letter came last spring, inviting her to transfer to the school on a full athletic scholarship for lacrosse, they had sat at the kitchen table for hours, trying to decide how the hell to react. A part of her thought it was a dream come true—Keating had one of the best teams in the country, and there were college scouts at all of their home games. Plus, her mother had gone to Keating, back when she was happy, before she became just a person in a photo whom Sadie could barely remember.

But the rest of her couldn't stop thinking about how wrong for her the school was. It was incredibly exclusive. The President's kids had

5

gone there, and they had an airstrip a few miles off campus for private jets. Tuition there cost more than most Ivy Leagues. It was a completely different world, and she wasn't sure she wanted to be a part of it. Still, they had eventually decided the scholarship was too good to pass up, and now here she was, driving through a posh Virginia suburb with her dad and her whole life in the back seat.

The houses on either side of them grew bigger as they left the center of town, each one massive and swollen, like each extra wing and balcony was built to accommodate another bulge in its owner's undoubtedly massive ego. There was no other explanation, she thought, for a house the size of a small shopping mall. They were set far back from the road, each one protected from the unwashed masses by a wide swath of grass so green and manicured it looked like AstroTurf. She saw swimming pools and tennis courts, and she even spotted a few polo players trotting their ponies around in one particularly large field. That was a first. The only polo players she saw in Portland wore goggles and Speedos and constantly complained about the effects of cold water.

The mansions thinned and finally disappeared, and an hour later they were driving through rolling green hills. They turned onto a narrow side road and passed a wooden sign that bore two crests, one for Keating, and one for its nearby brother school, DeGraffenreid Academy. The Keating crest was a shield decorated with what looked like a fox, a bunch of swords, and a knight's helmet. Sadie rolled her eyes. If it turned out jousting was part of the curriculum, she was going to have some serious second thoughts.

They followed the road for at least ten more miles, weaving through hills and forest until they started to smell the salt in the air. The trees were thicker this close to the coast, and the roads were dark and cool in the dense shade.

As they came around another bend, something on the side of the road caught Sadie's eye. It was a wooden cross that years in the damp forest had covered with moss. At its base was a single bouquet of roses that was slowly turning to dust. She watched the cross fade away in the Camry's rear-view mirror, until her dad patted her on the knee.

"You ready for this, kid?" he said, raising his eyebrows. "Because I think this is your stop."

He pointed ahead, and she saw the entrance to Keating Hall, every bit as stately and intimidating as it looked in the brochure. The gate was wrought iron with a heavy arch and stone pillars on either side of the doors. In the center were the initials GLK, for Gerald Leland Keating, the school's namesake and first headmaster. A stone wall snaked off into the woods on either end of the gate, encircling the campus on three sides.

On her visit to the school last spring, her host Jessica had told her the wall was originally built in the '20s after the then-headmaster's daughter had caused a huge scandal by getting pregnant after sneaking through the woods to Graff to see her boyfriend. Supposedly, he had kicked her out of school, sent her to live in a convent in Maine, then built the wall to prevent any future students from shaming the school like she did.

"The only direction we can go now without feeling locked up like a bunch of horny virgins is to the athletic fields or to the beach," Jessica had joked, rolling her eyes. "I guess the headmaster was worried about us slutting it up, but he wasn't too concerned about us drowning." She had grinned, and Sadie had started to think that life at Keating might not be so bad with Jessica around.

She had been so nervous on her way to Virginia to visit—she had fully expected her host to take one look at her mall sweater and dirty green tennis shoes and decide she wasn't worth ten minutes of her time. But she was so wrong. She had been sitting in the admissions office, staring at the pages of an old *New Yorker* when Jessica had marched in, scanned the room, and started toward Sadie.

"Oh my god, I so wish I was wearing jeans right now," she had said, and her words had echoed loudly against the vaulted ceiling. "So cute, by the way—are they Tate Denim? Love that super dark wash." Before Sadie could answer, she rambled on.

"This effing uniform skirt is so uncomfortable. They always brag about how they're designer, or whatever, but please—we all walk around here looking like we're wearing, like, the least sexy, sexy school-girl costume, ever." She made an exaggerated curtsy and showed off her conservative knee-length plaid skirt, navy blazer, white socks, and flat loafers. "Hot, right?" She had smiled and held out her hand.

"I'm Jessica. I'm on the lacrosse team, so Coach asked me to show you around and stuff. I'm from Illinois, so she thought we would get along—you know, not being east coasters and all. I don't think she realizes everything west of Virginia isn't just one big cornfield where everyone knows each other, but whatevs." She spread her arms wide. "Welcome to Keating."

They had talked all day as Sadie followed her from class to class, and by lunch she felt like they had known each other for years. Jessica was petite and pretty, with light brown hair, dark brown eyes, and a splatter of freckles across her nose, the kind of girl who looked like she was born to be a summer camp counselor and was probably really good at gymnastics. They had stayed up late in Jessica's dorm room, gossiping about guys ("Graff guys are terrible—they're like mini corrupt politicians in training"), teachers, and the other girls on the team ("Thayer's a bitch, but she's the best middie, like, ever, which makes it a little easier to deal with having her around"). By the time her dad had picked her up at the airport the next day, the idea of coming to Keating sounded almost tolerable. She had traded e-mails and texts with Jessica all summer, and Sadie was excited to see her again.

They pulled up to the gate and gave a uniformed guard their names. After a series of beeps, the doors swung open and they started the drive through campus.

Keating and Graff were some of the oldest schools in the country, and according to the brochure, Graff's original buildings had been occupied by Union troops during the Civil War. There was even an old military fort near the school's campus that overlooked the water. Keating had been built up a lot since then, and with all its red brick and dramatic columns, it looked like a sprawling Jeffersonian castle, tucked away on the Atlantic coast.

They drove through the grounds, passing first by the headmaster's house, a New England–style mansion with black shutters and a widow's walk on the shingled roof. There was a flashy yellow sports car parked in the driveway, and it looked so out of place next to the grand old house, it was like someone had pasted a full-color magazine cutout onto an old sepia photograph. As they made their way into the quad, her dad let out a low whistle.

"This place is incredible," he murmured, a little accusingly. "You just said it was 'nice.'"

Sadie sighed. It was beautiful, but it just didn't feel like somewhere she belonged. It was too perfect—so immaculate and contrived it was almost creepy.

The quad was a big oval of green grass dotted with shady oak trees and surrounded by the school's main buildings. At the center of one side was Sadie's dorm, a hulking mansion called Ashby that would house all of the junior and senior girls. In front of it, paths snaked across the grass, and everywhere there were small benches, lining walkways or tucked into little coves shaded with flowering vines. Each one was different, some iron, some stone, and branded with a little engraved plaque.

Jessica had explained they were all graduation gifts from former students. Some seniors gave money or rare books to the library, but others donated benches so the students who came after them would have somewhere to sit and stalk people online between classes. When she graduated, Sadie was hoping a card would suffice.

As they circled the drive, one bench caught Sadie's eye. It was small and concrete—more like a simple park bench than the legacy of some rich oil baron's daughter—but there was a huge bouquet of wilting calla lilies at its base. She thought of the sad little cross outside the main gates, and a chill rippled across her shoulder blades. Either dead flowers were another part of rich-people etiquette she just didn't understand, or the students at Keating were really big on memorials.

In front of Sadie's dorm, girls were already flitting back and forth from their cars to the front doors, stopping to hug one another, screeching like mating hyenas, and politely shaking parents' hands. Most of the cars were sleek black limos being dutifully unpacked by their uniformed drivers, and the rest were imposing SUVs in black or silver. They pulled up behind a Mercedes SUV with dealer plates and stopped the car, the Camry making its usual slow, sighing death rattle as the engine cut off. Her dad turned to look at her, his face expressionless.

"You know, it's not too late, Sadie May. We can turn this car around and drive all the way back to Portland." He paused, and a smile played at the edges of his mouth. "I might not even make you pay me back for gas."

She tried not to smile and let her head fall to the side. "Dad, I'm staying. Don't make this harder than it already is."

He broke into a wide grin. "All right, just checking. Let's unpack this luxury ride, shall we?"

Half an hour later, she stood next to the car and tried not to cry like a little kid getting dropped off at sleepaway camp.

"Call me," he said. "Every week. And don't smoke."

She laughed. "Come on, Dad. We both know what smoking would do to my mile time."

He held up his hands, palms out.

"Just had to say it." He took a last glance around the quad and slowly shook his head. "Oh, and don't go joining any of those creepy secret societies either. Or start playing squash. Rich people tend to have really weird ideas about what people should do for fun."

She arched a brow. "I'll be fine, Dad. This isn't a Lifetime movie."

He chuckled, then laid a big hand on each of her shoulders. "You know, your mom would be really proud of you for doing this. She always wanted the best for you." His voice broke, and she nodded. She could feel her eyes start to sting.

"And I'm proud of you, too. I love you, and I'm going to miss you like crazy. Try to have fun, though, okay? And don't forget why you're here."

He pulled her in for a big hug and then climbed into the driver's seat.

"Remember, kid: You're every bit as good as all of these girls, and you're probably a heck of a lot better than most of them. Don't forget that." He started the car, draped an arm out the open window, and called out, "Go get 'em tiger," as he drove off toward the gate.

She waved at his taillights, letting the realization sink in that she wouldn't see him again until Christmas. After the Camry was long gone, and limo after black limo had roared off behind it, she finally pulled herself away.

She followed two blondes as they glided up the steps toward Ashby's entrance, the heavy double doors yawning open to swallow them whole. At the top she squared her shoulders, and closed her eyes. Cool air billowed out onto the landing, raising goose bumps on her skin and pulling her forward. She took one more deep breath, opened her eyes, and stepped inside.

Chapter 2

She blinked. The inside was like a cross between a luxury hotel and the kind of rickety old mansion you would see in a bad horror movie—the kind where it's always raining and the characters get killed off, one by one, starting with the black guy and the girl with the biggest boobs. It was beautiful in a stuffy, old-fashioned kind of way, but it made her feel heavy, like the building had its own gravitational pull.

The small foyer opened into a wide great room with high ceilings, thick oriental rugs, and couches arranged in clusters around tiny coffee tables. Directly ahead was a marble staircase that curved up from the floor in two directions, each one leading to a different wing. She followed the matching blondes up the one to the right, swimming in the wake of their heavy perfume.

She found her room on the third floor and pushed inside. The other two beds were still empty, but she knew that wouldn't last. Room assignments at Keating were supposed to be random—part of the school's commitment to their "code of sisterhood" (Keating girls were all one family, regardless of age, race, or inheritance). But, the school was 95 percent white, and, according to Jessica, the girls from the richest families always ended up rooming with their closest friends. Which meant Sadie's roommates were probably going to be other scholarship kids—or lepers.

She shut the door behind her and sat down on one of the beds, a classic four-poster tucked into the corner next to a wide bay window. She glanced outside and watched as a girl in enormous sunglasses stood in the road with her hands on her hips. She was berating a chauffeur as he walked by, clutching a pink garment bag and shrinking away from her like she was contagious.

She sighed, her breath fogging up the antique panes. "Screw 'em, right Dad?"

Suddenly, she felt exhausted. They had been driving for three days, and she had barely slept. She reached into one of the big, plastic bags she had brought along, packed with bedding, picture frames, and useless little knickknacks her dad had convinced her she might need at school ("You definitely need a solar-powered flashlight, Sadie. What if there's a power outage?"). She pulled out her new, bright yellow comforter and threw it on the bed. Without even bothering to take off her shoes, she curled up right on top of the mattress and pulled it over her head.

In the warm, muffled darkness under the blanket, she tried to remind herself why she was here. Lacrosse, lacrosse, lacrosse. A college scholarship would make everything worth it. Even if she had stayed in Portland and managed to get into one of her dream schools, they would never have been able to pay for it. Keating was a good thing. As long as she survived the next two years.

She knew she shouldn't complain. Her dad made good money and she had always had whatever she needed, but when Sadie had been just a few years old, her mother had gotten sick. Not physically sick, like with cancer, but she was in and out of intensive therapy programs, rehab, and even psychotherapy, for years. Her dad had done everything he could to get her mom the help she needed, but by the time she died, all of their savings were gone and they had a long list of debts to pay. Now all these years later, she only had one image left from that day: her dad, sitting on the floor in the living room with the lights off, tears streaming down his face.

A squeal came from somewhere outside her blanket force field.

"Get your ass up, Sadie. I'd know those nasty old shoes anywhere."

Sadie peeked out from under the covers and saw Jessica standing in the doorway in a pair of crisp white shorts and a navy polo. Sadie jumped up and ran to the door.

"Oh my god, please tell me you're my roommate." She gave Jessica a big hug.

"I wish. They always put transfers together, so I'm guessing you'll be with two other new girls." Jessica jerked a thumb over her shoulder. "I'm down the hall with Madison Plath. Why don't they just kill me now and get it over with? She has her army of feng shui consultants in there right now trying to reorganize the place." She waved a hand at the empty beds. "Your roommates aren't here yet? That's kinda weird."

Sadie shrugged. "Who knows? Rich people are never on time, right?"

"Very funny." Jessica picked one of Sadie's pillows off the floor and whacked her with it.

"For your information, I've been here since noon getting my crap together and waiting for your ass to show up. And here you are, sleeping on a bare mattress with all your crap strewn around the room in plastic bags."

"Ugh, I know. I should probably hide the evidence that I bought all my stuff from Target, right? Just so they don't immediately realize I'm a charity case."

"Meh, who cares. Everyone Googles the new kids, so there's no point trying to hide it. Want some help unpacking?"

They spent the next hour arranging all of Sadie's clothes in the dresser, hanging her uniform skirts, blazers, and polos in the armoire, and trying to make the room feel like home.

"Posters help," Jessica said, nodding toward the empty walls. "Madison already covered, like, half the room in Fever Stephens glamour shots." She rolled her eyes. "It's weird staring at his creepy airbrushed abs all day, but at least I don't feel like I'm at my Nana's."

Sadie was pulling the last few items out of her duffel bag—a framed photo of her mom, dressed in yellow and holding a young Sadie on her hip, and a handful of medals from lacrosse tournaments—when they heard a knock on the door. It was three quick raps—authoritative, official. She opened the door to two imposing men in dark suits, each at least six feet tall with broad shoulders and dark glasses.

"You must be here about the aliens," she deadpanned. They didn't smile, but she heard Jessica suppress a laugh.

"Miss, please vacate the room," the one on the right barked.

The two men kept their chins pointed straight ahead as they talked, giving the impression they weren't really speaking to Sadie at all, but rather casting their commands out into the universe and just expecting it to obey.

"We need to do a sweep."

What the hell? She looked back at Jessica, who was sprawled on the bed on her stomach, paging through last year's Portland South yearbook. She just shrugged, but the expression on her face said this wasn't usual procedure.

"Uh, this is my room. Is something wrong?"

"It's protocol," the giant on the left said to the space a foot above her head. "Please wait outside."

It clearly wasn't a request. She stood in the doorway and hesitated, wondering if this was some sort of hazing ritual new students had to go through. What did they think she would bring, unauthorized snack foods? Counterfeit designer jeans?

Before she could decide how to react, a tiny woman wearing a sleek black suit squeezed through Right and Left and extended a small, bony hand. Her icy blonde hair was pulled back into a tight chignon at the base of her skull, and she wore high black pumps and nude stockings, despite the heat. Even with the heels, she just barely reached Sadie's shoulders.

"Hello ladies," she said in a thick English accent. She nodded to each of them without smiling. "I'm Ellen Bennett, and I apologize for this rudeness on behalf of my staff." She threw a look over her shoulder at Right, who cleared his throat in mild protest. "I'm the personal secretary and chief of security for His Grace Charles Windsor Everleigh the Third, Duke of Devonshire. His daughters, The Lady Gwendolyn Everleigh and The Lady Beatrix Everleigh will be your new flat mates. Now, which of you is,"—she paused and looked down at her clipboard—"Sadie Marlowe?"

"That'd be me," Sadie said, still absentmindedly shaking the woman's hand. Ellen gave her a tight smile and slithered her hand out of Sadie's grasp, drawing it back and holding it close to her chest in a fist.

"How grand." With a quick wave of her hand, Right and Left marched into the room, brushing Sadie aside in the process. Ellen walked in after them and cast a calculating glance around the room. Her eyes stopped when they landed on Jessica, still lying on the bed with her chin in one hand.

"Would you be so kind as to go back to your own room, Miss?" she said. "I need to go over some details with Ms. Marlowe and ensure the room is up to our specifications."

"I would be happy to," Jessica said, giving Ellen a sweet smile that dripped with sarcasm. She walked toward the door and made a gagging gesture only Sadie could see. Sadie bit her lip to hold back a snort.

"Ms. Marlowe, can you come over here please?" Ellen smoothed a pillow on the window seat and gingerly sat down, crossing one thin knee over the other and looking up with poorly concealed impatience. Right and Left were making their way around the room, peering behind the furniture and scanning the walls with a small black device. Sadie crossed the room and sat down, leaning back against the cushions and tucking her legs underneath her.

"What's up?"

Ellen looked at her for a moment, an odd expression on her face, then handed her the clipboard. She drew a black fountain pen from one of her blazer pockets and laid it on top of the form.

"I'll just need you to read this carefully, then sign it. It is very important that you understand every detail of the contract, so I would be pleased to answer any questions you may have." She didn't look pleased to be doing anything, so Sadie just nodded and started reading. The contract was some sort of confidentiality agreement, one that prevented her from, as it stated, "revealing to the press, the public, her parents, the other students, or any other interested party anything she learned specifically relating to her status as roommates of The Lady Beatrix Everleigh and The Lady Gwendolyn Everleigh." That and seven other pages of crap that didn't make any sense.

Sadie finished skimming it and looked at Ellen. "Um, I'm not really sure I want to sign this. I'm not even really sure what it means. Why would you need this?"

Ellen sighed heavily. "Ms. Marlowe, what do you know about the Everleigh family?"

Sadie hesitated. "Well, I know they're important enough to have bodyguards, and that their daughters are my roommates." She held up the clipboard. "And apparently they don't want anyone to know whether or not they wear embarrassing jammies?"

Ellen nodded gravely, ignoring her sarcasm. "Yes, Ms. Marlowe. They are important. His Grace is a very, very important man." As she said this, she puffed out her thin chest and squared her shoulders, as if she were expecting Sadie to be floored by the prestige of her position. "And privacy is of the utmost importance to the Everleigh family. Keating's code of sisterhood does not permit transfer students to live in private rooms, so we have been faced with a difficult situation." She looked hard at Sadie before continuing. "The Everleighs want some reassurance that you will appreciate the gravity of this situation, and respect their privacy as public figures and members of the English nobility. Do you understand?"

"Okay," she said slowly. "But I can't guarantee I'm never, ever going to talk about my roommates. I mean, I can't tell my friends what music they listen to or what we talk about? This is high school. That's kinda what we do."

"Well, you'll find a more worthwhile way to spend your time if you want to continue living in this room, and if you want the pleasure of the company of some of the most celebrated young women in England. I might suggest poetry or classical piano. Beatrix and Gwendolyn excel at both of those pursuits."

Sadie focused every bit of her energy on keeping her eyes from rolling into the back of her head. Her roommates were celebrated—celebrated, piano-playing, poetry-reciting British freaks who were definitely not going to be down for scarfing Cheetos and watching *Diva Divorcées* reruns after lights out. She could feel disappointment settling into her stomach like day-old Chinese food. If you couldn't OD on trans fats and trashy TV with your roommates, what was the point of boarding school at all?

Ellen paused, then spoke slowly and deliberately, her eyes never leaving Sadie's. "I would hate to have to request a transfer so early in the term," she said, cocking her head to one side. "It would be quite arduous for the administration, and I know they frown upon students who make trouble regarding the roommate system. The code of sisterhood is such an important principle for the Keating community." She paused again. "You're a scholarship student, aren't you?" She smiled sweetly, and her message was clear: You are expendable. You should think twice about making waves.

It was Sadie's turn to sigh. She flipped to the last page on the clipboard, uncapped the pen with her teeth, and signed her name. There was no turning back now, anyway. And if they were truly horrible, maybe she could sleep on a cot in the broom closet. That's probably where she belonged, anyway.

As soon as she lifted the pen off the paper, Ellen was all business. She grabbed the clipboard and clacked her way back across the floor in her impossibly high heels. She turned in the doorway, busily wiping the pen cap with a handkerchief she had produced from another pocket.

"My team will need another few minutes to sweep the room," she said with another icy smile. "Perhaps you and your friend should take this opportunity to have supper? They should be finished upon your return." With that, she turned and strode out of the room.

Sadie sat for a minute, a little stunned, as Ellen's muffled footsteps moved away down the hall. Her roommates were going to be two famous girls—not famous, royal—and she had just legally signed away her gossiping rights. In the high school hierarchy, she was pretty sure that made her just a hair above completely worthless. The twin giants were starting to throw stern looks in her direction, so she stood up and headed off towards Jessica's room. Contract or not, Sadie couldn't wait to see what she had to say about this.

Chapter 3

"Wow, and I thought Madison was bad," Jessica said. "I've heard rumors about things like that, but it's usually when the girl's mom's a senator or something. I guess being a Duke is kinda the same thing?"

"I guess," Sadie grumbled, still miffed about being blindsided.

They had left Jessica's room—a double just down the hall from Sadie's—and joined the steady stream of girls heading down to the Ashby dining room. At the bottom of the curving staircase, they turned away from the front door and continued through an archway leading toward the back of the building.

After the dusty gloom of the dark lobby, the dining room was almost jarringly modern. It reminded Sadie of the kind of swanky bistros that lined Pioneer Square in downtown Portland, with shiny maple tabletops and walls painted in warm tones.

Jessica scanned the crowd until her eyes settled on one table in a far corner of the room. The girls were talking and laughing loudly, and most of them were wearing fitted, kelly-green tank tops that read "Keating LAX" in big, white letters.

Jessica waved and a couple of the green tank tops shrieked loudly in response. "Come on," she said, linking one arm through Sadie's and rolling her eyes. "Time to meet the girls."

As they started across the dining hall, Sadie felt so many pairs of eyes on her that her cheeks started to flush. She pretended not to notice everyone at the lacrosse table was looking her way, but most of them weren't smiling.

"Hey, ladies. You all remember Sadie Marlowe, right?" All the dead eyes at the table transformed into big, phony smiles, and a few manicured hands fluttered in waves of welcome.

A tall, willowy blonde with thin, tanned arms and thick, pouty lips stood up and extended a hand.

"I'm Thayer Wimberley, team captain. Welcome to Keating." Her smile stretched wide over blindingly white teeth aligned in perfect rows. She tossed her head, making her long ponytail swish from side to side. "I hear you're quite the hotshot on the West Coast."

Sadie stretched her mouth into what she hoped was a less terrifying expression. "Thanks. I was all-state last year." She hesitated. "But obviously the competition isn't exactly the same as it is out here."

"No," Thayer said, cocking her head to the side. "It's not." She paused, just long enough for the other girls to start squirming uncomfortably. "But we're all super, super excited to have you here."

The whole table exhaled.

"Anyway, this is everyone." She waved a hand around, listing each girl by name as Sadie and Jessica plopped down into two empty chairs. Seconds after they sat, a waitress in a white, full-length apron quickly set their places with silverware and a white napkin monogrammed with the Keating crest.

One of the other team members, a black-haired girl named Grace, smiled at Sadie. "We really are glad you came. We've been needing another middie so, so badly—ever since Anna . . . " She trailed off, and Sadie saw Thayer's head jerk in her direction.

"Ever since Anna's been gone," Grace finished, hunching back over her food and shrinking into herself like a scared puppy. Sadie swallowed and looked around the table. Something had shifted. The girls fidgeted in their seats, and Thayer was still glaring at the top of Grace's head. Sadie noticed a few girls at neighboring tables had turned to stare, and the whole room felt quieter. The name "Anna" had dropped like a bomb on the cafeteria, one that spread silence and squirm instead of smoke and shrapnel.

"Anyway," Thayer said finally, cracking another wide smile, "I heard Jess got stuck with Madison Plath. My money's on her for the Keating Curse, so let me know if she starts, like, making voodoo dolls of everyone in the Harvard admissions department."

"The Keating what?" Sadie asked.

Thayer tossed her head. "What, they didn't put that in your scholarship pamphlet?" She smiled like it was a joke instead of an insult. She leaned forward and lowered her voice. "Girls at this school tend to . . . uh . . . lose it during college application season. The last whackjob threw herself in front of a car out on that road by the main gates, all because she didn't get into Princeton. And some girl in the '80s tried to drown herself and then ran away from school when that didn't take. The Princeton one was like eight years ago, though, so we're totally due."

"But Anna—" Grace spoke up again.

"Let it go, Grace," Thayer snapped, her voice like ice. "That was different."

Sadie looked at Jessica with wide eyes, but she just waved a hand. "It's a stupid rumor," she whispered. "I think the teachers keep it going just so they can scare people into finishing their applications early."

"But those accidents—they really happened?"

Jessica nodded. "And if there really is a link, I am just fine not knowing what it is." She shuddered and looked down as her phone vibrated on the table.

"Oh my god, Madison seriously just texted to tell me she's thinking about painting the walls pink," she murmured.

"You should listen to her, you know," Thayer said softly from across the table. Sadie looked around, but all of the other girls were too wrapped up in their own conversations to hear.

"Why wouldn't you want to know?" Sadie said. "I would."

Thayer's face was blank. "Sometimes ignorance really is bliss."

Before Sadie could respond, Thayer smiled and clapped her hands. "So do you guys like the new practice jerseys? We tested them out this morning."

Jessica punched a button and put down her phone. "You can't seriously have practiced already."

Thayer cocked her head to the side. "Oh, honey, all the local girls did a three-hour session as soon as we moved in."

The girl on Sadie's right, a pretty redhead with porcelain skin, nodded. "Coach is out for blood. She told Thayer we're doing the running test early this year just so she can make sure no one sat on their ass all summer."

Sadie felt a lump start to form in her stomach. Running test?

"When is it?" All the eyes at the table turned toward her. Thayer looked annoyed, like she had spoken out of turn.

"Monday."

Sadie sat back heavily in her chair. The other girls chattered on all around her, and suddenly she felt like her bright red tank top was oddly appropriate among the sea of green ones. She might have been recruited to play lacrosse, but she wouldn't be part of the team until she earned it—Thayer had made that much completely clear.

I am just as good as they are, Sadie thought, her dad's words sounding trite and ridiculous in her head. It was going to be a long week.

☙

The hallway was empty outside her room, but as she neared the door, she heard voices. She paused. Yup—English accents. Her shoulders sagged as she pushed open the door.

Their backs were facing her, but she could already tell everything she needed to know. Each girl was tall, thin, and dressed in a boxy tweed suit, one pale lavender and one pink. Their black hair was drawn up into buns, each one topped with an identical, tiny, white hat. They looked like Easter Brunch Barbies. With really weird taste in headware.

They turned slowly—and, for some creepy reason, in perfect sync—and Sadie stood awkwardly while they looked her up and down, slowly taking in her jeans, tank, and rumpled, wavy hair. She tried not to think about the ketchup she had dripped onto her thigh at dinner, or the zit she knew was developing right above her lip, but she could feel her cheeks burning. She was toast.

The girls smiled identical ladylike smiles, and Ellen Bennett appeared between them.

"Hello again, Miss Marlowe." She clicked her way across the room, nodding to Sadie over the top of her ever-present clipboard. "May I present The Lady Beatrix Everleigh." She swept an arm toward the girl in lavender, who dropped into a small curtsy. Sadie's eyes widened.

"And The Lady Gwendolyn Everleigh." Ellen motioned toward the one in pink, who did the same.

This was just too much. All three of them were looking at her expectantly, and she wondered how one was supposed to respond to such an introduction. Salute them? Bow? Drop to her knees and kiss their feet?

She panicked and did the only thing she could think of, bending her knees and bowing her head in a crude imitation of what the twins had done. She saw Beatrix bite her lip to hold back a sneer, and she felt her cheeks flush even hotter. She couldn't wait to tell her dad about this one.

Ellen looked annoyed and clapped her hands. "All right, I'll leave you three to get acquainted. Ladies, you have my mobile number should you need anything." She turned to Sadie and raised an eyebrow. "Miss Marlowe, please keep in mind everything we discussed."

With that, she swept out of the room. The door swung shut and the three girls stood still, facing off across the room. Beatrix cocked her head to the side, listening. As the last clack died away down the hall, she looked at Sadie, her face blank.

"I thought that frosty bitch would never leave."

In the next instant, the twins leapt into action, ripping off their gloves and blazers and shimmying out of their shapeless skirts. They were like little pastel Tasmanian devils—if Tasmanian devils had cleavage and wore ridiculously expensive-looking lingerie.

Sadie stood motionless, her jaw hanging open, and soon they had stripped down to matching sets of lacy underwear in pink and purple. They pulled out bobby pin after bobby pin, tossing each one on the floor in a pile with their tiny hats, then finally shook their heads until their hair cascaded wildly down their backs. At that point, the one in purple finally stopped moving and looked at Sadie, a toothy grin on her face.

"I'm Trix, and this here's Gwen." She jerked her head toward her sister, who had skipped over to a huge, full-length mirror in the corner of the room. Gwen was standing sideways on her tiptoes and staring intently at her reflection, one hand running across her flat stomach. She waved a hand distractedly, eyes never leaving the mirror.

"It's Sadie, right? Don't touch our shit, don't snitch about anything we do to Ellen, and we'll all get along fucking great," Trix said. She smiled again, one side of her perfectly pink mouth curving slightly upward. Then she turned and sashayed back to one of the beds, flopped down on her stomach, and pulled out a cell phone. Sadie's jaw dropped farther as her eyes zeroed in on a black orchid inked neatly on her lower back.

She forced her eyes up toward the ceiling as she tried to figure out what was weirder—the fact that her royal roommate had a tramp stamp or that she had just looked at that roommate's butt. Then she realized she should really be focusing on what was important: What the hell just happened?

"Uh, hi," she finally started, trying to sound about a thousand times more confident than she felt. *I belong here, right?* she told herself. *I hang out with royalty all the time, dahling—I just love tiny hats!* The room stared back at her, and she felt like she was completely invisible. Trix was already deep in conversation, talking so fast Sadie could barely catch what she was saying. Gwen was still studying the mirror, this time facing it with one hip jutted out and her lips arranged in a sensual pout.

Sadie sighed, grabbed her toothbrush, and took off toward the bathroom. An hour later, she was deep into a book when the lights shut off. She glanced at the clock radio she had plugged in next to her bed and groaned. It was 10 P.M. exactly. The twins had taken off minutes earlier, calling out something about going to the library. Sadie had just smiled and waved, but something about the amount of black spandex and bronzer they were wearing didn't really say late-night studying in the stacks.

Sadie closed her eyes and imagined she was back in her old room in Portland, with its boxy IKEA furniture and ancient yellow eyelet bedspread. It was her mom's favorite color, and she had never been able to bring herself to change it after she died. She saw her four walls against the insides of her eyelids—on one was a signed poster of the Northwestern Lacrosse team, and on another was a collage of photos and a cheesy Van Gogh reprint she couldn't seem to get rid of. She gathered her blanket closer around her body, held the image in her head, and finally she slept.

Chapter 4

Sadie tugged at the hem of her skirt as she made her way up the chapel's stone steps. She and Jessica wore the same navy blue and green uniform, but they couldn't have looked more different. Jessica's looked tailored and preppy, and Sadie felt like she was dressed up for Halloween in a sixth-grader's cheerleading uniform.

The pleated skirt was too short—it hit her awkwardly just one too many inches above the knee—and her polo shirt was somehow simultaneously too baggy and too tight in all the wrong places. She looked down as she climbed the last step and wrinkled her nose. The white knee socks were really more overgrown girl scout than over-sized cheerleader, but that really didn't help.

She had stared at herself in the mirror for at least five minutes that morning, trying to decide how to make her outfit look slightly less ridiculous. She tried sagging the skirt or rolling it up, but everything just made it worse. She could unbutton one more of the polo shirt's buttons and look like a cheap extra in a bad music video, or one less and look like a bible-camp counselor who was desperately trying to hide her chest acne. She was pretty sure neither of those was the ideal first impression. She finally decided to err on the prude side until she saw the other girls, but now she was in full panic mode.

Jessica stopped in front of the chapel door and sighed. "I swear Sadie, if you mess with that button again, I'm going to smack you." She glanced down at Sadie's chest and grinned. "And go with the skanky version. No one buttons up."

Once inside, Sadie felt like she was back in the dining room, walking the gauntlet toward the lacrosse table. As she and Jessica made their way down the aisle, each row's chatter quieted as they passed, then began again—louder this time—with a flutter of manicured hands over glossy lips.

"When does this new-girl stuff wear off?"

Jessica shrugged. "Don't worry, in a few days, everyone will go back to ignoring you, and it'll be just like you're invisible."

Were those really her two choices? Sadie looked to her left and saw Thayer sitting with Charlotte, a platinum blonde Sadie recognized from the lacrosse table. Both of them had hair perfectly curled in waves that looked like they took hours. Sadie raised a hand to wave, but Jessica grabbed her arm and pulled her into an empty pew.

Sadie settled in, taking in the soaring, vaulted ceiling and the floor-to-ceiling stained-glass windows. "So do we really have to do this every Friday?"

Jessica wrinkled her nose and pulled out a purple phone. "Yup. Every Friday morning, and again for special events and holidays. It blows, but at least our first class is a half hour shorter." She looked toward the ceiling and closed her eyes in mock prayer. "And thank god for Twitter."

Sadie giggled. "Tell God I don't think I can Tweet on my crappy flip phone." Jessica just grinned and started poking at her phone's touchscreen. "Holy crap, Charlotte just tweeted the most blatant humble brag ever."

Sadie slumped down farther in the pew and gazed up at the ceiling. Despite how weird everything at Keating was, she had to admit starting school on a Friday was a merciful touch. No matter what happened today, at least she would have forty-eight hours to get over the trauma before she had to do it all over again.

Jessica was still hunched over her phone, so Sadie kept herself busy by counting the bloody Jesus statues scattered around the church. She was at six when the building fell silent.

She felt a tug at her sleeve and looked around her to see the entire school staring open-mouthed down the aisle toward the chapel doors.

They were wide open, and the sunlight streaming through was so bright Sadie had to shield her eyes. She could just make out the silhouettes of two girls, but from the roar of furious whispers that was rising up around her, she had a guess as to whom they might be. As they started down the aisle, Sadie felt a blush creeping up her neck. Her slutty polo was the last thing anyone was going to notice.

The twins' skirts were the same plaid fabric as everyone else's, but they were cut low across the hips and fell in short pleats that barely covered their thighs. Their polo shirts were tight, and the necklines plunged so deep Sadie could see the tops of their bras—super subtle in neon orange and electric blue. Their hair was down and messy, and their eyes were rimmed in thick black liner. They still looked like Barbies, but different ones this time. Supermodel Barbies—or maybe porn stars.

"Uhh, are those your roommates?" Jessica stuttered. "You said they were twins."

Sadie snorted. "Yeah, that's them."

Jessica looked at her accusingly. "All you said was that they were uptight. And British!"

Sadie sighed. "Well, they were. Then they got naked, and they have tattoos, and they mostly just ignore me. It's a long story."

"Uh, I have time," Jessica hissed. "Why'd you let me blab about pancakes for twenty minutes this morning when you could have been telling me that you live with Gwen and Trixie Everleigh?"

Sadie raised her eyebrows. "You know them?"

Jessica's jaw dropped. "You don't? Sadie, you're from Oregon, not Mars. They're like, really famous. They're in the tabloids all the time. Last week Gwen was on the cover of *Fame* because she got super hammered at some club in London and flashed the deejay." Jessica lowered her voice. "And Trixie supposedly made a sex tape with one of those super-hot soccer—sorry, football—players, but no one's seen it yet." She looked at Sadie solemnly. "Her lawyers are suing the porn companies so they can't release it."

Sadie watched the twins with renewed interest. If the twins were tabloid fodder, it might explain all the drama with Ellen.

"Anyway, I want to hear all about it at lunch," Jessica said with a pout.

"Okay, but not when everybody is around. I'm not allowed to talk about them, remember?"

Jessica waved a hand impatiently and looked back toward the aisle. The twins were still making their way to the front of the room, relishing each pair of eyes that followed their every move. As they drew level with Sadie and Jessica's pew, Thayer appeared directly in their path, dragging a short brunette with long frizzy hair and big brown eyes that blinked rapidly behind thick glasses.

The twins glanced at each other and immediately looked bored.

"Hi ladies," Thayer said, her voice dripping with honey. "It is such an honor to meet you. I'm Thayer Wimberley, of the Philadelphia Wimberleys, and this is my friend, Edith Hemmings. Her father is the British Ambassador to the United States." She emphasized each syllable with immense satisfaction, linking an arm through Edith's. Edith just kept blinking, looking happy and terrified.

"We met last summer at the Queen's regatta," Edith blurted, a little too loudly. "Our daddies were at Oxford together."

Trix tossed her hair, and Gwen looked down at her nails. Thayer darted her eyes back and forth like a frog drooling over a particularly juicy pair of flies, but her smile was starting to fade.

"Sit with us?" Thayer finally finished, a little desperately. She motioned toward the group of girls seated behind her, and Charlotte and the others nodded excitedly. They looked like bobble-heads, with their wide, fake smiles and chins bobbing up and down as if detached from their bodies. The twins looked at each other, and Sadie saw a hint of a smirk pass between their identical lips.

They turned slowly back to Thayer in perfect sync, and Sadie could tell they were back in tiny-hat mode. They smiled sweetly, and Thayer arranged her crestfallen features back into their usual mask of smugness.

"We would absolutely love to sit with you, Thayer," Trix began. "You too, Edith. I'm sure we have just loads in common, and we really need to get in with the right sort here." She paused as Edith's eyes lit up, and Thayer opened her mouth excitedly to respond. "But see we already decided to sit with our roomie, Sadie Marlowe—of the Portland Marlowes?"

"Maybe next time," Gwen finished, giving Thayer a condescending smile. Then they flopped down in Sadie's pew and buried their heads in their phones.

"Social-climbing commoners," Gwen muttered, just loud enough for the rows around her to hear.

Left alone in the aisle, Thayer's smile disappeared, and she dropped Edith's arm like it was on fire. She straightened her shoulders and puffed out her chest, but her face was as red as a tomato by the time her skirt hit the pew.

"Hey, um, guys?" Sadie said. "This is Jess. Jess this is Trix and Gwen—my roommates."

They each looked up and gave Jessica a quick nod, their manicured fingers still jabbing away.

Jessica turned back to Sadie and mouthed, "Oh my god!" Sadie just shrugged.

They heard footsteps at the front of the room, and everyone turned back toward the podium. Sadie could see a man in an expensive-looking suit making his way up the dais. Sadie opened her mouth, but before she could comment Jessica held up a hand.

"Trust me," she said, rolling her eyes.

Headmaster Cromwell was one of the shortest, tannest men Sadie had ever seen, and he was so wide she was worried he would tip over and roll back down the steps like a runaway bowling ball. His suit was at least a size too small, but the rest of his outfit was perfectly put together—his tie and pocket square the exact shade of pink as the tip of his ruddy, bulbous nose.

"Way too much time on the yacht this summer," Jessica whispered under her breath. "And a lifetime of too much bourbon."

"Welcome ladies," the man bellowed. His voice echoed around the room's soaring walls and ceilings. "I trust that you all spent your summer enriching your minds and enjoying the sunshine, resting and readying yourselves for another year of learning at this fine institution." He paused and looked up expectantly, like he was waiting for thunderous applause. A few girls clapped politely, and Trix loudly snapped her gum.

"I'd like to welcome our new freshmen and transfer students, and I trust that your sisters have already done their part to make you feel like a part of our family. As we welcome you into our circle of trust, we hope that you will bring us into yours, as well." He cleared his throat. "I look forward to getting to know each one of you over the course of the school year. I wish to not only be your headmaster, but also your mentor and confidant."

Jessica made a gagging noise and Sadie bit her lip to keep from laughing. Somehow, Sadie couldn't picture herself going to Mr. Cromwell to talk about period cramps.

"My door is always open, and I hope you will all take advantage of it and come by to introduce yourselves."

Jessica leaned towards her. "Don't do that unless you want him to look down your shirt and then tell you your shoulders look tense." She shuddered. "He's a creep. And he's handsy."

"Mrs. Darrow, our Head of Housing and Social Development will now take you through the school rules and other items on this week's agenda. Enjoy your week, and I expect to see you all at the annual Kickoff Reception tonight at Cranston Field before the football game."

He stepped down from the podium, and a woman stepped up and took his place. She raised the microphone and sent screeching feedback echoing through the chapel. When the girls groaned and covered their ears, she looked up sharply. The noise stopped instantly. Sadie made a mental note to never break a rule. Ever.

The woman was at least six feet tall, and she wore a dark blue suit with an antique-looking brooch on the lapel. Her hair was pulled up into a tight—and sort of oddly terrifying—French twist, and she wore narrow glasses with wire frames. At last, she cleared her throat.

"Good morning, ladies. Welcome back, and of course welcome to all of our new students." She didn't smile. "We take the rules very seriously here at Keating. Please understand that we will not look lightly upon any infractions."

She took a deep breath. "Ms. Plath. Rule one, please."

Madison shot out of her seat. "Rule number one is to always act in the manner that is expected of a young lady of Keating Hall caliber. Keating girls are polite. They are eloquent, and they are never sloppy." As she finished, Mrs. Darrow cast a sharp glance toward the first row, and the girls all straightened up, throwing their shoulders back and crossing their ankles. She nodded stiffly and Madison sat down. She pointed at a senior Sadie didn't recognize. "Rule number two, please."

The girl stood. "Keating girls are always punctual, and they do not swear."

"Oh, for fuck's sake," Trix muttered. Sadie and Jessica both giggled, and Mrs. Darrow looked up. She cleared her throat loudly.

"Ms. Marlowe."

Sadie froze.

"I trust that you used the summer to develop a thorough understanding of the student handbook, as you were so instructed in your welcome materials. Can you give us the third rule, please?"

Sadie saw a flash of blonde hair as Thayer and Charlotte whipped their heads around, smug joy reading plainly on their faces.

Sadie swallowed and stood up. She felt hot and sweaty, her mouth packed with cotton balls. She pictured the leather folio she had paged through once, then tossed onto her nightstand months ago. It had sat there, untouched, until she had shoved it into her duffel bag last week.

"Whenever you're ready, Ms. Marlowe."

Sadie looked down at her hands. She remembered a list of rules—she had scanned it to make sure she wasn't going to get rapped on the knuckles for speaking out of turn in class—but it's not like she had memorized it. Jessica cleared her throat softly, and Sadie realized she was motioning something in her lap. She had taken a pen from her purse, and was holding it between two of her fingers. Something clicked, and Sadie looked up.

"Um, don't smoke, or any of that other trashy stuff."

Jessica winced, but Sadie thought she could see a hint of a smile tugging at the corner of Mrs. Darrow's mouth. "Close enough, Ms. Marlowe. Keating girls do not drink alcohol, smoke cigarettes, or partake in any other such unladylike activities. You may sit."

Sadie sank back into the pew and exhaled.

"It also goes without saying that there are no unsanctioned visitors, ever, on the upper floors of Ashby and McLaren, and girls will not be permitted to leave the dorms after lights out. Students are not to leave school premises without explicit permission, and access to the athletic fields and the beach is prohibited after supper has been served."

Jessica leaned toward Sadie. "Darrow is terrifying—seriously, do not let her catch you with a pack of cigarettes—but that last one's kind of a joke. All the upperclass girls sneak out."

Sadie nodded. The rules didn't sound so bad, and so far Darrow hadn't mentioned anything about public flogging, so that was a good sign.

"If you have questions about any of these rules, please direct them to your class prefects," Mrs. Darrow said. With that, she cracked a smile, and Sadie heard the whole audience exhale as one. Mrs. Darrow's eyes roamed the crowd until they found Sadie's. "Enjoy your first day, ladies. And good luck—some of you may need it."

❦

Back outside on the quad, Sadie pulled her creased paper schedule from her pocket and stared at it for about the twentieth time that morning. She was actually weirdly relieved that her first class was Calculus. Math wasn't exactly exciting, but at least it was universal. Sadie could rock a derivative at least as well as these rich kids could.

She headed toward the math building as a steady stream of plaid skirts spilled out of the chapel and fanned out across the quad. She spotted the pretty redhead from the lacrosse table walking up the steps ahead of her and followed her through the doorway. Once inside, she wandered along the dim hallways, taking wrong turns until she found the door marked 202. At first, she thought she still had the wrong room. Instead of the usual classroom setup—with desks in rows or, for the really hippie teachers, grouped into smaller tables—it was furnished with a big oval table surrounded by about ten chairs. She hesitated. There were four girls seated already, and they were busily arranging notebooks and pens on the lacquered surface. It looked like they were sitting down to a board meeting or something. The redhead was there, pouring herself a cup of coffee out of a giant thermos.

"Hey, it's Sadie, right?"

The girl smiled up at her and held out a tiny hand. "I'm Brett Whitney. We met at dinner last night?"

Sadie smiled and shook her hand. It was so dainty it made her feel like a giant. "Yeah. It's nice to meet you, um, again."

"You too."

Sadie sat down next to her and watched as Brett used a ruler to create a perfectly straight line along the top and left margins of the page. Brett finished by carefully printing the date at the top, titling it, "Calculus, Fall Term, Day 1." Sadie glanced down at her own notebook and scribbled the date at the top. Close enough.

As she finished, the teacher entered the room and took her place on one side of the oval. She dropped a heavy armful of books, causing Brett to squeak something in protest and clutch at her coffee cup to steady it. Sadie thought she saw a hint of an eye roll as the teacher waited for her to calm down.

"Welcome to Calculus, ladies," she said. Her gray hair was pulled back into a loose bun, and strands of it stood out in wisps around her face. She scanned the room, stopping as her eyes came to rest on Sadie's. She took a deep breath.

"Well, you must be the transfer. What brings you to Keating?"

Sadie sat up straighter in her chair. The teacher was looking at her with an odd expression on her face—something between wariness and disapproval.

"That's me." She gave a little wave. "My mom went here—Maylynne Anderson? Maybe you had her in your class?"

The teacher's eyes narrowed, and she stared until Sadie started to squirm. "Did you say Anderson?"

"Um, yeah," Sadie said, confused. "Did you know her?"

The teacher fumbled with the books on her desk for a moment. "I've been teaching here for twenty-five years, but I can't say I remember anyone with that name." There was an awkward silence, and finally the teacher clapped her hands.

"All right, we have so much to cover this term, so we won't waste any more time. Please open your books to chapter one." With that she turned toward the whiteboard and started scribbling with a blue marker. She barely stopped writing for the full hour, and when she finally turned around and dismissed them, Sadie's whole right arm ached.

She dropped her pen and stretched her palm, flexing her fingers and massaging her joints with her other thumb. The open page of her notebook looked like someone had chewed up a bunch of blue pens and then thrown up all over it. She looked over at Brett's notebook and blinked.

Brett was carefully placing six pages of perfectly legible notes into a binder, one that she had neatly labeled, "Fall Term: Calculus." She snapped the rings shut and looked up at Sadie. "So, what do you have next?"

Sadie pulled out her schedule and pressed it flat on the table. "Uh, English with Bergstrom."

"Oh, he's great. Come on, my class is near there. I'll walk you." She grinned. "If your sense of direction is anything like your penmanship you might have some serious problems getting there on your own."

The hallway was packed with girls in identical polos, making them look like a swarm of really preppy clones. As Brett wove her way through them, her deep red hair made her stand out. It was shaped into one of those perfect, pretty bobs you only ever see on people in ads for stuff like zit cream or tampons, and Sadie felt suddenly self-conscious about her wild, wavy mess. She ran a hand through it to try to smooth it down, but it was hopeless.

"So are you excited for tonight?" Brett said.

"Oh, um, yeah. That thing Cromwell was talking about?"

Brett's eyes lit up. "Nobody's told you about the Kickoff? It's so much fun, and it's the first chance you'll get to see the fresh meat at Graff." She grinned. "Got a boyfriend back home?"

Sadie laughed. Jessica had told her Graff students' egos were even bigger than the school's endowment, but she figured they couldn't be all bad. "Nope. So it's a football game?"

"Well it's not just a football game, it's the first social event of the year. The Graff team plays their rival from Maryland, and it's a pretty big deal. It goes back like, a hundred years."

They stepped out onto the quad, and Brett placed a pair of huge sunglasses over her eyes.

"Before the game there's a big reception. You have something cocktail, right?"

Sadie nodded confidently at Brett even though she had no clue what that meant.

Brett turned to Sadie and put a hand on her arm. "A good relationship with the right guy at Graff is really important. There are so many events where you need an escort, and if you don't have someone appropriate it can be super embarrassing."

Sadie just nodded. An escort?

"Anyway, this is you," Brett said, pointing toward a big stone building to their left. Bergstrom's on the third floor. See you tonight, then? I have a guy I want to introduce you to. I have a feeling you two might hit it off." She grinned wickedly, then turned and hurried up the steps.

Sadie waved and watched as she disappeared through the doors. She could just picture what this guy would look like—probably some social reject from Graff who wore boat shoes with crew socks and too-short shorts. But still, it was nice that Brett was looking out for her. Maybe Keating girls weren't so bad?

She walked through the building's doors and ran straight into two freshmen wearing diamond earrings the size of marbles. "God, watch out," one said, brushing herself off like Sadie had just spilled something all over her shirt. The other girl looked Sadie up and down and smiled sweetly. "Cute shoes. Didn't know they still made those." They pushed past her, and she could hear them laughing as they walked down the steps. Or maybe not.

Chapter 5

By the end of her last class, Sadie was exhausted. Her cheeks hurt from smiling, and her hand hurt from constantly scribbling notes. She staggered up the Ashby stairs to her room, collapsed on the bed, and stared at the crown molding on her bedroom ceiling. She had spent the whole day trying to navigate the huge campus, and she had been forced to introduce herself awkwardly in practically every class. It had been excruciating, and she was pretty sure no one cared where she was from and what she wanted to be when she grew up.

As the day went on, she had thought more and more about skipping the party and getting in a workout instead. The team's first practice was the next morning, and she needed to be ready. Plus, she had nothing to wear that would fit in with these girls, and she was pretty sure a sundress from two years ago didn't qualify as "cocktail."

"Damn, American girls really are lazy, huh?" someone said. "Shouldn't you be getting ready?"

Sadie picked her head up and saw Trix and Gwen standing in the doorway.

"I might not go."

Their jaws dropped. "Why wouldn't you? We actually get a chance to see some boys for once. You're going to get really sick of all the puss around here, you know," Trix said.

"Speak for yourself." Gwen stepped out of her uniform skirt and threw it on the floor. "She doesn't know anything about high school guys, anyway. Her last boyfriend was, like, forty." Gwen ducked to avoid a shoe Trix had sent sailing toward her head.

"I'm right about this, though," Trix said, distorting her lips into a perfect imitation of Thayer's smug pout. She flattened her voice into an exaggerated American accent. "All the men from Graff will be there, and it's important that we make the right impression." Sadie laughed and Trix broke character, her features settling smoothly back into place.

"Plus, if the Graffies suck we'll just get trashed and flirt with the alumni," Gwen added. "I heard half of DC is going to be there." Trix nodded emphatically, and finally Sadie gave in.

"Fine—but I'm going to look like an idiot going there in my jeans. What does cocktail even mean?"

Trix looked her up and down. "You're what, like a six?"

She threw open the double doors of her armoire and showed off a row of dresses in every length and color. "I'm wearing the silver strapless, but you can take your pick of the rest."

By the time Sadie recovered and started to thank her, the door had slammed and both twins were gone. She tentatively reached out a hand and touched one of the dresses—cobalt blue with a sweetheart neckline and tiny straps—and the fabric flowed through her fingers like mercury. It was beautiful, but there was no way she could pull it off. The material was so thin and clingy she would look like a big blue sausage—something she was sure Thayer would helpfully point out. She flicked through the others with the tip of one finger—there must have been fifty, all in fluttery, flimsy fabrics like silk and satin.

Finally her hand closed on something more structured, a sleeveless, buttery yellow cotton shift with a subtle floral print and a narrow belt circling the waist. She held it up to herself in the mirror and it looked about the right size.

She undressed quickly—she still wasn't quite used to the whole, "Oh, hey, I'm just standing here naked, want to compare bra sizes?" thing Gwen and Trix were obviously totally comfortable with—and slipped the yellow dress over her head. She stood on her tiptoes and looked in the mirror, turning to one side, then the other and smoothing the fabric down across her hips. It fit her perfectly, and she had to admit it looked pretty good. The print was elegant and subdued, but the bright color made it a little more fun, and the simple shape hugged her hips, making her look a little less like a ruler than usual.

The door banged open as Gwen and Trix strolled back in from the showers, and Sadie turned to face them.

"What do you think?"

They looked at her in complete silence. Trix looked confused, and for a crazy moment Sadie wondered if she had actually imagined the conversation where a member of the British nobility casually invited her to rifle through her closet. Then the twins burst out laughing. Trix leaned on the back of the chair and gasped for air, and Gwen collapsed onto her bed clutching her stomach.

"Is there a garden party tonight we weren't invited to?" Trix finally managed between loud peals of laughter.

Sadie turned back to the mirror. "What's wrong with it?"

Trix looked at her reflection over Sadie's shoulder and curled up her lip in distaste.

"I can't even believe Elsa packed that after I told her not to. That's one of the stuffy little shifts we wear when Mum makes us go to parties with the other royals. You look like you're about to go have brunch with the Queen, and that's not a compliment."

Sadie frowned. She did look a little bit like a politician's wife at a daytime fundraiser. She rolled her eyes at herself in the mirror. She couldn't even fake rich when she tried.

"Take it off," Trix instructed, plunging into the armoire. "What do you think, Gwennie, maybe one of those little white minis from last spring?"

Gwen frowned. "Nah, she looks too virginal already. We need to slut her up a bit."

"Hey!" Sadie put her hands on her hips. "I'm not virginal. Well, mostly. It depends whether you count—"

Trix held up a hand. "I don't need to hear about how many guys you've dry humped. And either way, that dress isn't helping." She reached back into the closet and pulled out the blue dress with the tiny straps. After a moment, she held it out toward Gwen.

Gwen nodded approvingly. "Sexy, but like, hard-to-get sexy. The hamburgers'll love it."

Sadie raised her eyebrows.

"American dudes. You know, meatheads."

Sadie grinned. It was oddly fitting, especially considering every guy she had ever dated had a tendency to smell like bacon and barbecue sauce.

Trix tossed the dress on Sadie's bed. "You're wearing that. Trust me, guys don't want a girl who looks like she's about to go to church, and every single one of these uptight little American girls is going to be wearing a dress that looks just like that yellow sack. Now go shower. We'll figure out what to do with that hair when you get back."

Half an hour later she sat in her desk chair while Gwen fluttered around her, wrapping hunks of hair around a huge curling iron. Sadie brushed a stray strand out of her eyes, and Gwen smacked her on the shoulder.

"Quit fidgeting." As Gwen picked up another lock and wrapped it expertly around the barrel, something occurred to Sadie.

"Hey, why are you guys here? At Keating, I mean. Wouldn't you rather be at Eton or Oxford or one of those famous British schools?"

Gwen snorted. "First of all, Eton is a boys' school and Oxford is a university. But we didn't really have a choice." In the mirror Sadie saw her eyes flick toward Trix, who was straightening her hair in front of the full-length mirror.

Trix turned to face them. "What Gwennie means is, we got kicked out of all the good schools in England, so Daddy sent us here to keep us out of the gossip rags and make sure we didn't embarrass him anymore." She shrugged and turned back to the mirror, but Sadie saw Gwen bite her bottom lip as she finished curling the last section. Gwen cocked her head to one side and stepped back.

"Not bad, right?" She looked back at Trix, who nodded in agreement.

"All right, bitches," Trix said, running the straightener once more over her side-swept bangs then dropping it on the floor. "Time to get dressed."

Once the blue dress was on—and fitting about ten times tighter than Sadie thought it would—Sadie blinked at her reflection.

There is no effing way that's me.

Sadie Marlowe was messy and tomboyish and, as another year of swimsuit shopping had sadly confirmed just two months ago, still pretty flat. But the person in the mirror was none of those things. She was hot—and girly—and even her boobs looked bigger. Maybe fashion designers really were magical. It would explain how they had managed to convince people to wear shoulder pads.

Suddenly Sadie was nervous. "Listen, guys, are you sure you don't mind me wearing your stuff? What if you want to wear this to one of the other dances or something?"

Trix rolled her eyes and Gwen started digging around in the bottom of her armoire. "Those dresses," Trix said, nodding toward the rack, "are just what we packed for fall. Our stylist sends us a new collection every season." Sadie's shoulders sagged, and she made a mental note not to ask any more ridiculous questions.

"Two final touches, and you're done," Gwen mumbled, pulling out two handfuls and darting back across the room. She had a pair of black pumps that looked like high-fashion bear traps in one hand, and a glass bottle filled with dull, amber liquid in the other.

"Put these on," she said, holding out the heels. She held up the bottle and smiled her crooked smile. "Two shots each, and then we'll go?"

She uncapped the bottle and threw her head back, taking a huge gulp. She swallowed and shuddered slightly, then passed the bottle to Trix. She took a smaller sip, then grimaced. "Fuck, Gwennie, why do you always have to buy whiskey? It's nasty." She held the bottle out to Sadie and they both looked at her expectantly.

She froze. She had gotten drunk exactly once, but it wasn't really an experience she was dying to replicate. Earlier that summer she and her friend Sarah had convinced Sarah's older brother to buy them a big jug of cheap pink wine that tasted like rotten grape juice. They drank the whole thing, washing it down with a huge bag of popcorn and a couple *Diva Divorcées* reruns. They had felt great for about an hour, then spent three times that long puking it all up in the bathroom. But what the hell—it was just a few gulps.

She grabbed the bottle and both girls cheered. The liquid scorched its way down her throat, and she immediately started coughing. Trix just snickered as Gwen threw back another huge sip. They passed the bottle around the circle one more time, then headed down the hall to pound on Jessica's door.

"I'm almost ready," she called as Sadie pushed the door open. Jessica was seated at her desk, carefully applying lipstick in a little vanity mirror. "Sorry, I know I'm running late—Madison left, like, twenty minutes ago." She paused and looked back over her shoulder.

"Holy crap, Sadie," she squealed, jumping up from her seat. "You look awesome. You guys all do." She hesitated, her face melting into a frown. "Do you think this is too casual? You look like you're going to a movie premiere or something, and I look like I'm going to an ice cream social." She put her hands on her hips. "Shit."

Sadie looked at Jessica's delicate floral strapless dress and nude wedges and smiled. She felt Trix's elbow dig into her ribs and smacked her away, trying to hold in a giggle. "You look great Jess, seriously. Gwen and Trix just wanted to see if they could make me look like a girl for once. You ready to go?"

Jessica looked doubtfully at her reflection, then shrugged. She grabbed a little blue clutch from the bottom of her closet, stuck it under one arm, and led the way back out into the hall.

Chapter 6

Outside, the afternoon sunshine slanted through the building's tall columns and spread across the manicured lawn. The air was just the right temperature, and a slight breeze ruffled the hem of Sadie's dress. For the first time since she had been at Keating, she felt a rush of happiness. Things were going to be okay here. She was going to make it.

They followed a brick path around the side of the building that led them out along the water and past a row of sandy dunes. A wave broke on the beach below them, and Sadie felt a faint spray of cool air.

They walked for about half a mile, the endless ocean on their right and dense forest on their left. The path was tightly packed gravel, and Sadie had to focus to keep from tripping in her torture traps. Ahead of them, a big group of freshmen walked with their arms linked, and wisps of laughter drifted back over their heads and down the path.

Even farther ahead, Sadie could see the old military tower standing guard along the water. It looked ancient, its ramparts beaten almost smooth by a hundred years of coastal winds. It was set far out on the water on a little spit of land, and the whole thing was covered with wet, spidery moss that seemed to choke more than cover. Sadie wondered if anyone ever went inside. For some reason, the thought made her shiver.

Before she could get any closer, Jessica turned left and followed a narrow path into the forest. They passed a sign that read "Cranston and Wimberley Athletic Complex," with carvings of each of the two schools' crests. Jessica busily explained to the twins that the two schools shared athletic fields, and the football stadium was located in between the two campuses. Sadie could tell she was nervous. She had barely stopped to breathe since they had left the dorm.

She could hear the band playing now, and familiar sounds drifted through the trees and drew them forward. Sadie thought about Friday nights at Portland South and felt another little tremor of homesickness. She and her teammates had always spent the game in the top row, away from all the smug football girlfriends who sat on the 50-yard line and proved ownership by wearing their boyfriends' spare jerseys. It was so medieval, Sadie had always expected them to start tossing favors onto the field and calling for jousts. Really, they just spent the whole game gossiping and sneaking sips of marshmallow vodka from their enormous purses.

At Keating, things were a little different. The girlfriends were still there, but the stadium was huge, with neat brick bandstands instead of rickety metal bleachers. Vendors with trays of lemonade roamed the aisles, and beyond the freshly painted end zone was an ivy-covered field house that probably contained all of the team locker rooms. Above it was a digital Jumbotron that showed the tanned face of Graff's quarterback in high-definition, each of his dimples at least a foot high. The field itself was an unnatural shade of bright green.

They walked toward the throng of students mingling on the sidelines as both teams warmed up on the field. Waiters in dark jackets circulated among the crowd, offering soft drinks to the students and cocktails to everyone else. All the Graff boys were in dress uniforms, and they looked eerily similar in their matching navy blazers, striped ties, and gray flannel slacks.

Before they had even reached the crowd, a cluster of senior girls lurched toward the twins, screeching compliments so loudly Sadie almost covered her ears. As the mob pulled them away, Trix and Gwen looked back and rolled their eyes. Sadie noticed they were both smiling, though. Widely.

Jessica made a choking sound that Sadie guessed was probably a laugh. "Guess Cromwell isn't wasting any time this year." Jessica pointed toward a group of men gathered a few dozen yards away. The headmaster had traded his snug suit for a smarmy velvet smoking jacket, and the glass he was clutching was filled almost to the brim with syrupy brown liquid. Two men that looked like clones of

Ellen Bennett's enforcers stood a few feet away from them, their wrists crossed and eyes constantly scanning the crowd.

"Who's he talking to?"

Jessica squinted at the group. "The old guy is Sumner Cranston—you know, as in Wimberley and Cranston? He's a senator or something, and the younger one is his son, Teddy. He's a big deal too, even though he's only like, forty-five. He's President Manning's chief of staff, and he knows, like, everybody in D.C."

Sadie just nodded, choking back a fresh wave of panic. Jessica rattled off the titles of guys who passed by the Oval Office every day on their way to the bathroom like she was talking about the sixth-grade student council. She was never going to get used to that.

"The Cranstons have been rich since like, the Middle Ages," Jessica went on, "so they do a lot of charitable stuff, too." She waved a hand around. "They built most of this stadium, actually."

Sadie raised her eyebrows. "You guys Facebook friends or something?"

Jessica snorted. "Thayer's dating Teddy's son, so she never shuts up about them." She rolled her eyes. "The Wimberleys are rich too, obviously. They donated the money for the rest of this place."

As Sadie watched the little group, Teddy turned his head toward them, sending a little jolt of electricity down the back of her spine. He murmured something in Cromwell's ear, and then all three of them swiveled to look. Sadie nudged Jessica with an elbow.

"What?"

She pointed back toward the group, but the moment had passed. The men were talking with their heads bowed, and Cromwell was gesturing wildly with his glass. She watched as some of the liquid sloshed over the edge and onto the field.

"Oh I know—he probably started right after Chapel this morning. Now come on," Jessica said, grabbing her arm and grinning as she pulled her toward the bleachers. "It's time for your social debut."

They found most of the team sitting in a lower section, sipping Diet Cokes and laughing with a group of guys in blazers. Brett introduced her to the Graff guys one by one, each of them standing up to firmly shake Sadie's hand. Before she got to the last one, a tall guy who looked like he was probably born in tennis whites, Thayer popped up next to him and put a hand on his outstretched arm.

"This is my boyfriend, Phineas Everett Cranston the Fourth." She emphasized the word "boyfriend," tightly clutching his elbow.

Sadie shook his hand awkwardly, jostling Thayer's claw up and down with it, and he smiled at her in a way that was almost a sneer.

"You can call me Finn."

He casually knocked Thayer's hand away, and it fluttered for a moment before settling on his shoulder instead.

"Finn's the starting attacker on Graff's team," she said. "He's already being recruited by Princeton, Virginia, and Harvard."

"Wow, that is awesome," Sadie said, the words tumbling out before she could stop them. "I'm dying to hear from Virginia, but it's hard to get scouted in Portland."

The sneer-smile widened. "So you're the transfer. We've been hearing about you for months."

Thayer huffed out a little puff of air and started dragging him toward the aisle.

"See you on the practice fields," he said, winking back at her as they walked away.

Sadie wrinkled her nose and turned back to Jessica and Brett. "Guys wink here?"

Brett grinned. "Not the ones you should pay any attention to. Just ignore Finn. He and Thayer have been dating since, like, eighth grade. Most of the other lacrosse guys are pretty okay, though." Her eyes wandered to one of the dark-haired guys on the bleachers. He caught her eye and smiled.

"Like Josh," she added, her cheeks flushing red. "He's taken though, too."

"Ohh, he's cute," Sadie said. "How long have you guys been together?"

"We just started before the summer, but it's really going pretty well."

Jessica grinned. "What she means is, she's totally freaking in love with him and has been since freshman year."

Brett started to scowl, then broke. "Okay yeah, she's right. But quit jinxing it. I don't want him to know that."

Jessica looked at Sadie and made a face. "You're lucky you weren't here last season. He would wait for her outside the locker room like a preppy little puppy every day after practice. It was gross."

Brett tried to look annoyed, but Sadie could see a smile creeping across her face. Her cheeks were almost as red as her dress.

"Okay fine, we're a little clingy. But I think it's romantic."

"Whatever, I think that's great. I'd love it if a guy did that for me," Sadie said. "The only thing my ex did for me was meet me at my locker and try to grope me before lunch."

Brett laughed. "Well that guy sucks. There are plenty of options around here, you just have to be able to weed out the jerks. For example—" She pointed to a guy with brown hair and sunglasses, standing in a crowd of Keating girls. "Take Chip Jennings. He keeps a book in his dorm room with pictures—you know, pictures—of all the girls he's hooked up with. If we ever catch you flirting with him, we'll probably kick you off the team."

Sadie wrinkled her nose. "Not my type. I hate guys who look like they take longer than I do to get ready."

Jessica pointed to the football field, where the Graff team was stretching in orderly lines. "And that guy up front, number twelve? Brent Taylor. Grace went to a dance with him last year, and he totally slipped something in her drink. She woke up the next day and couldn't remember anything that had happened."

"Scary," Sadie murmured.

"Oh, and not that he's available, but we should probably warn you about Finn, too," Jessica said. "He's the biggest dick of them all. Well, not you know, literally. Ew."

Brett frowned. "Finn's not so—"

Jessica cut her off. "He used to cheat on Thayer constantly, and he would never even admit they were really dating. Last year he dated like three other girls, then suddenly one day he and Thayer were back together, and they've been acting like Barbie and Ken ever since. Thayer of course pretends it never happened."

"Jeez, who did he date? I'm surprised Thayer let them all live," Sadie joked.

Both girls hesitated, until finally Jessica waved a hand. "No one you know. I'll tell you later."

"So, besides Josh, is there anyone who isn't a complete douchebag?" Sadie asked, looking out over the crowd of minidresses and blazers.

"Meh," Jessica said. "I'm sick of all of them."

Brett smacked her on the arm. "Do not listen to her. There are tons of guys you might like, especially on the lacrosse team. Did you meet Stephen and Morris back there?" Sadie nodded, remembering two guys who mentioned they played defense. "They're both pretty cool. And single. Oh! And then there's Jeremy, the new guy."

"Wait, what?" Jessica perked up. "Where?"

Brett pointed back to where Josh was sitting. Next to him was a guy with shaggy, dark blonde hair. He was sitting on the bleachers with his elbows on his knees, and he didn't look like the rest of them, like he was carefully considering everything he did, right down to which side he parted his hair on. His blazer was stretched tight against his shoulders and Sadie could see the outlines of his biceps under the fabric. She felt excitement bubbling up in her stomach. Crap.

"Cute, right?" Brett said. "Josh told me he's really good, too. He just transferred from some school in California. I heard his mom's like, some major up-and-coming movie producer. She made that indie film everyone went nuts over last year about the guy who ate himself to death on live TV. Maybe you guys'll have something in common?"

Jessica poked Sadie in the ribs. "Hey, if you don't want him, I'll take him. He's fucking hot."

Sadie bit her lip. "I guess he's pretty cute."

"Hey, the game is starting soon," Brett said. "Do you guys want to sit with Josh and me?"

"Sorry, we promised to sit with the twins," Sadie said. "But we'll find you guys after, okay?"

"Cool, see you later," she called, then jogged a few steps up the bleachers toward Josh and Jeremy. Jessica waved at Josh, and Sadie caught Jeremy's eye. Brett said something to him, and he looked back down at them and smiled. Sadie quickly looked away.

She started toward the next section of the bleachers, where she could see Gwen and Trix sitting in a circle of blue blazers. Nice work, idiot. She resisted the urge to pound her fist against her forehead. She was the worst flirt ever.

"He totally smiled at you," Jessica said, plopping down next to Gwen. "And you just ran away."

"He smiled at us, not at me. I'm sure Brett was just talking about us being on the team or something."

"Yeah, whatever. I know when I'm being smiled at, and that wasn't it." She grinned. "Don't be such a pussy. You're so talking to him at halftime."

Sadie tried to hold back a smile.

"Unbelievable. One stupid football game and you already have a crush on someone. I knew that would happen. And meanwhile, I'm totally going to end up going to all the events with Gene again."

"Gene?" Sadie raised her eyebrows.

"Ugh, do not ask. Trust me."

The whistle blew for the kickoff, and they all turned their attention toward the field. The game turned out to be really exciting, even though Gwen and Trix spent the entire time complaining about how confusing "American football" was. By halftime, Graff was ahead 14–13.

Jessica popped up out of her seat and stood on her tiptoes to peer over the crowd. "Let's go. You're not getting out of this. Actually, wait . . . damn it. He just left."

Sadie stood up and watched Jeremy's lanky stride as he made his way down the aisle and disappeared into the crowd. In response, her stomach fizzled with nervous, frustrated energy, but Jessica wasn't fazed.

"Nachos?"

During the second half, Sadie tried to keep an eye on Brett and Josh, but Jeremy never came back. When they finally caught up to Brett on the way back to campus, she told them he had left early.

"He said he was nervous about practice tomorrow and wanted to go over the plays again." Brett shrugged. "Can't say I blame him. I'd be nervous if I was the new kid, too. No offense."

Sadie groaned. "So I should be nervous?"

"Um, yeah. Especially for the test," Jessica cut in. "Have you been training?"

"Yeah, I guess. But I didn't even know about the test until last night."

Brett frowned. "Well, there's not much you can do about it now. Don't stress about it. I'm sure you'll pass. And if you fail, you just get to take it over again."

Jessica raised her eyebrows. "You do not want to do that. Trust me."

As they turned onto the beach road, Sadie looked back and saw the tower darkening as the sun dipped down behind the trees. She felt the knot in her stomach grow a few sizes.

The lacrosse team was the entire reason she was here, and failing the running test would be the worst possible way she could start things off. She would have to do everything she possibly could for the next three days to make sure that didn't happen—starting tonight.

ↄ

Over a disturbingly raw block of tuna in the dining room (Brett called it "seared"), Sadie pondered her plan. First, she thought about working out in Ashby's fitness center, but she knew that wouldn't be the same. She had to run outside—feel the turf under her cleats so the field wouldn't feel so foreign come Monday. She remembered their after-dinner curfew and the 10 P.M. lights-out time and took a deep breath. She was going to pass this test, even if it meant breaking a few rules.

After dinner she went immediately back up to her room, leaving Brett, Jessica, and the rest of the team watching TV in one of the common rooms. She slipped through the door and checked the clock. 8:36. Technically she wasn't allowed to leave campus after dinner, but as long as she made it back before lights out she would probably be okay. At least, that's what she had been telling herself for the last two hours.

She changed quickly into running clothes, then threw on a huge gray sweatshirt that hung down past her black running shorts. She sneaked a glance in the mirror to make sure her camouflage was effective. The running shoes were kind of a giveaway, but she would have to make it work. She grabbed a water bottle, clipped on her Shuffle, and headed back toward the stairs.

She followed an exit sign in the lobby down a short hallway until she found a side door. It was labeled as an emergency exit, but no alarm sounded when she cracked it open and pushed her way through.

Outside it was completely quiet, the campus dark and deserted. Still, she tiptoed silently until she made it down the hill to the beach road. When she was far enough away, she switched on her music and let it fill her head.

She broke into a light jog and slowly accelerated as she made her way toward the stadium. By the time she passed the wooden sign in the woods, she was hot and sweaty and gasping for breath. The humidity made the air feel thick, like she was drawing hot steam into her lungs. Running here might be more difficult than she had thought.

Just outside the stadium, she stopped to catch her breath and stripped off her sweatshirt. She leaned against a wall, and the brick spread a cool calm up and down her spine. Her head was aching, and she winced as she remembered the swigs of whiskey she had taken earlier. Finally, she stood up and took another few steps toward the turf.

The game had ended almost two hours ago, and a cleaning crew must have long since finished and left. The field was pristine, the moonlight casting it in a watery blue haze. But it wasn't empty.

A guy stood on the 50-yard line, hands on his hips with his back toward her. He wasn't wearing a shirt, and she could see the light reflecting off his broad, angular shoulders. Her breath caught in her throat as she recognized his shaggy blonde hair. Jeremy.

His chest was heaving as if he had just stopped to catch his breath. As she watched, he looked down at his wrist, pressed a few buttons on his watch, and then took off in a full sprint. He ran a few dozen yards, then cut back and sprinted toward the center of the field, brushing the turf with his hand as he turned. She watched, mesmerized as his legs and arms pumped hard through the humid summer air. He was fast—really fast.

He did six lengths before stopping, then checked his watch and put his hands behind his head. He stood there for a while, chest rising and falling as he caught his breath. For a few moments, she felt like they were the only two people in the world. Then he turned around.

She jumped and tried to duck back behind the wall, but it was too late. She felt excruciatingly exposed, like she had just been caught spying by someone in the middle of her own dream. He waved.

At a loss for a more appropriate response, she waved back. They stared at each other for a few moments, until awkwardness won out and she turned away. She abandoned her plan to do sprints completely, instead heading back toward the woods.

She ran along the path back toward the beach, and soon the crashing waves were loud enough that she could hear them over her headphones. She turned the music off and just listened to the rhythmic sound of her breathing, the rolling waves, and her footsteps pounding on the gravel. When she ran, she let her mind go completely blank, listening only to her body. She loved that feeling. She craved it. Even if it sounded like something only a hippie from Oregon would do.

She drew level with the Graff tower and slowed to a walk. She had never been this close to the tower before, and for the first time she realized how huge it was. The spit of land it sat on looked like it had once been paved with smooth stones, but now they were cracked and worn, and weeds had wound their way up through the fissures. She stood there for a moment in the dark, staring up at the black, hulking structure. She could have sworn she could see a hint of light glowing in one of the slits that served as windows, but she knew it was just her eyes playing tricks. A cloud had passed over the moon, and it was so dark, she could barely even see where the beach ended and the sea began. She turned her headphones back on and took off back toward Keating.

She was dripping with sweat by the time Ashby loomed into view. She thought about a long, hot shower and hesitated, tempted to head inside. Then she remembered Thayer's smug smile and thought about how much satisfaction she would get if Sadie failed. Instead she turned up the volume and sprinted back toward Graff.

Near the tower once again, she took off her headphones and doubled over, heaving, against a tree. As she waited for her pulse to slow, she heard an unmistakable sound: the crunch of gravel and the soft purring of a car engine.

Instinctively, she ducked a little farther into the woods. She angled herself so she could see a few hundred yards down the path. As she watched, a black SUV appeared on the road beyond the tower, crawling slowly along with its lights off. It was just a truck, like the kind a nighttime security guard might drive, but still Sadie felt goose bumps pushing up through her skin. She pressed her body even closer against the tree trunk.

When the car got to the tower, it turned onto the little spit of land, curved around the side of the building, and disappeared. She stepped out from behind the tree to get a better view, but the truck was gone.

She squinted at the tower windows, willing her eyes to see another flicker of light or movement, but there was nothing. Jessica had said the tower was abandoned, just some old, empty ruin that was too old to tear down and too expensive to maintain. Sadie cocked her head as she heard a car door slam. Or maybe not so empty.

Suddenly she was very aware of where she was—alone, in the dark, a mile from anyone she knew. The fear moved in quickly, flowing in icy waves from her chest out to the tips of her fingers. Her breath caught in her throat and she swallowed, willing herself to relax. She moved to slip on her headphones, but something stopped her. She froze, barely breathing until she heard it again. A twig snapping, then the soft crunch of gravel. Someone was there.

She heard another twig snap, closer this time, and she whipped her head in the direction of the sound. She knew she should run, but her legs felt weak and grounded, like the kind of half-baked paralysis that always happens in dreams. Somewhere far away, she heard the truck's engine roar back to life, and the sound brought the blood back into her limbs. She took a step toward the path, but she stumbled over a tree root and pitched forward into the darkness, branches scratching at her cheeks as she fell. As her palms hit the dirt, she cursed. Then, straight ahead, she saw them.

There were two, both dressed in black with hoods pulled low over their faces. They just stood there, staring at her as she tried to untangle herself. She tried to yell, but the sound died in her throat, nothing more than a sad, strangled whimper. One of them laughed.

She got to her feet and turned and ran deeper into the woods, falling forward blindly with her breath pounding in her ears. She couldn't tell if she was being chased—she just ran.

Finally she saw a glow of moonlight and broke through the trees onto the path. She doubled over, heaving and shaking in the dark. She tried to tell herself she had imagined them—she was delirious from the run, from the heat and the dark—but her hands were still trembling as she forced herself to put her headphones back in. She took a long, shaky breath, bouncing a few times on her toes. Then, just as she turned to run back to Keating, she felt a hand close down on her arm. This time she screamed.

Chapter 7

"Whoa, whoa, relax!"

The hand on her arm was gone as quickly as it had come, and she leapt back, bringing her fists up in front of her face like weapons. She realized she was shouting nonsense, like she was trying to intimidate a mountain lion. As her vision cleared, her jaw dropped open and her cocked fists wilted against her sides.

Her attacker, who was neither wearing a hood nor, actually, wearing much of anything, was cowering in front of her, holding up his hands like he was afraid she would shoot. In that moment, he looked even more terrified than she did.

"Damn it, I'm so sorry," he blurted, taking another step away from her. "I wasn't—I'm not—look, I go to Graff. My name's Jeremy."

"Holy creepy stalker in the woods, Jeremy," she yelled, jerkily wiping the cold sweat from her forehead. "You almost just gave me a heart attack."

Her heart was still pounding, and she could feel the adrenaline pulsing through her veins. "What the hell were you doing? I think I'm having heart palpitations—for real. If my left arm starts going numb, it's your ass."

He bit his lip like he was trying to hold back a laugh. "Deal."

He jerked his head back down the path. "I just came from Cranston-Wim. I tried to call your name, but I think you had your headphones in." He motioned to the ear buds that now hung limp around her neck.

"It's okay, I just . . . wow, I really thought I was about to get dragged off into the woods and chopped up into pieces."

"I know, I'm an idiot. I saw you run this way like half an hour ago, though, and you never came back even though you left this." He held up her gray sweatshirt. "It sounds so stupid now, but I was kinda worried. It's so dark out here."

She mumbled a thanks and took it back. She was glad he couldn't see her blush.

"What are you doing, anyway?" he said.

She sighed. "Trying to get ready for this damn running test. I'm new, and I don't like running on unfamiliar turf." She took a deep breath and looked down at her shoes. "Sorry about being so awkward earlier, by the way. I just didn't expect to see anyone else on the field."

He smiled. "No worries. It's Sadie, right? The transfer from Oregon?"

"Yup. Portland. You?"

"San Diego. I'm dreading our test, too. Everyone tells me it's brutal."

"Is yours on Monday?"

"Yeah."

"Ours, too."

They looked at each other for a moment. Sadie glanced at her watch.

"Well, I should really head back." She motioned toward the path. "But it was nice to meet you. I guess I'll probably see you on the field? Next time try not to unwittingly cause my premature death."

He smiled widely, and she felt her stomach flip.

"Definitely." He reached up and ran a hand through his hair. "At least I hope so. Good luck on Monday." He held up his hand in a wave and then turned back toward Graff.

She watched as he ducked under a few tree branches, her stomach now flipping around like a kid three doses behind on his Ritalin. She put her headphones in and turned back toward Keating. Double crap.

✧

"He said what?" Jessica screeched.

Sadie grabbed a striped pillow off of Jessica's bed and sat down, cross-legged, with it in her lap. "It wasn't that big of a deal."

"Oh screw that, Sadie. You're trying so hard not to smile right now."

Sadie grinned and hid her face in the pillow. "Okay, fine—it was pretty cute. But of course, I made a total ass of myself."

"No way. He said he was worried about you and that he hoped he would see you soon, so you basically have a date to the next formal already. Un-effing-believable." She crossed her arms and pouted.

Sadie swatted her with the pillow. "For all I know he'll turn out to be a complete douchebag who has pet names for both of his balls and talks about himself in the third person."

Jessica grinned. "Well, he does go to Graff." She yawned. "Okay, get out of my face already. I need to get some sleep. You should too. First practice is at 9 A.M. tomorrow. Breakfast at 7:45?"

"Sure."

"See you in the morning," Jessica called as Sadie shut the door behind her.

She padded back to her room. The hallway lights were dimmed, but she passed Madison as she was huddled in one of the window bays talking on a bright pink phone. Sadie waved, but Madison just frowned and tapped the face of her diamond-encrusted watch.

Trix and Gwen were both in bed when she got back from the showers, and she could hear one of them mumbling in her sleep. She sat down on her bed and cracked open her laptop to check her e-mail. She had one new message, but she didn't recognize the sender. It was from an anonymous Keating address, just a jumble of letters and numbers, and the subject line was a single word: Fate. Even stranger was the cryptic message inside.

> *We are all at the mercy of fate.*
> *Soon you will know yours.*
> *-Z*

Sadie's eyebrows slid toward the ceiling. If this was some kind of motivational message from the school, they really needed to work on their delivery. She was tempted to be creeped out, but she was just too tired and happy to care. It was probably a virus anyway, like one of those scams that e-mails everyone you've ever met an ad for generic Viagra and penis enlargement pills. She shut the laptop and lay back on the bed.

She hugged the covers close around her body, closed her eyes, and imagined herself back on the beach with Jeremy. She curled herself tighter into a ball and buried her face in her pillow, holding the image in her mind. Finally, she drifted off to sleep, the faint smell of salt still lingering in her nostrils.

&

When something woke her hours later, she assumed it was the twins. They had a habit of disappearing right after lights out and then showing up back in bed right around dawn, smelling like smoke and sweaty cologne. She blinked into the darkness and lay still, listening for their slurred whispers and sloppily stifled giggles, but all she heard was the sound of her own breathing and the slow creak of weight moving across old wooden floors.

She stopped blinking and opened her eyes wide, waiting for her pupils to dilate. The room was quiet again, and she told herself she had imagined it. She was still a little freaked out about what had happened in the woods, and she knew she was probably half asleep and dreaming. She closed her eyes and willed her body to unclench, focusing on letting each of her limbs sink fully into the soft mattress. She took a deep breath and tried to let her mind go blank.

Before she could exhale, the blankets and sheets were ripped off of her body. She opened her mouth to scream, but a heavy hand clamped down across her jaw, forcing her head back into the pillow. She tried to kick, squirm—anything to get the hands off of her—but they only pressed harder. As she struggled, a single thought ran through her head: Soon you will know your fate. She tasted something sharp and metallic just before the dark closed in.

&

At first, all she felt was cold. She was sitting on something hard—a bench, maybe—and her hands were tied behind her back. She was blindfolded and gagged, and some kind of strap was wound tightly across her rib cage. She could feel a rigid cuff wrapped around her upper arm, and the air around her smelled old and stale, like each breath she drew in hadn't been moved in a long time.

She squeezed her eyes shut and willed herself to wake up. Stuff like this only happened on detective shows and in cheesy CIA movies, and she was pretty sure some hot, muscle-y actor wasn't about to burst in with a SWAT team and rescue her. Some hysterical part of her almost wanted to laugh, but the rest was so terrified she could barely breathe.

She felt a puff of air on her neck, and she stiffened. She told herself it was the wind and repeated the word in her head, over and over, as if she could will it to be true. Then she heard the voice, just inches from her right ear.

"Just relax," it purred. It was male and patronizing. "We don't want to hurt you."

In her mind she was screaming.

She had seen enough low-budget horror movies to know those words usually led straight to death by chainsaw or pickaxe. The screams trickled out as pathetic whimpers, strangled by the wad of coarse cloth pressing against her tongue.

The voice began again. "At least, it's less messy that way." It laughed, and she screamed again in frustration.

"Just answer the questions, and you'll get to go home."

She stopped.

"Much better. I'm going to take your gag and blindfold off. Promise you won't scream?" The voice waited. She paused, trembling. Nodded.

She felt movement behind her head as someone untied her gag, then her blindfold. As the fabric fell away, she looked around frantically, searching for some sign of where she was. The room was dark, but there was a single, weak bulb hanging a few feet over her head. It cast a small circle of light around her, and beyond it she could just barely make out shapes in the darkness. There was something large and bulky in front of her, but nothing moved.

She craned her neck and looked behind her, but the voice and hands had slunk back into the shadows.

"Hold still," it said. "Look straight ahead. Speak only when spoken to."

She turned and faced the hulking shape, squinting into the darkness. She felt strangely calm now, and she wondered if this was what it felt like to be in shock.

Another bulb switched on ahead of her, then another, and a third, and things started to take shape. The mound in front of her was a large podium, set high on a dais three steps above her. There were three figures behind it, all in black robes with hoods pulled low over their faces. She blinked her eyes rapidly in disbelief. Either she was hallucinating, or she had been kidnapped by a satanic cult that watched way too many horror movies. She figured the odds were about even.

Then the center figure spoke. "Welcome, Sadie Marlowe. You have been summoned to prove your worth in front of the tribunal. We are the Moirae."

Sadie's jaw almost hit her chest. The voice was young. And female. The whole thing was some kind of sick joke—hazing, or just a really elaborate prank. Fear gave way to simmering anger.

"I am Clo—"

"What the hell is a Morray? Someone who celebrates Halloween all year round?" The words were out before Sadie could stop herself.

For a moment there was silence, and then one of the other hoods spoke up.

"It's moy-ray," second hood said, with a little huff. "Like the Greek—"

Sadie heard a loud thunk under the podium, followed by a little yelp of pain.

"Hey, I was just—"

"Shut. Up," first hood hissed. Another thunk.

Sadie was trembling again, but not out of fear.

"I am Clotho, the spinner, the giver of life," first hood started again, voice reverting to the low bellow she probably thought was super intimidating.

"I am Lachesis, the drawer of lots," second robe said, trying to match her tone and sounding like she might be having a mild stroke.

"I am Atropo, the inevitable." Third hood kinda pulled it off.

Finally all three spoke at once. "We are the Fates, gatekeepers of the Order of Optimates, protectors of the brotherhood, and avengers of those who move against us." Their voices echoed eerily in the drafty room. "You have been called before us to demonstrate your intelligence, your pedigree, your integrity, and your worth. If we deem you deserving enough to be one of us, you will be richly rewarded. If you are found wanting, you will be cast out. In either course, you will never speak of what has happened tonight. Swear upon your life, and the lives of your family members, that you will never breathe word of this to anyone."

As their last syllable died out, she had the oddest feeling the room was much larger than she had thought. She could hear a rustling that she had originally assumed was the ocean, or tree branches scratching against a window, but now it seemed unmistakably like the sound of bodies shifting in seats, like the soft white noise in the movie theater during a tense moment. Sadie swallowed, and she heard the voice behind her clear his throat.

"Whatever. I swear."

Her voice came out clear and strong, but her mind was working furiously trying to piece everything together. She thought about the cryptic e-mail, the cheesy dramatic robes, and her dad's joke about prep school secret societies. She wasn't sure whether to cry with relief or laugh out loud at the ridiculousness of it all. Minutes ago she was sure she was going to die, all for some stupid high school charade.

First hood looked to her left and right, then all three spoke as one. "The oath has been made."

Right hood, the one who called herself "the inevitable," spoke next. "If you break this oath, you will be punished—harshly and without mercy. Know that no matter where you are, or how long from this day, if you betray us, we will find out." She paused, and the room filled with menacing silence. "And we do not forgive oath breakers."

"The device you are hooked up to is a polygraph machine. The truthfulness of your answers will be recorded, and if we are not satisfied, there will be repercussions." She looked back to first hood. "Clotho—you may begin."

"What is your name?" she said. The bellow was back.

Sadie cleared her throat, forcing herself not to answer in the same ridiculous baritone. "Sadie. And yours?"

"Watch yourself," the voice hissed in her ear.

"Where were you born?"

"Portland, Oregon. It's fantastic this time of year."

This time his voice was harsh, biting: "Last warning, Sadie."

She clenched her teeth and leaned as far away from him as the ropes binding her would allow.

"How old are you?"

She sighed loudly. It was the middle of the night. She was cold, and the ropes around her wrists and ankles were starting to chafe. The cuff on her arm was making her hand go numb. And she didn't want to be in some stupid secret society, anyway.

"I'm twelve—I skipped a few grades. Is that a problem?"

The light above her head went out, and suddenly there were hands around her neck. She froze, eyes wide in the sudden darkness. The hands squeezed tighter, and she felt her lungs start to strain. The voice was there again, closer—hotter—against her neck.

"I warned you."

She felt beads of spit spraying against her earlobe. One of the hands slid forward until a thick arm was wrapped around her neck. As the grip circled tighter, it forced her chin upward until she was blinking at the ceiling, her mouth breathlessly pumping the air like a fish.

The terror was back now.

It squeezed harder, slowly crushing her throat until the blood was screaming in her ears and her whole face felt like it might explode through her eye sockets.

"No matter what you think you know about us—who we are, what we're capable of—know that you know nothing," the voice whispered.

She was getting dizzy, and the pressure was fading. She thought about her dad at home in their kitchen, and she was just starting to feel herself drift away when the voice whispered again, softly this time.

"Don't you ever forget that."

And then, as suddenly as they had come, the hands were gone and she could breathe. She drew in breath after breath, leaning forward and gasping into her trembling knees. The light above her head flipped on again, and she buried her face further into her lap. She clenched her eyes shut and willed herself to wake up back in her bed in Portland, realizing that the last two months had all been just a horrible dream.

Instead, first hood spoke: "We will begin again now. That was your only warning. Fail to show respect for this tribunal again, and you will be punished." She spoke the last word carefully, as if she relished its taste.

"Are you a virgin?"

Sadie should have been shocked, but at this point she was too far past that. She squinted in the dim light and tried to make out something, anything about the Moirae's faces, but all she could see was darkness beneath their black hoods.

"No sex." She felt the blood pulsing around the cuff that was still strapped around her arm. "Other things, though."

"What things?"

Sadie felt herself start to fold, the roomful of eyes boring into her like leeches.

"I dated a guy for a few months. We hooked up, just not . . . never all the way."

"Why not?"

"I wasn't ready, I guess. I didn't want to."

"Did he?"

"I guess."

"What did you do instead?"

Even after everything, she couldn't believe they were asking her this.

"Third base, a few times. Mostly just out."

"Did you like it?"

She couldn't take it anymore.

"I said, did you like it?"

The hand was on her neck again, playing with her earlobe, flicking it back and forth. She swallowed hard and tried to fight back tears.

"Fine. Yeah, of course I liked it. I'm not a robot."

"Have you dated other guys?"

Sadie shook her head.

"Speak your answers," the hood demanded. "Have you been tested for STIs?"

Sadie folded in on herself further. "No."

Right hood leaned over and whispered something in first hood's ear. They bent their heads together, then turned back to Sadie. This one wasn't a question.

"Tell us about your mother."

Sadie's anger flared, and her shoulders jerked back. They could humiliate her and scare her and do whatever else they wanted, but they didn't get to bring up her mom.

"No," she said, teeth clenched. "She's dead."

"How did she die?"

"She killed herself."

"How?"

Sadie shut her eyes tight but the tears were already flowing. They seeped out from under her lids and dripped down her cheeks. Her hands were tied, and she couldn't wipe them away.

"She hung herself at a hospital."

"You mean, a mental hospital?"

Eyes still closed tight. "Yes."

"Was your mom crazy?"

"She was depressed."

"Was she a drug addict?"

Tighter. "Yes."

The next time the hood spoke, her voice was louder, almost baiting. "Was she a whore? Addicts usually are."

Eyes open. Wide.

"No." Sadie spat out the word. "And my mom is none of your business."

The girl cocked her head to the side in a gesture that was both condescending and completely familiar. "Oh, honey. You have no idea how much it is my business. If your mom was a whore, how can we even trust that your dad is your dad? How can we trust that you are who you claim to be at all?"

Sadie took a deep breath, and when she finally spoke her voice was low and even, perfectly controlled. "My dad is my dad, and he's ten times the man that your dad will ever be. My mom was not a whore, and she died of a disease that has no cure. And you, Thayer Wimberley, can go fuck yourself. Next question."

She stared deep into the shadow beneath the girl's hood, the tears now dry on her cheeks. No one moved, and nothing but darkness stared back.

Chapter 8

She woke up feeling as if she had barely slept, her head pounding like her skull was suddenly two sizes too small. She felt like she was emerging from a bad dream, or from one of those drunken nights on TV where all the actor has left is a bunch of blurry flashes with nothing to connect them. It came back slowly—the hand over her face, the chemical smell, the dark room, and the voice spitting in her ear. She pulled the covers over her head and burrowed back into the darkness, determined to stay there until her dad could come and pick her up— take her away from here and never mention Keating again.

The questioning had gone on for what felt like hours. After her mother it was more questions about her past—whether she had ever stolen anything, whether she had ever cheated on a test, whether she had ever tried drugs or gotten drunk or been arrested. Then they had moved onto her family, asking questions about her relatives, how they died, whether they had had cancer, heart disease, questions Sadie barely even knew the answers to. She told them her mom was basically an orphan, that she didn't even know her maternal grandparents, but that didn't satisfy them. They had wanted to know everything about her, and by the time they were finished her head had drooped weakly against her chest, and her eyes had felt like they were filled with sand. Then, just as it had begun, it was over. The hands were on her again, pressing something cold and wet against her mouth. The voice was in her ear, and just as she was fading away she heard his last words: "Congratulations, Sadie Marlowe. You passed."

She snoozed her alarm clock until the last possible moment, then slowly dragged herself out of bed. Black spots crowded her vision, and she steadied herself on her desk until the room stopped spinning. As she trudged past the twins' full-length mirror, she caught sight of her dark, puffy eyes and pasty skin. This was going to be the worst practice ever.

The dining room was completely empty except for the group of girls at the lacrosse table. They were all in their practice uniforms—black, pleated skirts and the green tank tops they had worn Thursday at dinner. Sadie glanced down at her rumpled outfit and resisted the urge to walk back upstairs and go back to bed.

Instead, she plopped down at the table next to Jessica, who looked like she had rolled right out of bed and directly into her chair. Her hair was mussed, as if she had slept in her ponytail, and she peered grumpily down at her oatmeal through sleepy little slits. Sadie scanned the faces across the table. Brett's red hair was flawlessly French braided, but she had dark bags under her eyes.

Jessica looked up at Sadie and paused, a spoonful of oatmeal poised inches from her mouth. "Yikes. Exactly how long did you spend fantasizing about you-know-who last night? You look like you slept for, like, two minutes."

Sadie glanced around the table, but no one seemed to have heard. She cleared her throat loudly. "I don't know, Jess. For some reason I just couldn't sleep."

Most of the girls glanced at her with bored looks on their faces, but Brett kept her head down, staring intently at a grapefruit half like it was about to tell her the cure for cancer.

"It's okay, today's just a practice. You'll get through it," Grace offered.

Sadie forced herself to smile. "Thanks, Grace."

Jessica nudged her elbow as the servers finished setting her place. "Food'll help." She grinned. "You're going to need a lot of it."

In response, Sadie's stomach growled, and suddenly a big, greasy meal sounded like the best thing in the world. She trudged up to the buffet and filled a plate with heaping servings, stacking bacon on top of her scrambled eggs once it got too full. She was still angry, but at least the shot of saturated fat would help her think straight. She plunked the delicate china back down on the table and started shoveling.

"I hope you girls are ready for this," Thayer sang, sidling up behind them with Charlotte and two other seniors in tow. The girls drew back chairs, sending loud screeching noises through the silent room. Thayer sat down, her gaze crawling over their plates from one end of the table to the other.

"You all must be hungry," she said lightly. "I could never eat something so heavy before a practice." She tossed her thick ponytail over her shoulder, whipping a sophomore in the face in the process. "But maybe that's just me."

Out of the corner of her eye, Sadie saw Grace slowly put down her fork. Sadie picked up a strip of bacon and crunched into it loudly, chewing slowly with her eyes locked on Thayer's. Thayer met her gaze, and the corner of her lip curled up in a cold, knowing smile. Sadie stared back, but Thayer just blinked and smiled wider. Apparently they were going to pretend nothing had ever happened, and for now, Sadie could live with that. As long as Thayer and her creepy friends left her alone.

As Thayer and the others headed toward the buffet in search of egg whites, Sadie popped the last piece of bacon in her mouth and stood up. Seeing Thayer had sharpened her anger all over again, and now she could feel it stabbing her from the inside out. She looked over at Brett, Grace, and Jessica and arranged her features into a smile. "Want to head out early and warm up?"

೮౧

"Line it up, ladies!" Coach Fitz bellowed, blowing her whistle in three short blasts. The girls immediately sprinted to the 25-yard line and organized themselves into a perfect row.

Sadie fell in line between Jessica and Brett and imitated their posture—each girl was standing with her stick out in front of her, shoulders thrown back and head high. She half expected the coach to start barking orders like a drill sergeant, and her prediction wasn't far off.

"Welcome to your first practice of the year," the coach yelled. She stalked from side to side in front of them like a caged panther: head lowered, shoulders slightly hunched, and eyes narrowed. Sadie took a deep breath, trying to mitigate the simultaneous fear and excitement that was bubbling up inside of her. Coach Fitz had been a three-time All-American in college at Virginia, and she was a legend in lacrosse circles.

"I trust that you all spent your vacations wisely, and that you're in better shape now than when you left us in June. Many of you were on the team last year, but a few of you are new. Some of you were JV, and you think you have what it takes to move up to the next level. Some of you are transfers, and you're probably used to being the star." She stopped pacing and looked them slowly up and down.

"But no matter who you are, know this: Every second you are on this field, you will work harder than you would have ever thought possible. You will push yourself past your limits, find new limits, and then push past those. You will push yourself until you break, because you know that showing weakness is not an option. If you want to be a member of the Keating Monarchs national championship lacrosse team, you better want this, badly, and you better plan on showing me that passion every single day you are out here. If you don't want to eat, sleep, sweat, and bleed lacrosse for the next ten months, then I suggest you leave right now."

She paused and looked down the line of girls. No one moved.

"For those of you who choose to stay, lacrosse at Keating is not a spring sport. We will practice every Saturday morning until the season starts, and Thayer will run captain's practices during the week. I expect you all to go if you want to see the field come March. Understood?"

"Yes, Coach Fitz!" the girls yelled.

"Good." For the first time, she smiled. "Now we're going to play a little game."

Sadie looked down the line, expecting the girls to huddle up and be split into teams, but no one moved. Apparently it wasn't that kind of game.

"If you were a starter last year," Coach barked, "take a step forward."

Ten girls stepped forward, leaving the rest on the 25-yard line.

"If you were all-state, all-district, or all-league on this team last year, take another step."

Thayer, Brett, and another girl stepped forward again, leaving the rest of the girls in two lines behind them.

"If you were on the varsity team last year, step forward." Everyone except Sadie and five others stepped forward again.

"Now if this is your first year in the Keating lacrosse program, at any level, including summer camp, take one step back."

Sadie looked around, but no one met her gaze. She was the only one to step back.

"Now take a look around. Look at the girls in front of you, and those behind you. This is where you stand coming into the season, and anyone in front of you is your competition. If any of you girls back there want to make the team, you're going to have to overcome at least half the people in front of you."

Sadie forced herself to stare straight ahead. She was in dead last, with five rows of girls stretching ahead of her. One of the girls standing directly in front of Sadie looked like she was barely fourteen, and she was holding her stick awkwardly like it was a shotgun that might go off.

"For the girls in front, look behind you," Coach continued. "This is your competition, and you can bet they will do everything possible to break you down and take your spot."

She watched the girls crane their necks, and she felt her cheeks start to get hot. Thayer glared at her from her spot in the front row, that smug smile back on her face. Sadie knew the coach was trying to prove a point—show her she still had a long way to go, and that she couldn't relax just because she had been recruited. She squeezed her stick tighter, feeling its rough edges cutting into her palm. The pain felt good.

Coach Fitz blew her whistle and sent them on two laps around the field. As Sadie fell into step at the end of the line behind the little freshman, she stared at the coach as she passed. Throw whatever you want at me, she wanted the look to say. You won't break me that easily.

She could swear she saw a smile tugging at the coach's mouth before she turned away.

℘

When they finally called the practice, it was almost noon. Sadie's hair was dripping with sweat, and she collapsed on the ground and closed her eyes against the glare. A shadow loomed over her.

"Don't tell me you thought that was hard."

She opened her eyes to see Thayer grinning down at her, not a drop of sweat on her face.

"Yeah, it was fucking hard," Sadie said, still struggling to catch her breath. They had drilled for two hours, then spent the last hour doing interval training, switching off running the stadium stairs, doing ladder sprints on the field, and jogging around the track.

Thayer put a hand on her hip and laughed. "I almost can't wait 'til Monday. I'm betting you're the one who pukes."

Sadie sat up. "Okay, seriously—what is your problem with me?" She stood so they were eye level and lowered her voice. "You and your psychotic, sadistic friends got what you wanted last night. Now leave me alone."

Thayer raised her eyebrows, looking amused. "I can't leave you alone, honey. I'm your team captain—if you make the team, that is. And you had better start showing some respect if you want that to happen." Thayer stepped closer. "As for last night, we did get what we wanted. But trust me—leaving you alone is the last thing you want us to do."

She waved her fingers and jogged off toward the sideline, leaving Sadie alone on the field. She lay back down and forced herself to stare straight into the sun until her vision blurred. Monday was going to be hell.

℘

She had seen it during her visit last spring, but Sadie was still shocked at how nice the team's locker room was. Each locker was

73

more like a small closet, with a nameplate, open cubbies for toiletries, and a big hamper bin at the bottom that doubled as a padded seat. There was an entertainment center on one wall that the team used to view game footage, and down a short hallway there were showers and bathrooms that they shared with the other women's sports.

The girls who had been on the team last year all had assigned lockers, and they were already scattered around the edge of the room in varying states of undress. The others had camped out in empty spaces in the center, and the shy freshmen had gone to the bathroom to change in the stalls. Jessica waved Sadie over and motioned toward her locker.

"You can stash your crap in here 'til you get your own," she said.

If, Sadie added in her head.

As she changed, Sadie's eyes roamed the room until they settled on an empty locker next to Thayer's. All the unused lockers were blank, but this one still had a nameplate.

#11 Anna.

The locker looked used. A piece of green construction paper with "Anna" spelled out in bubble letters hung crookedly from a piece of tape against the back wall, and one white T-shirt sleeve hung out of the bottom bin.

"Hey, who's Anna?"

Jessica wrapped a towel around herself and started pulling bottles of shampoo and conditioner out of her cubby. "She was our teammate."

Jessica said it quietly, but Sadie noticed a couple of the girls glancing in their direction. Thayer slammed the lid of her locker closed and headed for the showers. The room suddenly felt a little smaller.

"Was?"

Jessica turned and looked her in the eye. "Later," she mouthed. Out loud she said, "Come on, I'll show you where the showers are. I'm going to have like six new zits by dinner if I don't get this sweat off me soon." She walked down the hallway, leaving Sadie alone in a room full of silence.

☙

She walked back to campus with Grace, Brett, and Jessica, and as they walked, the cool air breathed life back into her fatigued limbs. A breeze whistled through the tree branches, and instinctively she veered a foot or two closer to the other girls. For the first time since last night she thought about the two figures she had seen in the woods. She was sure now they had been following her, just waiting for their chance to make their move. What the hell was wrong with these people?

"What'd you think of your first practice?" Brett asked, bringing Sadie's mind back into focus. Practice had kept her busy, but now she could feel the rope binding her wrists, and the pressure of the polygraph cuff cutting into her arm. She rubbed the spot just above her elbow and forced a smile.

"It was good, I guess. Hard, but it's not like I'm surprised. Is Coach always such a hard-ass?"

"Pretty much," Brett said. "She was actually pretty mellow today, if that helps?"

Jessica shook her head. "You should have seen her last year after we lost to Hamilton. I thought she was going to pop a blood vessel right out there on the field. She ran us until Charlotte started having a panic attack."

Sadie groaned and rolled her eyes. "Great."

Jessica glanced down at Sadie's arm and raised her eyebrows. "Jeez, where'd you go to give blood—the butcher shop?"

"Huh?"

Jessica pointed to a spot just above Sadie's elbow crease. "You're all bruised. Happens when they poke around too much with the needle." She rolled her eyes. "I once had some nurse newbie prick me like twelve times before she found a vein."

"What are you talking abou—" Sadie looked down at her arm, but Jessica was right. There was a deep purple bruise that spread across the crease. She stopped walking and stared, bringing her arm up closer to her face. In the center of the bruise was a tiny red scab that looked inflamed. She felt a cold sweat break out on the back of her neck.

"You okay?" Jessica took a step toward her. "It's no big deal—really. I'm sure it's normal to bruise a little."

"But I didn't," Sadie murmured.

"Didn't what?" Jessica was starting to look worried. Brett just stared at Sadie with wide, unblinking eyes.

Sadie had the sudden urge to spill everything, but she swallowed it down and forced a smile. "Never mind. I totally forgot I donated last week—must have just taken awhile to show up." She heard Brett exhale.

She felt like she was going to throw up. Pranks were one thing, and she could handle them trying to scare her. But they had stuck a needle inside of her, and she had no idea why.

Jessica didn't look convinced. "You sure nothing else is wrong?"

Only everything, Sadie wanted to shout at her. *Everything is wrong.*

Instead she just nodded and started walking back toward Keating, forcing the other girls to jog a few steps to keep up.

Chapter 9

Sadie and Jessica spent the afternoon lounging in one corner of the quad, each with a pile of books spread around her in a wide arc. Sadie was squinting hard at the math book in her lap, but the formulas that were usually so familiar were swimming together, refusing to make sense.

She tossed the book to the side and leaned back, feeling the cool grass between her fingers.

"Hey, so can you tell me what the deal is with Anna? How come nobody likes to talk about her?"

Sadie had expected Jessica to get angry again, but she just sighed.

Jessica closed the book in her lap and took a deep breath. "Okay, you just have to understand that it's still hard for people to talk about it. One day she was here, and the next it was just . . . nothing. Most of the girls still haven't really made sense of it."

"Made sense of what? Did she quit the team or something? Transfer?"

Jessica looked up from her lap and met Sadie's gaze. "Sadie, Anna didn't leave. She's dead."

Sadie opened her mouth to respond, but nothing came out. She looked down at her hands and swallowed. "I'm really sorry, Jess. I honestly had no idea." She clapped a hand over her mouth. "Oh god. And I was in the locker room blabbering on about her in front of everyone." She covered her face with both hands. "I'm such an idiot."

"It's okay. You just didn't know." Jessica looked back down to the grass and picked a little white flower. She twirled the stem between her finger and thumb, then started pulling the petals off in bunches. "I just don't know why no one told you." She looked up again. "You never saw it on the news last year? It was a pretty big deal until they found her."

Sadie shook her head. "I guess I just missed it."

Jessica's eyes strayed across the quad, and Sadie watched as they landed on the bench she had noticed the first day. The bouquet of calla lilies was gone, but there was a bunch of white roses in its place.

Sadie frowned. "Hey, what do you mean before they found her?"

Jessica looked at the naked stem in her hand and tossed it back onto the grass. "At first, she just disappeared. It was March, so lacrosse season was about to start, and we were together all the time. We spent every afternoon at practice and most nights watching film or going over our plays. We ate every meal as a team. Then one night she went to bed, and when her roommate woke up Anna was gone. We thought maybe she had gone out for an early run or something, but then she didn't show up for breakfast, or class, or practice, or anything. We called her cell phone over and over again, but it always just rang and rang."

"Wow," Sadie murmured. Jessica was looking straight ahead, her eyes glassy and unfocused.

"They searched for weeks. First on campus, then at Graff. They spent two weeks just walking through the woods with a huge group of volunteers. Coach canceled practice so we could help. It was the worst feeling ever. Like, you were looking and you wanted to find something, but at the same time, you knew if you did it would mean the worst news in the world. They brought in dogs to search the woods, and then even the Coast Guard to check the water. Her parents hired people to investigate, but no one could find anything. It was like she just vanished."

She stopped, and her eyes were shiny with tears.

"They never found her?"

Jessica rubbed a hand over her eyes, smearing her mascara. "They looked and looked, and they never found anything. Not even a fucking shoe or her wallet or anything. They started thinking maybe she ran away, or was kidnapped or something. Then the cops started showing up less often, then not at all, and eventually it stopped being in the news every day. Then one day it was just . . . over. Some deep-sea fisherman found her body way offshore."

"Oh, god," Sadie whispered.

Jessica looked up, and they locked eyes. "They couldn't even tell what happened. Her body had been in the water too long." She shook her head and looked back out over the quad. She nodded toward the bench. "That was her favorite spot on campus. She liked to read there, even in the winter."

"Jess, I'm so sorry. I should never have brought it up."

Jessica sniffed and straightened up. She wiped her tears away with one hand and smoothed her ponytail with the other. She looked at Sadie and smiled weakly. "It's okay. I try not to think about it too much anymore, but whenever I do it's still really hard."

She took a deep breath. "Anna was really fun—you would have liked her. You guys even kinda look alike. She was tall, too." Her eyes welled up again, and she stopped.

"Well, if you ever want to talk about it, I'm here," Sadie said softly.

Jessica sniffed. "You know, since I'm already crying I might as well say this." She managed a weak laugh. "I'm really, really glad you're here, Sadie. Seriously. I like the other girls, but it's hard being around people you can't really relate to, you know?"

Sadie nodded.

"My family's rich, I guess, or at least most people would think we are, but I'm not like these girls. I don't go to the Hamptons every summer or get tickets to movie premieres or go to balls at the White House. It's easy to get lost in all that."

She looked up and met Sadie's eyes. "But you're different." She smiled. "You're more like me."

Sadie threw her arms around Jessica in a big hug. "You're practically the reason I decided to come here last spring."

"Really?" Jessica wiped her nose with the back of one hand. "You didn't think I was like, totally obnoxious, and that I talk too much and make too many awkward jokes?"

Sadie smacked her on the shoulder. "Please. I was just relieved you weren't a rich robot who thought I didn't deserve to be here."

Jessica's smile faded. "Well, you do." Her eyes followed a group of three sophomores as they walked across the quad. The sunlight glinted off their pale blonde hair—all three the exact same shade—and their shadows stretched tall across the grass.

"It's so strange when you start school here. You watch all of the girls walking around with their perfect designer outfits and haircuts, and they're all beautiful and smart and well dressed and well-spoken. And then it's parents' week, and all the families show up, and they don't even look real. All the dads wear expensive suits, and the moms are young and beautiful. It's like you're living in a movie, where everything is flawless and everyone wears tasteful pearls and it's all just perfectly as it should be."

She shook her head and laughed bitterly. "But then you start to see the cracks. You see the faces behind the facades, and they're ugly and sad and empty. The dads all cheat or get caught banging prostitutes or divorce their kids' stepmom for someone who just graduated from Yale, and the moms are all workaholics who take pills just to get through their eighteen-hour days, or they don't work at all and they're depressed or crazy or obsessed with their charity work because it makes them feel like they're more than just some rich guy's wife. You know Madison, my roommate? She pulls out her hair because she's so stressed all the time. She has to wear extensions because she's going bald, and her parents still give her shit if she doesn't get straight As."

She looked up at Sadie. "You're smart and pretty and fucking great at lacrosse, and you earned every dollar of that scholarship. Trust me, the more you get to know these people, the more you realize they're really not untouchable at all. They're just as screwed up as the rest of us—they just have better costumes to wear."

Chapter 10

It was almost 7:30 by the time Sadie forced herself out of bed. She had lain awake for over an hour already, her heart pounding and her stomach rolling with angry butterflies. It was Monday, the day of the test, and Sadie felt even less prepared than she had last week. Ever since Friday night, she had been waking up terrified in the middle of the night, sure there was someone in her room. Her dreams were stressful and restless, and every morning, the second before she opened her eyes, she saw a faceless blonde in a black hood.

She showered and dressed quickly, then flipped open her laptop to check her e-mail. The only message she had was from Thayer letting them know practice had been pushed back half an hour. She groaned in frustration. All that meant was an extra half hour of torture before she was put out of her misery.

She spent the morning trying to concentrate on calculus and physics, but all she could think about was practice. Her stomach felt empty and tense, squeezing tighter and smaller as the day went on. When the last period was finally over, she took the steps up to her room two at a time. As she changed, she tried to pump herself up by blasting some music and visualizing herself passing the test. It didn't work.

She took her time getting there, trying to enjoy the sun and the wind on her face. She told herself it was just another workout; she had done this a million times. But she couldn't keep the nerves out—not for the best high school lacrosse team in the country.

She walked onto the field at around 3:30, with plenty of time before practice was supposed to start. But something was wrong. The team was already on the field, and Coach Fitz was standing on the sidelines with a stopwatch around her neck. Her two assistants stood next to her and busily scribbled on their clipboards. The Graff team was sitting in the bleachers, waiting their turn, and behind them was a little cluster of men in suits, watching the practice from far up in the stands.

Her stomach turned to water as the realization hit her. Thayer hadn't e-mailed the whole team. It was an act of sabotage, and Sadie was the only target.

She immediately broke into a sweat, and her heart felt like it was beating directly behind her eardrums. On the field, Jessica was motioning to her frantically, waving her arms and pointing at her nonexistent watch. Sadie dropped her bag at a run and joined the others, so nervous she felt faint.

What felt like seconds later, Coach blew the whistle and signaled for the girls to line up. They took their usual positions on the 25-yard line.

"Welcome, ladies," Coach yelled. "Today is the conditioning test. Most of you will pass, but some of you will not. I see some of you didn't deem it necessary to take full advantage of warm-ups today, and that has been noted." She looked Sadie in the eye, but Sadie stared back, her chin high. "Those of you who don't pass will retake the test every Saturday morning until you pass or give up. Until then, you will not be allowed to practice. This year's test will be harder than last year's, so I hope you're all prepared."

Sadie heard a few of the girls groan.

"This year's test will contain two parts: a speed test and a long-distance endurance test. The speed portion will be a series of six three-hundred-yard shuttles completed in twenty-five-yard increments. To pass you must complete each shuttle—that's twelve lengths—in less than seventy-two seconds. The endurance test will be a two-mile run on the track that must be completed in under fourteen minutes.

"As is our tradition at Keating, you will run the test in order of increasing seniority. This means Marlowe, Harris, Brownley, Reid, Thomas, and Helms, you six are up first on the sprint."

Sadie followed the five other girls as they trudged toward the other end of the field, where the assistant coaches had set up two lines of bright orange cones 25 yards apart. The field felt a mile wide, and with each step her heart pounded faster, until her whole ribcage seemed to vibrate. As she placed her toe on the starting line, everything seemed to slow. The sounds around her fell away, and she saw nothing but the cone in the distance. She took a deep breath, feeling her lungs expanding and swelling against her chest, and then the whistle blew.

☙

She passed.

All the girls who had been on the team last year did, except for Jenna, a senior and the team's backup goalkeeper. When it was all over, the Graff team took the field and Sadie followed the rest of the team as they staggered back to the locker room. Jenna was crying uncontrollably as they walked, but nobody had the energy to console her.

When she got to the showers, she stepped into the closest stall and closed the curtain behind her. She turned the shower on full blast, twisting the dial all the way to the right so the water ran ice cold. She stepped under the spray and let it wash over her face. She stayed there for a long time, until her teeth started to chatter.

Most of the girls were already gone, but Jessica and Brett were still waiting by their lockers. She dressed quickly, and they made their way back out to the field. The Graff team had started their test, and she scanned the players until she saw Jeremy's shaggy blonde head a few inches above the rest. He was in the middle of a 300-yard shuttle, and she felt her cheeks flush as she flashed back to Friday night. She looked away, putting the image out of her mind.

As they passed the bleachers, Coach Fitz waved at them to stop.

"Marlowe, can you come up here for a minute?"

Sadie looked at Brett and Jessica, who both shrugged.

"You passed," Jessica said. "What's the worst she can do?"

Sadie sighed. "See you back at the dorms, then?" They nodded and waved. She watched their backs as they made their way down the sideline, then turned into the aisle.

"Have a seat, Sadie," Coach said, her face expressionless behind her dark sunglasses. Sadie sat down and swallowed, trying not to think about the answer to Jessica's question.

"So, how have you been settling in?"

"Everything's been good so far," Sadie said slowly, anxious to see where this was going. "I'm still adjusting, but classes have been going okay." When the coach didn't respond she added, "The girls all seem really great, too." That part was a lie.

"Good. Glad to hear that." Coach pulled off her sunglasses and smiled. "I wanted you to know I was impressed with you today. It's rare for a transfer to come in so well prepared, and you definitely proved that you worked hard over the summer."

Sadie exhaled, feeling the stress finally leaving her body.

"I saw some game film from the Oregon State Championships last year, and you have a lot of potential. You'll still need to earn your place on the starting squad—your scholarship doesn't guarantee you playing time—but I'm confident that you can do that, as long as you're willing to work hard." She looked at Sadie and raised her eyebrows. "Are you?"

"Absolutely, Coach," Sadie said, a smile spreading across her face. "Lacrosse is the reason I'm here."

"That's what I was hoping to hear." She leaned down and grabbed two items out of a box at her feet, then handed them to Sadie. They were two articles of clothing—a kelly-green tank top and a black pleated skirt. Sadie bit her lip to keep from grinning as Coach slipped her sunglasses back on. "See you next Saturday," Coach said.

Chapter 11

The next few weeks passed by in a blur. Sadie went to class, ate her meals with the team, and spent nights studying in the lobby with Jessica and Brett. A few nights a week after curfew, she would sneak out for a run along the water. But she didn't see Jeremy again. She tried to pretend she wasn't hoping to run into him, but it was always in the back of her mind.

On Sunday nights she would call her dad and tell him about the week. He would ask about lacrosse practice and tell her a few stories about what was going on in Portland. He would make jokes about how strange her classmates must be, and she would deflect them so he wouldn't worry, all the while thinking in her head that he had no idea how right he really was. Thayer hadn't spoken to her about anything other than lacrosse since that first practice, and that was just fine with her.

One Saturday morning, the dining hall was oddly empty before practice. Not a single one of her teammates was there yet, even Brett who was always so early for everything that Sadie wondered if she ever even slept. Sadie sat down to eat a bagel, but by the time she was done she was still alone. And nervous.

Thayer hadn't tried to mess with her in weeks, but maybe she had just been waiting until her guard was down. For all she knew, Coach had scheduled an earlier scrimmage and Sadie had conveniently been left off the e-mail chain. The thought made her feel ill. She gathered up her things and jogged all the way to the field.

It was empty. The field was completely still except for a few early fall leaves that tumbled in the wind. She sank down onto the lowest bleacher and dug her phone out of her pocket.

"Where are you? No one's at the field," she texted Jessica.

Her response came back a few minutes later: "Canceled. Don't you check your e-mail? Go back to sleep, you skank. XOXO"

Sadie shook her head. She had checked her e-mail, and apparently she had been conveniently left off the chain—again. She started the walk back toward the woods. As far as pranks went, this was pretty weak, even for Thayer.

At the edge of the trees, she stopped. There was a small white envelope pinned to the trunk of one of the oaks that lined the path. Her name was embossed on the front in big, black letters.

Sadie looked around uneasily, but everything was still. She walked closer. Inside the envelope was a piece of heavy cream stationery with a note.

You've proven your worth. Now give us a chance to prove ours.
The locker room. 9 A.M.

It wasn't signed, but Sadie knew who it was from. Them. The Order of Optimates, or whatever the hell their dumb name was.

Sadie let her head fall back and stared at the sky. The practical part of her—the part that knew reality TV was the beginning of the end and that Wheaties covered in her usual two scoops of sugar probably wasn't actually the breakfast of champions—knew she didn't want anything to do with whoever had written that note. But she had to admit she was a little curious. What kind of group would go to all the trouble they had to scare her? Who were they? What did they want?

For a moment she played with the idea of going along with it, just to find out more. Then she saw Thayer's face in her mind—or at least, the shadow of Thayer's face buried under her black hood—and she heard those words again. *Was your mother a whore?*

Sadie ripped the paper in half and dropped it on the ground, making sure to leave a muddy footprint across its face as she continued down the path.

"Sadie, stop."

She knew that voice, but it wasn't the one she was expecting. She whirled around angrily to see Brett standing behind her, breathing heavily with a pleading look on her face.

"Don't do this. You don't know what you're giving up."

Sadie shook her head slowly. "You're one of them?"

Brett took a step forward and reached out to her. "Yes, but it's not what you think—"

"Okay, so you guys didn't kidnap me, strap me to a chair in a dark, scary room, and try to humiliate me in front of a room full of people?" Sadie's voice cracked, and she took a breath. The next sentence came out softer—angrier. "And your creepy friend didn't choke me until I almost passed out? 'Cause that's what I think."

Brett's whole body seemed to sag. "You're right. You're completely, 100 percent right. The whole ceremony is ridiculous. And the Moirae are assholes." She held up her hands. "I'm not one of them, I promise. But it's just the way we do things. It's been that way for a long time."

Sadie wasn't impressed. "Look, I just don't want anything to do with it, okay? Pick someone else." She turned away from Brett and kept walking.

"We can't. It has to be you."

"Whatever," Sadie called over her shoulder. "Still don't care."

"You were chosen by blood, Sadie. You're a legacy."

She said the words so quietly that Sadie barely caught them. She stopped.

"What did you just say?"

Brett took a step closer. "Your mom was one of us."

Sadie shook her head. "No way. I don't believe you." From what she could remember, her mom wasn't exactly the kind of person who would have joined something as pretentious and ridiculous as a secret sorority.

"I can prove it."

"But she was nobody. She was here on scholarship, just like me."

Brett frowned. "Sadie that's not—" She cut herself off, a frown deepening between her eyebrows. "Look, the others can explain everything." She could see Sadie weakening, and she smiled encouragingly. "Just give us a chance. Hang out with me today. We're not doing anything scary. No ropes, no polygraph, no dark rooms, I promise."

"No Thayer?"

Brett bit her lip to hide a smile and shook her head.

"Fine. But I swear, any tricks and I will never speak to you again. Seriously."

Brett grinned widely and grabbed her arm. "Deal. Now come on—I have some things I want to show you."

☙

Inside, the locker room was completely dark. Brett positioned Sadie in the center of the room and ran off down the hallway.

"Ready?" she called.

"That depends," Sadie yelled back.

The lights flipped on. On the floor in front of Brett's locker were three enormous shopping bags with brand names Sadie had only ever seen in magazines. Hanging inside was a long black garment bag and the most beautiful ivory wool coat Sadie had ever seen. It definitely looked like something Brett would wear. And something Sadie would defile with ketchup or coffee (or both) within about five seconds.

Sadie frowned. "You went shopping?" She couldn't figure out why Brett would go to so much trouble just to show off her haul.

Brett appeared back in the doorway with a big grin on her face. "You are so weird sometimes, Sadie." She swept an arm toward her locker. "It's not for me—it's all yours. Now change. We need to hurry if we're going to make it to the pad in time."

Brett set to work tearing apart the shopping bags and throwing items of clothing at Sadie. She struggled into a slinky cashmere dress that fit her like it had been hand knitted by magical fairies, a pair of chocolate suede ankle booties, and a drapey gold necklace and matching earrings. From the last bag, Brett lifted a huge purse that she cradled as carefully as a newborn.

She handed it to Sadie, her voice dropping to a deferential whisper. "Do you know what this is?"

Sadie shrugged. "A bag?"

Brett gasped and hugged the purse to her chest. "Do not let it hear you say that." She shook her head, then handed it over. "Just be careful with it. Samantha French carries that handbag, you know."

Sadie barely had time to loop the bag over her shoulder and glance in the mirror before Brett dragged her out the door.

&

"This is a joke, right? Are you tricking me into being a contestant on a dating show or something, 'cause I'm not really interested in dating a thirty-year-old with Ken-doll hair, spray-on abs, and the personality of a cardboard cutout."

Brett laughed. "It's just faster, okay? It's not like we do this all the time." She hopped up into the helicopter and extended a hand for Sadie. "Are you ready to see what you're getting yourself into?"

Sadie paused. The chopper blades were whirring overhead, and the sound made her feel dizzy and heady. For a moment, she wondered how the heck she had ever gotten to this moment, standing on a helicopter pad in $600 shoes. In the next second, she decided that right then, she didn't really care.

"Come on, Sadie," Brett said again. "You're ready for this." Sadie took her hand and let herself be pulled on board.

A shiny black car met them on the outskirts of D.C. The driver tipped his hat to Brett and took off without even waiting for a destination.

As they settled into the plush seats, green forests gave way to shining metal and glass downtown, then the redbrick row houses of historic Georgetown. They kept driving, winding up into rolling hills. Finally, they pulled up to a modern wrought-iron gate that stretched between two stone pillars. The driver mumbled a few words into an intercom, and the gate swung open.

A huge stone mansion unfolded in front of them, surrounded on all sides by manicured lawns. The house had a wide porch that was lined with benches and rocking chairs, and the grass was dotted with cherry trees. People in pairs milled around the grounds or sat in the cool shade of the porch, some reading or playing games. The sun was shining and a cool breeze ruffled the ivy that clung to the mansion's walls. It looked like paradise.

"Where are we?" Sadie asked, looking closer at a nearby man and woman until she realized why they all looked so similar. They were all wearing the same subtle shades of blue, green, and lavender. Hospital patients.

Brett just linked an arm through hers and led her up the brick path toward the door.

"I want to show you what you have a chance to be a part of. All the good we do—all the good you can do if you become one of us. You ready?"

Sadie nodded, and they passed through the doors into a cool, high-ceilinged foyer. There was a small reception desk on one side, and a young woman in a pale blue sweater smiled up at them. Above her on the wall hung a brass plaque engraved with the words, "Enlighten the people, and tyranny and oppressions of body and mind will vanish like spirits at the dawn of day."

"Good afternoon, Ms. Whitney. Will you be touring the North Wing today?"

Brett nodded and the woman clicked on her headset and dialed. As she waited, the woman kept stealing glances in Sadie's direction until she started to squirm. Finally she murmured a few words, then hung up.

"You're all set. Dr. Kent will meet you on the second-floor landing." She turned to Sadie and smiled again, with just a hint of something playing at the edge of her features. Sadie couldn't put her finger on it, but she looked almost . . . excited. "Welcome to Dawning House, Ms. Marlowe. Please let me know if I can assist you with anything at all during your time here."

Sadie thanked her and followed Brett up a curving staircase. The click of her new heels echoed loudly against the marble.

Dr. Kent was petite and brunette, and she wore a stylish wrap dress under her white lab coat. She shook both of their hands and smiled broadly. "Good to see you, Ms. Whitney. We missed you over the summer." She turned to Sadie. "Your friend's been a great help to us here at Dawning. I hear you are also interested in volunteering at the center?"

Sadie paused, and Brett squeezed her elbow just slightly. "Yes, definitely. It's a beautiful facility." The doctor seemed pleased, and she gestured for them to follow as she clicked off down a long gleaming hallway.

First, she led them down the hall to a large, high-ceilinged room decked out with comfortable chairs, couches, a large-screen TV, and Ping-Pong tables. "One of our many patient lobbies," she said, gesturing toward the TV. "As you can see, our patients are never bored." She smiled, and Sadie noticed the center had every gaming console she could think of.

Dr. Kent ushered them back into the hallway, but not before Sadie noticed something that flooded her mind with uncomfortable memories. The huge, antique-paned windows were beautiful, but they were also lined with metal bars. Sadie swallowed the memories back down and cleared her throat.

"What kind of patients do you typically have here, Dr. Kent?"

Dr. Kent whirled around, stopping suddenly in her path. "Typically, we handle substance abuse cases, but we are open to healing of all kinds."

Sadie blinked. "So this is a mental hospital."

Brett coughed uncomfortably next to her, but the doctor seemed unfazed. "We prefer to think of ourselves as a comfortable environment that is most conducive to mental, emotional, and physical healing." She leaned in conspiratorially. "But yes, that would be correct in the common vernacular." She smiled again and practically bounced down the hallway. "Now come on, I'd love to show you our new patient rooms."

They spent another half hour touring the hospital, but with every new room there was a new memory. The cheerfully painted hallways triggered flashes of cold linoleum, and the clean, crisp white linens in the bedrooms made her see dingy municipal hospital sheets. Every detail was soothing and beautiful. She couldn't wait to leave.

When they finally said goodbye and emerged onto the porch, the sunshine soaked into her skin like a salve. "Mind giving me a sec? I'm just going to run to the ladies'." Brett hurried back inside, and Sadie sank down gratefully onto a small wooden bench. A patient and one of the nurses shuffled by in front of the porch, and the woman stared at Sadie with wide, unblinking eyes.

Sadie nodded hello, and the woman smiled back. "Don't let them take you into the basement," she said, the smile still plastered across her face.

The nurse put an arm around the woman's shoulders and ushered her away. He looked back at Sadie and gave her a sympathetic smile. "Alzheimer's," he mouthed.

Sadie leaned back and closed her eyes. In the dark behind her eyelids she saw the last time she visited her mom. She had waited in the hallway outside her room for a long time, watching hollow-eyed nurses shuffling back and forth with papers and pills. When her dad finally waved her inside, she barely even recognized her mother—so pale and thin inside her papery white robe. She had been so heavily medicated she barely knew who Sadie was. Her dad didn't say a word the entire way home.

Sadie tried to focus on taking deep breaths, each one pushing the memory back down a little farther, but something interrupted her thoughts. Someone was crying.

A few yards away on the porch was a little girl Sadie hadn't noticed before—no more than eight or nine—sitting with her knees drawn up underneath her. She had tears streaming down her cheeks.

Sadie looked around, but none of the staff members were close by. She stood up and took a few steps toward the girl.

"Are you okay?"

The little girl didn't respond. She just stared out into the garden, her eyes glassy with tears. Sadie sat down next to her.

"You know, I still remember what it was like." Sadie paused, and the girl sniffled again. "Visiting."

The girl turned, and for the first time Sadie saw how piercing and blue her eyes were. The girl wiped a hand across her cheek, rubbing away the tears. "Who were you visiting?"

"My mom."

"Me too," the little girl said, her voice small.

"It'll get easier."

The girl nodded, but Sadie could see she wasn't convinced. "Your mom's in really good hands. This is an incredible hospital."

"Do you think they can make her better? She was in another place before . . . a not so nice place . . . and it didn't work. She was still sick, but Dr. Kent said they could help her here for free."

Sadie saw the entrance to her mom's hospital, all cold concrete and flat fluorescent lights. She blinked the image away, and her eye wandered across the grass to where two patients sat, sunning themselves on Adirondack chairs. They looked so peaceful, but still she didn't want to lie. This girl didn't need one more person giving her cheap, empty hope.

"My mom never did. But she wasn't here, and this place seems different. Your mom is exactly where she needs to be."

The girl smiled hesitantly, just as a new tear slid down her cheek. "Thanks." She bit her lip and fumbled with the hem of her pink sweatshirt. "Will you wait with me until she comes out?"

Sadie smiled. "Sure." The girl reached out and took her hand. It felt so tiny.

A door behind them opened.

"Cassandra?"

Sadie and the little girl both turned toward the voice. There was a woman standing with a nurse in the doorway, a wide smile on her face. Her brown hair was pulled up into a neat ponytail, and her cheeks were flushed with pink. She looked happy and alive.

The girl jumped up and ran to her, and she knelt down, enveloping her in a huge hug. The girl was crying again, but it felt different. It felt like relief.

Sadie stood up to give them some privacy, and as she walked away she heard the mother murmuring softly. "Mommy's going to be okay now, Cassie. Everything's going to be okay."

❦

She was standing at the porch railing, watching the mother and daughter as they walked through the garden, hand in hand, when Brett called to her from the doorway.

"Want to sit and talk for a bit?" She pointed back to the bench. "My feet are killing me in these heels."

"Sure." Sadie looked down at her new boots. She wiggled her toes and realized they were numb. "Mine too."

"So are you doing okay? I know this is probably weird for you."

Sadie took a deep breath. "I'm okay. It just brings back a lot of stuff I don't really like to think about." She looked sideways at Brett. "Why'd you bring me here?"

"We wanted to show you what we do—what we're really about, beyond the ceremonies and the gifts and parties and everything else." She gestured to the manicured grounds. "We fund projects. Help people. We make things better."

"So this group—whoever you are—you all volunteer at this hospital?"

Brett paused for a moment, lifting her chin and gazing out over the gardens.

"Actually, we built it."

Sadie sat back, stunned. Maybe she had misjudged them. The rituals were stupid—and any group who chose Thayer to be a member had some serious problems—but they were making a difference. They were using the power they had to help people. That couldn't be all bad.

"So this is the group's thing? Helping people through rehab?"

Brett shook her head. "The Sullas have lots of interests—"

"The whats? I thought you called yourselves the Order of Optimus or something?"

Brett grinned. "Optimates." She waved a hand. "It's a really old name that means 'Best Men.' Within the group, we just call ourselves the Sullas—long story. Anyway, once you're in, you'll have access to a lot—money, resources, connections. Some people have a pet project they pursue, and the Dawning House was one of them."

Sadie nodded. "So whose project was it?"

"Sorry, Sadie. Can't tell you anything about the other members. But I can say he had personal reasons. His girlfriend from a long time ago had problems with this kind of thing. It messed him up, and he swore he would help other people with the same issues."

For the first time, Sadie felt a twinge of excitement. She was being given the opportunity to be a part of something huge, a part of something that was helping make sure no one else ever went through what she did.

Brett stood up and carefully brushed off her dress. "Ready to go? The hard part's over. Now we eat."

An hour later they were lounging over sushi and champagne at a fancy restaurant in Georgetown. The waitress hadn't even carded them—apparently carrying a $4,000 handbag meant nobody asked questions. The feeling was a little intoxicating, like she was invincible and could do whatever she wanted.

By the time they were landing back at Keating, the chopper blades beating loudly overhead, Sadie was completely drunk—on champagne, and on the overwhelming momentum of everything that was falling into place around her. At the same time, it all felt a little wild, like something had been set in motion that was too powerful for anyone to stop. But maybe that was just it—the power was running straight through her, and for the first time Sadie realized how much she liked that feeling.

Chapter 12

A week later, Thayer waltzed into the dining room looking even more smug than usual. She hadn't said anything to Sadie about the canceled practice, or about anything Sadie had seen in D.C., but every once in a while she caught Thayer watching her, an odd expression on her face. Sadie was getting the feeling there might be more to Thayer than the standard-issue entitled heiress she seemed to play so well, but she still didn't want anything to do with her.

That morning her cheeks were flushed, and she held a huge bouquet of roses cradled in one arm like the runner-up at a small-town beauty pageant. Her followers trailed behind her, screeching even louder than usual, jockeying for position and tossing their shiny hair in each other's faces.

Before Sadie could ask, Jessica let out a groan. "Every effing year. Like anyone here gives a crap that Finn invited her to a fifteenth dance and gave her a forty-seventh present that his dad's latest personal assistant-slash-mistress probably picked out anyway."

"I don't know," Brett said. "I think it's kind of sweet. At least he's romantic."

"Yeah well, easy to say when you have a date. When you don't, this whole thing feels like a regularly scheduled kick in the face." Jessica slumped down in her chair.

Sadie flashed her a sympathetic look before Thayer's envoy closed in.

"Hey, laaadies," she cooed. She thrust the flowers forward like a woman offering her baby up for baptism. "So pretty, right? Finn is such a sweetheart. I just can't get him to stop spoiling me." She slithered into one of the chairs as her sheep performed their usual standoff—each one trying to grab the closest seat while keeping up the constant stream of phony compliments they were always lobbing at each other. Their restraint was actually kind of impressive. Sadie was sure one day someone was going to throw an elbow and end up spraying blood all over the dining room floor.

"So," Jessica said, with obvious sarcasm. "How. Did. He. Do it? We're all just dying to know."

Thayer's blue eyes narrowed to slits. "I would be, if I were you." She leaned back in her chair and tossed her hair over her shoulder, revealing a giant diamond earring. Reverential gasps echoed around the table. "I don't really want to tell the whole story now, though. It's so long, and I mean, it's really not that exciting. Once you've had a boyfriend as long as I have, this kind of stuff just starts to feel"—she curled her lip and shrugged—"average."

All around the table, faces fell. "Tell us! Tell us!" the chorus kicked in.

Thayer broke into a coy smile. "But then again, I guess it's selfish of me to deny you single girls the chance to live vicariously." She looked pointedly at Jessica, then launched into a story that spanned breakfast, the walk to chapel, lunch, dinner, and half of practice the next morning. By the time they all straggled into the locker room, Sadie could recount the name of the jeweler who had designed Thayer's new diamond earrings, the model of the limo Finn had used to deliver the gift, the name of Finn's family's private "suit guy," and all twenty-seven of the sappy texts he had sent her, verbatim, since Friday morning.

In the shower, she let the hot water pound against her forehead, drowning out all the other girls' voices as they carried over the tops of the stalls and mingled with clouds of steam. Afterward, she dressed and hurried out the door, calling to the other girls that she would wait for them on the bleachers. Brett tossed her a knowing look, and Jessica yelled, "Just want some fresh air, huh?"

Sadie ignored her, but as the door swung shut she heard her call out, "Tell Jeremy I said hi."

The weather had turned in the last week, and the autumn air felt cool and crisp as she walked toward the bleachers. She pulled her jacket closer around her body and climbed a few rows up.

After that first night on the field, she had been sure she would hear from Jeremy. She had made excuses to run back to her room between classes to check her e-mail and carried her cell phone with her at all times, even though he didn't even have her number. And every time she had checked and found nothing—no e-mails, no texts, not even a lame wall-post—she had hated herself just a little more.

Lately she had stopped hoping for contact, but she couldn't help looking for him whenever she got the chance. She scanned the players on the field—all alike in their white mesh jerseys and forest green helmets—until she found number forty-two. Just finding him in the crowd was enough to make her pulse speed up. He was still there, within reach, and if he turned around she could imagine he just might be looking at her, too.

She heard steps on the bleachers above her and turned to see a man making his way down from the knot of alumni that always sat near the top. When Sadie had asked about them weeks earlier, Brett had just waved a hand and said they were boosters—"lacrosse types, you know?" Sadie hadn't, but she hadn't pushed it, either. She just figured they were having some serious trouble moving past their glory years. Most high schools had a few.

She turned back to the field and leaned forward, resting her chin on her knees. Forty-two was lost in a huddle now, so she settled in to wait.

"Sadie Marlowe, right?"

It was a deep voice—smooth, with the kind of aristocratic southern accent she had adopted in her head when she read *Gone with the Wind*. She looked over her shoulder. He was tall and tan, dressed in a slim-cut navy suit with no tie. He held out a hand.

"Teddy Cranston."

She took it silently, too confused to formulate a proper response. Instead she just stared.

He had a square jaw, blue eyes, and blonde-streaked yacht club hair, the kind that looked like it was continuously being tousled by some phantom ocean breeze. He was the type of guy who would play the lead in a cheesy rom-com—he would be excruciatingly charming and witty, and she and her friends would make fun of everything he said.

"Mind if I join you?"

She opened her mouth to answer, but he was already folding himself into the seat next to her. They sat for a moment and gazed out across the field. She floundered for something to say.

"You're Finn's dad, right? You built this stadium."

He laughed. "My family did. I'm just a Graff alum who really loves the Monarchs." He held out his right hand, showing off two huge rings. One had a gleaming green stone with a yellow gold monogram, and the other looked like a class ring, with a shiny black stone rimmed with diamond chips. He pointed to the latter. "National Champs, 1988," he said, puffing out his chest. "And you, if my intel is correct, are the new transfer."

She relaxed. This made more sense. Booster talk. She mustered up a smile. "Yeah, from Portland."

"So how do you like playing for Keating so far?"

"Oh, it's been great. I'm just really excited for the season to start. And it's an honor to play for Coach Fitz," she parroted. Boosters always wanted to hear the same thing: Everything's great! This is our year!

"Yes, she has done a lot for the program. Then again, Keating and Graff have always had stellar lacrosse teams." He looked down at his hand and flexed his fingers so the emerald glinted in the sun. "Eighteen national championships in the past twenty-five years." He looked at Sadie. "We have high hopes for you helping to continue that legacy."

"Thanks." She paused, floundering for a way to deflect the compliment. "I just hope I can compete. Lacrosse is a whole different world on the East Coast."

"That's true. But you girls have been working hard in the off-season, I'm sure." He smiled and patted her knee, his hand lingering just long enough for her to feel the heat from his palm spreading across her thigh. He stood up.

"I just wanted to say hello. I make it my business to know everything about this lacrosse program, and you're a part of that now." He reached out his hand. "Welcome to the family—I'm sure you'll do us proud."

She shook his hand again, then watched as he climbed back up the bleachers, turning back just in time to see Jessica bounding up the bleachers toward her. She was two minutes into a rant about something Thayer had said in the locker room before Sadie finally shook herself back into focus.

"Hey, why would Teddy Cranston know who I am?" she interrupted. The look on Jessica's face changed from annoyed to incredulous in an instant.

"Ooh, you met Teddy Cranston? Hot, right? In a weird, old-guy kinda way. He looks like a movie star. I cannot believe he and Finn came out of the same gene pool." She craned her neck around and looked back up at him in the stands. "I mean, how did that happen?"

Sadie shrugged. "He just like, came down and introduced himself. He said he heard I transferred and wanted to say hi. It was weird."

Jessica shook her head. "I've been here for two years and none of the Cranstons have ever even looked at me. Well except Finn, but, ew." She shuddered. "Anyway, Teddy is always at games and stuff. I guess it's not that strange that he would know who you are. It was a big deal when they announced that you were coming." She looked sideways at Sadie. "Don't act like you don't know that." She grinned and Sadie laughed.

"Whatever," Sadie said. "And he can't be that old," she added. "What do you think, forty-five?"

"Maybe. He's married though. Hands off, you little skank."

Sadie's jaw dropped and she shoved Jessica in the shoulder. "Oh my god, so not what I meant. Gross. He's my dad's age."

Brett sat down and started carefully picking invisible lint off of her cable-knit sweater.

"Hey, Brett, what do you think about Teddy Cranston—would you do him? Sadie thinks he's old."

Brett's shoulders tensed, and she turned and scowled at Jessica. "You know, you can be really immature sometimes, Jess."

She turned back to face the field and Jessica made a face. "Hey, I wasn't the one flirting with him, but whatevs," Jessica said.

Brett raised an eyebrow at Sadie. "Teddy talked to you?"

She shrugged. "Just for a second." Brett bit her lip, and there was something in her expression that Sadie couldn't quite identify. Brett noticed Sadie watching her and arranged her features into a wide smile. "Well, I'm sure he just wanted to meet the new recruit." She winked. "Everybody does."

Jessica stood up and patted her stomach. "Let's go. I'm effing starving."

The Graff team was grouped around the water cooler as they walked by, and as Sadie watched, Jeremy turned his head and met her eyes. For a second he did nothing, then held up a hand and waved, just a hint of a smile playing at the edges of his mouth. Sadie smiled back and linked one arm happily through Jessica's.

"Don't think I didn't see that, you little hobag," Jessica said, without turning her head.

∾

Sadie came back from dinner that night to an empty room. She hadn't seen the twins in the dining room, and she realized that lately, she hadn't seen much of them at all. She would sometimes see them lazily sipping coffee in the dining room in the afternoon, looking disheveled and sleepy, like grumpy cats. She almost never saw them after dinner though, and if they didn't duck into the room at three minutes to 10 P.M., they stumbled in hours later, carrying their red-soled platforms and slurring their words like drunken British frat boys. She never asked them where they went, and some nights they didn't come back at all.

And yet, somehow they hadn't gotten caught. Mrs. Darrow supposedly did random bed checks, but they hadn't had one since the first week of the semester. She remembered Ellen Bennett and the clack-clack-clacking of her heels. It made her wonder how much power that woman actually had over this school.

Sadie sat on her bed and stared at the empty room. It was only eight, but Brett had left the lobby early to work on a physics lab, and Jessica and Grace were writing essays. The rest of the team was in the TV room watching a *Diva Divorcées* marathon, and Sadie had barely gotten through three minutes of it without feeling like she was going to spontaneously combust.

Her eyes fell on her running shoes piled in the corner of the room, and she stood up.

ભ

The quad was quiet, but she still skipped from shadow to shadow until she was safely on the beach. Once on the path, she broke into a run, drawing in the salty air and feeling the wind whipping through her hair. It felt good.

Her muscles ached, but as she worked she felt them start to release. She could feel her stiff joints loosening, her stride falling easily into the familiar rhythm. She pushed herself faster than usual, letting all of her confusion and excitement and anxiety fuel her until it burned up like candle wax, leaving nothing behind but hot beads of sweat that dripped down her forehead.

She took the path to the stadium and jogged across the turf to the 50-yard line. Her sweatshirt felt heavy and damp, and she stripped it off and dropped it in a pile on the grass. She finished four 300-yard sprints before she finally collapsed onto the ground, breathing heavily and closing her eyes.

She lay there for minutes, her mind finally quiet and her body screaming in pain. She thought about nothing except the drawing in and out of breath, and for once everything was still.

When her limbs stopped burning, she sat up. The wind picked up around her, and she shivered as goose bumps pushed up through her skin. She picked up her damp sweatshirt and glanced at the field house. The lights were on. She thought about a hot shower and dry clothes, and within seconds she was walking across the grass toward them.

She rounded the building and tried the door to the locker room, but it wouldn't budge. She cursed under her breath and walked to the front entrance, but that was locked, too. As a last resort she tried the door to the Graff lacrosse locker room, and the knob turned easily. She whispered a thank you to whichever forgetful employee had decided to slack off that day and stepped inside.

She paused in the hallway and listened, but everything was quiet. Suddenly curious, she looked around; the foyer was identical to theirs, down to the ugly gray industrial carpeting and the green and blue painted trim on the walls, but the air was different. Instead of the usual scent of shampoo and flowery shower gel, all she could smell was feet.

She jogged away from the smell down a narrow hallway that seemed to lead in the right direction. She was getting colder, and she was nearing a full sprint when she rounded a corner and smacked, face- and boobs-first, into a wall of abs.

"Oh! God, sorry, I . . . " She blinked at the pecs that stared back at her at eye level, realizing they looked oddly familiar. She jerked her head up and saw Jeremy looking down at her in surprise, a wide smile spreading across his face.

"Okay, now that time you scared me."

She opened her mouth to respond, but then her whole body froze up. He had caught her on impact, and now his hands rested loosely on her lower back. Her palms were flat on his shoulders, and he was radiating heat like he had just stepped out of the shower.

Her face flushed, and she forced herself to breathe. She looked up again and he was still smiling down at her, a look of amusement on his face.

She quickly stepped back. "Sorry, I didn't know anyone was in here." She squared her shoulders and tried to regain some composure, but she knew she was blushing. She remembered her sweaty, probably now kinda see-through tank top and crossed her arms awkwardly over her chest. "Our door was locked."

He laughed. "No problem. I heard you coming down the hall, so you didn't really scare me. I just expected it to be one of the other guys, not, you know, some girl who was obviously trying to sneak in here to catch me in this vulnerable state." He pointed to his towel, and it took all of her focus to keep her eyes above waist level.

Her jaw dropped. "I was not!" Then she caught sight of his grin and gave up. "Oh, shut up." They stood there for a second, grinning stupidly at each other, until he broke the silence.

"So, um, why don't you go do what you need to do." He looked down at his towel. "I should probably put some clothes on before you completely lose control."

"Very funny," she deadpanned. She shrugged and tipped her head to the side in mock scrutiny. "To be honest, it's not even that impressive." It was such a lie, it felt like sacrilege.

His jaw dropped in horror. "Oh man, don't say that. I just spent, like, twenty minutes doing abs, and I don't think I have any more in me." She shrugged and he laughed. "Okay, go do your thing—perm your hair or whatever. I'll wait for you back here."

"Pfff, please." She started to walk towards the door, then stopped. "Wait, you'll what?"

"I'm walking you back to Keating," he said, a grin spreading across his face. "It's dangerous out there."

After she showered, she dug through Jessica's locker and pulled out the only clean thing she could find—one of the "cute" workout outfits Jessica claimed her mom was always sending her. This one was a pair of stretchy, hot pink yoga pants and a matching zip-up that seemed designed specifically to show maximum cleavage while you downward dogged. It was a little embarrassing, but then again if Jeremy had a secret trophy-wife-after-Pilates fantasy, it was definitely his lucky day.

She found him sitting on the ground in front of his locker, a ragged-looking paperback spread open on his lap. He looked up and raised his eyebrows, but she held up a hand.

"I know. I don't have my own locker yet, and it was either this, putting my sweaty clothes back on, or swiping someone's game uniform."

"Actually I was just going to say that I like it. I think my sisters would be really jealous."

"Oh yeah? And how old are they?"

He grinned. "Nine and eleven. Big Barbie fans."

She made a face, but before she could respond he stood up. She had been standing over him, and suddenly he was so close she could smell that distinctive boy-after-shower smell, a mix of lingering heat and Axe shower gel. It made her feel dizzy.

"I'm just kidding, you know. You look great—you always do."

She crossed her arms over her chest to keep from reaching out and grabbing him. "Oh yeah? And you've seen me what, like twice?"

"Well, yeah. But . . . you're around." He shrugged his shoulders. "Our teams share a field, you know? I'm not blind."

She smiled to herself and followed him out the door and across the stadium. They reached the end of the turf and turned right, following the path out to the beach.

"You're really great by the way," he said. "At lacrosse. You have a wicked side arm shot."

She looked at him, but she couldn't make out much more than his profile in the dark. "Thanks." She bit her lip to keep from smiling too widely, but still she felt like she was skirting dangerously close to jack-o'-lantern territory. Any minute her hysterical excitement would light her up from the inside and give her away.

They both fell silent, and she realized it was her move. "So—" she started, hoping she would come up with something by the time the "o" limped off her tongue. "How's school?" She bit the inside of her cheek in frustration. Rough choice.

"It's pretty good," he said. "The guys are all cool—well, most of them—and I like my classes. My roommate's great, too. You know Josh, right?" She nodded. He was silent for a moment. "To be honest, I really thought I'd hate it here."

They were on the beach path now, and she could tell he was looking out over the ocean. His face was in shadow, but she could see the curve of his jaw lit up in the moonlight. A part of her—the same part that led her subconscious through the same cheesy dreamscape every night—wanted to lean in and lick it.

He looked back at her. "This place isn't really, me, you know?"

Something about his expression made her hold his gaze. "I know exactly what you mean."

"Thought so." Something in him seemed to relax, and he started to whistle quietly, hands jammed in his pockets. They reached the turnoff toward Keating's campus, and he stopped.

"Hate to say it, but I think this is where I turn around. I hear Cromwell doesn't take kindly to Graffs on campus after dark."

Sadie rolled her eyes. "Probably not."

For a second he was quiet, and she could see the moonlight tripping into a tiny divot that was deepening between his eyebrows. He opened his mouth, then seemed to change his mind.

"Well, thanks for walking me home," she said, too loudly.

"Anytime. You know, if you ever want to work out after hours you should text me first."

She raised her eyebrows. "Is that a euphemism?"

He grinned wickedly. "Nope. I'd be happy to kick your butt in some 300s any time you want."

"You wish." She had just started to turn away when she felt a hand on her arm.

"Hey, wait a sec."

She turned, and he was so close she could feel his body heat.

"I've been wanting to do this for a while, and I know it's probably too late now—I'm guessing at least three guys have asked you already but,"—he paused—"is there any chance you would want to go to the Autumn Ball with me?"

There was a smile on his face, but she could see something else there too, just a shadow of uncertainty that weighed on his features.

He's nervous. Suddenly she wanted to laugh out loud.

Instead, she smiled. "Hell, yeah."

He laughed, clearly relieved, and she smiled wider.

"Okay, then. Well, I'll call you next week—we can figure out the details." He gave her a mock salute. "Good night, Sadie Marlowe."

She waved and watched as he walked away. After a few steps he turned around and she could see him grinning as he called out, "Just don't wear that outfit to the dance, okay?"

Chapter 13

The next morning she woke up feeling tired, sore, and completely irrationally happy. It had been after ten when she got back, but she had padded down to Jessica's room anyway, the news bubbling up inside of her and threatening to overflow. She had run in and spilled everything, even before Madison could whip off her eye mask and yell at them for waking her up.

After she had huffed and sniffed and flopped over on her other side, they talked in hushed whispers for another hour, Sadie analyzing every detail and Jessica asking follow-up questions like an investigative reporter. When they had finally exhausted everything from his smell to his clothes to his exact quotes ("Did he say he saw you, or did he say he watched you, 'cause like, ohmygodsoawesome or like, easy psycho, you're so not giving him your skin for a lady-suit"), they adjourned the strategy meeting, and Sadie had tiptoed back to her room. She was asleep by the time her head hit the pillow.

She spent most of breakfast in a happy fog. She sat at her usual table, listening to the girls chattering on about "Jailbait Jenny," Keating's and Graff's latest sex scandal. Some freshman had gotten caught in one of the senior Graff dorm rooms doing what was probably making out but depending on who you listened to could also have been dry humping or filming a soft-core sex tape for his YouTube channel. She was already gone, whisked away early that morning by her father's chauffeur and leaving nothing but gossip as evidence of her stay at the illustrious Keating Hall.

The noise floated over her and around her, and she uh-huh'ed and totally'ed at all the right moments, but she was too busy looking around for Brett to really commit to Jenny's roast. She hadn't had a chance to talk to her alone since their trip to D.C., and she had so many questions, she felt like she couldn't concentrate on anything else. What happened now? Was Sadie going to be invited to join them, and if so, did she even want to?

Brett never showed at breakfast, and instead of slipping in beside Sadie at chapel, out of breath and sneaking bites of low-carb English muffin from her bag, she never showed up there either. Sadie didn't think much of it until the bell rang for their first-period calculus class. Brett—and her pencil case, ruler, and notebook, all set in perfect parallel formation on the oval table—was still nowhere to be found.

After an hour of rational functions, she resigned herself to waiting until lunch to launch her verbal assault. When Brett still hadn't shown by dinner, she interrupted Charlotte midway through a rave about the new eyelash glue her makeup artist had sent her to ask where Brett was. The table stared back at her, a dozen sets of eyes wide as cows', mouths robotically chewing their organic, fat-free, low-calorie cud.

"Uh, where have you been all day?" Jessica whispered. "Brett's, like, really sick or something. She's in the nurse's office, and they won't let anyone see her."

Charlotte perked up. "I heard it's mono or herpes or something. Whatever it is, it's super contagious. That's why no one can go in."

"It's not herpes, Charlotte," Jessica shot back. "She's no Jailbait Jenny."

"Hey, I'm just saying what I heard." She pursed her lips and shrugged her thin shoulders. "I mean, it's not like she's Josh's first."

Eyes all around the table widened, and Jessica's narrowed. "At least Brett can remember her first, Charlotte."

Before Charlotte could respond, Jessica slung her oversized purse over one arm and stood up. "And you're going to feel like a real asshole if Brett's really sick." She stomped away, but Charlotte just shrugged and looked bored. Sadie followed her out the door, and she heard the table behind her dissolve into laughter.

She caught up with Jessica in the lobby, and they sunk down into big leather armchairs in their usual corner of the room. The spot was their observation deck—far enough from the couches that their voices didn't carry to where the rest of the girls usually sat, but close enough to keep an eye on the natives in their natural habitat. Brett, Sadie, and Jessica spent most nights after practice draped on the furniture, studying or pretending to, and tonight things felt all wrong without her there.

"What was that about?" Sadie asked, as she leaned her head back against the cushions.

"Ugh, Charlotte's always such a bitch about Josh. She's still so bitter that he dumped her in seventh grade."

"What about Brett though—we really don't know anything?"

Jessica shrugged. "I guess not. I ran into Coach after lunch, and she said Brett didn't want any visitors. Maybe she just has strep or something, so she can't be around people for a couple days?" She cocked her head to the side, then suddenly widened her eyes. "Ew, maybe it's lice? I totally had that once when I was little. Got it from my brother. If you tell anyone I said that I'll definitely murder you in your sleep. But anyway yeah, I'm sure she's fine. We'll go check on her tomorrow—maybe we'll be able to see her then?"

Sadie just nodded, but she knew she couldn't wait that long.

Half an hour later she was jogging across the quad toward the infirmary. Down a narrow hallway, she found a nurse's office and poked her head inside. A plump woman in an old-fashioned nurse's uniform was sitting at a desk, reading a paperback. Sadie cleared her throat, and the woman looked up in surprise.

"Didn't see you there, dear. Can I help you with something?" She reached a hand toward Sadie's forehead, but Sadie shook her head.

"I'm actually looking for my friend, Brett Whitney. She came in last night, I think?"

The woman's smile faded. "Oh, I'm very sorry, dear, but Brett isn't taking any visitors right now."

Sadie frowned. "How come? Is she contagious?"

"Oh no, she's not sick." The nurse paused. "She had a bad fall and she's pretty bruised up. She just isn't really up for seeing anyone yet."

Sadie bit her lip, weighing whether or not it would be worth just making a break for it. The woman didn't exactly look like a sprinter.

"You know, you look very familiar," the woman smiled, but she had an odd look on her face. "Did you have a sister who was a student?"

Sadie shrugged. "Nope. Only child."

"Ah well, there's something about you—just feels like I've met you before. I'm Nurse Brennan, by the way." She held out a small plump hand.

"Sadie Marlowe." They shook hands, and Sadie could still see the woman studying her face intently. "My mom was a student, though. Like twenty years ago."

The woman's eyes widened. "That must be it! What's her name?"

"It was Maylynne—" The nurse's eyes got so wide that Sadie cut herself off. "What?"

The woman busied herself smoothing down a page in her book, but Sadie saw a shadow pass over her face. "Nothing, dear. She always seemed like a very nice young lady. I'm glad she got herself sorted out."

Sadie raised her eyebrows. "What do you mean?"

The nurse gave her a hard look. "She was a patient of mine for awhile before she left Keating. It was right after her accident—I'm sure you've heard the story."

"Actually, I haven't."

"Oh . . . "—she squirmed uncomfortably—"well, she was swimming with some friends at the beach, and she got too close to the rocks near that old tower. Nearly got crushed by the waves."

She must have seen the look of horror on Sadie's face because she patted her arm. "Gave me quite a fright, but she was lucky. Just a broken leg and some bruised ribs." Nurse Brennan cocked her head to the side. "You know, you really do look just like her. Same pretty blue eyes and wavy blonde hair—must be those famous genes."

Sadie's head was spinning. How could her dad have never mentioned her mom's accident?

"You sure you're okay, hon'? I could take your temperature just in case."

Sadie forced herself to smile. "I'm fine, thanks. I'll just come back to check on her tomorrow."

She never got the chance. The next morning when Sadie and Jessica walked into the dining room, Brett was sitting alone at their usual table, slumped over a half-empty mug of coffee. Her red hair had fallen forward over her face, and it looked like it hadn't been washed in days. Sadie immediately moved toward Brett to give her a hug.

"Brett, are you okay?"

Brett didn't look up, but she jerked back in her chair, as if her entire body was flinching away from Sadie's touch. "I'm fine," she mumbled. "Sorry. I'm just, um, still contagious. You shouldn't touch me."

The girls exchanged glances over her bowed head, but Jessica just shrugged. Sadie decided to keep what Nurse Brennan had said to herself. If Brett was lying to them, she figured there must be a good reason.

After the servers had set their places, Sadie tried again, quieter this time.

"Look, are you really okay? We were worried about you. Nobody knew what happened. And you seem a little . . . down."

Brett sighed. "It was just a stomach bug or something. I'm really okay." When they didn't respond, she straightened in her chair and ran a hand through her hair, pushing it back off her face. Sadie barely stifled a gasp.

"Then what happened to your face?" Jessica cried, bits of egg dribbling out of her mouth. Brett's eyes were pink and bloodshot, and there was a dark purple bruise spreading across one of her cheekbones.

Brett was smiling, but something was off. Her mouth stretched wide, but her eyes were dull. "Oh, it's nothing,"—she laughed—"I got dehydrated from all the throwing up, and then on my way to the nurse's office I fainted and hit my head on the edge of a table. I'm fine, really."

Grace jumped up from the table. "I'm going to get you some ice—that looks like it's still swollen."

Brett waved a hand. "It's just a bruise." She smiled her ventriloquist smile again. "I'll survive."

Jessica shrugged and started in on a piece of toast, but Sadie watched as Brett bowed her head back down and stared into her mug. She glanced at Brett's right wrist and frowned. A month ago Josh had given her a diamond Tiffany bracelet for their six-month anniversary, and she had barely taken it off since. She even wore it to practice, tucked under a terry-cloth sweatband so it wouldn't get scratched. Sadie watched as Brett lifted her hand and brushed a stray lock of hair behind her ear. There was a thin red welt around her pale wrist, but the bracelet was gone.

Chapter 14

The next weekend, it snowed. Sadie pulled open the curtains, saw the flurries gathered in the corners of her window, and barely suppressed the urge to get back in bed and stay asleep until next spring. "How the hell is it already snowing?" she yelled at the windows. "It's not even Thanksgiving yet."

She was answered by two muffled groans coming from somewhere beneath the twins' pastel comforters.

She was supposed to meet Grace, Brett, and Jessica in the dining room at ten so they could have breakfast and head into town to shop for dresses, and it was already almost 9:30. She sat down on the window seat and surveyed the room.

Over the last two months the twins had managed to cover their side completely with discarded clothes, candy wrappers, and half-empty cans of Red Bull, and now the mess was spreading into her space like a fungus. There were at least three different pairs of black leather and suede boots crinkled in sad little piles on the floor, and a pair of shredded fishnet tights hung off the back of Sadie's computer chair. She picked it up with two fingers and shot it towards Trix's desk like a slingshot. It landed on the top of a closed laptop. Sadie didn't think it had been opened in weeks.

More and more, she was starting to wonder if the honorable Duke Everleigh was actually just paying Keating to babysit, with the implicit understanding that an education would be a welcome side effect if they happened to go to class.

After a minute, she spied the leg of her favorite jeans sticking out from under a pile at the bottom of her closet. She grabbed them, threw open the doors of her armoire, and pulled out a white tank top and a chunky gray sweater. She tossed the whole pile on her unmade bed, then laid the ivory coat carefully across her chair before heading to the showers.

Forty-five minutes she stood with the others by Ashby's front door, shivering and watching as their breath gathered in a steamy cloud over their heads.

"Seriously, Brett, if this car doesn't get here in five seconds, I'm going back inside to watch TV," Jessica said, jamming her hands deeper into the pockets of her North Face jacket.

"It'll be here soon." Brett checked her watch. "I told the car service 10:30 and it's only, like, 10:28."

Sadie shook her head. "I still can't believe we're taking a limo. Couldn't we have just called a cab?"

"Oh, quit whining." Brett smiled. "It's included in the cost of tuition. If we didn't use the cars we would actually be wasting money."

"Besides, there are no cabs in Foxburg," Jessica said. She wrinkled her nose and imitated Charlotte's southern drawl. "I mean, seriously y'all, I would die before I let my Chanel coat touch the inside of a taxi."

"There it is." Grace pulled back the cuff of her glove to check her watch. "It's 10:30, just like you said." Jessica and Brett exchanged sarcastic "I told you sos" and begrudging "whatevers," and the four of them ran toward the car.

While the car wound its way through the hills toward Foxburg, they all chatted about what they were looking for. Brett wanted something strapless and "Audrey Hepburn-esque," and Grace wanted something blue. Jessica claimed she didn't want anything, but Sadie knew she was lying. A sophomore named Stephen had asked her to the ball yesterday after practice, and she had been struggling to keep up her grumpy ruse ever since.

"What about you, Sadie? If you want to top that sexy little napkin you wore to the welcome reception, you're basically going to have to go in a thong and pasties," Brett teased. "Josh said all the guys were talking about you at practice the next day."

Sadie pressed her lips together. "I don't know—I mean, what do you wear to a ball? All I can picture is like, Cinderella's dress from the Disney movie."

Jessica straightened in her seat, wrinkled her nose, and pursed her lips in her usual Darrow impression. "A floor-length gown, preferably in a winter fabric, is most appropriate." She held up one finger. "And remember, beauty is about class and elegance, not . . . skin." The girls dissolved into laughter.

"Okay well, whatever the hell that means," Sadie said, "I guess that's what I'm getting."

Jessica relaxed back into a slouch and smiled. "Good, 'cause we're almost here."

They turned onto Foxburg's main street, and Sadie pressed her face to the window. The sidewalks were bustling with couples clutching huge cups of coffee and women pushing strollers the size of small golf carts. The snow was just starting to stick, and the cobblestone streets were dusted with a thin layer of white.

The car dropped them off in front of a store with huge glass doors and faceless mannequins in the windows. Sadie followed the others inside, then tried to resist the urge to immediately back out again. The store was total chaos—there were at least four other groups of Keating girls inside already, and the salespeople were darting frantically from one rack to the next, carrying hangers of sequined gowns like white flags of surrender over their heads.

"This is worse than the Portland farmers' market," Sadie said. "And you do not want to get in between yuppie hippies and their raw-milk sharp cheddar."

Brett hooked an arm through hers and propelled her forward. "We only get one day to shop, so it's either dealing with this or dancing with Jeremy in your dress uniform."

Sadie pictured the thick velvet jumper and starchy blouse Keating girls reserved for chapel on holidays and shuddered. "Fine. But I'm not picking anything out. I'll try on, but that's it."

Brett looked at her sideways. "Like we would have let you choose your own dress anyway. Nice coat, by the way." She grinned and dragged Sadie toward the fitting rooms.

The first three dresses she tried on were awful. One was silver and slinky, but it ended about six inches shorter than where it should have. The second had plenty of length, but the material sagged on her chest like it was made for someone who was planning on smuggling exotic melons inside her strapless bra. The third was so tight she could barely get it up past her thighs. She gave up and stepped out of it, tossing it aside so it fell in a twinkling gold heap on the floor.

Before she could yell to Brett for some new options, her phone jingled. She glanced at the screen, but she didn't recognize the number. She flipped it open.

"How's shopping going?"

She typed out a reply. "Meh. All this stuff is made for girls with double-Ds. Who's this? Don't have your number saved."

She threw the phone back into her purse and surveyed the damage in her room. All of the hangers were empty, and she was out of options.

"Hey guys?" she called through the velvet curtain. "This really isn't working. None of this stuff fits me."

Jessica yanked back the curtain in one swift movement.

"Hey!" Sadie cried, crossing her arms over her bra.

Jessica grinned. "Whatever. Sorry if a couple old sales ladies see your perfect body." She held out something black and sparkly. "This was like eight inches too long on my stumpy legs so it'll probably be just about right on you. What do you think of this one?" She twirled and showed off the red minidress she was wearing. It was silky and flirty and just scandalous enough to drive Darrow nuts.

Sadie laughed. "It's perfect. Stephen might have a hard attack."

"That's the plan." Jessica grinned, then caught herself. "Or not, I don't care." She turned and flounced away toward the full-length mirror.

"Hey wait," Sadie called. "Did someone on the team get a new phone or something? Who has an 858 area code?" Jessica looked over her shoulder and shrugged, and Sadie's phone beeped again. As soon as she flipped it open, she wanted to die.

"It's Jeremy . . . Josh told me you guys were shopping today. He asked Brett for your number . . . hope you don't mind."

She felt her cheeks flush as she pounded her forehead with the heel of her hand. She sat down to type a reply, but the phone beeped again.

"And for the record, I'd take yours over double-Ds any day."

She bit her lip to keep from grinning. "Sorry, shopping is the worst. Got any preferences?" She glanced at the dress debris on the floor, then added: "Right now we're looking at black sequins or gold sequins, with varying levels of slut-itude. Up to you."

His reply came back immediately.

"Anything but hot pink spandex, and I'll be happy."

She rolled her eyes and tossed her phone back into her purse. The dress Jessica had given her was hanging on the wall, and she stared it down like an opponent in a boxing match. The design was pretty simple—no scary studs or ruffles—and the sparkle factor was subtle enough. Plus, if Jessica had liked it, it couldn't be all bad. She took a deep breath, then lifted it off the hanger and over her head.

As soon as she felt the dress fall down over her hips, she knew it was perfect. The fabric was smooth and supple, with one strap that gathered at her shoulder and skimmed down gracefully to the floor. It was just tight enough to show off her curves, and a spattering of tiny sequins made it glow under the dim fitting-room lights. As much as she hated to admit it, it was beautiful.

She turned and looked at the back, and she drew in a quick breath as she noticed the train. She imagined what it would be like to feel Jeremy's hand on the small of her back, and a shiver crawled down her spine. She shook herself and rolled her eyes at her reflection. Before she took the dress off, she picked up her phone.

"Don't worry, I think I just found something. It's black, and it doesn't even come with matching velour sweatbands. I think you'll like it."

"Hey, ready to go?" Brett called from outside the curtain.

"Yeah, one sec."

Brett called back that they would meet her up at the register, and she carefully changed out of the dress and back into her clothes. As she shrugged her coat back on, her phone beeped.

"Can't wait."

She held back a smile as she draped the dress carefully over her arm and headed to the front of the store.

"Find everything okay?" The young woman behind the register eyed her over a pair of chic, dark-rimmed glasses.

"Uh, yeah, thanks." Sadie plopped the dress onto the counter and busied herself with digging her wallet out of her purse. She had purposely avoided looking at the dress's price tag, but she was just hoping it would be under $300. She hadn't spent much of her allowance since she had been at Keating, but anything more than that and she would be stuck paying her dad back until senior year.

The woman glanced at her computer screen. "That will be twenty-three-forty-seven, please."

Sadie frowned. "Wait, twenty-three dollars? For the dress?" One corner of the woman's raspberry-tinted lips curled up into a smirk.

"No, sweetheart," she cooed. "The dress is two thousand, three hundred, and forty-seven dollars. It's a Marchesa," she added, as if she had just explained that it was made of solid gold.

Sadie's jaw slackened, and she felt the blood rushing into her cheeks. The credit card she had clutched in her hand—"For emergencies, only," her dad had said, "as in, you realize you're deathly allergic to the East Coast and need to fly home before your esophagus closes,"—had a $1,200 limit. And she was pretty sure a date didn't count as life threatening, anyway.

"Um, hold on a sec." Her voice cracked like a choirboy's whose balls were starting to drop, and she dug frantically through her purse just to buy herself some time. She felt tears starting to sting the backs of her eyes, and for the first time since she had arrived, she knew she was finished. She didn't belong with these people—not even Brett or Jessica, no matter how many meals they shared or practices they sweated through together. Where Sadie was from, $2,000 was a year's worth of groceries, not a few yards of glitter.

Her eyes started to well up, and she mumbled something else about her credit card without meeting the woman's eyes. She was debating whether it would be more embarrassing to explain herself or just sprint for the door, when she felt a hand on her arm.

"Hey, Brett," Brett said, emphasizing the name with an exaggerated smile, "I just realized I never returned your Amex. Thanks for letting me borrow yours. I have simply got to remind Daddy to send me a new one as soon as he gets back from Dubai." She turned her dark brown eyes toward the saleswoman and slid a shiny black card across the counter. "I'm such a spaz, I must lose my wallet every other week."

The woman nodded slightly, looking disappointed, and swiped the card through her machine. Sadie's palms were still sweating, but her pulse was slowing down. As the woman packed the dress into a garment bag, Sadie turned to face Brett.

"You seriously cannot do this—it's way too much."

Brett just smiled. "I can, and I just did." The woman wordlessly handed over the bag, and Brett reached around Sadie and took it. She linked an arm through Sadie's and steered her toward the door. As it swung open and a bitter gust of wind drew them out into the snow, she leaned in close and whispered, "Just think of it as another gift from some new friends."

Chapter 15

Even at 9 A.M. on the Saturday of the dance, the dining room was frantic. Most of the girls already had their hair up in curlers, and a few of the freshman were shuffling around the buffet in salon slippers. Sadie almost choked on her oatmeal when one stumbled on her foam sandal and sent a bowlful of melon balls rolling across the hardwood floor.

She sat back and pushed the bowl away. She was so nervous, each spoonful she forced down felt like a rock landing in the pit of her stomach. For the first time, she noticed how empty their table was. "Hey, where is everyone?"

Jessica shrugged, but Brett gave her a wry smile.

"Eating on the day of the dance? What are you guys, amateurs?"

Jessica rolled her eyes. "She's right. Thayer and the minions never eat before dances. They claim it makes your stomach stick out, but really, it just makes them act like even bigger bitches than usual. I guess if I had to go to dances with Finn, though, I'd be acting like a bitch too."

"Yeah, what's his deal?" Sadie said.

"He's not that bad," Brett said thoughtfully. "He's just, you know . . . a rich kid. Guys like him grow up with no one ever saying no to them. And his family is kind of intense."

"Whatever," Jessica said. "I just know he gets drunk at every dance and then starts hitting on everyone while Thayer gets pissed and follows him around like an angry sheepdog."

"Really?" Sadie said. "So he's seriously not that into it?"

"Not at all. They're practically an arranged marriage—both their families have been close for generations—but Thayer total-ly bought into it. She thinks they're the modern-day Romeo and

Juliet—although, that really just shows how much she doesn't pay attention in English class. I don't think he really cares. He just gets her those presents all the time to keep her happy and keep his family off his back."

"Wow," Sadie said, feeling almost sorry for Thayer. Her relationship was as fake as her extensions, and everyone knew it but her.

"All right, let's go," Brett said and stood up. "The guys are picking us up at five, so that only gives us, like, six hours to get ready." She took off toward the door, leaving Sadie to wonder whether or not she was being sarcastic. Ten minutes later in Brett's room, she found out the answer.

"Okay, here's how this is going to go." Brett pulled up a spreadsheet on her laptop. "We'll all shower now and blow-dry. At noon, Ken and Jesse are getting here to do our hair—my mom's treat. She practically pays them as full-time employees anyway, so it's no big deal. Sadie and Grace, you guys go first since your hair's long and will probably take a while. Jessica and I'll go next. By the time you're done the ladies from LaBelle should be here, and they'll do your manis and pedis. We'll go when you're done, then we can all go put on our dresses, come back here for makeup at 3:30, and all be ready for pictures and stuff at 4:30. Sound okay?"

The girls nodded.

"Okay, guys. Break."

Out in the hall, it was quiet—way quieter than it had been during midterms. As Sadie walked, three girls slipped out of one of the rooms, their hair in Velcro rollers and green masks smoothed over their noses and chins. They padded quickly down the hall, short pastel robes fluttering behind them, and disappeared into another room.

The next three hours passed by in a blur, and at 4:30 they met back in Brett's room. Sadie was already exhausted, but she couldn't believe the transformation. They all looked fantastic, and she noticed even Jessica couldn't resist sneaking glances of herself in the mirror. They spent the requisite fifteen minutes fawning over each other's hair and nail polish, then argued over who looked prettier and whose dress made them look skinnier. When they were done, Brett broke out the champagne.

"Courtesy of Ken and Jesse," she said with a grin. "They smuggled it in for us."

She popped the cork, and they all shrieked and frantically pulled their skirts away from the frothy bubbles that spilled over the top. Brett poured the champagne into two empty water bottles, a green Keating mug, and her silver pencil cup, and they toasted clumsily and chugged it down. For something so pretty, it tasted like fizzy old shoes.

"Who wants the last glass?" Brett said, tipping the bottle and shaking the dregs. Grace and Jessica shook their heads, and she looked at Sadie expectantly.

"All you, Sadie. You look like you need this a lot more than we do."

She let her breath out in a rush. "Oh my god, you guys—I am dying. Does it really show that much?"

Brett handed over the champagne. "Kinda."

Sadie plugged her nose, threw her head back, and chugged the rest of the bottle. When she came up for air, they were all grinning at her.

"Better?" Grace asked.

Sadie paused. "Can't tell yet. Ask me in ten minutes."

"Why are you so nervous, anyway?" Brett asked.

Jessica made a face. "Oh, I don't know, she's only going with the guy she's been completely in love with—and practically stalking— since school started."

Sadie smacked her on the arm. "I'm not that pathetic." She laughed. "Okay, maybe a little. But I also just—" She looked down at her gown. She gathered the fabric in her hands and shrugged. "I'm not going to have any idea what I'm doing tonight. The last dance I went to was in our gym, and I was wearing jean shorts."

"Okay, we'll talk about the fact that you actually ever thought it was okay to wear jean shorts later, but for now, you should not be worried. At all." Jessica smiled. "It's just the same old people from Keating and Graff that you see every day. Remember how ridiculous

Charlotte looked last Saturday during practice when she was prancing around in her push-up sports bra trying to get the Graff team's attention? And remember those dumb freshmen that tried to get a tan in the quad a couple weeks ago when it was like, sixty degrees outside? Yeah. Those are the people you're worrying about embarrassing yourself in front of. You'll be fine, I promise."

Sadie sighed. "Thanks, Jess. But what if I'm not wearing the right thing? Isn't this a little . . . much?" She looked around the circle, eyeing Jessica's red mini, Brett's chic, black strapless gown, and Grace's simple blue column. "I feel like I'm way too dressed up."

Grace, Brett, and Jessica simultaneously burst into laughter.

"You really don't have any idea what you're walking into, do you?" Jessica said. "Trust me, half of the girls out there will practically be in wedding dresses, and a few of them will actually be in wedding dresses. With tiaras. And maybe diamond-studded veils, just for kicks," she added. "You look perfect—as always, you little skank." She grinned.

"Okay, fine. No more whining, promise." Sadie finally felt herself start to relax, and she could feel a warm little glow spreading throughout her body. Maybe Jessica was right. For the first time that night, she started to feel excited.

Brett glanced at her laptop. "Eek, you guys, it's time to go. The guys should be here in,"—she checked her watch—"eight minutes."

When they reached the top of the staircase, Sadie could see the rest of the students already gathered in the lobby, huddled excitedly in groups and whispering behind shielded lips. She felt a hint of nervousness creeping back up, but she forced it down. The shit-talking was practically wafting around the lobby like poisonous gas, but she realized for once she didn't care.

The four of them settled into their usual spot in the corner of the room, and a minute later, Mrs. Darrow hovered over them.

"I specifically remember telling you ladies that this would be a black-tie event," she said, brow even more furrowed then usual. "That means length, and that means elegance. This event is at the Hay-Adams, and you, Ms. Harris, are sorely underdressed."

"Oh, really?" Jessica looked down at her dress in mock horror. "Well I guess I could go put on my dress from last year's Spring Gala. It's right upstairs in my closet." She smiled sweetly and looked up at Mrs. Darrow through big, watery brown eyes. The other girls snickered. Last year, Jessica had made her dress herself—using black duct tape—and Mrs. Darrow apparently hadn't been amused.

She didn't take the bait though, and instead she just pursed her lips. "That won't be necessary," she said. "You'll just have to,"—she wrinkled her nose distastefully—"make do."

After a sneer, she addressed the rest of them. "You all look beautiful, by the way. Perhaps you could lend your friend some guidance when it's time for the next event?" They all nodded solemnly, and she looked satisfied. "Now, your escorts are here. Please remember your manners, and keep in mind that you'll be representing Keating tonight." With a last disdainful glance at Jessica's bare, tanned legs, she headed off toward another group of girls.

Sadie's stomach tightened into its usual knot as she walked toward the door, one elbow linked through Jessica's. Together, they pushed through the door and stepped out into the night. As the door swung shut, blocking out the chatter of excited voices and the smog of over-applied perfume, everything was suddenly still. The quad was dotted with rings of light from each of the old-fashioned, but LED-retro-fitted, street lanterns that lined the circular drive. Snow was falling in soft flakes, and the lawn was a flawless sheet of white, save for a narrow path of footsteps leading from Ashby's steps to the road. With the stillness all around them, Sadie felt a calm start to spread over her. It was a beautiful night—she felt beautiful—and she was about to go to a ball at one of the most famous hotels in the country. The champagne felt pleasantly warm in her stomach, smoothing over the jagged edges of her excitement with a fuzzy confidence that took the place of her nerves.

They stood at the top of the steps in their gowns, blowing heat into their cupped hands, until the door of a sleek black limo opened. One by one, their dates stepped out into the snow.

Josh was first, and he walked straight up to Brett and kissed her full on the mouth. She kissed him back—a little awkwardly, Sadie noticed. She leaned slightly away from him at impact and then forced a smile as they parted. Brett had been her usual impeccable self since that morning two weeks ago in the cafeteria, and she had even been wearing her tennis bracelet again, this time with matching diamond earrings. But still, something had shifted.

Jessica's date was next, and he looked surprisingly handsome in his black tux. He was nervous, though, and his voice cracked as he tried to tell Jessica how nice she looked. She just grinned and marched him back down the steps to the limo, throwing Sadie and Grace a smile and an awkwardly concealed thumbs-up as they climbed inside.

Next was Grace's long-time boyfriend, Eric. He was tall and lanky, and apparently a nationally ranked chess player, but Sadie had only met him a few times. He nodded to Sadie before politely taking Grace's hand and leading her down the steps. Whatever disadvantages Brett claimed Graff guys suffered from their privileged upbringing, Sadie thought, they sure had impressive manners when they chose to show them off.

Finally, the door opened and she saw Jeremy unfold his six-foot-four-inch frame and step out of the limo. He paused for a moment, their eyes meeting across the expanse of snow, and it took her breath away. He looked, for lack of a more eloquent description, so hot she could barely stand it. And then he smiled.

He strode up the path, stomping his way through the fresh snow, and took the steps two at a time. When he reached her, he came so close she could feel his breath on her cheeks.

"Hi," he said simply, and grinned.

She smiled back up at him and swallowed, all of her energy going towards resisting the urge to wrap herself around him.

"You look beautiful," he said. He stepped back, making a show of admiring her dress. Then he spread his arms wide. "Like the penguin suit?"

She laughed. "You look great. Way better than all the other guys wearing the exact same thing."

"Thanks. I spent at least five minutes picking it out." He grinned. "Okay, now show me your shoes," he said, crossing his arms in front of his chest.

She pulled up her skirt a few inches and stuck out a glittery black sandal. "Why? Are feet, like . . . your thing?" She grimaced, but he just nodded his head in mock seriousness.

"Just as I suspected." He looked out over the snow, then back at her mostly-bare feet. "Looks like I'm going to have to carry you." He grinned again and swept her off her feet, lifting her easily like she weighed no more than a basket of laundry. He squeezed her affectionately, and she felt a surge of excitement pass through her. As they neared the car he looked down at her. "You were right, you know."

She stared up at him, her eyes jumping from one pupil to the next and finally settling on a space somewhere near his chin. Their faces were so close she felt exposed, like he could see right through her mask of makeup and straight down to her shaky core. She was acutely aware of every part of her that was touching him—his arms across her back and under her knees, and her arm wrapped tightly around his neck.

"About what?" she asked.

"The dress. It's perfect."

❧

The Hay-Adams was grand and elegant and a little stuffy, just like everything associated with Keating and Graff. The limo dropped them off under the wide portico, and a swarm of bellhops in starchy uniforms instantly manned the doors. She and Jeremy followed the others through the lobby, up a small flight of stairs to an elevator, and then out into the ballroom. It was elaborately decorated with shades of gold and cream, and there were huge white flower arrangements on every table. Sadie realized it looked exactly how she pictured Thayer's house might look on an average Tuesday.

The guys led them to a table just off the dance floor, and they all found their seats while their dates took off toward the bar. Sadie sank into one of the chairs and scanned the room. Once her eyes adjusted to the glare of the aggressive floral arrangements, she was genuinely surprised. While the ball felt totally different from her dances back home, in some ways it was exactly the same. Or at least, the cast of characters were all there, just in more expensive outfits.

In the center of the room, the tipsies were already on the dance floor, making their best effort to grind to the tasteful, predinner music. The deejay wasn't even on the stage yet, and Sadie watched as a sophomore in a tight white dress struggled to gyrate in time to instrumental jazz. In less than an hour, they would all be stumbling around, barefoot and humping each other, doing the faux-lesbian thing.

The rather-be-studyings and the too-cool-for-dancings were seated at the tables farthest from the dance floor, heads bowed in conversation or boredom. They would take the first limo ride back as soon as it seemed socially acceptable, and spend the whole drive passionately discussing how little they cared.

The jocks were nowhere to be seen—they were probably all packed into the bathrooms doing shots—but their table was already littered with crumpled tuxedo jackets. At Sadie's old school, they usually lost about one article of clothing per hour, but the Graff guys seemed to be setting a more ambitious pace. At this rate they would be in slacks and bowties, grinding on the dance floor like a bunch of male strippers, before dessert was even served.

And then, of course, there was Thayer and Finn. They staged their entrance ever so carefully to guarantee the whole school would be forced to acknowledge their presence as they elevated the event from simple gathering to religious experience. Sadie had to admit, though, they made Portland South's own Veronica Madden and Brendan Wyckoff look like amateurs.

They swept in dramatically, and their entourage's chattering increased sharply in volume as soon as they crossed the ballroom's threshold, inevitably calling the whole room's attention to their group and the intense amount of fun they were having. Thayer was wearing a gown that could only be described as fantastic, with a train at least six feet long and an intricate texture made up of a million different pieces of gold fabric. Something about it looked distinctly familiar, but Sadie couldn't quite place it.

"Oh my god, she didn't . . . " she heard Jessica say from over her shoulder.

Something in Sadie's head clicked. "Wait . . . is that—"

"The dress Samantha French wore to the Oscars?" Jessica finished, her voice rising incredulously.

"The one-of-a-kind gown that was part of Zachary Kane's final collection before he died," Brett said softly, her jaw hanging open. "It's usually displayed at the Met."

"Can't she just take a day off for once?" Jessica muttered. "It must be exhausting."

"Hey, who cares," Sadie lied. "Everyone in here is thinking the same thing we are. She tries way too hard, and nobody likes that."

"Nobody except for everybody at Graff. Guys eat that shit up."

"Yeah, well, the one guy she wants to pay attention to her won't. Plus, we have dates that actually like us. She should be jealous of us, not the other way around."

They grinned at each other, each pretending they were convinced.

"Okay, whatever. We're here to have fun," Brett said, tucking a lock of hair back into her updo. She picked up an empty water glass and held it up in a mock toast.

"To Sadie's first dance in something other than jean shorts," she yelled. The girls burst out laughing, toasting their empty glasses in the center of the table like drunks at Oktoberfest.

"What's so funny?" Josh asked. Jeremy handed Sadie a wine glass filled with Diet Coke, brushing her fingertips with his as he passed it off.

"Oh nothing, just that Sadie wears jean shorts," Jessica said, dissolving into laughter again. Jeremy cocked an eyebrow.

"Pink jumpsuits and jorts? I might have been wrong about you."

"Oh, shut up. At least I don't wear the same sweaty blue Cubs hat to practice every single day," she teased.

"Ah," he said, suddenly looking smug. "So you noticed."

"Uhhh, maybe—" she trailed off, realizing she had basically just admitted she was a stalker. She felt her cheeks flush, and she looked down at her plate.

"Busted," he said quietly. When she finally looked up he was smiling at her, with just a hint of something else in his eyes.

"So, why the Cubs, anyway?" she asked, hoping to leave the moment behind as soon as possible. "You said you were from San Diego."

He nodded. "My dad's from Chicago. We go every time they face the Padres—been doing it for as long as I can remember." He laughed. "The Cubs lose almost every time, but it doesn't matter. You ever been to a game?"

"Not really. Portland's not exactly huge on professional sports. I went to a Giants game once when I was little, but I don't really remember it."

He nodded and looked toward the dance floor. "Maybe we can go sometime when the Cubs play the Nationals?" He said it so casually, she had to take a deep breath to keep calm.

"Sure. But if you wear that sweaty hat, I'm definitely wearing my jorts."

❧

The next three hours were so much fun she started to get nervous. Dates were never this fun. They were awkward, sweaty, boring, or at the very least kinda stressful. But everything felt right. Everyone danced—even Brett—and Jeremy was always close, leading her onto the floor or making her laugh while they sat at the table and watched.

This was the point in the night where the prince was supposed to turn back into a frog—try to grab your boob, or slyly put his hand on your crotch while you were kissing like he was hoping you wouldn't even notice. This was when the rom-com façade fell away and you remembered he was a seventeen-year-old asshole who was probably just counting the minutes until he thought he might have a shot at getting laid. But nothing went wrong, and finally Sadie relaxed.

After the next song ended, the guys went for refills and Sadie went to look for the restroom. She found a door in one corner daintily marked "Ladies Water Closet" and stepped into a small lounge. The air was heavy with potpourri and a cluster of frilly upholstered chairs beckoned to her aching feet. She sank gratefully onto a love seat covered in red and ivory toile and waited for the feeling to creep back into her toes.

Before she could relax, the door swung open and Finn lurched into the room. As he crossed the threshold, the toe of one shiny dress shoe caught on the carpet, and he stumbled, then steadied himself with one hand on the wall. His hooded eyes scanned the room, and when he saw Sadie, his mouth stretched wide.

"Sexy Sadie," he said, stretching her name out at least two extra syllables. He stood with his eyes fixed on her, his body swaying slightly.

"Uh, hey Finn. You know, the men's room is next door."

He just looked at her, grinning stupidly. Finally she sighed and stood up. "Finn, you are in the women's bathroom." She enunciated every word slowly, like she was talking to a small child. "You need to leave." He blinked lazily and took a step toward her.

"I know where I am." He lurched forward again.

"Whatever you say, champ. I'll walk you there." She took his arm and tried to turn him around, but he resisted, stumbling in the wrong direction and then wrapping an arm around her waist. "Come on Finn, help me out here," she grumbled, struggling to stay upright as he leaned into her.

Suddenly, he pushed forward and she lost her balance. Both his arms wrapped tightly around her back and they stumbled like clumsy ballroom dancers across the room. After three quick steps, she felt her back slam into the wall, and the air rushed out of her lungs.

Finn was in front of her, his full weight pressed against her chest, and his face was inches from hers. She turned away to the side and felt his hot, sour breath on her temple. She struggled to breathe, and he laughed, softly, deep down in his throat.

"Finn, this isn't funny. I know you're not too drunk to stand up, so get off of me." He leered at her, and she felt his hand groping up the outside of her thigh.

"You're going to tell me you don't want this? Every girl at Keating wants it, whether she knows it yet or not."

She put her palms flat against his chest and pushed as hard as she could. He tipped backward and stumbled against one of the couches, finally collapsing onto the cushions.

"Fuck, Sadie." He struggled to right himself, and the stupid grin was already spreading back across his face. "I just wanted a little preview." His eyes traveled up and down her body, and he ran his tongue over his bottom lip. "Can't wait to see what's under that dress."

She shoved him again, and he fell back on the cushions. "Try that again and all you'll be seeing is the tip of my kneecap in your Cranston family jewels." As she stormed out of the bathroom, she could hear him bellowing with laughter, still sprawled on the love seat with one leg hanging off the side. Outside the door, she paused and leaned against the wall, gulping in deep, ragged breaths. She forced herself to unclench her fists and ran a hand carefully over her hair.

"Hey, there you are. I was starting to think you decided to ditch me for one of the football players." Jeremy jerked his head toward a bunch of hulking Graff guys gathered around a nearby table. They had stripped down to their tuxedo vests, adding their shirts to the growing pile of jackets. He rolled his eyes and muttered, "Meatheads."

Sadie forced herself to smile. "Nope, I was going to go to the bathroom, but it was, um, occupied." She pointed at the door as it opened and Finn staggered out.

Jeremy raised his eyebrows. "I heard he was a bad drunk, but jeez." They both watched as Finn made his way across the dance floor, Thayer marching after him, her fading smile looking increasingly forced.

"Hey, want to go upstairs? I have a surprise for you." He put a hand around her waist and pulled her toward him.

And there it was. His inner frog jumping out and ribbiting all over everything.

"Upstairs?" She narrowed her eyes and stepped back out of his grasp. She could feel the anger bubbling back up in her throat, and her hands curled back into tight fists.

"Wait—what's wrong? I just meant we could see the view."

"The view? Does that line seriously work?" It came out louder than she meant it to, and the meatheads were starting to stare.

He opened his hands, palms facing her. "Hold on, Sadie. Back up. What's wrong?"

"You just asked me to go upstairs . . . at a hotel. On our first date, or whatever this is."

He held her stare for a second, then burst out laughing. His whole body shook with the force of it, and she could feel her anger sublimating into rage.

That was it. As he laughed, she saw Finn's wide, stupid grin and felt his hot, beer-sour breath on her face. She could still feel his hand greedily pawing at her leg, trying to burrow its way under the fabric. She was just a joke to them.

"You know what, screw you." She turned on her shaky heel and stomped toward the door. She needed a coatroom, a hallway, anywhere she could shut herself in a corner and let the disappointment wash over her.

She was just steps outside the ballroom when he caught up. He touched her arm. She stopped but she didn't turn around.

"What," she spat, pulling her arm away.

"Sadie, I'm really sorry. I swear, for whatever reason, I just keep doing really dumb things around you—startling you, or saying the wrong thing, or insulting you by accident."

Reluctantly, she turned to face him. He ran a hand through his hair and fiddled with one of his cufflinks. He wasn't laughing anymore.

"When I said I wanted to go upstairs, I meant I wanted to go up to the rooftop terrace. It's kind of a Hay-Adams thing—at least, that's what Josh told me. He said you would really like it. It's supposed to be pretty, and you can see the White House."

His voice was a little desperate, almost pleading, and as she looked into his eyes, something clicked. The room started to spin as she realized her mistake, and she would have punched herself in the face if she thought she could get enough momentum to actually do some damage. Thayer was constantly talking about her wedding—how amazing her dress would be and how Finn would propose. Whenever she talked about it, it always, always happened on the Hay-Adams rooftop. She had some elaborate plan for exactly how Finn would lure her there, how he would surprise her by covering the roof in a blanket of white roses, and how he would propose with a four-carat Harry Winston canary diamond with a platinum band.

Jeremy was looking at her—a little panicked, a little amused, mostly nervous. He was leaning slightly away from her and flinching, like he expected her to kick him in the shin.

Instead, she smiled.

She didn't know what to say, and instead just blurted out the first thing that came into her head. "I just don't want to have sex with you . . . " she trailed off, eyes widening. "I mean, I do just . . . hypothetically, at some point—oh, god." She gave up, and they both burst out laughing.

"So, now that we've covered that . . . want to go to the roof?" He offered her an elbow and she took it, letting him lead her back to the elevator.

To his credit, the view was beautiful. The city lay spread out beneath them, and the White House glowed under a dusting of new snow. She leaned on the railing and turned to face him. "I'm really sorry about that." She turned and looked out over the city. "I have no idea why I reacted like that, I'm just always so worried that people here don't take me seriously—like I'm this trashy skank from the middle of nowhere who doesn't belong. And then I couldn't figure out why you would even want to go with me—I mean, I'm sure you could have asked anyone—and then you said that thing about going upstairs and I just freaked out." He leaned his elbows on the railing and looked thoughtful.

"A trashy skank, huh?"

She laughed. It sounded so ridiculous now. He turned to face her, and she looked up, shivering slightly as a single snowflake landed on her bare shoulder. He shrugged off his jacket and draped it over her, then let his hands slide down the sides of the coat and settle on her lower back. Her throat immediately went dry.

"Look Sadie, I like you. And I don't think you're a trashy skank; I think you're cool. You're funny, and you don't try to be anything you're not. All these people, they're always trying to convince you of something—that they're richer than everyone else, or that their family has more influence, or that they're happy all the time. Sometimes I just want to cut the power, you know, shut everyone off. But there's no on/off switch. That's just who they are. And in the middle of all that noise, you're just you."

She swallowed. "I like you, too."

He stared back and inside her head she was yelling at him to kiss her. Another snowflake drifted down and settled on Jeremy's eyebrow, and she watched as it melted and disappeared. Instead, he spoke.

"Tomorrow—you guys can leave campus if you want on weekends, right?"

She nodded.

"Go out with me? On a real date—you know, where we wear normal clothes and do something trashy like eat pizza and see a movie about aliens."

She smiled. "Absolutely."

He exhaled and ran his palms up and down the outsides of her arms. "I know you must be freezing, and that was the end of my big speech, so . . . do you want to go back inside?"

He took a step away toward the door and reached a hand back for her. She glanced at it, hesitated for a moment, and then her instincts took over. She grabbed his hand and pulled him back toward her until their bodies collided. She wrapped her arms around his neck, stood on her tiptoes, and kissed him. His lips were warm and smooth, and she felt his arms immediately circle her waist. His breath was hot. Before she could stop herself, she leaned into him and felt his body press back against hers.

After what felt like hours, he finally pulled back, a huge grin plastered on his face.

"Okay, so that was kinda trashy."

She punched him in the arm. "Oh, whatever. You couldn't pull the trigger, so I did." She grinned. Subconsciously she licked her lips, and he laughed.

"That good, huh?"

She shrugged happily. "You taste like cinnamon." She reached up and pecked him again, then grabbed his arm and dragged him back toward the elevator.

Chapter 16

The limo dropped the boys off first, then made the short trip back to Keating. Jessica was imitating Finn's drunk dance moves, and Grace and Brett were laughing hysterically, but Sadie was so distracted she had to remind herself to laugh and nod at all the right times.

When they pulled through the gates, the campus was dark and quiet. They piled out of the limo and picked their way through the slush, squealing as the cold seeped into their shoes and ran between their toes. At the top of Ashby's steps, Brett glanced back at Sadie.

"Hey, did you forget your purse?"

"Oh crap—must have left it in the limo."

They all hesitated, shivering, in the doorway.

"You guys go ahead." Sadie shooed them inside. "I'll meet you upstairs."

She turned and ran back toward the car, her skirt bundled around her knees. She tapped the limo on the trunk just as the driver started to pull away, then crawled back inside and felt around the carpeted floor with her hands.

"Where is that damn thing?" she mumbled. It was Gwen's, and she figured chances were pretty good it wasn't something she could replace. Finally, she felt her fingers close around the satin clutch, and she started to back out of the limo on all fours.

She had one foot on the ground when she felt the hood slide down over her head. Someone shoved her from behind, sending her sprawling face first across the leather seats. She heard the door slam as someone climbed in after her, and the engine purred as the limo pulled away.

"What the hell, guys. Again?" Sadie struggled to right herself, pulling the fabric of her dress down over her knees. "Is this seriously necessary?"

The limo was quiet.

She sighed and crossed her arms tightly over her chest. "You could have just texted me like a normal person. You don't have to kidnap me every time you want me to go somewhere."

Still nothing.

"Okay, fine. Don't say anything." She reached back and fiddled with the knot at her neck until two hands closed down on her wrists.

"This is just how we do things."

This time the angry hiss was gone, and he sounded perfectly calm.

"Fine. But if you try to strangle me again, I'll kick your ass."

She heard a low chuckle.

"We have to scare you. That's the fun part."

The car slowed and stopped.

"So what now?"

"Now," the voice said slowly, "we make you one of us."

∾

The car door opened and she was passed from one pair of hands to the next as they led her down a flight of steep stairs and through a doorway. The air was cold, and she thought she could hear the rumbling of the ocean.

She heard the creak of another door opening, and a voice told her to sit down. She sank back onto surprisingly soft cushions. The door closed.

She listened, but the room was still. After a minute, she reached up and untied the hood. She pulled it off and blinked into the darkness.

"Boo."

The lights flickered on, and she saw Thayer sitting across from her on a white love seat, her legs delicately crossed and a glass of champagne in one hand. She had changed out of her massive gown and was now dressed simply in a white linen shift. Her hair was down, and it fell around her shoulders in waves. Sadie looked around.

They were in the center of a small, white room. There was a large armoire behind her, and on the other side of the room was a big three-way mirror. In front of her was a small glass coffee table, on which sat a bottle of expensive champagne and an empty flute.

Thayer leaned forward and filled the glass. She held it out to Sadie.

Sadie shook her head. "Look, are you finally going to tell me what this is? Some kind of club or something? I'm tired of not knowing what's going on."

"Relax, Portland. Champagne first, then I'll tell you what you need to know."

Sadie took the glass and sipped.

"So basically,"—Thayer leaned forward and lowered her voice—"everything you've heard is true. The rumors about us, all the power we have, it's all real."

Sadie looked at her, her face blank. "Okay, what?"

Thayer sighed. "You've never heard the rumors? God you really are small town, aren't you? I told them this was a mistake."

Sadie leaned back against the cushions and took another sip. "Fuck off."

Thayer cleared her throat and stretched her lips into a tight smile. "Fine, sorry." She smoothed out the skirt of her dress with one bony hand. "Here's what you need to know. We,"—she motioned around the room, as if it were filled with people—"are the Order of Optimates. Technically I guess we're a secret society, but we don't like to call it that anymore. Skull and Bones ruined that for everybody, and we're not a bunch of lame frat guys sitting around making up secret handshakes, you know? We matter. We have a plan."

She paused for dramatic effect, and Sadie threw back another gulp of champagne.

"Really? You're still pretending you're not impressed? Sadie, our members are everywhere. We're Wall Street CEOs, Supreme Court Justices. We're the founders of Omnitech and Rothschild

Industries—even Britton Cunningham, that kid who practically invented the Internet. We're everywhere, Sadie, and we can do whatever the fuck we want."

Her cheeks were flushed and her eyes were glassy and wide. "We own this country, and we're about to make you one of us."

"So, you're a bunch of spoiled rich kids throwing your power around? I thought the point was to help people."

Thayer looked exasperated. "Of course. You saw the hospital, and that's only the beginning. We fund lots of projects. Last year our inner-city literacy program taught hundreds of kids how to read, and we've donated millions through various charities." Thayer looked anguished. "Do you know how bad it is out there? People are getting poorer and sicker and less educated, and no one's stepping up to help." She settled back in her chair, her features smoothing out like ripples in a pond. "We're stepping up. That's the main goal—we're trying to make the world a better place. And in the meantime, we get to do some seriously cool shit."

Sadie cocked an eyebrow. "Like what?"

Thayer grinned. "Whatever you can think of. We're American royalty, Sadie. There are no limits."

"Okay, but that's just it. Why me? I'm not like you—I'm not rich. My dad's no one. I'm not even on the freaking honor roll."

Thayer shrugged, but Sadie saw the corner of her mouth curve up in a smirk. "We don't make the decisions. The Sullas are based here, at Graff, but that's only the beginning. Our network goes way beyond this campus—all the best prep schools are used for recruiting, and we have members all over the country.

"The older members have the real power. The real Order is, like, decades of the richest and most powerful people in the world. They make the selections—sometimes a few kids a year, sometimes no one—and they're always inducted in pairs. Sometimes they're heirs from powerful families,"—she laid a hand delicately on her chest—"like me. Sometimes they're geniuses or talented athletes who they think will make something of themselves. And sometimes they're legacies, like you. They choose whoever can strengthen the Order the most, whoever can carry on the tradition and help make them even more powerful than they already are."

Sadie leaned forward. "My mom. She was really a member?"

Thayer nodded. "She was inducted in '87. And honestly, it's not that surprising. Like they could resist inducting a Ralleigh. Not for prestige, obviously, but their fortune alone made it worth it."

Sadie frowned. "What do you mean, a Ralleigh?"

Thayer arched one thin eyebrow. "You're joking, right?"

Sadie sighed. "What now?"

"Your mom's maiden name was Ralleigh—"

Sadie shook her head. "It was Anderson—"

"As in, Pennsylvania Ralleighs."

When Sadie didn't react, she threw up her hands.

"They own the largest diamond mining company in the world, Sadie. They basically own half of Africa. Your mom was one of only two heirs—how can you not know that?"

Sadie's mind raced. Her dad had told Sadie her mother had cut ties with her family sometime after high school. He had always said she didn't have any grandparents on her mom's side, but Sadie had always just assumed that meant they were deadbeat alcoholics or something.

Sadie shook her head. "We don't talk about her much anymore." Her voice came out small and hollow.

Thayer's face softened. "Look Sadie, this is what she would have wanted for you—to follow in her footsteps." She leaned forward. "I know I haven't been that nice to you, but I just fucking hate new girls. Especially hot new girls who happen to play the same position I do. You came in here so cocky, with your slutty British roommates and your sad little scholarship and your fancy borrowed clothes. You didn't know your place." She grinned. "But now you don't need to. We know who you really are, and your place is here, with us." She spread her arms and smiled wider.

"Those idiots who follow me around every day, Charlotte and the rest of them—they're nothing. I won't even talk to them after graduation. The Sullas are my real friends—my real family—and we'll be there for each other for life."

Thayer sat back, finally satisfied. "So what do you think? Are you ready to do this?"

Sadie took a deep breath. "I don't know . . . I mean, why? What's the point?" She thought of the picture on her desk, her mom in yellow, smiling and laughing. She wondered if she had been that happy here as one of them. She looked down in her lap, and her gaze lingered on the slight shadow of a bruise that still spread across her inner elbow.

"What's the point?" Thayer sounded incredulous. "I don't think you understand. This is huge. This is your whole life. This is the end of your family's debt and a guaranteed scholarship to any school in the country. It's a job in whatever field you want—connections to the wealthiest and most powerful people.

"You think people turn into billionaires by accident? It's not like my family won the lottery. You get rich by being smart. Knowing the right people and making the right connections. Billionaires breed more billionaires." She smiled. "And let's just say the Order has a whole fucking lot of billionaires."

Sadie thought of her dad, all of their financial problems, and her eyes started to sting. She thought of her mom, happy and sitting on this same couch, before anything went wrong inside of her head. She thought about how people had looked at her in Portland after her mom was committed, how people still looked at her when they found out her mom was a drug addict. She thought of not fitting in, of never being good enough, and she thought about never feeling that way again. In her mind, she heard the chopper blades whirring over her head and adrenaline surged through her veins.

"All right." She smudged her tears across her cheek and raised her chin. For the first time in a long time, she felt strong. "I'm in. What do I have to do?"

Thayer picked up the champagne bottle and refilled Sadie's glass. "You just have to drink this. We'll do the rest."

Chapter 17

"I look like a bride at a cult wedding," Sadie deadpanned. "With a serious virgin/whore fetish."

She looked in the mirror again and sighed at her reflection. Thayer, Brett, and the three other Keating members had spent the last half hour prepping her for the induction ceremony, and she was having some issues with their artistic vision. Her hair hung in loose waves around her face, and she was dressed in a bikini so small she might as well have been naked. Over it she wore a flowing white robe that billowed around her as she walked. She had a ring of white flowers on her head.

Brett stood next to her, hands on her hips, but Sadie could tell she was holding back a laugh. "This ceremony is like a hundred years old, okay? And I'm sure this will come as a surprise to you, but a bunch of dudes made it up. Now just go with it." She paused then, an odd look on her face. "It's actually kind of . . . interesting."

Thayer leaned in toward Sadie. "What she means is, it's sexy. Besides, you should be happy they added the bikini in the fifties, because before that you would have been naked under there. You're being reborn, you know?" She motioned to Sadie's half-empty glass. "Now chug the rest so I can fill you up again."

Thayer's phone buzzed and tinny strands of music spilled from her purse. She met Sadie's gaze in the mirror and raised her eyebrows. It was time. Sadie nodded once.

"Okay everyone, time for The Bonding."

"The what? Are you sure I'm not about to become some guy's sixteenth sister-wife?"

Thayer pinched Sadie's elbow and led her to the door. "Wait in the hallway until someone comes for you." Her voice was sharp now; she meant business.

"Don't make noise, don't ask questions, just do everything exactly as you're told." She held up a white silk scarf and made a twirling motion with her finger.

Sadie turned to face the door, and the fabric settled over her temples. Thayer yanked it once, hard, and she winced.

With Thayer guiding her elbow, they stepped outside the door. "Any last questions?"

"Uh yeah, what the hell am I walking into, and why am I dressed like I just left a soft-core porn shoot?"

The door slammed, and Sadie was alone. The thick wooden door and stone walls snuffed out the sound from the white room, and the hallway was unnervingly quiet. A breeze crept along the narrow corridor and blew the flimsy robe off her bare legs. She shivered.

She squinted into the darkness that spread out in front of her. The white scarf must have been more symbolic than functional, because she could still make out the lanterns that lined the hallway. She heard footsteps behind her. The voice was back.

"You ready?"

"Do I have a choice?"

That mocking laugh again. A hand found her arm and tucked it under an elbow.

"Let's walk."

Up and up they went, spiraling upwards in a slow, lazy circle. The low rumble of the ocean faded and fell away, until all she heard was the muffled crackling of flames.

"Wait here."

Standing there silently, nothing beyond the gauzy white fabric but darkness, she realized she was drunk. Excitement bubbled through her veins, and she felt like she was watching herself from above, like she was in a dream and she could do whatever she wanted and nothing bad would happen. She was happy, nervous, and nauseous. The emotions mixed in her stomach and fermented, boiling down to a steady hum of anxious energy.

Footsteps echoed, and the voice was at her side again.

"We're going to walk straight into the room, and when I stop, you stop." It was a whisper now. She nodded inanely in the darkness. She took a deep breath, and as she exhaled, they started forward.

She stumbled slightly as they crossed a stone threshold. Her feet felt foreign and uncooperative, and they were slowly going numb as the cold of the stones seeped into her soles.

As they walked, she felt space. The air had room to shift here, and an almost imperceptible breeze played on her bare legs and stomach. After the cramped passageways and stairwells, the feeling of empty volume was intimidating. She felt watched, and completely alone.

She could hear the wind howling outside. With the sounds of the ocean and the curving stone staircase, she knew where they must be: the tower.

After twenty paces, the elbow slipped away and she stopped. She glanced to the left and right, but the room was black as pitch. She listened for whispers and shuffling feet, but heard nothing. Everything was still.

Directly ahead of her, a flame appeared. It was small, match-sized. With a blue flare of phosphorous, it became two. The flame moved inches to the right and flared again. Around in a circle the flame went, multiplying with each step. She followed it with her eyes until it disappeared behind her, and soon she was surrounded by a ring of light about ten feet across.

A low voice broke the silence.

"In the beginning, there was only chaos—a dark, primordial void." The words bounced around the room, and she knew it was him again. The voice.

"Then, out of the void appeared Night and Erebus, the unknowable place where death dwells. All else was empty—silent, endless, darkness."

She recognized the words of the Greek creation myth. With a low hiss, each of the tiny dots of light grew larger, and soon she could make out a hood above each one, hanging low and menacing over a masculine chin and cheekbones. She counted them, one by one. There were twelve.

"Then, somehow, love was born, bringing the start of Order. From Love came Light and Day, and then Gaea, the earth, appeared."

The voice grew slowly louder, and it echoed around the room until she felt surrounded by his words.

"As descendants of Gaea, the twelve Titans ruled the world. The Titans were ruled by Cronus, father of the first Olympians. Cronus feared his children would overthrow him, so he swallowed them, one by one, after they were born. When Cronus's wife Rhea bore her sixth child, she wrapped a stone in swaddling clothes, and Cronus swallowed the stone instead. That child was Zeus."

Ahead of her, the circle of light began to move. It bulged, then split and separated. Darkness flowed into the circle and snuffed out the little visibility she had. She heard footsteps, and the flames returned, barely illuminating the figure who had joined her in its center. He stood at least seven feet tall, and he was wrapped in a heavy black robe. In the dim light, she could see that a hood hung low over his face. He looked huge, and a creeping fear started to take hold at the base of her spine.

"Zeus grew handsome and strong, and with the help of Rhea, he freed the rest of his swallowed siblings and overthrew the Titans, beginning the age of the Pantheon, the all-powerful Gods of Olympus."

A low murmur filled the dead air. The twelve faces surrounding her were chanting, but it was so soft she couldn't make out the words. It was almost a whisper, barely audible above the wind whistling outside. The voice continued.

"Zeus, king of all Gods and ruler of all men, became infatuated with a beautiful Phoenician princess who went by the name Europa. On a warm, spring day he set out to seduce her. Knowing she would be frightened by the beauty and power of him in his true form, he disguised himself as a white bull. He mixed himself in with her father's flock of cows as she played nearby with a group of other maidens."

The dark figure pulled back his hood and his robe fell away. Involuntarily, she gasped. He wore a loose-fitting pair of black pants, and his skin glowed in the flickering candlelight. On his head he wore a white mask that covered his eyes and cheekbones and cast the rest of his face in shadow. A giant bull's horn curved up from each temple, giving him the illusion of being incredibly tall. He was beautiful and terrifying, and she felt her pulse quicken, out of fear or excitement, she couldn't tell.

"Europa and the maidens were drawn to the bull, noticing his spotless flanks and powerful muscles."

Sadie felt a rustling at her side and realized she was surrounded by figures in white robes. They had flowers in their hair and small white masks covering their eyes. One of the girls squeezed her elbow softly. Her face was blank, but something about the gesture was reassuring. Sadie noticed her dark red hair and the fear started to seep out of her body.

She felt herself being propelled forward. They walked toward the boy in the mask, fanning out and encircling him, a small circle of white inside the ring of flames. They took her hands and placed them on his chest, moving them in slow circles. The chanting continued, louder now. Whatever it was, it wasn't English.

The girls had surrounded him, and they were running their hands across his back and ribs. They were chanting too, their lips moving in unison beneath their masks. She looked up at him through her gauzy blindfold and realized he was staring at her intently. She couldn't see his face, but she could hear him breathing, hard and a little ragged.

She looked down at her hands on his chest and realized she was trembling. His skin was so hot she could feel the heat seeping into her palms and spreading down her forearms like hot oil. The chanting grew louder.

"Encouraged by his gentle nature, Europa climbed upon his back and rode him through the fields of wild flowers and onto the banks of the ocean."

Sadie paused. The girls had surrounded her again, and six pairs of hands turned her so the man was on her left. She felt hands on her shoulders, and the robe fell away. Then, with one swift motion, he swept her up into his arms and walked back the way he had come, the circle parting to let them through. He squeezed her softly with both arms, a gesture that felt oddly familiar.

"When they reached the waves, the bull continued across the ocean, taking her with him to the island of Crete, where he seduced her and made her Queen."

He carried her up a short flight of steps, and she realized the flames were following them, guiding their way and then fanning out in a circle around a sort of altar, a raised platform draped in heavy dark fabric. Before he laid her down, he leaned down and brushed her lips with his.

She tensed and he pulled away. He stared down at her. There was a question in the look, like he was waiting for something from her, some kind of sign.

She bit her lip and noticed a familiar taste she couldn't quite place. His face was still close, and she could feel his hot breath on her cheek. She breathed in deeply, trying to force the nerves and the fear back down into the depths of her stomach. She smelled cinnamon. Something inside her gave way, and she felt like her skin was on fire. Jeremy.

She squeezed the arm around his neck, and he exhaled. She could almost see the tension leaving his body in waves. The flames were all around them now, and he placed her softly on the altar, laying her head down on a silk pillow. As the chanting grew louder still, it quickened and the words reverberated rapidly around the stone walls. He stood over her, and she could still smell the warm scent of his breath on her face.

The chanting was so fast now that the sounds ran together. The noise pounded in her ears, and she felt the vibrations deep in her chest. When the chanting was so loud and so fast she felt like it would swallow her up, he leaned down and kissed her, again.

Without thinking, she arched her body up to meet his and parted her lips. The chanting grew louder and faster, so loud they must have been yelling. Then, in one split second, the chanting stopped and the flames blew out, plunging the room into total darkness. They parted, and the only sound she heard was their breathing, loud and raspy in the sudden silence.

As she lay there, she was filled with a sense of foreboding. Had they done something wrong? She felt hands underneath her shoulders, and someone guided her up off the table and onto the floor in front of the altar. Someone told her to kneel, and she did, sinking down into the carpet. With a pang of embarrassment, she realized what she had just done, kissing Jeremy in front of a room full of faceless people. She smiled to herself, and she was surprised to realize she didn't care. She couldn't wait to do it again.

The voice spoke again, filling the silence.

"Sadie Marlowe and Jeremy Wood, you have been invited to join the Order of Optimates. In embodying the spirits of those who came before us, the almighty Gods of Mount Olympus, you have sealed yourselves within the Order, as members and standard bearers for all eternity. Do you solemnly swear to uphold the values of the Pantheon, maintain loyalty to your brothers and sisters of the Olympiad, use your strength, intelligence, and power to further the goals of the Order, and protect the secrecy of this body upon penalty of death?"

Silence filled the room, and then Jeremy spoke. His voice was calm and clear.

"I do."

A hand tapped her on the shoulder. She took a deep breath.

"I do."

"We offer these neophytes to you, Zeus, for judgment. Do you find them worthy?"

She was confused. She waited, but no instructions came. After what felt like minutes, she heard a series of scraping noises, somewhere high above them. She heard rustling, as if a group of people were getting to their feet, and a new voice spoke, older and deeper this time. "We do."

There was another pause, and then the voice continued.

"The seal has been made. Let them have light."

She felt the blindfold fall from her eyes and bright lights flared on overhead. She heard champagne corks popping. People cheered.

Brett was at her side, helping her up, and she rushed her down the steps to where a group of girls in white robes stood laughing and filling glasses of champagne. She recognized Thayer's long blonde hair, and a few of the other girls looked familiar. She searched the room fruitlessly for Jessica's light brown hair, and a pang of disappointment settled deep down in her stomach. She looked back over her shoulder and saw Jeremy in a circle of guys in black robes, hoods pushed back off their faces. They clapped him on the back and took turns earnestly shaking his hand. He looked up and met her eye, and the corner of his mouth drew up in a smile. She turned back toward the group, and Thayer handed her another glass of champagne.

"Congratulations," she said, raising an eyebrow. "Have fun?"

Sadie's cheeks burned, but she was too happy to be angry. "That obvious, huh?" She laughed, and Thayer clinked her glass before walking away. She looked around her, taking in the cavernous room. It was cylindrical, and above them she saw a wide balcony cut into the stone wall. She could see a hall lined with flickering lanterns and dozens of chairs, but they were empty. She remembered the voice and quickly scanned the room, but whoever it was was gone.

Brett appeared at her side and enveloped her in a huge hug.

"You could have at least warned me about Jeremy, you know."

Brett cringed and spread her hands.

"I really, really wanted to, but I couldn't. I would have been punished." As she said it her eyes went to the balcony. Sadie frowned. Punished?

Suddenly she felt a little ill. "Wait, did Jeremy know? Is that why he asked me to the dance?"

Brett opened her eyes wide. "Oh, no. He didn't know you were going to be here either—this whole thing between you was a complete coincidence. Worked out well for us, though." She grinned. "These things are a lot more fun when people get into it. You should have seen Finn when he and Thayer got initiated—I swear he was disappointed he didn't get to feel up some random stranger."

"Yikes."

"Really, we have no part in choosing new members anyway." Brett jerked a thumb toward the balcony. "The senior members do that."

A girl Sadie recognized as one of the senior prefects joined them, linking an arm conspiratorially through Brett's.

"You're lucky, you know. They always initiate one member from Graff and one from Keating at the same time, so the guy could be anyone." She grimaced. "I got initiated with Brent." She rolled her eyes and looked over at a guy Sadie recognized as the football player Jessica had warned her against. "I'm Lillian, by the way. Ready to meet everyone else?"

She spent the next half hour shaking hands and meeting people whose faces were already vaguely familiar. They were all notable students at Graff and Keating, heiresses or athletes or prodigies.

Next, they led her down to another room they called the salon. It was richly furnished and softly lit, and an oddly modern gas fireplace blazed on one side. Everything was leather or brocade, and the walls were lined with huge oil paintings in heavy gilded frames.

At around 2 A.M., someone brought out a platter covered with food, and the members flocked to it like pigeons to scraps of bread. Sadie was sitting on one corner of a sofa next to Brett, and another member, a junior named Olivia whose father was a Supreme Court justice, was sprawled on the other end, one bare foot kicked carelessly across Brett's lap. The two of them were passing a bottle of champagne back and forth and arguing over which members were going to hook up that night. Brett was making a convincing case for all three of the table dancers when Sadie interrupted her.

"Hey, where's Josh? I feel like he hasn't been around all night."

Brett shrugged and waved a hand. "He's just doing his own thing." She chugged another gulp of champagne.

Sadie scanned the room and saw Josh standing with Jeremy near the food. As she watched, she saw him glance at Brett. There was an odd look in his eyes, but before she could decipher it he looked away.

Olivia sniffed the air and struggled to sit up. "Hey . . . chicken." She lurched to her feet and grabbed Brett's arm. "Come on Brett, let's get some chicken."

Sadie watched the two girls stagger across the room, giggling and swaying like drunks in a three-legged race. She laid her head back on the cushion and closed her eyes, relishing the first moment she had had to herself since the ceremony. She felt someone sink into the cushion next to her and opened her eyes. Jeremy.

Her body responded instantly to his closeness, and she leaned toward him.

He grabbed her hand, and she could see his face was flushed. "Come somewhere with me?" He jerked his head toward the others. "No one will notice."

She nodded, her eyes locked with his, and let him lead her out of the room. As soon as the door closed behind them, she grabbed his arm and pulled him to her, wrapping her arms around his neck. They leaned against the stone wall and kissed until they stopped to catch their breath.

His eyes flashed as he looked down at her. "I've been waiting to do that all night." His voice was hoarse. "Come on." He took her hand and led her down the hall, feeling along the wall for doors as they went. Finally he found one that opened and pulled her inside.

They tumbled into the room and stumbled over a small table. She laughed, but Jeremy looked at her anxiously until she reassured him she was okay. She looked around and realized they were in the dressing room she had used earlier. She remembered the couch and grabbed Jeremy's arm to steer him toward it. She started to sit down, but he stopped her.

"Wait, Sadie, hold on a second." As she watched, he took a deep, controlled breath. "I want you to know I'm not, you know, expecting anything. I know tonight was crazy, and we've had lots of champagne and everything, but I just wanted to get away so we could talk. Everything just happened so fast, and I wanted to tell you something."

She smiled. "I know. This has been pretty nuts, right?" She sank down onto the couch and pulled her legs up underneath her. "What did you want to tell me?"

"I just wanted you to know I'm excited about all of this, but I'm also really glad it was you in there." He grinned and raised an eyebrow. "Now we're linked forever. Whether you like it or not."

She laughed. "So did you know? I mean, about any of it?"

He shook his head. "Not really. They told me the basics tonight, but I still feel like it's barely started to sink in."

"Did they tell you much about the Order? Like, what the point of it is and what they actually do?"

He looked thoughtful. "I guess it's sort of like a frat, only stronger. The members all help each other out—they're in the same social circles, they give each other jobs, finance each other's companies—you know, all that stuff." He shrugged. "So this has been going on for the two hundred years since it was founded, and they've managed to get members in most of the most powerful companies and all the branches of government. It's just a really loyal group of rich and powerful people, and wealth and power breeds more wealth and power." He shook his head again and looked at her. "Blows your mind a little, doesn't it?"

She gave him a wry smile. "No kidding. And here I thought you just had to invent something cool like Post-its or blankets with sleeves."

She sighed and leaned into him. "I guess we shouldn't complain, though. We're on their team now." He put an arm around her and squeezed, then leaned down and kissed her. He tipped her slowly back onto the cushions, and she let the last bit of anxiety drain out of her as she kissed him back.

Chapter 18

She groaned and rolled over, pulling her blanket over her head and trying to fall back asleep. Her head was pounding and her stomach felt like she had spent the night chugging seawater. What felt like seconds later, she woke up again to someone banging on her door.

She heard the old hinges creaking open, and someone jumped onto the bed next to her.

"Rise and shine, bitch. Time for practice."

Sadie didn't move. Maybe this was a bad dream, and she would wake up soon and feel fine. Then someone yanked the blanket off her face, and she saw Jessica grinning at her from the foot of the bed. Jessica's smile faltered.

"Jesus, Sadie. No offense, but you look like crap."

"Thanks," Sadie croaked, throwing an arm over her eyes. "Why is it so bright in here?"

"Uh, 'cause it's ten o'clock, otherwise known as half an hour before we have to be in the gym for conditioning or Coach kills both of us." Jessica jumped off the bed and started rummaging through the piles on Sadie's floor. "Where's your bag? I'll pack it for you while you brush your teeth."

Sadie pulled herself up and rubbed her eyes. She still felt like someone was playing the bongos on her temples, and her skin was clammy and cold. She pointed to a black duffel in a far corner of the room, and Jessica started tossing things into it.

"God, I completely forgot practice was on Sunday this week. I'd rather do anything than run right now."

"What's wrong? Hung over or something? You totally look hung over. Oh, and by the way, don't think I didn't realize that you and

Brett never came upstairs last night." She pouted a little. "You could have just told me if you wanted to sneak out to meet Josh and Jeremy."

The night came back to Sadie in a rush. The ceremony, the voice, the people on the balcony. The dark dressing room. Jeremy. Her body felt warm at the thought, and she smiled.

"Okay, you are seriously grinning like an idiot. That good, huh? Now get up. You can tell me about it on the way."

They got to the gym with minutes to spare, and Thayer was already leading the rest of the team through warm-ups. Thayer caught Sadie's eye and nodded slightly. Sadie scanned the court, but Brett wasn't on it.

"Hey, did you wake Brett up?"

"I tried. She wasn't in her room." Jessica was sitting on the front row of bleachers, lacing up one of her tennis shoes. "Sounds like she had an even better night than you did."

Sadie frowned. "I guess. She's never late, though."

Jessica shrugged. Coach whistled for them to corner up, and they dropped their bags and joined the rest of the team.

That day she was. Instead of running with the team, Coach made Brett spend the whole practice doing laps around the gym. She shuffled slowly along with her head down.

The rest of the team ran for an hour, alternating sets of suicide sprints with lunges, push-ups, sit-ups, and squats. By the eighth sprint, Sadie was trailing a half step behind the other girls in every round. Her legs felt thick and leaden and her headache had retreated from her temples and settled low and heavy around the base of her skull. Seconds after they crossed the baseline, the whistle blew and they dropped to their stomachs for a round of push-ups. Her arms felt strong, and she completed the set quickly. Coach blew the whistle again and the girls lined up on the baseline, sucking in oxygen in short gasps.

"Sadie, I better not see you in last again," Coach barked. Sadie nodded but looked straight ahead, avoiding her gaze. The whistle blew, and they took off.

She pushed hard, pumping her arms and willing her legs to move faster, be stronger, push harder. At the first turn, she was in the middle of the pack. She dug in her toes, grazed one hand along the gym floor and turned, lunging back toward the other end of the court. She passed two girls who were slow to turn and kept going hard, ignoring the pain. By the next turn, her legs started to give, and she could feel her body losing power. By the last length, she felt like she was running in mud, and she crossed the baseline a split second behind Jenna, the second-string goalkeeper, in dead last.

The whistle blew again, and she started a set of lunges, following Thayer as she led the group to half-court and back. They paused for two counts at the bottom of each lunge, allowing the burn to soak in and take hold. By the end of the set her legs were shaking, and she doubled over and breathed hard, hands on her thighs. The blood rushed into her head and brought a fresh wave of pain. She stood up straight and bit down on her lip until it faded. The whistle blew again and they took off. She crossed the line a full step behind the last of her teammates.

They all collapsed to the ground for a round of sit-ups, grateful for the chance to rest their legs. They waited for the whistle to sound to signal the start of the set, but instead they heard Coach's voice.

"Again. And if Sadie still can't keep up, we'll do it again. And again." Everyone groaned and Jenna shot her a dirty look. She struggled to her feet.

Thayer stepped off the baseline in front of the girls and put a hand on her hip. "Coach, why should everyone who's in shape be punished because Sadie can't lay off the cheeseburgers?"

Coach sighed and held up her hand. "Get back in line, Thayer. Our team is only as strong as our weakest player." She looked straight at Sadie. "And for some reason, today that's you." She raised her eyebrows, and Sadie dropped her eyes to the floor.

So much for the Sullas being Thayer's family. Apparently she and Thayer were only friends behind generations-old stone walls. She looked down the line and saw Thayer whisper something to Charlotte.

As Sadie watched, Charlotte's eyes widened and she shook her head. Thayer spat out a few more words, and Charlotte turned away. Just then, Thayer met Sadie's gaze and winked. The whistle blew.

Sadie put the pain out of her mind and pushed hard, but still she felt herself losing ground. Her thighs burned, and her throat felt like it was filled with hot sand. As she made the turn at half-court, she saw Charlotte stumble and slow down. Encouraged, she tried to pick up speed. In the final sprint, she barely passed Thayer, who was furiously pumping her arms despite rapidly falling behind. She crossed the line third to last.

"Much better, Sadie. Everyone give me fifty sit-ups, and then Thayer will lead you in a cooldown."

She breathed a sigh of relief and collapsed gratefully to the ground. Apparently, Thayer was going to live up to her promise of sisterhood after all.

When they were done, Sadie sank down onto the bleachers and put her head in her hands.

"Feeling better?" Jessica asked.

"I'm alive, but I don't think I could have done another suicide." She crushed her paper cup and threw it in the trash, glancing around for Brett. She needed to get her alone. She wanted to talk about last night, and it was killing her that she couldn't tell Jessica.

"Yeah, that was weird. Charlotte and Thayer are usually really fast." Jessica frowned. "No offense. Think they did that on purpose?"

Sadie laughed to hide her smile. "Do you really think they would do that for me? Charlotte probably just tripped because she was trying extra hard to beat me."

Jessica looked unconvinced.

"Trust me, I just got lucky." She didn't want to lie to Jessica, and that was true—she was lucky, just not in the way she was implying.

She stood up and looked for Brett. Most of the girls were still scattered on the bleachers, catching their breath and sipping Gatorade. Something caught her eye near the entrance, and she looked just in time to see Brett's red ponytail disappearing out the door.

She saw Thayer standing alone at the cooler and mumbled something to Jessica about getting a refill. She got in line behind Thayer as she filled a paper cup.

"Hey, thanks for doing that." Thayer shrugged, but she didn't turn around. "You're family. If you ever need anything, I'm here." Thayer gulped down the contents of her cup and started filling it again.

"Actually, I was hoping you could tell me something. I'm in now, so no more secrets, right?" Thayer glanced around them, but no one was close enough to hear. She turned to face Sadie.

"Sort of. What do you want to know."

"A few weeks ago, after the meeting with the Fates, I woke up with a bruise, like I'd given blood or had an IV or something. What was that about?"

Thayer shrugged. "Honesty isn't the only thing they test for that night. We don't really know details—the senior members keep most of that stuff quiet—but I know they have to make sure everyone's, you know, a good fit."

"Meaning what?"

Thayer smiled. "Like I said, they don't tell us everything right away. But they will. Just be patient—they'll answer all of your questions eventually." She looked Sadie in the eye. "Trust me, okay?"

Sadie sighed and nodded. She felt a little better, but she still wished she knew more. "Okay. Thanks."

"No problem. Now ignore everything I'm about to say," Thayer said. Louder, she said: "I don't know if you're hung over or what, but I don't want to see you coming in last again. Ever. Understood?"

Sadie heard the room go silent, and she could feel the rest of the team staring. She clenched her teeth. "Understood."

With her back turned to the rest of the girls, Thayer grinned. "Good. Now don't make me tell you that again."

❧

Sadie was trudging back to Keating with Jessica when her phone jingled. She flipped it open, and felt a smile spread across her face.

"Feeling okay today? My head feels like it's going to explode."

She typed out a quick response.

"Rough wake up but feeling better now. Practice sucked."

His response came a minute later.

"Ouch, ours isn't until noon. Last night was worth the headache though, right?"

"Definitely."

"Good. Me too. Still on for tonight?"

&

Jeremy picked her up at five o'clock. She hurried from the door to the limo, clutching her hood around her face to keep out the cold. Inside the car was warm and dry, and she sighed gratefully as she sat back against the smooth leather.

She looked at Jeremy and feigned shock. He was wearing a simple white T-shirt, his Cubs hat, and jeans. "So this is off-duty Jeremy? I can't even believe they let you off campus like that." She stuck her nose in the air. "You hardly look like DeGraffenreid material."

He grinned and nodded toward a black wool coat that lay in a heap on the seat next to him. "The coat was my camouflage. Sure you don't want to reconsider? You know, now that you've seen me without my rich-kid costume?"

"Nah, I like it." She scooted a little closer to him on the seat. "So what's the plan?"

He took her to Lou's, a tiny, hole-in-the-wall brick building on a small side street in downtown Foxburg. The sign above the door was a wooden carving of a plump tomato that read, "Lou's Pizza: Since 1937." He told her it was the best pizza he had ever had, "outside Chicago, obviously."

They sat together in a cozy wooden booth near the back and ordered a thin-crust pizza with sausage, mushrooms, and peppers. It was sizzling hot when it got to the table, and Sadie immediately reached for a piece.

"Wait!" He held up a hand. "It's not ready yet."

She watched as he picked a large slice and slid it onto a plate, leaving a trail of thick, melted cheese. Next, he picked a shriveled, light green pepper out of a small bowl and held it up like an offering.

"The secret ingredient," he said.

He used a knife to carefully slice off the tip of the pepper. Then, squeezing it like a lemon, he drizzled the spicy juice all over a slice. He finished it off with a sprinkle of Parmesan cheese, then finally slid it toward her.

She looked at him expectantly, but he just stared back. "Are you really going to watch me eat it?"

He grinned. "Just the first bite."

She picked up the steaming slice and bit off the tip. He leaned forward, crossing his arms on the table like a little kid waiting for seconds.

"Great, right?"

She chewed, purposely avoiding his gaze. The pizza was good—hot and cheesy, with just the right amount of sauce—and the hot pepper juice added a spicy kick at the finish.

He laid his hands flat on the table and leaned even farther. "Come on, Sadie—you're killing me."

She put the slice back down on her plate and took a deep breath. "Okay fine, you're right. This pizza is ridiculously awesome."

He exhaled loudly and settled back into his seat. "Thank god. If you didn't like Lou's, we might have had some issues." Satisfied, he performed the ritual all over again and dug in.

They were debating over whether to have thirds when an enormous man in a big white apron walked over to their table and slapped Jeremy on the back. He had bushy gray hair with eyebrows to match, a ruddy red nose, and deep laugh lines carved in both cheeks.

"How's the pizza tonight, eh?" He spoke with a heavy Italian accent.

Jeremy leaned back and patted his belly. "Great, as always. Thanks, Lou."

The man smiled widely and put his hands on his hips. "Good. You going to introduce me to your girlfriend?"

Her cheeks burned, and she opened her mouth to correct him, but Jeremy was unfazed.

"This is Lou, he owns the place. Lou, this is Sadie, she goes to Keating."

Lou raised his bushy eyebrows. "Keating, eh? Did you know that girl who disappeared last spring?"

She shook her head. "I'm new this year, I just transferred in."

He nodded. "Tragic. The whole town was devastated. Sometimes I wonder what's going on over there."

"At Keating? What do you mean?"

"Well, you know, people around here talk. It's a pretty small-town atmosphere." He glanced at Jeremy and shrugged a half-hearted apology.

Jeremy started to speak, but Sadie cut him off. "Like what?"

"Oh, you know, it's not the first time a student has ended up . . . in trouble. There was that other girl too, back in the '80s. Can't remember her name, but she was one of those heiresses, you know? Family was always in the news."

Sadie frowned. The Keating curse. She wondered exactly what "getting into trouble" was a euphemism for.

"What happened to her?"

He shrugged. "They never found her. But don't you worry about that. All the schools are having problems these days—kids getting into drugs and sex and vampires and stuff. I'm sure what happened to the Ralleigh girl was just a sad accident."

He waved a meaty hand to dismiss the subject, but Sadie's throat had instantly gone dry.

"What Ralleigh girl?"

"Oh—Anna Ralleigh. That was the girl who died last year."

Sadie's tongue felt thick and clumsy, and she was starting to feel dizzy. "Her last name was Ralleigh?"

"Listen, I should never have brought it up." He put a hand on each of their shoulders and smiled. "Have a great time on your date. Come back and get some pizza soon, all right? Just don't bring any of your snooty friends—those rich brats never tip." He grinned, then turned and ambled back toward the kitchen.

Sadie sat back heavily in her seat. She told herself it was a coincidence—that Ralleigh could be a common name. But something about it made her stomach turn. "Have you ever heard any of that before?"

Jeremy was busy pulling another slice out of the pan. "Not really. I mean, I heard about Anna. Everyone was still talking about it when I got here. But I've never really heard about anyone else. It's sad, but that shit happens, right? The other thing was probably just some tragic accident, too."

Sadie thought about the moss-covered cross on the side of the road near Keating's main gate. "Or another suicide."

Jeremy took a bite and chewed. "Actually now that I think about it, they do talk about girls not being able to handle the pressure and losing it during finals. They joke about it, the Keating Curse or something dumb like that, but it's just people talking. I didn't think they meant, you know, really losing it."

She frowned, and Jeremy looked surprised. "Hey, don't worry about it. It's probably nothing. I've only even heard that once or twice. Besides, Lou probably just means students who drop out or cause a huge scandal by going to UC Santa Barbara instead of Princeton." He smiled. "Besides, no talking about Keating and Graff tonight, right?"

Her head was spinning now, and part of her wanted to sprint to the kitchen to ask Lou more questions. Instead, she forced herself to give him a convincing smile.

"You're right. No Keating, no Graff, just jeans, pizza, and slumming it with the other common folk."

He laughed, and she grabbed another slice. They ate the last two pieces, then walked the few short blocks down the street to the movie theater. Foxburg had an old-fashioned theater with velvet seats, a big, red curtain, and an organ pit that dated back to the days when the theater showed silent films. Now, it mostly showed indie movies and slightly older releases for five bucks a ticket. When they were about a block away, he nonchalantly took her hand. He didn't let go until the credits rolled.

ॐ

She got another e-mail from the Sullas a few weeks later. It was a Thursday, and she was in the lobby with Grace and Jessica, slumped in an armchair with her laptop propped open on her lap. She was 2,000 words into a 2,500-word essay on Nabokov, and she was debating trying to get away with using 500 words' worth of quotes from the book to fill out the rest. She leaned her head back and sighed, rubbing her temples with both hands.

"You know, maybe a creepy pervert who's obsessed with a teenager is just a creepy pervert? Why do we have to write papers about him?" she said aloud.

"Tell me about it," Jessica muttered, her hands still moving along her keyboard.

Sadie was about to shut her laptop when an e-mail notification popped up on her screen. It was another e-mail from Z—whoever that was.

The salon
2 P.M.
Saturday
-Z

She looked up and glanced around the room. Instinctively she hunched over the screen, as if someone would see right through it and discover her secret, but nothing had changed. She spent the next hour staring at her essay and wondering what Saturday would bring.

At nine, the lights dimmed, and she closed her computer and made her way up to her room. As she put a hand on the doorknob, it opened from the inside and Trix came stumbling out. Judging from her outfit, she was just leaving.

"Oh, hey Sadie," she said as she brushed by her in the doorway. Sadie smelled pungent smoke mingling with her perfume. "I'm just headed to brush my teeth." She jerked a thumb toward the bathroom down the hall and smiled widely. "I'll see you later."

Sadie just waved and shut the door behind her. With the twins, Sadie had realized the best way to deal with them was to just pretend she believed them, no matter how ridiculous their stories were. Lately, she was pretty sure they were both spending every night in the dorms at Georgetown, but they still gave her a convenient excuse every time they ran into each other in their room. They would say: "Oh, hey, Sadie. I haven't seen you in days—I feel like I haven't left the library in ages," even as they changed out of the mini-dress and heels they had clearly been wearing since the night before.

She dropped her laptop on her desk, then peeled off her sweat-shirt. As she collapsed on the bed, she winced as the old springs gave way with a loud whine. She thought for a moment, then flipped open her phone.

"Get the e-mail about Saturday? Any idea what's going on?"

She sent the text and settled down to wait, curling up under the covers with her phone inches from her nose. It buzzed a moment later.

"No clue. Some kind of event? Josh said they get invited to lots of stuff in the city. Have you heard anything?"

"Not really. Haven't gotten the chance to ask yet, though. What are you up to?"

"Just got in bed. About to start watching a movie."

"Oh, sounds fun . . . What movie?"

"Probably *Rocky*. Hulu's streaming the whole series for free this month."

"Nice. Never seen it—supposed to be good, right?"

"You've *never* seen *Rocky*? We might have a problem."

"Haha, I'm not really into boxing. Or sweaty guys with weird accents . . ."

"Okay, now you're just trying to piss me off. *Rocky* is the ultimate sports movie. And you call yourself an athlete . . . Check your e-mail."

She pulled her laptop off of her desk and opened it, navigating back to her e-mail inbox. A few moments later an e-mail from jwood@degraffenreid.edu popped up. It was a link to a Hulu page with the movie embedded in it.

"What's this?"

"Watch the movie with me?"

"Uh, I wish. There's no way I can get out of here right now."

"Ha, that'd be nice. But I just meant with me, at the same time, on your laptop. It'll be like a date, and you won't even have to worry about me trying to get to second base."

I'm an idiot, she thought.

"Sounds good to me. Should I start it now?"

"Yeah. And prepare to have your mind blown. Just don't judge Rocky by his tight '80s sweatpants—I think they were considered manly back then."

She plugged in her headphones, turned off the lights, and settled back against the pillows to watch. Halfway through the movie and about two dozen texts later, she made a mental note to ask her dad about her cell phone plan. If she didn't have unlimited texts already, she was definitely going to need them.

Chapter 19

At 1:30 that Saturday, she stood in front of her closet and stared at the rack of T-shirts, sweatpants, and rumpled jeans. She was wondering what, exactly, one was expected to wear to one's first official secret society meeting if such a meeting took place in the afternoon. She couldn't exactly Google that one like she did every other social occasion at Keating that required a nonsensical dress-code label like "cocktail casual" or "white tie." She finally settled on some jeans, a navy blue sweater, and some brown leather boots Gwen had casually discarded a few weeks before.

"Want these? I'm sick of wearing them," she had said, before unceremoniously dumping them at Sadie's feet. They were $400 riding boots that looked like they had barely been tried on, much less worn enough to be given away. Sadie had simply nodded, wide-eyed, and Gwen had walked away like she had just given Sadie something as worthless as a spare square of toilet paper.

She threw the outfit on, brushed her hair, and pulled on a wool hat. She glanced out the window and saw rain falling fast and heavy. She sighed—the walk to the tower was not going to be fun.

She slipped down the stairs and padded across the thick carpet. She had a hand on the front door, when she heard Jessica's voice.

"Hey, Sadie! Wait up." She was standing in the doorway to the TV room in sweats and a giant fuzzy pair of slippers. "Where are you going? I just texted you earlier—Madison's screening her entire collection of Fever Stephens movies. There's so much unintentional comedy, I can't even stand it. Come watch?"

Sadie shook her head. "Sorry, Jess, I really have to get to the library to finish that paper." She grinned. "It does sound tempting, though."

Jessica pouted. "Okay, fine. But want to do pizza and a movie tonight? There's a double feature at the Foxburg Theater, and I really need to eat something way greasier than all that gourmet crap they serve in the dining room. You in?"

Sadie thought for a moment. She had no idea how long this meeting would last, but she figured she would at least be back within a few hours. "Meet you in your room at six?"

"Deal! Good luck with your paper, you big nerd." Jessica smiled and spun around on one slipper, disappearing back into the room.

Sadie exhaled. She felt terrible lying to Jess, but she was glad they would get to spend some time together tonight. With everything that had been going on lately, they had barely had time to hang out. She waited until she heard the sounds of the TV starting up again, then slipped out the door.

❧

It was cold and wet along the path, and by the time she reached the tower her hair hung in ragged clumps beneath her hat. She had wondered how she was going to make the long walk between Keating and the tower without anyone wondering where she was going, but the weather took care of that for her. The fog rolling off the ocean was so thick she could barely see more than ten yards ahead.

When she got to the tower, she stood dumbly in front of it for a few moments, realizing she had no idea how to get in. She thought back to last Saturday. She had been blindfolded, but she remembered walking down some steps and through a door.

She wandered around the building until she found a small staircase carved into its side. At its base was a heavy wooden door with a rusty iron knocker in the center. She frowned. It looked about a million years old, and if she didn't know any better, she would have thought the whole thing had probably been rusted shut for decades. With one mittened hand, she tried the handle. It didn't budge.

She tried the knocker next, but it barely moved. She took a deep breath, then grabbed the knocker with both hands and pulled as hard as she could. A little trickle of dust rewarded her for her efforts, but nothing else moved. She put her hands on her hips and sighed.

For a moment, she indulged in a crazy fantasy that last weekend had all been one really long, vivid dream, and now she was just some psycho crawling around an abandoned old army fort like a schizophrenic who had stopped taking her meds.

She pulled out her phone to text Brett or Jeremy, but she didn't have any service. She stepped back up to the door and pounded on it with one fist. It made a low, dull thumping sound.

She stepped back again and waited. Nothing. She took off her mittens, took a deep breath, and pounded again with both fists.

"Uh, what are you doing, crazypants?"

She turned around, a smile frozen on her face. Thayer, Olivia, and Lillian stood at the top of the stairs, looking at her like her fantasy might actually be coming true. They were all perfectly dressed in wool coats and cashmere scarves, and somehow they were totally dry.

Sadie tried to run a hand through her hair, but all she succeeded in doing was tangling it further and soaking her mitten with slush.

"I, uh, forgot how to get in." She gestured lamely toward the locked door with one dripping paw.

Olivia stepped forward. "Actually, hon, I don't think you ever learned."

She knelt down to the right of the door. At about knee height, there was one stone that looked cleaner than the rest. She pulled what turned out to be a thin metal facade, and it swung open like a tiny kitchen cabinet. In the hollow behind it was a black metal box with a single blinking red light. She reached into her pocket and pulled out her wallet.

Confused, Sadie watched her fish out a silver credit card and wave it in front of the box. The light turned green, and Sadie heard a sequence of low beeps followed by the soft scraping of metal against metal. Olivia swung the little door shut and stood up. She nodded toward the door.

"Go ahead."

Sadie tried the handle, and the door swung open easily. She looked at Olivia in surprise.

"Your Visa opens the door?"

Olivia snorted and walked into the building with Lillian a few steps behind her.

Thayer walked down the last few stairs and handed an identical silver credit card to Sadie. "It's not real, see?" Sadie flipped it over, and the back was blank. "It's a smart card—all the members get them. You'll get yours today. You wave it in front of the sensor, and it unlocks the door."

Sadie handed the card back and followed Thayer inside. When she pulled the door shut, she heard the same soft scraping sound. A chill went through her as she realized that the mechanism was locking them all in, too.

Thayer pointed to a small black box on the wall to the right of the door. "Usually I wouldn't bother pointing this out, but since I can totally picture you standing here for hours trying to figure out how to get out, here's how you unlock the door from the inside. You use the card the same way, just on this little box right here." She looked at Sadie and raised her eyebrows. "Just make sure you're never the last one in here if you don't have your key. There's no other way out except the door that leads to the roof, and it's not like there's a fire escape."

Olivia giggled. "One time sophomore year Rob Nicholas and I got locked in here overnight."

Thayer tossed a sheet of blonde hair over her shoulder and pursed her lips. "From what Finn says, you and Rob sure made the most of that."

Olivia sniffed and Sadie saw her jaw tighten, but she just hooked an arm through Lillian's and turned and walked away.

"So what if we did?" she called over her shoulder. As they continued down the hallway, Sadie watched their shadows stretch, distorted, along the curved stone wall, then finally disappear.

"You should really take a car next time you have to get here," Thayer said, wrinkling her nose. "Just have it drop you off at the gate and then just walk around the edge of the grounds."

Sadie groaned inwardly as she tried to wring out the ends of her hair.

"Plus, you look completely ridiculous." Thayer took a step forward and Sadie flinched, but her face had softened. "Look, I know why you're here. Legacies almost always get in—keeping the right families in power is one of the most basic principles the Order is built on. But there are still some people who don't think you're Sulla material. So just try to fit in, okay? Fake it 'til it starts to come naturally."

Sadie nodded, and Thayer seemed satisfied.

"All right Portland, let's go. If we leave the guys in there alone too long without some supervision they'll be hammered before we can even get anything done."

The start of the meeting felt suspiciously like Sadie's tenure as secretary of her sixth-grade student council. Thayer and Finn sat on two cushy armchairs that they turned to face the rest of the group, while the others sat on couches and the floor. Thayer even took roll, and there was something hilarious about watching her hunch over a plastic clipboard while entrenched in a century-old secret lair. Then they issued Sadie and Jeremy their credit card keys.

As Finn handed her the card, he met her eyes. "If you lose this, I'll kill you," he deadpanned. Sadie laughed, but he just stared. She watched as his eyes panned down her neck and settled on her chest, and she adjusted her sweater awkwardly as she walked back to her seat, trying to keep the disgust from showing on her face.

Thayer tossed the clipboard aside. She stood up, put her hands on her hips, and scanned the group. Her eyes hovered on Sadie's for a moment, and she pursed her lips. Sadie self-consciously sat up straighter.

"Okay, guys, here's the real reason we called this meeting. The White House's Holiday Gala is tonight, and we're all going."

The last sentence ended in a shriek, and the other girls bounced up to join her, jumping up and down and squealing like hungry seals jostling for fish. The Graff members all tried to keep it dignified by just lazily slapping each other on the back and hiding their excitement behind clenched jaws and upturned chins. Finn and Brent went immediately to the large liquor cabinet and started pulling out bottle after bottle of whiskey, lining them up on a table like bowling pins.

After about a minute, Sadie realized she was the only one still sitting. She looked around nervously, and for the first time that day she noticed Brett. She was curled up on the corner of a couch near the back of the room, her legs drawn up tightly beneath her. She was staring into space, and her arms lay limp on the couch at her sides.

Sadie stood up to talk to her, but Jeremy appeared at her side.

"Pretty amazing, huh? I've never been to the White House."

Sadie shrugged and tried to look bored. "I've been a few times. Would you believe the First Lady had the nerve to serve us an overdone filet mignon? I mean really."

They grinned at each other until Thayer clapped twice, loudly, in the front of the room. The din boiled down to a low hum, and she started to bark directions like a grade school teacher.

"Girls, my aunt pulled us a bunch of dresses, and they're on racks in the white room. Pick whatever you want, but try not to puke all over it, especially if it's a Valentino. We almost burned that bridge for good last time." She looked pointedly at Olivia, and a ripple of laughter went through the group. Olivia crossed her arms in front of her chest.

"Fuck you, too, Thayer," she muttered. Lillian sympathetically patted her on the arm, and Thayer continued.

"After we pick dresses, we'll do hair and makeup in Foxburg—I made us all appointments. Guys, your tuxes are hanging in the closet. No switching out your shoes or accessories. Contrary to what you may think, you look like assholes when you try to make tuxes look cool. We'll meet back here at five for the drive to D.C."

Jeremy grinned down at her. "Well, I guess I'll see you later?"

She smiled. "Can't wait."

She followed Thayer down the hall to the white room, but today it looked drastically different. The love seat and chairs were all gone, and in their place stood four silver racks packed with glittering and gleaming fabrics in dark, rich tones.

The girls fanned out against the wall in front of the racks, and Thayer took her place facing them. Directly in front of Sadie was a rack filled with dresses in varying shades of deep, shimmering blue. She reached out a hand to touch one, but Thayer threw her a look so scathing she jammed her hands into her pockets and stepped back.

"Okay, so you guys know how this works. We'll go by seniority by order of induction, so Sadie you're last even though you're a junior." She tilted her head toward Sadie and mouthed an exaggerated, "Sorry."

Sadie was actually relieved—maybe there would only be one dress left by the time it was her turn and she wouldn't have to pick anything out. The dresses might as well have been dozens of near-identical screws at a hardware store; they all looked about right, and about the same, but she knew if she picked the wrong one everything would fall apart.

Thayer was pointing to the rack on Sadie's far left. "We have, from left to right, Valentino, Marchesa, Oscar de la Renta, and, of course . . . Chanel." The girls made swooning noises as each designer was announced, and by the time she said "Chanel" in a low, deferential whisper, Sadie thought they might actually faint. Somehow, they stayed standing, but they staggered on their feet like drunks.

Thayer pointed to an enormous garment bag hanging alone at the back of the room. "I've already picked my dress, obviously, so Lillian, you're up next."

Sadie watched each girl file through the racks of dresses, quickly and confidently, then select one and carry it toward the mirrors.

It was as if they had already seen them all before, and they knew instantly which one they wanted. Some left the wall at a jogging pace, zeroing in on a single slip of fabric with the determination and unwavering accuracy of a homing missile. They would clutch the prize to their chest and sneak furtive glances back toward the group, then slink off to the mirror to admire their catch. By the time they got to Sadie, there were still dozens of dresses on the racks, and she was at a complete loss.

She walked slowly toward the rack on the right and the shades of blue that had caught her eye earlier. She carefully picked one up, noticed a gash of triangular cutouts across the dress's midsection, and quickly put it back. She hadn't shown her stomach in anything other than a bikini since her first-grade ballet recital, and she didn't plan on breaking that streak tonight.

She stepped back and surveyed the racks. She was tempted to just pick one at random, but she remembered Thayer's warning in the hallway: Fit in. Fake it if you have to.

She took a deep breath.

"They won't bite, you know."

She looked up and saw Olivia, a look of amusement on her face.

Sadie raised her eyebrows. "Are you sure? Because that black one with the studded shoulder pads looks like it might."

Olivia laughed. "Yeah, well, don't pick that one." She held up the dress and shuddered. "This is so fug. Sometimes I don't know what the hell these designers are thinking." She put the dress back and turned to Sadie. "So, I take it you're not really into shopping?"

Sadie looked down at her rumpled outfit. "That obvious, huh?"

"Not at all, actually—I like the way you dress. It's very . . . West Coast–casual. Sort of purposely messy in a cool, irreverent sort of way."

"Oh, yeah, disheveled chic is kinda my thing," she said sarcastically. A look of confusion passed across Olivia's face, and Sadie wondered if she had somehow been sincere.

"Anyway, you look a little lost. Want some help?"

Sadie nodded, and Olivia turned and walked down the line of gowns, trailing one finger along the edge of the racks. She walked the full length of the room twice, then stopped and pulled out a long, navy blue column that glimmered in the light. She stared at it for a moment, her brows knitted together in concentration, then held it out to Sadie with a smile.

"Definitely this one. Blue's your color."

Sadie took the dress and carefully draped it across her arm. The bodice fell from points at each shoulder, then dove into a deep, plunging neckline. Bands of glittering jewels crossed the dress at the waist and again below the hip, where the skirt spread out in a flurry of tiny, delicate pleats that fell to the floor. It looked like the kind of thing a Rockefeller heiress would have worn to a speakeasy in the '20s. Just holding it made her feel a little giddy.

"Wow, Olivia—this is perfect. Thank you."

She waved a hand. "No problem. If anything'll make you fit in at the White House, that dress will." She grinned. "Plus, it'll make your boobs look hot."

⚬

After the salon, the girls piled into a waiting limo and headed back toward Keating, excitement rippling between them like their eyelash extensions were electrically charged. The girls all chatted and laughed and tried their best not to squash their updos against the leather headrests, but Brett was quiet. She spent the ride staring out the window, her chin in her hand, and Sadie could tell something was wrong. Her clothes were wrinkled, and underneath the thick layer of makeup, Sadie could see her skin was pale and waxen. She looked dull and empty. Closed for business.

Sadie looked around the car. The other girls were distracted—talking over each other and singing loudly along with the music. She placed a hand softly on her arm. Brett flinched and pulled away, but then her eyes seemed to clear, like she was just waking up from a dream. She shook herself slightly and stretched her mouth wide in an unconvincing grimace.

"What's wrong, Brett?"

Her smile faltered, then stretched even wider.

Sadie squeezed her arm. "I'm serious. Don't tell me it's nothing."

"What? I'm just tired." Brett waved a hand and looked back out the window. "School stuff. I've been pulling all-nighters."

Sadie frowned. "You haven't been yourself in weeks. I barely even see you. Even before the initiation—you're never in the dining room, and you missed calculus twice last week."

Sadie saw Brett's jaw tighten, but her voice was calm.

"That's not true—I see you at practice all the time. I just really need to focus right now."

"On what? Finals aren't for weeks. And you're just . . . you're different. You're quiet. And I can't remember the last time you mentioned Josh. Is something going on with you guys?"

Brett turned her head sharply and looked Sadie in the eye. Her smile was tighter and smaller. "We're fine. Look, sorry if I can't hang out in the dining room with you guys or sit around wasting time in your rooms. College applications are due soon, and I really need to be perfect."

Sadie paused. "You mean your applications need to be perfect?"

Brett sighed loudly. "Yes, Sadie. That's what I said." She turned back to the window and crossed her arms over her chest. Sadie noticed that she was distractedly scratching a spot on her forearm.

"I just need to get accepted to Yale and get the hell out of this place," Brett muttered.

Sadie looked down and grabbed Brett's hand. "Brett, you're bleeding," she whispered. "What did you do to your arm?"

Brett looked down at the bright red line spreading slowly across the sleeve of her white sweater. She said nothing, but yanked her hand away from Sadie's and tucked it back against her chest. She looked out the window.

"None of your fucking business, Sadie."

Sadie recoiled as if she had been struck.

Past Brett, outside the window, Sadie saw the enormous houses roll by, one by one, in blurs of red brick and white columns. They passed a large mansion with pillars three stories high, and an enormous stone house that looked like it belonged on an English moor. She remembered three months ago when she had driven down this road with her dad. She had wondered then what went on behind those walls, what kind of people could possibly live inside something so massive. But now she was glad she didn't know. If these houses were anything like the students at Graff and Keating, their facades were meaningless.

She shuddered. The outside was the only thing about these people that was predictable. Once you got beneath the surface, there was no telling what you might find.

☙

When they got back to the tower, the sky was slowly darkening over the ocean, and everything was so gray it was hard to tell where the sea stopped and the sky began. A cold wind blew across the water and buffeted the stone building from all sides, and she could hear it howling as she followed the rest of the girls down the hallway.

The guys were already there, gathered around the liquor cabinet filling up flasks and slipping them into the breast pockets of their tuxedo jackets. Within three of his long strides, Jeremy picked her up and twirled her around in his arms. Despite herself, she giggled, then struggled back to her feet.

"Watch it, dude," she joked, straightening her skirt. "This dress costs more than my dad's car."

"You look amazing."

"Thanks, I could really get used to wearing shit like this all the time."

He laughed. "You're lucky. Tuxes are literally the most uncomfortable thing in the world. Well, maybe not literally, but you know—they blow." He pulled at his collar. "I'm basically being slowly choked to death."

She reached up and adjusted his collar. "Yeah, well, you don't look uncomfortable."

He wrapped one arm around her back and pulled her in close. "Thanks." His voice was husky, and seconds later he was kissing her.

"Jesus, Jeremy, she's not even drunk yet. Save some energy for later."

They broke apart to see Finn standing next to them, his face just inches from theirs.

"Maybe we'll all have some fun once we finish these." He held up two flasks, one in each hand, and grinned.

"Knock it off, Finn," Jeremy said, pulling her in closer.

Finn turned his gaze toward Sadie and raised his eyebrows. He ran his tongue over his bottom lip suggestively and slowly looked her up and down.

"Fuck off," she said. "I wasn't interested at the formal, and I'm not interested now." He shrugged and held out the flasks, one to each of them.

"Whatever. It'll happen. It always does." They took the flasks, and Finn turned and addressed everyone. "Cars are here, ladies and dicks," he yelled. "Let's move out."

❧

After the first half hour, the flasks were nearly empty and the liquor had the rest of the drive to work its way into their veins and settle in for the long night ahead. By the time they passed the first security checkpoint, Olivia had settled into a pattern of a few minutes of slumped silence, followed by a loud hiccup and then peals of hysterical laughter. She would exhaust herself, then slump back against the seat and start the process all over again.

The car slowed to a stop in front of the second security checkpoint, and they all piled out. Sadie looked around. It wasn't the grand entrance she was expecting, but she could see one wing of the White House looming above them.

Ahead was a small booth staffed by a woman with a sleek black ponytail, the kind of person who looked like she had marched out of the womb with a clipboard and a tiny cell phone. Two guards stood on either side of her, their arms crossed and their chins thrust aggressively into the air. A blue carpet led past the booth and around the side of the building to the entrance.

At Thayer's command, the members organized themselves into couples and lined up in front of the desk. Thayer and Finn gave their names first. The woman bared her teeth in what Sadie assumed was a smile, welcomed them, and immediately waved them through.

A few other couples sailed through next, but when Olivia and Brent stepped forward, Olivia hiccupped loudly, clapped her hand over her mouth, and sputtered with laughter. Brent put an arm around her waist to steady her, but the woman frowned. She scrolled through the list of names on the tablet and murmured a few quiet words into her mouthpiece, holding up one finger for them to wait.

Olivia fell silent and pouted. She looked over her shoulder at Sadie and rolled her eyes exaggeratedly. "So rude," she slurred, just as one leg buckled and she collapsed against Brent's side.

A moment later, the woman pursed her lips and looked up. "Against my better judgment, welcome to the White House, Ms. Spencer and Mr. Taylor." She waved them through without smiling.

"Finally," Olivia huffed loudly as she strolled past.

Sadie cringed and stepped forward.

"Are you also personal guests of the Cranston family?" The woman didn't look up.

"Uh, yeah—I think so."

Her eyes flicked toward Sadie. "You think?"

Jeremy cleared his throat and squeezed Sadie's arm. "Yes, ma'am. I'm Jeremy Wood and this is Ms. Sadie Marlowe. I believe you'll find us on that list without any problem at all."

She spoke a few hushed words into her mouthpiece, then waved them through with a stiff nod. As they passed, she put a hand on Jeremy's arm.

"Look, you kids clearly have friends in high places, but if your friend pukes on the president or any members of Congress, it's going to be my ass on Monday. Keep an eye on her."

Jeremy nodded solemnly, and she let him go. They walked quickly down the lit path and stifled their laughter until they rounded the corner of the building.

Chapter 20

The first time she caught a glimpse of the President, Sadie gasped audibly. President Manning was taller than she had expected, but it was him—the President of the United States—sipping champagne out of a flute just like the one Jeremy had handed her seconds before. He was about fifteen yards away from her, his head bowed in discussion with two other men, and she was surprised to realize he looked so . . . normal. He was just one guy in a tux in a room full of them. She wasn't sure what she had been expecting, but it was a shock.

Brett stood next to her, a full champagne glass in her hand. She was staring, glassy-eyed, in the President's direction.

"Pretty crazy, right? We're actually at a party with the President," Sadie said. "My dad's going to be so jealous."

Brett just stared and shrugged. "Yeah, it's pretty cool, I guess."

Sadie blushed. "You've probably seen him tons of times. I bet I'm the only one in here who doesn't consider this, like, an average, run-of-the-mill Saturday night."

Brett turned to her and raised her eyebrows. "I doubt it." She waved her flute in a slow arc, motioning toward the crowd mingling in the elegant ballroom. "All these people just live for this shit." Her voice was hard. "Being here means something to them, all right. It means they matter."

Sadie looked at Brett, and as she watched, her face suddenly changed. Seconds earlier her cheeks had been flushed, and the fire in her voice had shown clearly on her face. Now the color was gone, siphoned by some force Sadie couldn't see. She looked flat and lifeless.

"Brett—what's wrong?" She followed Brett's unblinking line of sight back toward the President. She frowned. Nothing had changed.

At that moment, one of the men he was speaking to turned toward them and for the first time she saw his face. She recognized the strong jawline and sandy hair immediately. It was Teddy Cranston, and the gray-haired man next to him was his father.

Her face registered surprise, and she turned back to Brett. "Hey, that's—" She trailed off. Brett was already gone.

Sadie circled the ballroom three times looking for her, and by the time she gave up she had downed her second glass of champagne. She glanced around for a sign for the bathrooms, then tapped the shoulder of a woman standing nearby in a long silver gown. The woman turned and looked her in the eye—she had shiny brown hair and perfectly rouged cheeks, and something in Sadie's mind tried to push its way through the champagne fog. Sadie was sure she had seen her before, but she wasn't sure where. Recognition flashed across the woman's face, and she turned away without saying a word.

"What, rich people never have to pee?" Sadie muttered to herself as she made her way through the crowd. Eventually a waiter pointed her toward a small alcove, and inside she found two large white doors primly labeled with brass plaques.

Once inside the stall, she sank gratefully onto the seat. Then she looked down.

"Oh, come on!" she said, unable to help herself. "At the White House—real freaking poetic," she muttered. She looked around the stall. The tiny satin clutch Olivia had lent her was useless; she could barely have fit a tampon in there even if she wanted to. She needed to find something—right away. She was not going to be the girl who got her period on Chanel.

She exited the stall and scanned the bathroom for the ubiquitous metal box. She found nothing on her initial sweep, and began a more thorough search, checking under the sinks and in each corner of the room. Finally, she gave up and threw her hands in the air. "If we had a female president, there would be some freaking tampons in this bathroom," she said aloud.

"Amen to that," said a voice behind her, followed by a loud chuckle.

Sadie's cheeks instantly started to burn. "Oh, um, sorry," she called. "I didn't realize anyone else was in here."

She heard a flush, and a woman emerged from the last stall. She was wearing a simple black dress, and a small diamond stud in each ear sparkled in contrast with her dark skin. "Don't apologize—that's the best laugh I've had all night." She approached the sink and flipped on the tap. "Plus, you're probably right. I bet they have cold beers and ESPN in the men's room." She grinned, then opened her clutch and pulled out a tampon. "Don't sweat it. We've all been there."

Sadie exhaled. "Oh god, thank you."

When she was finished, the woman was leaning toward the mirror, tracing her lips in deep red. Sadie glanced at her reflection as she washed her hands, and the woman smiled.

"That's a really beautiful dress," she said. She pressed her lips together. "How did someone as young as you manage to get ahold of Chanel's spring collection before some Hollywood starlet snatched it up?"

Sadie blushed and looked at the floor. "A friend lent it to me."

The woman raised her eyebrows, and Sadie felt embarrassment washing over her.

"I'm really not that into fashion. Wearing this kinda makes me feel like I'm in a costume or something."

A corner of the woman's mouth turned up in a half smile. She lowered her voice conspiratorially. "Don't tell anyone, but this is the eleventh White House function I've worn this dress to." She hooted with laughter. "A plain black dress no one remembers is a poor White House reporter's best friend." She stuck out a hand. "Charlie Ronson. I cover the Hill for the *National*."

Sadie shook her hand. "Oh, wow. I know who you are. My dad quotes from your columns all the time." She adjusted the bodice of her dress nervously. "Sadie Marlowe. I, uh, crash White House parties in borrowed clothes because I happen to know someone with connections."

Charlie raised her eyebrows. "Must be some connections. Let me guess, Keating Hall?"

"How'd you know?"

The woman laughed. "Wild guess. So how'd you end up there? Don't take this the wrong way, but I've been covering D.C. royalty for a long time, and something about you just doesn't seem like the type."

Sadie smiled. "Lacrosse scholarship. I just transferred this fall. Are you an alum?"

The woman threw her head back and laughed. "Please. I went to public school in Chicago. I may report on the upper crust, but I've always been an outsider looking in. I'm an explorer—navigating unfamiliar territory and always taking copious notes."

Sadie snorted. "Sometimes I feel like I'm part of some weird experiment, like Jane whatshername and the chimps. I like to think I'm the scientist and they're the monkeys, but honestly, I'm not even sure anymore."

Charlie eyed her curiously. "You know, I know exactly what you mean."

"Is it fun, though? Your job? I've always thought it would be pretty cool to be a reporter."

Charlie looked thoughtful. "I don't know if I'd describe it as fun, but it's rewarding." She reached into her purse and pulled out a small piece of paper. "Here. Take my card. If you ever want to check out the newspaper industry for yourself, give me a call. I can take you around the office, show you how we get things done."

Sadie took the card. "Wow, thanks. My dad's going to die when I tell him."

"It was nice to meet you, Sadie Marlowe." She waved a hand and started for the door.

"Hey, Charlie?" Sadie called. "This is kind of embarrassing to admit, but I always thought you were a guy, you know? I mean . . . a man."

Charlie's eyes sparkled. "Can't say that's an accident. One thing I wish someone would have told me when I was your age is a male name on a resume will get you far, especially in this town. They can't keep you out of the boys' club if they don't know you're not a card-carrying member." She grinned. "Now go have fun. I may be on the clock, but you and that dress should be on the dance floor."

She swept away toward the door, leaving Sadie slightly stunned and still holding her card.

⁂

On the way back she stopped at the bar and ordered a Coke. Champagne was so deceptive—it went down like Sprite, and then ten minutes later everything around her would be spinning and her hands would look weird. She wasn't sure she liked the feeling.

"Aren't you a little young to be at the bar?" The voice was smooth and rich. She forced a smile.

"Hi, Mr. Cranston," she mumbled. "It's just a Coke, I would never—"

He laughed. "Relax. I'm not here as a chaperone. And you should call me Teddy." He took another step toward her and leaned an elbow on the bar. A wave of his cologne surrounded her, making her feel a little dizzy.

She exhaled and forced her shoulders to un-hunch.

"So, are you having fun? I trust my son is behaving himself?"

"I am, thank you. And yeah, Finn's great," she lied. So far he had spent most of the night trying to grope one of the first daughters on the dance floor while Thayer glared at him from across the room. "I heard you got us our tickets tonight. That was really generous of you."

He waved a hand. "You deserve it, and it's never too early to start meeting the right people. Have you been mingling?"

"A little," she lied again. "I just met Charlie Ronson, she's really cool."

He nodded politely. "If there's anyone in particular you would like to shake hands with, just give the word and I'd be happy to make the introduction. If you're looking for a summer internship or the chance to be a congressional page, we can definitely make that happen."

"Thank you, I'm sure I'll take you up on that."

He held her gaze. "And of course, if there's ever anything else I can do for you, feel free to ask."

Before she could respond, the bartender returned and looked questioningly at Teddy.

"Bourbon, splash of water, two cubes." The words rolled off Teddy's tongue like warm milk.

Sadie picked up her drink and turned to leave. "Have a good night, Mr. Cranston. Thanks again for inviting us."

"You know, Sadie, I didn't see it before, but you really remind me of your mother tonight. Especially in that dress—she always liked wearing blue."

The words fell like bricks on her chest. She set her glass back down on the bar with a loud thump. "You knew my mom?"

He looked surprised. "Of course. I assumed you knew that."

She shook her head.

"We were in school together. Well, she was at Keating while I was at Graff. Class of '89."

Sadie looked up again, and she was surprised to see that his face had stiffened. There was a tightness about his jaw, and his eyes mechanically followed the bartender's movements. For the first time, she realized how blue they were, like the ocean.

"It was a real shame what happened to her," he said, his voice flat. "She was a beautiful young woman who could have had a bright future ahead of her."

Sadie swallowed hard. "Did you know her well?"

His face was still. "I did."

He smiled widely then, and it was so sudden it was like his expression had cracked into a million pieces. "We dated, actually."

Her mouth dropped open. She searched her brain for an appropriate response, but found nothing.

He touched her arm. "That was a long time ago, though. Enjoy your evening, Sadie." And then he was gone. She stood, motionless, at the bar until the bartender plunked down Teddy's bourbon and looked at her with eyebrows raised.

"He left," she said.

The bartender shrugged and turned away. She grabbed the bourbon, leaving her untouched Coke on the bar in a puddle of its own sweat.

∽

It was raining again by the time they rolled quietly through the gates of DeGraffenreid's main entrance. After a few terse words from Finn, the driver flipped off his lights and drove stealthily through campus toward the tower.

Inside the salon, Brent and Connor flipped on the enormous gas fireplace and the room slowly started to heat up. They lounged on couches and on the thick carpet, drinking and smoking.

Sadie was lying on a leather couch with Jeremy beside her, his fingers tracing a long, slow path down her bare arm. She could feel the heat from the fire licking at her skin, and she felt heavy, happy, and warm.

"Hey, you're empty," Jeremy said, gesturing to her glass.

She looked at it lazily and laughed, tipping it upside down. "Don't we have butlers or something for this? Butler!" She tried to snap, but her fingers felt like rubber.

He grinned and sat up. "You know, I think they're starting to get to you."

She jabbed him softly in the ribs and feigned shock. "Yeah, says the guy who spent all night following Finn around and shaking hands with senators."

He stood up and held out his hands, palms up. "Guilty. I figure if I'm at the White House I might as well make a few friends, right?" He took her glass. "Be right back."

Sadie propped herself up on an elbow and watched him walk away. He had ditched his tie and jacket and rolled up the sleeves of his crisp white shirt. She grinned widely, then caught herself and quickly bit her lip.

She struggled to her feet, and for the second time that night, she realized she had no idea how to get to the bathroom. The room spun around her, and she reached out a hand to steady herself on the couch's armrest.

The hallway was cold and damp, and she shivered as a slow breeze blew past her. She made her way along slowly, running one hand along the inner wall to keep her steady. The first three doors she found were locked and rusted shut, and behind the fourth was the white dressing room. She found herself back at the salon door and turned this time toward the narrow winding stairs. The only time she had ever been off this floor was the night she was initiated, and her skin tingled with residual energy as she climbed upward.

On the next floor the hallway stretched dark and shadowed in two directions. She chose left and walked on, tiptoeing from one circle of light to the next. She knew she didn't really need to be quiet, but something about the chilly darkness just made her feel like the stillness shouldn't be disturbed.

After a few yards she breathed a sigh of relief. She could hear a low murmur of voices, and she knew she must be close. Light glowed softly under the next door, and she pushed it open.

As her eyes swept the room, she froze. At first, she just saw skin and limbs and leather, but when her mind made sense of the images she wished she could break it up again and put it back in pieces.

It was a small room, lit by dim lanterns, and in the center was a low wooden table. On the table was a round mirror covered with a dusting of white powder, and there was a black leather couch along one wall. Olivia lay sprawled across it, one leg splayed open with her foot hanging slack in the air. Her eyes were closed and her head hung limply to one side, damp hair hanging across her face. Her dress was bunched up around her thighs.

"Get the hell out of here," someone yelled, and everything snapped back to focus. Finn was hunched over the table and Brent and Josh sat on the floor nearby. They were all staring at her, and they all looked angry.

"Oh god, sorry," she mumbled, stumbling backward out of the room. She ran down the hallway and ducked into the first door she saw, slamming it behind her and leaning her back against the cool surface. She breathed hot, fast gasps into the darkened room and tried to push the image out of her mind. When she started feeling dizzy, she slid down the wall and put her head on her knees.

After a few minutes she struggled to her feet and blinked at the darkness. She could tell she was in a large room, but she couldn't make out anything else. She felt along the wall until she found a light switch and flipped it on.

She knew immediately where she was, and she looked around, suddenly intrigued. The altar was on a raised platform in the center of the room, and tonight it was covered in heavy black cloth. On top of it sat a huge leather-bound book, open on a polished marble stand.

As she got closer, she realized the pages were covered with columns of small, inky script—lists of names, each with a corresponding year. She stood over the book and traced her finger down the last column. Her body tensed as she saw her own, Sadie May Marlowe, right below Jeremy's at the bottom of the page. She was the last one.

Instinctively she looked around her, but the room was empty. She turned back page after page and watched as the classes of the last ten, then twenty years flew by. When she got to the members from 1987, she skimmed down the page.

There it was. And wasn't.

The name listed read Maylynne Hester Ralleigh. She realized she had been holding her breath, and she let it out in a long, slow whistle. She stared at the page for a long time.

Thayer had been right—Sadie was the one who didn't know her own mother's real name. She blinked back the tears that sprang up behind her eyelids. What the hell was going on?

She forced herself to look away and turned the pages back. She felt her mom pulling farther and farther away from her as the pages turned, and she felt the pain of her loss all over again. When she got to the most recent page, she turned it carefully to make sure she didn't rip the heavy paper. Her eyes were blurred with tears, but as she laid it flat, a name just four lines above hers swam into focus. She leaned closer to make sure, but it was there, in ink just as permanent as her own.

Anna Francis Ralleigh.

She frowned. Sadie blinked again as something tugged at the back of her mind. If this was the same Anna—the girl who had disappeared last year—then two former members of the Optimates were dead. She turned the pages back again, just to be sure, holding her breath until she saw the proof. But it was right there, in black and white: Ralleigh.

Two members were dead, and they were related.

Sadie stepped back from the book. Suddenly she didn't want to touch it.

She was still standing in front of it, staring like it might suddenly burst into flame, when she heard the door open.

"Fuck, Sadie," said a raspy voice. "I've been looking all over for you."

It was Josh. His hair was rumpled and his eyes were wide and rimmed with red. He was fidgeting, and his whole body seemed to buzz with nervous energy.

Before she could speak he held up his hands. "Don't say anything. I know how that looked." He came toward her at a jog, and instinctively she stepped back. Her hip smacked into the table with a loud thud, and she winced in pain.

"I didn't even really see anything, Josh," she said. "The light, you know, my eyes hadn't adjusted."

He bounded up the steps until he was standing just inches away. "You're lying." He looked her square in the eye. "We didn't do anything she didn't want to do. You know what she's like—she'll give it to whoever wants it."

Sadie stared back. "She didn't look like she was giving anything."

He laughed without warmth. "Please. You don't get that hammered without knowing what it means."

Anger welled up in Sadie's stomach, and her throat suddenly felt tight. "So that gives you the right to—"

Fire flashed in his eyes, and suddenly she was scared to say it. She looked away. "You know what, it's none of my business." Even saying the words made her so angry she wanted to scream.

"You're Brett's friend." He paused and ran a hand anxiously through his disheveled hair. "It was stupid, I know. But she won't find out, and you're not going to tell her. I'll make it up to her, I promise."

He grabbed Sadie's wrist and squeezed, hard. "You won't tell her, right?" His hand was cold and slick with sweat. The scene flashed back through her mind, and her stomach rolled. She couldn't talk about this anymore.

"I won't."

He let her go, but he didn't step back. He was still staring at her, red faced and glassy-eyed, his sour breath in her nostrils. Her eyes slid down and fell on the book.

"So, this has all the members in it, right?"

Josh looked over his shoulder and seemed to relax. "Oh, yeah. Cool, right? That book's like a hundred years old or some shit." He flipped to the beginning. "You have to see this." The first few pages were filled with text, and he pointed out the group's mission statement and the script they read at the induction ceremony. "You know, all that stuff they say about brotherhood and Zeus and whatever," he said. She nodded. He turned one more page and pointed. "There— look at the first member."

She squinted at the book, then scoffed loudly.

Josh looked at her incredulously. "What's so funny?"

"That's some kind of joke, right? I mean, come on."

He shook his head. "No way. He was the original founder. It's changed a lot since then obviously—Keating and Graff didn't even exist yet—but he started it."

She still didn't believe it. "Thomas Jefferson? As in, *the* Thomas Jefferson? The Declaration of Independence and Monticello—that guy?"

He grinned. "Yeah, Sadie. Look."

She looked at the page again and saw the name scrawled in large, familiar letters. She shook her head. "How?

"Well, it's a long story. It's all in the book, though." He tapped the yellowed pages with one finger.

"Give me the shortened version."

He scratched his head and took a deep breath. "Okay, um, so you know about frats and sororities, right?"

She nodded.

"They're kind of like secret societies—they have handshakes and clubhouses and secret initiation ceremonies—but they're like, the most watered-down, pseudo-secretive, uber-powerless piece-of-crap versions of what they could be. They don't have power for shit. They're just a bunch of middle-class douchebags in Abercrombie ties blowing each other while wearing black robes and calling it tradition."

She raised her eyebrows.

"But when fraternities started, they actually meant something. TJ was in the first frat in the country—this club at William and Mary called the Flat Hat Club. Sounds lame, I know, no idea why they didn't call it something more badass. Anyway, it was modeled after European secret societies—you know, the Freemasons, and the Knights Templar, all that conspiracy shit—but they didn't really do anything. It was just an underground group of elite dudes, and they did, like, charity work and hung around talking about history and whatever."

He was talking so fast, Sadie could barely understand him, but at least his eyes were on the book. She took a tentative step farther away from him, and he kept talking.

"So when he graduated, he complained about how it was cool and all, but they didn't actually have any real purpose, so he decided to found one at his high school that actually meant something. Then a couple of his sisters got married or died or whatever, and he got like, really fucking lonely. And depressed. So he got really into it. He liked going there for debates and intense discussions—he was into all that shit, you know?—and they really only kept it secret because they thought it was fun. Eventually, that school closed and the members moved it to their new school, Montgomery Academy, and it continued from there. It was there for a long time, until the fucking Yankees took over the school buildings to use them for barracks during the Civil War.

"After that was over, Graff was built on the same land as Montgomery and all the richest families started sending their kids there, so it was natural for the club to be revived with Graff as its new home base. This building is the only part of the old army fort left, so the Sullas took that shit back and claimed it for their own. This is where it gets really good, though."

He turned and looked at her just as she edged away another few inches. He frowned.

"Where are you going? This is the coolest part." He pulled her back toward him, gripping her arm so tightly it hurt.

"Tensions were so high after the war, and everyone in the South wanted to make sure the major southern families stuck together. But no one could get caught doing anything that went against the Union, so they had to be really careful. That's when shit got real. It got really exclusive, and really powerful, and that just continued, for decades and decades. And here we are. Oh, and all that Greek shit from the initiation? TJ had a huge boner for the Greeks. You've been to UVA, right? He probably went from six to midnight every time he walked through that quad. Anyway, like fifty years ago the new leaders realized just how powerful they had become, so they started a new plan."

He leaned toward her and lowered his voice. "The real plan."

His hand was still on her wrist, and she could feel her fingers starting to go numb. "What plan is that?"

He leaned even closer, and Sadie could see that his eyes were wide and out of focus. "Taking over the world."

He laughed then, loud and sudden, and dropped her hand so he could turn the book back to the most recent page. She opened her mouth to speak, but he cut her off.

"Look, it's all in here. Read it if you don't believe me. This isn't just the member directory, it's a log. Jefferson wrote the first part and the other members added to it as they went along." He skipped forward a few pages and pointed to an inky block of text.

"See, that's when they moved to Montgomery." A dozen or so pages later there was another paragraph. "And that's when they moved to Graff. This is real shit, Sadie."

He was really excited now, and suddenly he was jogging back down the steps and across the room. He stopped in front of a four-foot-long wooden musket that was mounted on the wall over a plaque. It had a menacing-looking bayonet that jutted from the tip of its barrel, and she could see light glinting off the polished steel.

"This," Josh said, out of breath now, "is a Confederate freaking musket from the Civil War. After the war the members of the Order swore they would shoot any weak-ass Yankee who corrupted this sanctuary again." He looked at her and grinned. He made the shape of a gun with his right hand and pointed it at her chest. "It's loaded."

She stepped back.

"What the hell, Josh? Why would they keep that in here? I mean, they wouldn't shoot anyone now . . . "

He sighed. "'Cause it's a Civil War musket, Sadie," he said, emphasizing every syllable. "It's badass. And honestly, no one can get in here. This shit is airtight. But if they did, they would be in for some serious pain."

Josh was still staring at the gun, but his grin had faded. He was vibrating with energy, and Sadie knew she had to get out of there. Fast.

She shivered. "You know, Josh, it's pretty cold up here. I'm going to go downstairs." Without waiting for a response, she turned and ran for the door. As she opened it she sneaked a look back at him, but he was still staring, enthralled, at the mounted gun.

When she got to the salon, she still couldn't get the images out of her mind: Olivia's limp leg, Josh's glassy eyes, the book. She walked immediately to where Jeremy was standing and collapsed into him.

"Whoa, whoa," he said, laughing. "Where have you been? Thought you got lost or something."

She pressed her cheek against his chest. "Or something. Let's just sit for a second, okay? I'm really tired."

He looked down at her in surprise. "You okay? You're freezing." He sat back on the couch and she folded herself in next to him.

"I'm okay, I promise."

But she wasn't. Her mind shuffled through the images until it settled on one, replaying it over and over again like a broken record stuck on a single, discordant note.

Anna Ralleigh.

Maybe the curse was real. She shivered involuntarily and felt Jeremy's arms tighten around her. It was something else, though, something much darker than anyone knew. Sadie suddenly had the awful feeling it had nothing to do with finals or college applications, and everything to do with Sadie's family—which one, she wasn't sure. Either the Ralleighs, the family she never knew she had, or the Sullas, the new family she had sworn her loyalty to for life.

"Sadie, you're scaring me. You look really freaked out."

She shook her head. "It's okay, I think I just need to relax for a minute." She tried to laugh. "Probably just had too much champagne." It was true—or at least, it had been an hour ago. Now she felt completely sober, like she was seeing things clearly for the first time.

"Let me get you a soda. It'll help settle your stomach and stuff."

She nodded and settled back against the cushions. She watched him make his way across the room toward the bar, stepping over the empty bottles and pillows that littered the carpet. She tried to shut her eyes for a minute, blocking it all out so she could think, but the darkness just made her panic. Everything was all wrong, and she didn't even know where to start.

She looked over at the bar again, and her heart stopped. Jeremy wasn't alone—Finn and Josh were with him, and they looked angry. Finn was gesturing wildly, and Josh was bouncing anxiously on the balls of his feet. All three of them glanced toward her, and she quickly closed her eyes, pretending to be asleep. This was bad.

"Drink this, okay? It'll help."

When she opened them, Jeremy was settling in next to her.

"What was that about? I saw you guys arguing."

Jeremy rolled his eyes. "They're just coked out. Josh was rambling about something, and Finn was being his usual belligerent self. Don't even worry about them."

He held out a glass, and she took it. Jeremy put his arm around her shoulders and squeezed, and she forced herself to take a deep breath. Everything was going to be okay. She was sure there was some explanation for all of this, but she would find it tomorrow. Now, she just needed to get out of here, and get some sleep. She tipped the glass back and took a small sip.

"Is it okay if we leave soon?"

"Definitely. How about you finish that, and then I'll walk you back?"

Sadie nodded, and his arm squeezed tighter. More than anything, she just wanted this night to be over. As she tipped the glass back again, she saw Finn and Josh, still standing at the bar. They were staring in her direction, and they were both smiling.

Chapter 21

It was after noon by the time she woke up, but she felt like she hadn't even slept. Her head was pounding so hard she gasped. She squinted up at the ceiling, and the two names swam immediately in front of her eyes. She shut them tight, but the image remained.

Something was wrong. Her stomach rolled, and her limbs were heavy and sweaty under the tangled sheets. She knew she had had too much to drink the night before, but this hangover felt different. Her whole body felt achy and bloated, and her stomach was cramping so painfully she had to curl into a ball until the muscles relaxed.

When the pain finally faded, she struggled to her feet and limped down the hallway to the bathroom.

She didn't even remember leaving the tower—the last thing she could picture was sitting on the couch with Jeremy with so many awful new thoughts running through her head.

When she saw herself in the mirror, she flinched. Her hair was tangled up in the remnants of last night's elaborate twist, and the makeup had melted off of her face like candle wax. She had thick slashes of black under each eye, and her dark, stained lips looked grotesque against her puffy, pale skin.

She took a long, hot shower, then padded back to her room.

Her phone was buzzing on her desk, and Trix and Gwen both had their pillows folded over their heads. "Make it stop," one of them moaned.

"Sorry, guys," Sadie mumbled, picking it up and silencing it. She had three unread texts—all from Jeremy.

"Where'd u go?" the first one said, followed by two more asking if she was okay, and if she had made it home. They were all from after 1 A.M. Her stomach hardened into a knot. She felt terrible.

She typed out a quick response:

"Sorry . . . did I leave without saying bye? Can't really remember."

She lay back on her bed, covering her face with a pillow and willing the pounding in her head to go away. She felt the mattress give as one of the twins bounced onto the bed next to her, and a fresh wave of nausea coursed through her.

"Spill it, Yankee."

Sadie lowered the pillow to see Trix sitting on her bed, puffy-eyed and sleep-haired. "Spill what?"

Trix rolled her eyes. "You were out even later than we were last night. Come on, don't hold out on me." She pouted. "Where were you, and why didn't you invite us roomies?"

Sadie raised her eyebrows. "I got home at, like, one. You guys have an early night or something?"

Trix giggled and shook her head. "No way. You must have had even more fun than I thought. We got back at three and you still weren't here."

Sadie frowned. Jeremy's texts were from hours before then. Where had she been?

Her phone buzzed and she reached for it. "You completely disappeared. Went to find Thayer and then never came back. Everything okay? I was worried."

She glanced back at Trix. "Sorry, guess I lost track of time. I was just at Graff."

"I knew you were more fun than you looked!" Trix grinned and bounced up and down on her bed. "Hey Gwen, did you hear that? I told you she was fun."

Gwen just groaned and rolled over.

"Uh, thanks," Sadie said. "Are you sure I wasn't here until after three?"

Trix nodded. "It was more like five. I know because you were so wasted you tripped over that pile of clothes over there and woke me up. You are one sloppy drunk."

Sadie paused. She remembered everything before going back to the salon—if anything, she had been too sober to handle everything that had happened. But after she talked to Jeremy, everything just stopped. Four hours were just black.

Trix pointed gleefully to Sadie's arm. "Look, you even have a bruise. Battle wound!"

Sadie turned over her forearm. There was a dull purple smudge that circled her arm like a bracelet. But it wasn't from tripping and hitting something. Sadie forced a smile, but inside she was screaming. What the hell happened last night?

"Guess you're right—sorry I woke you guys up."

Trix stood up and stretched. "No worries. Just invite me next time." She strolled back to her bed and collapsed onto it, sending a few items of clothing cascading onto the floor. "And tell your sexy boyfriend I said hi." She pulled on an eye mask. "He's a good one. He walked you back to your room and everything."

"No way, he said—"

Trix rolled to face the wall. "Don't bother denying it—I heard a guy's voice before you came in. No way you would have made it back on your own like that, anyway."

A guy's voice. Outside her room, at 5 a.m., four hours after she left Jeremy in the tower. The seasick feeling in her stomach intensified, and she couldn't shake the dread that was surging over her. What had she done? Her phone buzzed again, and her hand shook as she picked it up. She took a deep breath and opened the message.

"Plus, I'm supposed to walk you home after we get wasted in our secret society's clubhouse after partying at the White House. It's a pretty key part of every high school boyfriend's duties."

Boyfriend. If Sadie hadn't felt so terrible, she probably would have been jumping up and down. Instead she was just numb.

"Are you sure I left that early? I can't believe I can't remember. It's a little scary."

After she clicked send, she scrolled back through her texts from last night, praying there would be some clue about what she was doing.

She rolled through with a sense of foreboding—she wanted to know, but at the same time, she had a feeling she didn't. She remembered the image of Olivia passed out on the couch, so limp and defenseless. What if she had cheated on Jeremy? Or worse?

Before Jeremy's first text was another from a number she didn't know. The time stamp said 12:55 A.M.

"Portland—meet me in the hall. Have to tell you something."

She frowned. It had to be from Thayer. But why? Last Sadie remembered seeing her, Thayer was sprawled on a couch with Lillian listening to Fever Stephens on repeat. Plus, she had never even texted Sadie before. Why now?

Sadie glanced at the text again as she snapped the phone shut, and the sight jarred something loose in her memory. The image came over her suddenly, and she sank back down on the bed under the weight of it. It was a hallway, bright and artificially lit, with double doors at one end. The left door had a tiny black rectangle in the center, and she was rushing toward it, faster and faster, until the doors swung open and swallowed her up. Then, just as suddenly, the memory was over.

Sadie blinked, feeling uneasy, like waking from a dream. She couldn't remember anything else, but the image left her with a feeling that was unmistakable. Fear. She took a deep breath and clasped her hands together to keep them from shaking.

She stood up, pressing a finger to her temples as they pounded even harder. She needed answers, and apparently Thayer was the only person who could give them to her.

She dressed and went downstairs, twisting her wet hair up into a messy bun as she tried to keep the room from spinning all around her. Every step was agony, and she couldn't believe how much her body hurt.

In the dining room, Sadie filled a cup with coffee, dumping in cream and sugar until it was almost white. She glanced toward the stack of fresh bagels, but even the sight of them made her nauseous. As she waited for the feeling to pass, she heard a voice behind her.

"Good morning to you, too." She turned around and saw Jess, sitting alone at a table. There was a plate of pancakes in front of her, but it looked untouched.

"Oh, hey." Sadie brushed a wet strand of hair out of her eyes with the back of one hand. "Sorry Jess, I didn't see you."

"In a hurry?"

"Actually, yeah." Sadie shifted her weight awkwardly and waved her bagel toward the door. "I have to talk to Thayer about something."

"Right. You look like shit, you know that? Where were you last night? We were supposed to go to a movie, remember?"

Sadie closed her eyes. The movie. She had spent the night at a party with Finn and Thayer and completely forgotten about her best friend. She hadn't even thought to send her a text. What was happening to her?

"God, Jess, I am so sorry. I forgot all about the movie . . . I, um, I felt sick. I just stayed in my room." Her head was still pounding, but lying to Jess felt even worse.

She arched an eyebrow. "You seemed fine when I saw you. And I came by your room. You were gone."

Sadie sighed. "I guess I was in the infirmary then. I don't know what time I went—I can't remember."

Jessica's face went slack with disappointment.

"Look, I'm sorry I can't eat with you, but I promise I'll see you later, okay?"

Jessica sawed off a chunk of pancake with the edge of her fork. "Whatever, Sadie."

Sadie watched her jam it into her mouth and chew, and a part of her wanted to sit down and explain everything. But she couldn't deal with that right now. She had so many questions from last night, and Thayer could only answer one of them. She turned and left the dining room, leaving Jessica staring sullenly at the wall.

She pulled out her phone and texted the unknown number. "Can you meet me in the lobby? It's Sadie—need to ask you something."

While she waited for a response, she walked down the hall to the computer lab. She logged in, then stopped for a moment, staring at the browser's blank search field. She had tried to find out more information about her mom so many times, but every search had come up empty. It was like her mother hadn't even existed before she married her dad, and now she knew why. She had been searching the wrong name.

She put her fingers on the keyboard and typed: Maylynne Ralleigh.

She hit enter and closed her eyes. When she opened them, the screen was filled with headlines from the late '80s. Her eyes skimmed over the words, each one hitting her like a punch to the gut. "Heiress attempts suicide" . . . "rumors of depression and substance abuse." A little further down the page, they started to change. "Estranged heiress disappears" . . . "Diamond scion deemed runaway" . . . "Police called off search." Apparently Sadie wasn't the only one who didn't know the whole story about her mother's life. At some point after she left Keating, the Maylynne Ralleigh everyone else knew simply ceased to exist.

She sat back in her chair and rubbed her eyes. Everything was changing so much. Her mother wasn't who she thought she was, and if that was true, what did she really know about anyone else? Thayer, Finn, Josh, or Brett? Even Jeremy.

A horrible thought had been playing at the edges of her mind since she woke up, threatening to break through. Again, she pushed it away.

Instead, she leaned forward and typed in a new name. This one came back with even more results.

There were headlines from all the local papers, first about Anna's disappearance, then some speculating about what had happened to her, everything from a kidnapping to running away. She clicked on one of the pieces and waited as it filled the screen.

She skimmed through it until she got to the last paragraph, when her breath caught in her throat.

Ralleigh's disappearance is not the first for her family. In an eery coincidence, distant relative Maylynne Ralleigh disappeared shortly after dropping out of Keating

Hall in 1988. At the time of her disappearance, May-
lynne Ralleigh was heir to a substantial portion of the
family's inheritance. She was eventually deemed a run-
away, and her current whereabouts remain unknown.

Sadie took a deep breath. If no one had any idea who her mother
had been, how did Thayer know? How did they even find her? On a
whim, she typed in another name.

She watched as the screen filled with headlines of a different sort:
society page captions, political puff pieces, and charity function
announcements, each accompanied by a photo of him, always smiling.
There was one of him shaking President Manning's hand, and another
of him posing with his father at some sort of White House event. In
both photos, he was in a crisp navy suit, always with the ubiquitous
flag pin politicians wore because they thought it proved something.

In the third photo he had his arm around a petite woman with
blonde hair cut in a sharp bob. She read the caption: "White House
Chief of Staff Theodore Cranston and wife, Pamela Cranston." She
scrolled through page after page of photos until she felt a tap on her
shoulder. She turned to see Thayer standing above her, a smirk on
her face.

"Doing a little light research?"

"Oh, yeah, just, um, surfing around." She groaned inwardly as she
minimized the window. "Er, you know what I mean."

"Sure, whatever." Thayer sat down next to her and leaned in conspiratorially. "How'd last night go? You guys bang or what?"

"Uh, no . . . wait, why would you ask that? Did someone say we
did?"

Thayer's face fell. "Boring. And no. No offense, but you banging
or not banging anyone isn't exactly scintillating gossip." She turned
away from Sadie and booted up one of the other computers. "Plus, it's
already obvious you guys are going to pick each other, so who cares?
It's only fun when people have to fight for it."

"What do you mean, pick each other?"

Thayer grinned. "You'll find out."

"Um, okay. Well speaking of, uh, gossip . . . Why'd you text me last night? About having something to tell me?"

Thayer raised her eyebrows without looking away from the screen. "Why would I text you?" She waved a hand. "Again, no offense obviously."

"I don't know, but you did." She held up her phone so Thayer could see the screen.

"Nice try, Portland. That's not even close to my number. Now leave me alone. I have shit to do."

Sadie's breath caught in her throat, and her head was pounding so hard she could feel a sweat breaking out on her temples. "But I just texted you back. How'd you know to meet me down here?"

"Didn't. Drunk Olivia spilled Red Bull on my laptop last night. Now do you mind? I have a paper due."

"Oh." Sadie's eyes slipped out of focus as she tried to make sense of what she was hearing. Someone else had texted her pretending to be Thayer—but why? She opened the window back up to close it, but something caught her eye. It was one of the society pages that had come up in her search—a story on some event from earlier that November. She scrolled through the photos of people in suits and fancy gowns. The last image on the page was small, but in it was a woman with brown hair and rosy cheeks. She was holding a little girl's hand—the girl was only nine or ten, but she was perfectly polished in a blue dress that matched her eyes.

They both looked familiar, and Sadie clicked the photo to enlarge it. As the image filled the screen, something in Sadie's mind finally cleared.

It was her—the woman she had recognized last night—and she finally knew where she had seen her before. It was the woman from the hospital who was supposedly a drug addict, one so far below rock bottom she had had to turn to a charitable foundation for help putting her life back together. And here she was in a photo from a charity event two weeks ago, healthy and smiling in a Chanel suit, a glass of champagne clutched casually in one hand.

Sadie read the caption: "Evelyn Cranston, and niece, Cassandra Cranston." Cranston.

Sadie stood up and backed away from the screen. None of it was real. The little girl's story, so much like Sadie's mom's, but with such a different ending. It was all a setup to convince her to believe in the Optimates and all the good they were supposedly doing.

Sadie pressed her fingers into her temples and willed her stomach to stop rolling and folding in on itself. She knew this all had to be connected—the Sullas, the hospital, the only memory Sadie had from last night. Where had she been for four hours? And if Thayer hadn't texted her, who had?

"Hey, psycho. Can you take your hangover somewhere else? You're making it kinda hard to focus."

"Sorry," Sadie mumbled. She opened her eyes to see Thayer shaking her head.

"You know, you look like you're going to hurl. You really need to figure out how to handle your booze."

Another wave of nausea broke over her, and she clapped a hand over her mouth. As she turned and lurched toward the door, knocking her chair over in the process, she heard Thayer call: "Don't forget to hold back your hair, hon'."

She made it into the bathroom just in time. She hunched over the toilet and heaved, over and over until her stomach was still. She sank down onto the floor and leaned her head back against the wall, closing her eyes. In that moment of darkness, she finally let the thought that had been nagging her since that morning take shape. There was no way she had been as drunk as Trix said she was, and she remembered every second of her conversation with Josh just minutes before everything went blank. She thought about Olivia, how lifeless she had looked on the couch, and a cold fear spread over her. She put her head in her hands. Stuff like this didn't happen in real life—it was only on dramatic teen soap operas and cheesy after-school specials about the horrors of binge drinking. But there was no other explanation. She had been drugged.

And that wasn't even the worst part.

Her mind kept sticking on the last thing she remembered before the white hallway: Jeremy, standing with Finn and Josh and arguing about something—just minutes after she had seen them doing whatever they did behind closed doors. Then minutes later, handing her a Coke in a bright red cup. "Drink this," he had said. "It'll help you feel better."

She drew in breath after deep breath, listening to the sound of the water rushing through the pipes behind her. She had underestimated them all—Finn and Josh, for how far they would go to keep her quiet, and Jeremy, for what he would be willing to do for his new brothers. He wasn't who she thought he was, and for all she knew, this had been part of the plan all along. Maybe this was what the Sullas did, and by the time the girls realized what had happened to them, they were in too deep with their new "family" to tell anyone.

She wanted to cry, but she was so spent she didn't have any tears left. She sat there, heaving with dry sobs until she finally stopped sweating, and her hands steadied. She dialed Jeremy's number and waited while it rang. When it went to voice mail, she hung up. Instead, she typed out a text.

"I know what you did." Her hands shook again as she pressed send, but she was angry now, and with it came a new sense of calm. She stood up, slowly, and washed her face and hands in the sink.

As she glanced at her face in the mirror, she saw the blurred memory once again. The white hallway, clean and tiled and fluorescent. The white double doors with the small, black rectangle, and Sadie rushing toward them until they swallowed her whole. Just like with the woman in the photo, Sadie just knew. She had been there last night. Dawning House.

She didn't know how the hospital fit into this, but she had to find out. Before she could even dry her hands, she was running toward the dining room and reaching for her phone.

"Thank you for calling Regency livery, can I have your last name, please?"

"Marlowe. First name Sadie."

"Thank you, Ms. Marlowe. What time will you need to be picked up?"

"Now, please."

"I'll have a car out to Keating as soon as possible."

"Just hurry."

She clicked the phone shut and dropped it in her purse just as she pushed through the dining hall doors.

"Jess!" she shouted, drawing a stern look from Mrs. Darrow, who was sitting at a table near the door reading a newspaper.

Jessica stood and threw her backpack over her shoulder. "I have a paper to write."

"Jess, wait. I'm sorry. I know I acted like an ass before, but . . . I'm in trouble. I really need your help." Her voice shook, and Jessica's face instantly changed. "Please?" It came out barely more than a whisper.

Jessica came toward her at a run. "What's wrong?"

Sadie grabbed her arm and started pulling her toward the door. "I'll explain everything on the way, okay? We'll have plenty of time."

"Where are we going?"

"D.C."

෨

As soon as they were safely outside the Keating gates, Sadie told her everything. About the first time she was kidnapped by the Sullas, the ceremony with the Fates, and the trip she had taken with Brett to the hospital in D.C. She told her about the woman and the charade the Sullas had put on to convince her to join. When she told her about the helicopter, the expensive clothes, and Thayer's speech about family, she could see the hurt straining Jessica's features as she realized she had been passed over. Still, she pushed ahead.

She told her about the bruise she had found on her arm after that first night, and the tiny injection mark that she couldn't explain. She went over the initiation ceremony after the dance, and Jessica's jaw dropped as she told her about Jeremy, the other members, and the nameless gallery of elder members that watched from above. She told her about the White House party, about seeing the Cranstons with the President, and the look of fear that she saw in Brett's eyes before she ran away. Finally, she told her about the text and the fact that she had disappeared for more than four hours last night, with no idea where she had been except for a terrible gut feeling.

When she finished, Jessica just stared at Sadie for a full minute, opening and closing her mouth like a fish. When she finally formed a question, it was a simple one.

"Why?"

"Why what?"

"Why are you telling me all of this? I mean, these people sound completely insane . . . won't you get in trouble for telling someone who doesn't belong?"

Sadie eyed the driver in the front seat and lowered her voice.

"Like I said, I needed your help. And also . . . I left something out."

Jessica shifted uneasily, like she wasn't sure she wanted to hear anything else.

"I think there's something else going on, something way bigger than charities and parties and making connections. I have this memory—not even a memory really, almost like a scene from a dream that I can't really grasp. I'm rushing down a hospital hallway toward a white door."

"A nightmare?"

Sadie shook her head. "It was more than that. I think they took me somewhere last night, and"—her voice broke—"I have to find out what they did to me."

Jessica gazed out the window for a moment, then suddenly her eyes cleared. She leaned toward Sadie.

"What do you need me to do?"

⁓

They split up at the door, Sadie tucking herself into the shadows on the porch and Jessica breezing through.

"Hi there, I'm hoping you can help me with something," Sadie heard Jessica say in her best future-president-of-the-Junior-League voice. "I was walking by the grounds just now, and I saw one of your patients drop this on the lawn."

Sadie peeked through the doorway as Jessica held up the diamond pendant she had been wearing just a few minutes earlier. "I was hoping to get it back to her."

The woman at the front desk tapped away on her keyboard while looking up at Jessica and smiling. "What did the patient look like?"

"Oh, I got a great look," Jessica said. "She was brunette, maybe mid-thirties, and she was wearing a white robe over a hospital gown."

The woman's smile faltered a bit and she stopped typing. "Well, all of our patients do wear the same gowns. Do you have a name?"

"No, sorry. But I did hear her say something about a daughter named Cassie. You must have names of family members in there, right?"

Sadie held her breath. If she was wrong about all of this, she would never hear the end of it.

The woman looked up at Jessica, her mouth a grim line. "I'm sorry, we don't have any patients matching that description." She held up one index finger. "Can you stay here for a moment please?" She started dialing her phone, her eyes never leaving Jessica.

Shit. Sadie hadn't even thought about what would happen if the staff members knew about what the Sullas had done during her visit. *Now, Jess,* she thought. *Do it now!*

Sadie heard a crash as a silver cup filled with pens teetered off the desk and clattered to the floor.

"Oh, I am so sorry! That was so clumsy of me," Jessica cried. "Here, let me help."

"Stay there, please. Miss," the woman snapped. "I've got it." She sighed loudly and ducked behind the desk to collect the silver ballpoint pens that were rolling in every direction on the floor. Silently, Sadie made her move.

Jessica turned and saluted, grinning, as Sadie ran past her, taking the stairs two at a time.

Just as Sadie reached the landing, the woman's head popped up. "Did someone just come in? I thought I heard footsteps."

"No ma'am," Jessica said, her eyes wide and innocent. She casually leaned a hand on the desk and sent a stack of files crashing to the floor. "Oh, gosh," she said, putting her hands over her face. Sadie heard the flutter of papers settling on the floor as she slipped through the doorway and onto the second floor.

She combed each of the four floors, walking hallway after hallway, but she still couldn't find the door. Everything felt wrong, too—the hallways too wide and the ceiling too high. She stopped at a window and rested her forehead on the glass. Maybe she had been wrong about everything? The thought made her feel crazy, like she belonged inside one of these rooms instead of out roaming the halls.

She decided to do one more sweep, and when she emerged on the ground floor, she walked slowly, trying to take in every detail. This floor was less polished than the rest, like a staging area for the rest of the hospital. She didn't see any patients, and most of the doors led to broom closets, or offices filled with old filing cabinets. The lights were dimmer down here, and it was colder, too. Sadie pulled her sleeves down over her hands and hugged her arms close to her body. She could feel goose bumps rising on her skin.

In the middle of the long hallway, there was a long white curtain that hung from the ceiling all the way down to the floor. She paused. It was odd—a curtain covering a wall—and on a hunch, she walked closer. As she watched, a slow breeze passed behind the curtain, ruffling the heavy fabric so that it rolled like waves.

Sadie took a deep breath and looked behind her, but the hallway was quiet. Quickly, she slipped behind the curtain and waited for her eyes to adjust.

She had expected to see a door, or maybe another long hallway, but instead she was on a small landing. A staircase descended down a few feet in front of her, growing darker and dimmer with each step. With a flash, she remembered her first visit to the hospital. The woman in the garden's voice echoed in her head. "Don't let them take you into the basement." She exhaled, willing her nerves to stop screaming, and climbed down.

There was another door at the bottom of the stairs, and she didn't even hesitate. The knob turned easily, and she stepped into a bright hallway, a smaller version of those on the upper floors. It was pristine, and the floor gleamed like glass. Against the far wall, at least fifty yards away, was a small white door, unmarked, except for a small black rectangle in the center.

Sadie swayed on her feet and leaned back against the wall for support. It was all real. She had been here last night.

Before she could calm down, she saw the door at the end of the hallway start to open. She ducked back into the stairwell and pulled the door shut just as a pair of men in white lab coats emerged into the hallway.

She watched through a crack in the door, listening for wisps of their conversation, but she couldn't make anything out. As they neared the door she was forced to retreat back up the stairs. She hovered in the darkness just inside the curtain and stood completely still as the door opened. If they looked up, it would all be over.

They paused. "I'll notify the boss—let him know the procedure was successful," one said.

The other gave him a mock salute and grinned. "Let him know that if he happens to keep sending us hot ones, that's just fine with us. Maybe a brunette next time, though."

They both laughed, and Sadie's stomach felt like it was filled with ice water. Barely breathing, she stumbled back through the curtain.

"Hey, what was that?" she heard the taller one say behind her.

She ran. She didn't care that patients were staring, or that one of the doctors tried to stop her as she passed. She just ran and ran until she was flying through the foyer, ignoring the woman at the front desk, and pushing her way out the front door.

When Jessica saw her face, she started running too, and they didn't stop until they got to the front gate and then two blocks down the street, where Sadie finally collapsed into a heap on the curb.

They sat there for what felt like an hour. She told Jessica what she had heard, and how she still had no idea what she was dealing with. Now, she wasn't sure she wanted to know.

When the sky started getting darker, they finally stood up. "I didn't want to mention it before, but our car left us," Jessica said.

"It's okay, we'll just call another one." Sadie flipped open her phone. She had six unread messages from Jeremy. She erased them all without reading a word.

Jessica looked uneasy. "I don't know—it'll take them a long time to get out here, and we're supposed to be back on campus in,"—she glanced at her watch—"two hours."

Sadie shook her head, picturing the twins as they stumbled into the room at four A.M. "Trust me, curfew is not an issue."

Jessica raised her eyebrows. "The faculty is in on this thing too?"

"I don't know. Either that or they just look the other way. I just know that last night I didn't get home until five, and no one said anything."

"Well, we still have to get back eventually. Want me to call Regency?"

Sadie shook her head. "I have a better idea."

಄

While they waited for the twins' driver to pick them up, Sadie flipped open her phone. She had learned so much about her mom in the last week, and now truth and lies had all blurred together. She wasn't sure she could believe any of what Thayer had told her anymore, or even what she had read online. She had to talk to someone she could trust.

"Hey, kiddo." Her dad sounded so happy, she felt terrible. "I'm so glad you called—I missed you last week."

She pounded her fist against her forehead in frustration. "I'm really sorry, Dad. I was just so busy with homework I didn't have time."

"Hey, that's okay. You've got to keep up with the kids whose private tutors do all their work for them, right?"

She laughed weakly, then winced. Even she could hear how half-assed it was.

"Hey Sadie May, what's wrong?"

"Oh, nothing really. I'm just tired."

"Ah. Big night last night? Did you go into town with Jessica and Brett?"

"Yeah, we saw a double feature," she lied. "Ate too much popcorn and then stayed up way too late."

She hesitated, trying to decide how to bring it up, but her brain was so fried she couldn't think.

"Dad, I know about Mom's family."

The phone was silent.

"Oh. Well . . . " He trailed off and sighed. "I knew eventually someone at Keating would mention that to you, but I was hoping it would be later rather than sooner."

She didn't respond, and eventually he continued.

"You have to understand, Sadie. This was your mother's choice. By the time you knew her, she didn't want to be Maylynne Ralleigh, the heiress, anymore. She wanted to be May. My wife, your mother, her own person. That's the mom she wanted you to know, and it's never been my place to change that."

Sadie wasn't convinced. "But they were her family. How could she just leave them behind like that?" *Like she left us?* She bit her lip to stop the tears from flowing.

"I know it's hard to understand, but the Ralleighs are a powerful family—you must know by now what they do, the business with the diamonds—and your mom didn't agree with any of it. She was an idealist, and their business takes a certain . . . hardness. I really don't know the details about what happened between them. May didn't like to talk about it, and it made her sad so I didn't push it. I just know they had some kind of falling-out after she figured out where the diamonds came from, and when she turned eighteen they disowned her and she them. After that she didn't consider herself one of them anymore. I never met her parents or the rest of her family, not even on our wedding day."

Sadie took a deep breath as she felt her eyes start to well up. Jessica put an arm around her shoulders and squeezed, and the tears spilled over. She cried for who her mom was and what she had been through, and for her own failures—falling for this whole scheme and convincing herself that belonging to this group was important. She had been neglecting everyone who actually mattered—her dad, Jessica, her friends back in Portland—all for people she couldn't even trust. Just because they had given her a taste of things she had never even thought she wanted: wealth, power, status.

"Are you there, Sadie? Talk to me."

"I'm here, Dad. Sorry—I'm really, really glad you told me. I just needed to hear the truth."

She paused, not sure how far she was ready to take this yet. "There's something else, too."

"Anything. Nothing but the truth from now on, I promise."

"I . . . " she stalled, trying to figure out how to make sure he didn't immediately hang up and call the psych ward. "Some weird things have been happening."

"Like what?"

The rest tumbled out in a rush. "I met some people. They knew mom when she was in school, and there are all these creepy coincidences —like a girl who was related to mom died last year and she committed suicide too. And things have been happening that made me think these people—the ones who knew her—might have had something to do with her death. I don't really have proof yet, but I just don't trust them—"

He cut her off. "Whoa, Sadie, slow down, okay? I'm not quite following."

"I don't think she killed herself, Dad. I think someone hurt her. Or at least, something happened to her when she was at Keating that messed with her head."

The line was silent for a moment, and she held her breath.

"Sadie, I'm so sorry. I knew sending you to that school was a bad idea, but you were so excited. I don't blame you for having these feelings, it must be so strange to be somewhere where she had such a history. But I think you need to know the whole story.

"Your mom was troubled. You know about her drug abuse and her depression, but what you don't know is that day at the hospital—it wasn't the first time she tried to commit suicide. She was sick when I met her. I knew it, but I loved her anyway."

"But, they must have done something to her—to make her sick—"

"Sadie, stop. You can't let yourself get too wrapped up in this. I understand how you're feeling, because I went through it too. But she had a disease, one that ended with her attempting to take her own life, and not for the first time. It's not your fault, Sadie, and nothing we do now will change what happened."

Sadie was stunned. "When? When was the first time?"

"Promise me you won't read too much into this?"

Sadie nodded inanely.

"It was while she was at Keating."

Sadie felt like the pavement was falling away from her, and she put her head down between her knees. She felt Jessica hugging her shoulders, and she leaned into her.

Her mom had tried to commit suicide at Keating, just like Anna Ralleigh.

She heard the nurse's voice in her head. *She got too close to the rocks near that old tower. Nearly got crushed by the waves.* It was too much of a coincidence. Two Ralleighs, two members of the Optimates, and two suicide attempts. It was all too much.

She sat up.

"I think I need some time, Dad . . . I'll call you in a few days, okay?"

"Okay, sweetheart. Please call me, though. I need to know you're okay. I know this is a lot to take in."

"I will Dad. 'Bye."

She hung up, and Jessica's eyes widened.

"What was that about? Is everything okay?"

Before she could explain, a black limo pulled up and one window rolled down. Trix stuck a cigarette out the window and yelled, "Get in, hookers."

"I'll tell you on the way. You're going to want to be sitting down."

Jessica raised her eyebrows. "What about the twins?"

"I'm telling them too. We're going to need more help if we're going to have any shot at doing this."

"Doing what?"

"Finding out what they did to me. And making sure they never do it again."

⁂

To their credit, the twins took it a lot better than Jessica had.

"Bloody Americans, always trying to copy everything we do," Trix muttered between guffaws. "We were doing secret societies before your big old shopping mall of a country was even invented."

Gwen just rolled her eyes. "So this secret group—they're how old?"

Jessica leaned forward. "Like, two hundred years or something. Isn't that crazy?"

The twins looked at each other and shrugged. "Call me when they get to an even five," Gwen said.

Sadie felt anger flare up in the pit of her stomach. The whole idea might sound stupid—and to someone who grew up hearing legends about Freemasons and the Knights Templar, it probably was. But this group wasn't a joke. They might be killing people.

"Look, are you guys going to help or not? I'm not really in the mood to be laughed at. They took me last night, and they can't just do that. I don't even know what I was doing for four hours . . . they could have . . . those men . . . "

She couldn't even say it. She didn't want to. She turned to the window and bit her lip, hard, to force back the tears.

She felt a hand on her shoulder.

"Sadie." She turned to see Gwen, her face settled in smooth lines.

"We're sorry—it's just . . . it's a lot. If this were coming from anyone else at this school, I wouldn't believe it. But I believe you."

Sadie frowned. "Why?"

Gwen shrugged. "Every other roommate we've had has tried to use that status to get something. Money, or attention, or favor with our family. But you didn't even suck up to Ellen. You're a good roomie, even if your accent sounds like you're talking through a mouth full of nacho cheese."

She set her mouth into a hard line. "Now whatever you need, we'll do it." She glanced at Trix, who gave a small, almost imperceptible, nod.

"We happen to know a little about what it's like to not have complete control over your life, but we know a lot more about how to handle it."

Sadie raised her eyebrows. "And how's that?"

One corner of Gwen's mouth curled up into a smile. "By getting the bastards to back the fuck off."

Chapter 22

"Guys, this plan is so good." Jessica grinned widely as she looked around the circle. When they had gotten back to Keating the night before, they had agreed to go on as normal for a few days while they tried to figure out their next move, but Jessica hadn't even made it past breakfast the next morning. "I have a plan," she had whispered under her breath between bites of scrambled egg. "Your room at 8 P.M."

"What is it?" Sadie asked, back in their room, later that night. She knew she sounded a little too eager but part of her was glad for Jessica's impatience. She had to know what happened to her in that place, and she had to know soon.

Jessica flipped open her laptop and turned it around so they could see the screen. It was a newspaper article from the *National*: "Dawning House Winter Benefit set for December 12th."

"I saw some invitations on that receptionist's desk when I was trying to distract her, so I looked it up last night. They're having a big fundraiser next weekend."

Trix raised her eyebrows. "And?"

"And we're crashing."

The twins dissolved into laughter and Sadie put a hand on Jessica's arm. "Jess, it's a good idea, but we can't exactly sneak in anywhere. They're, you know—"

"Super famous? I'm aware. And for the record, three months ago you had never even heard of them."

Trix gasped and looked at Sadie accusingly. "I knew I should have let them release that sex tape," she said, pouting.

Jessica's jaw dropped. "The tape is real?"

Trix smirked. "No comment." Gwen just rolled her eyes and mouthed, "No."

"Anyway, I'm not a complete idiot. Hear me out. I've thought this through," Jessica said.

Sadie nodded. "We're listening."

"Okay, so we all have different cover stories. Sadie, you have to convince the Sullas to go. Tell them you want to support the hospital because it'll give you closure or something." She waved a hand. "Or just tell Thayer rehab is Samantha French's favorite cause, and I'm sure she'll be all over it."

She turned to the twins. "You guys will go as . . . duh . . . your-selves. Unlike Sadie, most people don't live under an Oregon-shaped rock, so we have to assume everyone will recognize you. You can pre-tend you're interested in becoming benefactors or something, right? It'll probably just look like a good PR move because of all your, um, negative press about partying."

Trix looked thoughtful. "Actually, our parents would probably love that. I'll tell Ellen to get us tickets."

Jessica nodded and sat back, looking satisfied. "See, it's good, right? I have a plan for once we're all inside, too, but we can get to that later."

Sadie took a deep breath. This sounded like it could actually work. "Wait, what about you, Jess?"

She grinned. "Mine's the easiest. I'm just going to walk in."

Sadie raised her eyebrows. "Uh, I think your master plan may be flawed. The other members know you."

Jessica waved a hand. "Doesn't matter. I'll be invisible."

Sadie burst out laughing, but Jess just rolled her eyes and went to Sadie's closet. She rummaged through the rack before pulling out a pair of black pants and a collared white shirt. She held them up to her body.

"See?"

Sadie could see the twins breaking into broad smiles. "Wait, I don't—"

"She's going to dress like the party staff, French Fry," Trix offered, clapping her hands. "It's genius."

"But—"

"When was the last time Thayer actually looked at the person connected to a platter of hors d'oeuvres, Sadie? I'm thinking never." Jessica threw the clothes on Sadie's bed. "Plus, it's our only option. I'm not letting you sneak around in there alone, and Trix and Gwen have to stay at the party to distract people. Don't you want to find out what they were doing in that basement?"

Sadie hugged her knees to her chest. "More than anything. But I don't want to put you guys in danger." The weight of what she was asking her friends to do settled on her chest like a stone. Considering what she thought this group had done to one of their own, who knew what they would do to an outsider who tried to break in? She shook her head.

"I can't ask you guys to do this. I don't even know what I was thinking yesterday."

Gwen sat forward. "We want to help, Sadie. We want to get these assholes."

She shook her head. "You don't get it though. This is my problem. I was the one dumb enough to join this group, and we could get in real trouble." She swallowed. "We don't even really know what we're dealing with yet, but we could go to jail. These people are powerful." She lowered her voice to a whisper. "They might really hurt us."

Gwen's eyes flashed. "It's not just your problem. You may have been inducted into this secret society thing a month ago, but we've been in one our entire lives. We were born into it, and we can never get out." Her voice sounded hard and bitter. Trix put a hand on her shoulder, but Gwen just shrugged it off. "Do you have any idea what it's like to be a member of the nobility?" She spat out the word, like it had gone rancid on her tongue. "They tell us how to live our lives, down to what we can wear and who we can associate with. My parents shipped me all the way out here to Hamburgerland just to keep me from being who I am, and there's nothing I can do to stop it. But you can."

She stood up and stomped to the door, blinking away tears. "I'm going out for a cigarette," she mumbled. In seconds she was gone.

"Whoa. What was that about?" Jessica asked.

Trix sighed and picked at a thread on the carpet. "The real reason we're here instead of in London."

"What do you mean? You guys didn't get kicked out of all those schools?" Sadie said.

"Well, yeah. But there was more to it than that. Our parents were worried about a scandal, so they figured the farther away we were, the better." She rolled her eyes. "Anything to keep the family reputation intact."

"They just sent you away? All because of the tabloids?"

She shook her head. "Gwen told them something—something she didn't want to hide anymore. Something she shouldn't have had to hide in the first place." She squared her shoulders. "They tried to send her away, but I told them it was either both of us, or neither. We're twins, you know?" She smiled ruefully. "Package deal."

Jessica shook her head. "Wait, why would they want to send her away? No offense, but she always seemed like . . . you know . . . the conservative one."

Trix arched an eyebrow. "Hey, I take that as a compliment. But this was about something else." She stopped and looked each of them in the eye. "If this gets out, I'll know where it came from. And Sadie, with that contract you signed, Ellen would literally own your ass for decades. We're talking indentured servitude. In Siberia. Probably without food or water, and definitely without a Bloomingdale's."

They both nodded solemnly, and finally Trix shrugged.

"Gwennie likes girls. It's no big deal, but our parents couldn't handle it. They tried to set her up with some of the other royals, you know just for appearances, but she refused." She waved a hand around the room. "And now here we are."

Jessica's jaw dropped. "Those assholes!"

Trix laughed weakly, nodding. "That about sums it up. You get it now though, right?"

Sadie looked her in the eye. "Yeah, I do. I just still don't know how to thank you guys."

Trix waved a hand. "Don't. Gwen's the one with the sob story—I'm just in this for the chance to watch this whole thing blow up in Thayer's face, preferably in the press so she can see what it feels like." She grinned. "Plus, I've been dying for something exciting to happen around here. Georgetown guys are fit and all, but so, so boring. If I have to hear "Hoya, Saxa" one more time I'm going to scream. Now, let's talk wardrobe for this thing. I'm thinking sequins."

 જી

After Jessica left, Sadie lay on her bed and stared at her phone. She had three unopened texts from Jeremy, but she couldn't bring herself to respond. She didn't know what to say to him. She knew he would try to explain what had happened, but she couldn't trust him anymore, and she couldn't bear to just go on pretending everything was okay. Finally, she flipped open her phone.

She scrolled through them all. The first two were from yesterday, asking if she was okay and begging for her to call him. The third was from earlier that afternoon.

"Please call me—I'm really worried about you. I've been asking around, and I think I know what happened. We really need to talk."

Sadie exhaled. She knew she was being cruel, but she couldn't face him yet. As she was staring at the last text, her phone buzzed in her hand and a new message popped up.

"Can you meet me in your locker room? I know you don't want to see me, but it's really important. This isn't about us. You really need to hear this." Fear closed around her heart like a fist. He knew something.

Then another text came through. "It's about Saturday night. I know what they did to you."

 જી

The grass was stiff with frost, and she could feel each blade as they crunched under her shoes and gave way. The wind picked up around her, howling through the trees, and she shivered. She jogged faster.

She had told Jeremy she would meet him in an hour, but she had been so anxious she had decided to get a run in first. She had so much nervous energy she could barely stand still, and her mind was so jumbled she couldn't think.

She had already done the length of the beach three times, and she still felt tense. She reached Keating again and turned around, focusing on her breathing and the dull thud of one foot after another. She tried to focus only on the road ahead of her, blocking everything else out. In the dark, though, the long path looked almost like the dim hospital hallway, and she felt her mind pulling back to that night. Her eyes blurred, and the vision closed in around her. She felt like she couldn't stop, and just like in the dream, she barreled toward the door at the end of the hallway, and whatever awful thing lay behind it.

She forced her eyes closed and the vision fell away, but her toe caught on a crack and she stumbled, landing roughly on her knees. She collapsed onto the ground and just breathed, ignoring the slush as it seeped through her clothes.

When she finally made it to the locker room, it was still empty. She sat down to wait, leaning back against one of the lockers. Her head had been such a mess for two days now, and she still couldn't make sense of anything. She knew the Sullas had taken her, and she knew where, but she still didn't know why.

She had been assuming it was some kind of revenge for what she had seen—a threat to show her how easily they could get to her. But then why the hospital? And what had the men in the basement been talking about? She thought of her conversation with Josh—the way his eyes had glazed over as he talked about the history of the Sullas, and the future. "We're going to take over the world," he had said. Remembering the statement, she started to laugh at its ridiculousness.

She doubled over and laughed harder, but there was no joy in it. The stress and fear had all bubbled up until the pressure was so high she felt like she would burst. She had to let it out, and she shook until she wheezed, the sound echoing around the empty room.

Her whole body trembled until finally she was spent, and she sat back, exhausted. She wiped the tears away from her eyes, and they felt dry and raw. She blinked until her vision cleared, and when the room swam into focus, she saw a single word, written in girlish bubble letters.

Anna.

The sign was still there, hanging from its single square of tape like a dilapidated shingle. It had held on defiantly for all these months, as if determined to be the one thing that could keep her memory alive. Sadie had been so preoccupied all day with her own problems, she hadn't even thought about Anna's. She still didn't know what had happened to her, or to Maylynne, and what it had to do with the Sullas. She felt the weight of it all crushing down on her again, and her skin itched like she had had too much caffeine. She couldn't sit still any longer. She had to do something.

She stood up.

Anna's locker was still full of the usual trimmings—a bottle of lavender-scented shampoo, a purple loofah that had accumulated a thin layer of dust. Sadie reached into the cubby and felt along the back wall until her fingers closed around something metal. It was a tiny gold stud.

She placed the earring carefully back where she had found it and opened the hamper at the bottom of the locker. A scent wafted upward—it was weak, but it was a living smell, sweat and skin and detergent. It was Anna.

She sank to her knees and went through the clothes inside, one by one. There were two Keating T-shirts, one green, one white, and an old gray sweatshirt. She laid the clothes neatly beside her on the floor. She didn't even know what she was looking for, and part of her felt intrusive, like she was watching a stranger who thought she was alone. But Anna hadn't been a stranger, Sadie told herself. She had been family.

She took out the last item, a single white sock, and laid it next to the others. There was nothing there—no letter from beyond the grave, no eerie, cryptic messages scratched into the wood with a bloody nail. Sadie leaned over the hamper and laid her forehead down on her arms. The scent had already started to disperse, released back into the ether, and she felt its absence like a loss. She wondered what Anna had been like.

She sat up and shook herself. She needed to focus. She needed to find out what Jeremy knew, or if he really knew anything. He had refused to tell her anything via text.

She picked up the pile of clothes and placed it back in the hamper. It looked too neat, too artificial, and she toppled it with one hand. She watched the sock as it came to rest in one corner, and she paused. The crack between the base of the hamper and the walls was uneven, slightly larger in this corner, like it had shifted away from the wall. She slid a fingernail under the hamper lining and pulled. The panel was cheap particle board, and it curled up just slightly, but the heavy clothes weighed it down. She emptied the hamper, a little frantically, and tried once more. She pulled harder, and the seal gave way with a crackling sound, like chipping paint. Pain pulsed through her finger and she gasped. Her nail was split down the center, and bright red blood seeped out and pooled at the cuticle. She clenched her hand into a fist and looked down. She stopped breathing.

The base of the hamper was rough and unfinished, with a wavy line of hardened glue that wound around its border. But it wasn't empty. Near the corner was a photo on newsprint, grayed and creased along the center. Her mother's face smiled up at her, younger than she had ever seen her. She was wearing a coat and had the collar drawn up around her face, and she was surrounded by a crowd, like she was sitting in the bleachers at a football game. It must have been cold, but she looked happy.

Sadie picked up the photo and held it closer. She told herself not to hold it too tightly, but still her hand shook. In the photo, Maylynne had her arms wrapped around two people on either side of her. On her left was a girl her age, with long, straight hair that was blowing back off her face. She was smiling and clutching Maylynne's arm, leaning into her like a best friend. Or a sister.

On Maylynne's other side was someone so familiar, Sadie's brain almost couldn't process it. The square jawline and country club haircut were so similar that at first she thought it was him. He had the same haughty look in his eyes, and that same easy, effortless confidence that could only come from a deep understanding of exactly where you came from, and exactly where you were going.

He had his arm around Maylynne's back, and Sadie could see his fingers digging into the fabric of her coat on her opposite shoulder. She looked back to the woman on Maylynne's left and squinted at the photo. She tried to imagine her face older, the bones a little more prominent, the skin stretched and taut, but nothing came. She looked slightly off, like Sadie had seen her before, but not like this.

"Sadie, I'm so glad you came. I am so sorry, I don't even know where to start."

Sadie dropped the photo and turned, covering the open hamper with her back.

"How about you start with Saturday."

Jeremy came toward her in three long strides, and instinctively she backed away.

He held up his hands. "Please just listen, okay? I swear I didn't know what they were doing, and I couldn't stop it." He sank onto one of the benches. "When I think about what they did to you . . . " He trailed off and put his head his hands. He was shaking, and Sadie could see the knuckles on one of his hands were bruised and scabbed. She looked away.

"What did you put in the drink, Jeremy?" Her voice was cold, but she didn't care.

When he looked up, there were tears in his eyes. "Nothing—you have to believe me. It was just Diet Coke—you were so freaked out, and I just thought you needed to sober up. It usually helps."

Sadie's shoulders sagged. Jeremy looked beaten down, almost haggard. He looked so tired, and something inside her crumbled and started to give way. But she wasn't convinced.

"Finn and Josh—what did they say to you?"

He shook his head. "I thought they were just hammered, but they were babbling about you snooping around and seeing things you shouldn't have seen. I told them you were just looking for the bathroom—I thought it was nothing." He pounded the heel of his hand into his forehead. "I should have known what they were going to do."

She sat down next to him.

"What did they do, Jeremy? I have to know."

He looked up and took a deep breath. "They put something in your drink. I didn't see them do it, but Finn was bragging about it the next day. He said it was time for you to make your donation—become part of the family or something, it was so creepy. A few minutes after I gave you the soda, you got that text from Thayer, and then you disappeared. I thought you just went back to the dorms, but I should have looked for you." He reached out and took her hand. "I am so sorry. I'll kill them for this."

She pulled her hand away. "So wait, you think this was all just about Finn and Josh drugging me so they could . . . do things?"

He nodded, and she could see that he was barely holding it together. "I know it sounds crazy, but they've done it before. Those guys are scum. Please Sadie, you have to stay away from them."

Sadie shook her head. "I know. And you're not crazy, but I think it's bigger than that. I think they drugged me so they could take me somewhere."

He looked up. "What do you mean?"

She took a deep breath. "Now you're going to think I'm the crazy one, but I'll tell you everything I know. I can't believe I thought you were part of this, I just . . . I didn't know what to think, and I was so scared—" Her voice caught, and she felt Jeremy's arms wrap around her. She tried to resist, but it felt so good to let go that finally she collapsed into him. She let him hold her for a long time, until her shoulders stopped shaking.

Over his shoulder, she saw Anna's locker, and instantly her mind went back to the photo. What had Anna been doing with a picture of her mother? And not a framed, family photo, but a scrap—something she had ripped out of a newspaper. It didn't make sense . . . unless.

Sadie pulled back and closed her eyes. Maybe Anna had been trying to figure out what had happened to Maylynne, too? She was as much related to her as Sadie was, and as far as she knew she had been missing for twenty years. It wasn't hard to imagine that she must have been curious. Anna probably hadn't even known she was dead.

She felt herself start to shake all over again.

She opened her eyes and saw Jeremy facing her, one hand on each of her shoulders. He was shaking her lightly, his eyes searching her face. "Sadie, where'd you go just now? What's going on?"

"It's my mom." She looked toward Anna's locker. "I think Anna was looking for her, and now Anna's dead. They did something to her, too, and I think I'm next. Someone's trying to cover up what happened to her when she was here, and they'll kill to make sure whatever it was stays buried."

Jeremy let her go, and she could see the fear in his eyes. "Wait, slow down. What do you mean?"

"Look, I don't remember anything that happened after I left the tower on Saturday, but the twins said I didn't get home until five. That's at least four hours after I left the salon. Then I remembered this one flash, like a white hallway that I was rushing down." She took a breath. She knew she was rambling, but it was like blood from a wound. It wouldn't stop.

"I went to the hospital on a hunch. I just had this feeling that was where I'd been, and I found the hallway from the memory I had. They kidnapped me, and they did something to me, but I still don't know what it is."

Jeremy's body tensed, but he didn't speak.

"And I saw the book—the one in the big room in the tower, where they keep all the names of the past members. And I found my mom's and Anna's, and they were related. She was my cousin, and they're both dead." She put her head in her hands. "Something terrible is going on, but nothing makes sense. I just can't help thinking that something horrible happened to my mom while she was here, and Anna was killed because she started looking into it. And now . . . they must think I've been doing the same thing, and they're coming after me next."

She looked up at him, ready to defend her theory, but he wasn't laughing. He was sitting still, and his hands were trembling—with fear, or anger, she wasn't sure.

"The worst part is, I think it might have something to do with Teddy Cranston. He told me he and my mom dated, and I just found this picture of them together. I think Brett is afraid of him too, but I don't know why. Does that sound crazy?"

Jeremy shook his head. "There's something seriously wrong with Finn. That had to come from somewhere."

Sadie nodded. "See what you can find out from Josh, okay? About Teddy, the Sullas, the hospital—anything. We just need to know more. I have all these details and loose ends, and something stinks, but I feel like I'm missing the biggest piece."

"Okay, I'll do what I can. And I can ask the other guys too. They all talk too much, especially when they're drunk. It'll be hard though, unless I know what I'm looking for."

Sadie took a deep breath. "Okay, here's what I know so far."

෴

An hour later she finally stopped talking. Jeremy just nodded, over and over, and she could tell he was trying to keep calm. His body was perfectly still, but his hands were clenched into tight fists. When she was done she felt deflated and weak, like all of the secrets she had been carrying around for two days had filled her with hot air. Now, without them to prop her up, she could barely keep her eyelids open. She felt them sag, and Jeremy helped her stand up.

"Let me walk you back to Keating, okay? I need to process all of this anyway, and we can figure out what to do in the morning."

She opened her mouth to tell him about their plan to sneak into the hospital, then stopped. It was a huge risk, and if anything went wrong, she didn't want the Sullas to think he had been in on it.

Instead, she let him lead her out across the turf and through the trees to the oceanfront path. The moon was still high overhead, and the waves relentlessly pounded the sand.

Jeremy stopped walking, and she felt his hand slip from her grasp.

"Hey, what is that?"

She turned, crossing her arms tighter in front of her chest to keep out the cold. "What's what?"

He nodded toward the surf. "Out on the beach."

Sadie strained her eyes wide and stared into the darkness. The sand glowed almost green in the moonlight, but all she could see near the water's edge was white froth.

Then the light shifted, and she saw a glint of red.

"Oh my god," she said. Then she was running.

Chapter 23

She ran wildly—down the edge of the grassy dunes and toward the water, kicking up sand and strands of shriveled seaweed as she went.

By the time she reached the edge, the water was almost to Brett's knees. Sadie plunged in after her, gasping as the icy water seeped through her running tights and filled her shoes. Her feet went instantly numb, but she could hear Jeremy splashing right behind her.

"Brett, what are you doing?" She was screaming, but her voice barely carried over the roar of the waves. Brett took another step forward, waving her hands, palms down, over the surface of the water in a slow arc. It was like she was in a trance, conducting an orchestra only she could see.

Sadie grabbed her arm and held tight. She could already feel the current pulling at her knees, drawing Brett away from her. Brett winced in pain, but she didn't turn around.

"Come on, Brett—we have to go back!"

Brett shook her head, so small it was almost imperceptible. "We can't go back," she whispered, and the words were gone as soon as they left her lips, lost in the wind and the waves.

Sadie took her hand. It was cold and hard, like polished stone. "Brett, please." Her voice was pleading. The numbness was creeping up her legs, and the lower half of her body felt heavy and foreign.

Just then she felt Jeremy's hand on her arm. Wordlessly, he scooped Brett up and threw her over his shoulder, turning and charging back toward the sand. Sadie ran after him, willing the feeling back into her legs.

They ran all the way back to the locker room, Brett slumped like dead weight against Jeremy's back. Sadie trailed behind, trying not to watch Brett's arms as they dangled and swayed. The skin on her fore-arms was tinged with blue.

When they finally pushed through the door, Jeremy laid Brett on the floor near the showers, and she immediately rolled away from them and faced the wall. They both collapsed onto the ground, gasping for air.

"Leave me alone," Brett whispered to the wall. "You should have left me."

They sat her down in the shower, turning the head so that the hot water beat down on her legs. Jeremy left them to change into dry clothes, and Sadie sat there with her for what felt like hours, until the color finally returned to Brett's cheeks and the room was filled with hot steam.

"Do you want to tell me what happened back there?"

Brett shook her head. "It doesn't matter."

"This can't be about finals."

"No."

"What's wrong then?"

She shook her head again. "I can't tell you."

"Look, you don't have to. I already know there's something going on, but it's not too late to get away. It's not too late to get out."

"I already made my choice."

"Brett, they didn't give you a choice. They tricked you, just like they tricked me, with smoke and mirrors and all those promises. But you can get out."

She shook her head. "You don't get it."

"Yes I do. I know that what the Sullas are doing is bad. They did something to me on Saturday night, and they're probably doing it to you, too. We can help you—just tell me what it is."

Brett looked her in the eye, and all Sadie could see was pain. "I'm not talking about the Sullas, I'm talking about him. I picked him in the Pairing, and we're a good match. Teddy said it's too late to switch."

Nothing she was saying made any sense. Sadie reached up and turned off the faucet.

"Let's get you dry, okay?"

Brett nodded.

"Thayer mentioned the Pairing earlier—what is that?" She peeled off her wet jeans and wrapped a towel around her chest.

Brett struggled with her wet clothes, facing away from Sadie. "It's a tradition—the Sullas think it's important to use relationships to keep the family strong."

Sadie squinted at her through the steam, but all she could see was a pale wash of color.

"What do you mean, relationships?"

"You know, love . . . marriage."

"Are you seriously telling me they tell us who to marry?"

Brett shook her head. "We get to choose. But you have to stay in the group. I mean, what else are you going to do anyway, marry some random guy and then carry this secret around your entire life? It would never work. It makes sense, really. It's smart."

Sadie was glad the steam was too thick for Brett to see her face. She was so brainwashed, she didn't even realize she was being controlled. Brett turned away from her, and Sadie could see the outline of her narrow back. But something was off.

"Hey Brett, come here—are you sure you're warm enough?" The skin on her back looked mottled with blue, like a corpse.

Brett moved closer. "Yeah, I'm fine. And it's my fault, not theirs. I didn't have to choose him."

"Choose who?"

Brett stepped out of the fog and Sadie gasped. She was wrapped in a fluffy white towel, but underneath it she was skin and bone. Her shoulders were covered with bruises, some a fresh, deep purple, others older and fading to yellow and green. Her clavicle jutted out from her chest like an empty shelf.

"Who did that to you?"

She shook her head. "No one. I don't want to talk about it." She sighed and forced an empty smile. "Look, I'm okay. I kinda freaked out back there—I'm really stressed and I haven't gotten much sleep the past few weeks. Can we just go back now? I'm tired."

"No way, Brett. We have to at least take you to the nurse. You could have hypothermia. Or that thing mountain climbers get where their toes turn black and fall off."

"Sadie, I'm fine. It's not like I tried to kill myself."

Sadie's throat went dry. She stood up so they were eye to eye, the steam swirling around them in heavy wisps.

"Yeah, Brett, you did. It's forty degrees outside and you just decided to walk into the freezing cold ocean in the middle of the night. You're not okay."

Brett squared her shoulders and lifted her chin, then crumbled. Her face broke, and she folded in on herself like a dying flower. Her shoulders sagged, and tears ran down her cheeks. "I didn't want to die, I just . . . wanted to feel something else. I couldn't take it anymore."

Sadie grasped her hand and Brett squeezed it. She looked up and her eyes were wild.

"But I can't face it right now. They'll ask me a million questions and do tests and . . . they'll send me away. The Sullas won't trust me anymore. And he'll know I told. Don't make me go, Sadie. Please!"

"Who's he? Whoever he is, I can help you. You can get away."

Brett's eyes grew wide and she shook her head. "I don't want to. He loves me, it's just . . . it's only once in awhile. When he drinks. I just need to be better when he's in those moods. I always say the wrong thing."

"He loves you? And this is how he shows it?" She lowered her voice. "Look, we're getting out of the Sullas, and you can help us."

Brett dropped her hand and stepped back. "Why would I want to do that? Why would you?"

She looked so scared that Sadie felt herself starting to give. "Okay, okay, forget I said anything. I just want you to be okay. I'm trying to be a good friend."

"You are. You saved me. I don't know what would have happened if you and Jeremy hadn't . . ."

She threw her arms around Sadie and sobbed. Sadie patted her back, trying not to feel the sharp bones of her shoulder blades.

"Okay. We can go back to Ashby, but tomorrow you have to make an appointment to talk to someone, okay?"

Brett nodded against her chest.

"We'll figure it all out tomorrow," Sadie said again, not really sure whom she was trying to convince.

*   *   *

On the walk back to Keating, Brett told them both more about the Pairing. It was an unofficial tradition—there was no dramatic ceremony, no binding record—but members of the Sullas all paired off by senior year. After that the path was clear—Harvard or Yale, a European grand tour, law school or business school, a proposal. Brett said the pairs never broke—that would be considered disloyal. The Sullas liked stability. They liked their members to do what is expected of them.

Brett looked longingly out over the water as she recited these rules, and Sadie had to force herself not to grab Brett's arm, tethering her to land and to life. Even so, she felt the weight of Brett's words settling over her. What is expected of them.

With one careless decision she had signed away her entire life. She had no control over her present, that much was clear after Saturday night, but she didn't own her future either.

Brett went on. Those that didn't find a pair at Graff had to hope they would find a straggler from another school—one of the other recruiting grounds for the Sullas—who hadn't matched either. But from what Brett said, at that point you would be lucky to find someone who didn't chew with his mouth open or pick his nose when he thought no one was watching. Sadie didn't mention that anyone would be an upgrade from Brett's current match. From everything she knew now, he was a monster.

"If you leave high school without a pair, you're screwed. Everyone knows that," Brett said. Sadie could practically see her usual facade building back up around her. Her hair had dried into subtle waves, and with her bruises hidden underneath a black warm-up jacket, she was again transformed.

Sadie tried not to mention the obvious. If Brett was planning on staying with Josh, then she was already screwed. But she talked like she was one of the lucky ones. She had a suitable match—a good family, a respected name, a membership in the Sullas—and that was all that mattered.

"My parents didn't even meet until years after high school," Sadie said. "I thought that was normal." She thought of the photo back in the bottom of Anna's hamper, with Teddy's smiling face and gripping fingers. Maybe Maylynne had left because she wanted her future back.

"Yeah, well look how well that turned out."

Sadie made a noise like she had been punched.

"Sorry, that was a terrible thing to say." Brett rubbed her temple with one hand and closed her eyes. "I'm just so tired."

Sadie felt Jeremy squeeze her hand reassuringly. He had been so quiet since they found Brett, but he was still there and that was what mattered.

"So who else is paired? Thayer and Finn, I guess. That one's obvious," Jeremy said, clearly trying to steer the conversation back toward safer ground.

"Not as obvious as you would think. He took a long time before he finally ended up choosing her."

"Who would he have chosen instead? I thought they were basically engaged at birth."

Brett shook her head. "He hooked up with a few girls. Olivia for a little while, then a few others. Even Anna. I forgot about that— lots of people thought he was going to choose her before everything happened."

They kept talking, but Sadie wasn't listening. She forced her feet to keep moving, but all she could hear were Brett's words echoing in her head. The pairs never break. If Finn had chosen Anna, where would that have left Thayer?

They were nearing campus, and instinctively the three of them veered farther into the shadows as they walked.

She went through the motions of saying goodbye to Jeremy and walking Brett to her room, but everything around her seemed muted. Her voice sounded tinny and far away as she told Brett she would come by first thing in the morning, and she floated down the hallway, her footsteps making no sound.

When she finally collapsed onto her bed, she had so many thoughts swirling around in her head, she could barely breathe. She knew now that Jeremy was on her side, but there was still so much to do. She had to convince the Sullas to go to the benefit. She had to find out what was going on in that basement, and she had to figure out why Anna had a picture of her mother and Teddy stashed away in her locker. More importantly, though, she knew she finally had the ability to do those things. She had help—Jeremy, Jessica, the twins. She didn't know if she could trust anybody else, but at least it was something.

She curled into a ball, hugging her arms to her chest. She could still feel the bruising around her wrist, where Josh had gripped her so tightly it had left a mark. She tried to remind herself that whatever she was facing, what Brett was going through was worse. She had promised her whole life to someone, and already, she had seen how much that promise would cost.

❧

At practice the next day, Brett wouldn't meet Sadie's eyes. She didn't blame her, and she tried to give her space. But now she couldn't help but notice the long-sleeved shirt she wore under her jersey, and for the first time, she understood its purpose. It was armor—not to protect her body, but to uphold her facade: the perfect student with the perfect boyfriend. It was all a lie.

She dawdled in the locker room, sending Jessica and the other girls back to Keating ahead of her. Jessica had given her a questioning look, but she had gone anyway. The four of them had arranged to meet later that night to go over the plans, and by then Sadie had to let them know if she had managed to convince the Sullas to go. She still hadn't managed to get Thayer alone, and she wasn't sure how she was going to do it.

The way things turned out, it was easy.

"Hey, Portland," Thayer said, her words echoing around the empty room, "ready to meet your maker?"

"Is that a drinking game?" she deadpanned.

Thayer rolled her eyes. "It's time for you to meet the elders at the tower. Remember when I told you they'd tell you more about the Sullas when they thought you were ready?" She swept an arm dramatically toward the door. "It's time."

Sadie had to force herself to walk slowly in line with Thayer's pace, but she wanted to sprint. She wasn't sure if she wanted to run toward the tower or away from it, but her body just wanted to move. She was finally going to get some answers.

They climbed up to the third floor, passing the cavernous ceremony room, and the small room Sadie had walked into looking for the bathroom. The door was open and it was dark inside, but she shuddered when she saw the leather couch.

They stopped in front of an unmarked door. It looked just like the rest, but it was fitted with a modern lock. "This is you. Don't embarrass me, okay?" Thayer smiled. "And congrats. This means you're officially, officially in."

Sadie raised an eyebrow. "I thought that's what the whole white-robed, bovine-fetish wedding ceremony was about?"

"Very funny. You were in then, but now you're going to find out exactly what being in means." She fluttered her hand in a wave and turned back toward the stairs. "Have fun."

Sadie squared her shoulders and turned toward the door. As she raised her hand to knock, the door opened. Teddy smiled at her and extended a hand. "Welcome to the inner circle, Sadie. I have so much to tell you both."

Sadie shook it and peered past him into the room. It was an office, decorated like the salon with a rich, oriental carpet and a huge desk made of polished wood.

"Us both?"

Someone stepped out from behind Teddy and held up a hand. She was so glad to see Jeremy, she almost collapsed.

Teddy waved a hand toward two chairs. "Have a seat."

He took his place behind the desk, and for a moment no one spoke. Sadie's eyes wandered the room, settling on a marble bust set into an alcove cut into the stone wall. The man's nose was missing, replaced by a jagged gash of raw stone, and his eyes were blank spheres that looked ghoulish in the dim light.

"Beautiful rendering, isn't it?"

Sadie blinked. Teddy was looking at her, an amused smile on his face.

She nodded. "Who is it?"

Teddy glanced back at the bust. "Lucius Cornelius Sulla—celebrated Roman general and a personal hero of my father's. He's become something of a mascot around here."

He looked at her expectantly. "He looks very . . . heroic." She heard Jeremy stifle a laugh.

"Yes, he does. Okay, let's get to it," Teddy said, leaning forward. "Two weeks ago, you both became a part of something, but I'm sure you have lots of questions about exactly what that is. I'm sure you've heard snippets about our goals, maybe you've read our mission statement in the logbook, but you haven't heard the whole story."

Sadie found herself nodding along, maybe too eagerly, and Jeremy reached out and took her hand. She took a deep breath and forced herself to relax.

"As I'm sure you can understand, we have to be very careful about who to trust, and simply taking our oath doesn't guarantee you'll be worthy of becoming one of us. You two have taken many tests already. The interview with the Fates, the initiation ceremony, the White House event. You've both performed well."

Sadie shifted in her chair. She didn't like to think about herself being constantly evaluated. She thought about her trip to the hospital with Jessica. How closely had they been watching?

"Why don't you tell me what you've heard so far, so I know where to start."

Sadie glanced at Jeremy and he nodded to her to start. "Well, the point of the Order of Optimates is to make the world a better place."

He looked thoughtful. "That's true. Has anyone shared with you how we are planning to go about that?"

"Through philanthropy projects, like the hospital." She couldn't resist mentioning it, but Teddy didn't even flinch.

"Also true. We sponsor many projects, all unified by the single goal of helping others, and improving our positioning." He leaned back in his chair, lacing his hands casually behind his head. "Do you two read the news?"

"Sometimes," Sadie said. Jeremy nodded.

"And what do you usually see?"

They glanced at each other, but Teddy continued before they could answer. "I'll tell you what you see. Discord. Brutality. Degradation." He sat forward, his face suddenly flushed with color. "This country is in crisis. The global economy is as close to complete collapse as it's ever been. People are getting poorer. They're getting dumber. They're getting fatter. They're dying earlier of what should be preventable diseases. And genetic conditions—Alzheimer's, cancer, autism—are only getting more prevalent, when we have all the tools we need to eradicate them."

Sadie just blinked.

His eyes flashed. "We have all this potential, but no one is doing anything about it. No one is taking the initiative."

He smiled, then, and Sadie felt a cold fear seeping through her body, for a reason she couldn't quite explain.

"Well, we're taking it."

Out of the corner of her eye, she saw Jeremy shift in his chair. "What do you mean, exactly?"

His smile dropped, and his face became a somber mask. "This country was built on the idea of a better future. As I'm sure you know by now, this group was founded by one of the country's founding fathers, and through the years, we've always felt it was our duty to protect those ideals. And the United States is failing. The political system isn't working. We fight and bicker and take sides, and nothing gets done. The health-care system isn't working; we spend $150 billion a year on costs directly related to obesity, a condition that should be 100 percent preventable. Hell, the people themselves aren't even working. Unemployment rates are close to 10 percent." He stood up suddenly, and Sadie felt herself involuntarily shrinking away from him.

He came around the desk and perched on its edge.

"Look, democracy has failed. That became clear a long time ago, but now we're seeing the real effects. The recession is the beginning, but it's only going to get worse. We need change—real change, and the Sullas are offering a solution. We're building a new group of leaders, one that can step in once the current regime can no longer handle their responsibilities. That day is fast approaching."

Sadie was stunned. The Order of Optimates. Best Men. She had always thought the name was just another manifestation of the group's apparent obsession with Greek and Roman culture. But it was literal.

"You're building a new ruling class." Her voice was incredulous, but he mistook it for awe.

He nodded. "We have been for decades. And we're almost ready. But that's not the whole picture."

"You may have wondered why you were chosen over others—why we looked so deeply into your family histories, and why certain steps were taken during your vetting period that may have seemed odd to you."

He paused for effect, and his eyes were wide with excitement so naked and unchecked it was almost sexual. Sadie looked away.

"In the Order, genetic diseases don't exist. No Alzheimer's, no cystic fibrosis, no Down's syndrome. Our cancer rates are less than half that of the general population. We've screened every member and weeded out any potential risks. It's why we monitor the pairings so closely. We have to make sure you're a strong match."

Sadie shook her head. It was all too much to take in.

"But that's eugenics."

He nodded emphatically, as if she had just answered a question correctly in class.

"And it's wrong."

He cocked his head to the side and looked almost sympathetic. "I can understand why you would think that. It's what we've been taught. But in this case, I think it's fair to say the ends justify the means. We're using the process for good, and as the majority of the world's population has gotten weaker and sicker, we've only gotten stronger. One day soon, when they need our help most, we'll be there to lead them."

Sadie thought about Josh's speech in the ceremony room. It felt like weeks ago.

"So the goal of the Optimates is . . . saving the world."

Teddy turned to her, a strange look on his face. It looked suspiciously like respect. "Exactly, Ms. Marlowe. We are saving the world—one generation of superior leaders at a time."

She almost gagged.

He walked back around the desk and sat down. He spread his hands. "Now do you have any other questions for me?"

"Are you the head of the Sullas?" Sadie blurted out. She couldn't stop herself.

He laughed. "Not yet. My father fills that role, but as I'm sure you've heard, he'll be running in the presidential election next term. When he wins, it will make our transition to power that much smoother, but in the meantime, the position is too visible. I'll be taking his place."

Sadie couldn't take it anymore. She felt like the walls of the tower were closing in around her. She stood up.

"Thanks. I feel much better now—now that I understand what our goals are. But I think I should get back to studying."

He put up a hand. "Of course. One more thing, though. I know it's premature, but I wanted to let you both know that the elders approve of your pairing, should you choose to pursue it."

Sadie tried not to let the disgust show on her face. He was basically telling them they could mate. She hadn't felt this awkward since her dad had fumbled his way through "the talk" in eighth grade.

"Your blood tests revealed no genetic red flags, and all signs point to incredibly healthy offspring. Your children would be an asset to our family."

Oh god. Blood tests. She remembered the very first night with the Fates, when she had woken up with an injection mark and a bruise on her inner elbow. They had taken her blood. She felt violated in a way that was almost indescribable. They had been inside of her and taken something that wasn't theirs.

She felt herself start to sway, and then Jeremy was at her elbow. She heard him say goodbye to Teddy and nodded along, letting herself be steered outside. Soon they were descending the stairs, then walking along the path, and finally she was climbing the stairs to her bedroom.

She collapsed onto her bed. It was barely dinnertime, but she couldn't function. She had thought they had a plan she was comfortable with, but now the stakes had changed. She didn't just need to get out—she needed to stop them. She lay awake for hours, ignoring the twins as they came and went, ignoring the texts she got from Jeremy, and trying, failing, not to think about what she was going to do when she woke up. Finally, long after the room had darkened to pitch and the noises in the hallway had fallen silent, she slept.

Chapter 24

The site of the hospital gate made Sadie's stomach roll, but she forced herself to smile along with the rest of them. It had been a long limo ride, and most of the girls were already a few glasses deep into bottles of champagne. Sadie had been nursing the same glass since they left. She needed to be sharp.

The way it turned out, it hadn't been hard to convince the Sullas to attend the fundraiser. Once Trix and Gwen had pledged their donation to the event, the hospital's PR machine had run with the story, and Thayer had immediately decided they all simply had to go.

She had left Gwen, Trix, and Jessica in her room earlier that day. Sadie knew they were all a little scared, but she could tell they were trying so hard not to show it. She had told them about her meeting with Teddy Cranston, about the plan, the genetic testing, and what might be in that basement. They had all nodded along, the excitement slowly leaching out of their faces and giving way to fear. She had been afraid they would back out. She had almost hoped they would. But they were committed.

When Sadie had left, she had turned in the doorway and glanced at her friends. Trix and Gwen had gone for the full celebrity look, with chic cocktail dresses, big hair, and full makeup. Jessica was already outfitted in her waiter costume, with a pressed white shirt and black slacks. With the dorm room as a backdrop, they had all looked like they were dressed up for Halloween. Sadie hadn't been able to help but grin.

Trix had caught sight of her and frowned. "What are you waiting for, Yankee? You're going to be late."

Sadie had waved a hand. "I know, it's just . . . you guys are the best, you know that?"

243

Trix had just scoffed. "Obviously. We're English."

Jessica had just grinned and given her a mock salute. "See you on the other side, Agent Marlowe."

Now, as she circled the edges of the party, she caught a glimpse of Jessica as she breezed through the kitchen doors, a tray of empty glasses balanced on one hand. Sadie caught her eye, and she winked. So far so good.

Thayer and the rest of them were hovering near the door, and Sadie knew they were staking out the twins' arrival. Sadie didn't think the twins had ever said more than two words at a time to Thayer, but from her Facebook page and her Twitter feed, you would think they were best friends. No doubt tomorrow they would be on the front page of every tabloid, with Thayer's face not-so-subtly wedged in between theirs in every shot.

"Did your roommates say when they were going to arrive?" Thayer called, a tinge of annoyance in her voice. "It's almost time for the charity auction."

Sadie shrugged. "They were getting ready to go when I left." She glanced through the open front doors and saw blue lights flashing. She had to bite her lip to keep from grinning. "Actually, I think that might be them now."

Thayer let out a tiny, high-pitched screech, like a teakettle boiling over all at once, then composed herself. She smoothed down her dress, tousled her hair, and marched into battle.

The twins had gone all out—they had arrived with an entourage of three limos and a police escort—and at least half of the party spilled out onto the circular drive to gawk at their arrival.

Sadie hung back by the entrance, watching as the press photographers swarmed.

The twins emerged, looking surreal and otherworldly, like nymphs in questionably appropriate black spandex. They looked like they were dressed up to go clubbing, rather than to attend a charity event, but that was all part of the act. They were going for maximum attention, and it was working.

After they had posed for a few photos, Trix held up a hand. "Wait! We simply can't let you take any more until we get our good friend Thayer Wimberley in here. Thayer!" she called out, but Thayer had somehow already appeared in between them, grinning ferociously like a lion who had just stumbled upon a herd of sleeping buffalo.

After a few more, Gwen called the rest of the members over, chatting animatedly with the photographers about what good friends they all were. The performance was so over the top, Sadie could hardly believe they didn't see through it. Then again, being near the twins always seemed to give people some kind of contact high, and right now, all of the Sullas were completely stoned.

"Care for a canapé, Miss?" Someone whispered in Sadie's ear. She turned to see Jessica holding a tray of crackers and salmon mousse.

"Scurry along, wench. I'm busy being charitable."

"Very funny. The disguise totally worked, though. I may stick around after we're done just so I can get my share of the tips."

Sadie smiled, but she could feel her lips starting to tremble. "You ready?"

Jessica popped two crackers in her mouth, then dumped the tray unceremoniously behind a planter.

"Oh yeah," she said, dabbing at her mouth daintily with a cocktail napkin. "Let's infiltrate this bitch."

❧

Getting out of the event was so easy it was almost embarrassing. Everyone, down to the security staff, was still distracted by the twins' display, and they simply walked through the ballroom, slipped through a side door, and found themselves on the second floor's main hall.

"Where to next, double-0-seven?" Jessica said. "You said there was a hidden stairwell?"

"Follow me."

She led Jessica down a flight of stairs to the ground floor, their footsteps echoing around the stairwell and bouncing back, making it sound like they were being followed. The hallways were completely empty, but she could see shadows moving across the little viewing panes in the doors of the patient rooms. As they passed one, a pair of eyes watched them silently through the small square window.

"This place is such a horror movie," Jessica said, shivering. "I feel like we should be wearing cheerleading uniforms or something. People are always wearing cheerleading uniforms right before they get stabbed."

Sadie gritted her teeth and walked a little faster. "Not really helping right now, Jess."

"Sorry. My mom always says I ramble, but I don't do it on purpose. It's just when I get nervous—"

"Jess," Sadie hissed. "We're sneaking around here, remember? No talking."

"Right." Jessica nodded. "Complete and utter silence. From here on out. Which is also totally just like a horror movie."

Sadie gave her an exasperated look and pointed toward the wall. "We're here. There's a landing behind that curtain, which leads to a stairwell, which leads to a door, another hallway, and then whatever creepy torture dungeon they took me to." She laughed, but even she could hear how fake it sounded. She put a hand up to draw back the curtain, but Jessica touched her arm.

"Are you sure you want to do this? You could just leave—transfer to some boarding school in Chicago and never look back. I'd come with you! The winter sucks, but the food's good. You like hot dogs, right?"

Sadie shook her head. "Running away isn't an option anymore. They went to all that trouble to get me here, and I don't see them letting me just leave. And I know what happened to the last two members that made trouble."

Jessica looked uneasy. "You still think they had something to do with Anna's death?"

"More than ever. Plus, they did something to me down there. And I have to find out what it was."

Jessica nodded. "Okay, let's do this."

They ducked through the curtain and tiptoed down the stairs toward the crack of light that shone under the basement door. When they got to the bottom, Sadie took a deep breath and turned the handle.

It didn't move.

She tried again, but still nothing.

"What's wrong?"

Sadie jiggled the door again in frustration.

"The damn door is locked."

Jessica's jaw dropped. "Are you kidding? After all that?"

Sadie shook her head. "It was open before . . . I didn't even think about it." She collapsed against the wall next to the door and slid down, resting her head on her knees. "We have to get in there. I can't go back to Keating without knowing." She had been waiting seven days for this, and each one had felt like an eternity. She couldn't stand it.

Just then, as if in slow motion, the handle started to turn. For a split second, Sadie was elated—they were going to get in! Then the rest of her brain caught up, and she had to force herself not to jump up from the floor and fling the door wide open. She and Jessica locked eyes in the dark, and Jessica's mouth started to open.

"Oh, shi—"

Before she could finish, Sadie pulled her down onto the floor and pressed her hand over her mouth. At the exact same time, the door swung open, trapping them in the tiny space between the door and the corner of the stairwell.

Eyes wide open in horror, they both watched as the door drifted slowly back away from them, exposing them inch by inch to whoever was on the other side.

Then Sadie heard footsteps. A man in a white lab coat was making his way up the stairs, his head bobbing slightly in time to the music that was blasting through his headphones. It was so loud she could hear the bass pounding, and he executed a pretty embarrassing air guitar on the landing before disappearing behind the curtain. Sadie and Jessica stared in shock at each other for a moment, then Jessica lunged forward and grabbed the door handle, catching it just before the lock clicked back into place.

She pumped her other fist in the air. "That's why I kick ass every practice in one-on-ones, Sadie. Catlike reflexes!" Sadie clapped a hand over Jessica's mouth again, but she couldn't help but smile.

"There could be other people around," Sadie said in a whisper. She pushed her shoulders back and took a deep breath. "Now stay behind me."

As soon as the door shut behind them, they were plunged into darkness. At the far end of the hallway, a thin line of weak light bled underneath the double doors. Without giving her fear time to sink in, Sadie took off.

Even without any lights, she could see herself rushing toward the same door from the dream, the small black rectangle growing larger and larger. She pushed the image out of her mind and forced her feet to keep moving forward. Finally she got close enough that she could make out the words on the door: "Restricted Area: Hospital Personnel Only."

Everything around her seemed to slow down as she placed her hands flat against the double doors. She took a deep breath, and she could hear her heart beating in her ears, low and even. Jessica was right behind her, and her breath was warm on Sadie's shoulder. As she exhaled, she pushed.

The first thing she felt was cold. A whoosh of air surrounded her as the doors swung open, sucking the breath from her lungs and pulling goose bumps up through her flesh. She stood grounded in the doorway, somehow unable to take that final step.

She had come so far, and she was so close to finding out what was going on. And now she couldn't do it.

Jessica walked a few tentative steps into the room, then turned back toward Sadie. The backlighting in the room cast her face in shadow, but Sadie could feel the fear in her voice. "Sadie come here."

"What is it?"

"Just come."

Jessica pulled her through the doorway, breaking the spell. The room was freezing, and the only light was tinged with blue, emanating from a wall of sleeping monitors that hung above a desk. The effect made her feel like she was underwater. She floated forward.

The room was long and narrow, with metal filing cabinets stacked chest-high along each side. At the far end of the room, near the computers was something that made the skin on Sadie's whole body itch with fear.

It was a long table, padded, with arms that split out from the sides like a cross. A circle of spotlights hovered over it like ravens over a bleeding carcass. Instruments and machines converged on it from all sides, and at the foot end, two metal arms jutted out to either side. Stirrups.

Her knees started to shake, but Jessica grabbed her before she fell.

"What is this place?"

"I don't know yet." She took a deep breath and turned away from the operating table. "But I didn't come all this way not to find out."

She started with the filing cabinets. She yanked open the closest one, and inside were neatly stacked files, each one marked with a name. She skimmed over the tabs with one shaky finger.

"Oh my god."

"What is it?"

Sadie held up a thick file. "It's Thayer's."

She spread the contents on the floor—a stack of papers covered with small type and what looked like medical charts, some smaller sheets with handwritten notes, a DVD marked with a date, and a photo. Thayer stared up at them from the floor, her face smiling directly into the camera.

"Whatever they did, they did it to her too," Sadie murmured, flipping through the printed pages. "Do you think there's any way she knows about this?"

Jessica shook her head. "Who knows? Nothing Thayer does makes sense to me. I mean, she makes out with Finn. On purpose."

Jessica picked up one of the handwritten sheets. "My dog has better handwriting than this. I can't read any of it." She peered over Sadie's shoulder. "What's all that stuff? Looks like blood work."

Sadie was holding a page covered with a list of medical-sounding terms, each one with a corresponding number.

"Blood work?"

"Yeah, you know, when your parents go in to get their cholesterol checked or whatever. They get a big printout like that. My dad always brags about his for like three days afterward because he's convinced his coconut-kale smoothies are, like, the secret to everlasting vitality." She pointed to a line on the paper. "See, that's her cholesterol level, which . . . yikes." She shook her head with mock sincerity. "Skinny fat is an epidemic."

"They told me they tested our blood to make sure we were eligible to reproduce," Sadie said. "God, I can't even say that without feeling like I'm in a late-night movie on the Syfy Channel."

"Wait, Sadie." Jessica held up a piece of paper. "I don't think that's all they tested."

It was covered with a series of lines, almost like a barcode, but with little dashes of varying widths in multiple columns.

Sadie shook her head. "What is that?"

"Assuming the many hours of cop shows I've watched make me a legitimate expert—and they should—these are the results of a DNA test."

The Sullas had her DNA.

Suddenly Teddy's comments about creating a new class—a new race—didn't sound so overblown. How far were they planning to go?

"Whatever they were testing for, looks like she passed," Jessica murmured, showing her a second page. It showed a list of genetic conditions and a series of percentages that detailed Thayer's risk for each condition. All the numbers were tiny, and at the bottom was a black stamp. "Suitable."

"Wait, what are we doing?" Sadie dropped the pages and ran down the line of filing cabinets, pulling open one drawer after another until she found what she was looking for. She pulled out the file and spread it on the floor. The DNA testing form looked a little different—simpler, with fewer measurements—but she recognized the barcode pattern. She flipped to the last page and scanned to the bottom. She stared at the words while the room spun around her, pitching and rolling like she was in the eye of a storm.

"She failed the test."

"Wait, what? Who?" Jessica glanced up from Thayer's chart, and when she saw Sadie's face she dropped everything and went to her side.

"My mom."

She showed Jessica the last page. Her risk was high in multiple categories, and at the bottom was a single word in bold capital letters. **UNSUITABLE**.

"What does this mean? Do you think this is why she ran away?"

Sadie closed her eyes. "I don't know, but . . . this doesn't make sense. It doesn't fit. Unless—"

Anna's folder was filed right in front of Maylynne's. She grabbed for it eagerly, forcing herself not to rip the thing apart in the process.

"What are you looking for?"

She talked as she scanned the pages. "Maybe they couldn't just let Maylynne go. She knew too much after going through the initiation process. Then when she didn't pass, maybe they decided to get rid of her. They . . . I don't know, they tried to kill her, or they got her hooked on drugs and messed her up so badly no one would believe her even if she tried to talk. Then she ran away."

"Jeez." Jessica glanced around her then, and Sadie felt a new fear settle over them like a fog. She could taste it—sharp and metallic like undercooked meat. "And?"

"And if that's what happened to my mom, maybe the same thing happened to Anna." She swallowed. "They were family, after all. It would make sense if they both failed."

She flipped to the last page and scanned to the bottom.

"Damn it." She smashed her fist against the filing cabinet, and the crash echoed loudly around the room. "This can't be right."

Jessica leaned in over her shoulder. "She passed."

Sadie closed the file and dropped it back in the cabinet.

"Do you want to look for yours?"

She shook her head. "I already know I passed. I just need a second to think." Sadie leaned her head against the cool metal, forcing her breath to slow and her mind to grow calm. Every time she thought she knew something, things changed. If her mom hadn't passed, what did they even want with her? And if her mom had been unsuitable, why wasn't she?

"Hey Sadie, you might want to come over here."

Jessica was across the room, standing in front of one of the doors that led off the main room. It was the source of the cold draft—Sadie could feel the cold air flowing toward her now, and the room grew colder with every step. She hugged herself as she stepped through the doorway.

The room was long and narrow, with shelves lining the walls. A thick fog swirled along the floor and crept toward them like a living thing. Sadie lifted a foot. "What is this stuff?"

"Dry ice." Jessica's voice was flat. She was standing in front of one of the shelves. They were stacked with small metal canisters, each one like a big silver thermos with a little white label. Jessica reached a hand back and took Sadie's arm, drawing her toward the shelf. She squeezed. "Look."

Sadie squinted. "What does it say? It's so dark in here."

Jessica pulled her closer. The canister was labeled with a series of symbols that looked mildly familiar, like she had seen them a million times at the doctor's office, but never really bothered to look. One was the biohazard sign, but she didn't recognize the others.

"They're eggs, Sadie."

"Like, for scrambling? Why would they—"

"No. Eggs." Jessica's voice was soft. "My mom went through IVF when they were trying to have my little brother. This is how they store them."

Then Sadie was a million miles away. The operating suite, the puncture marks in her arm, the pain in her stomach, that feeling of fullness and emptiness at the same time. She ran her fingers over the label to make sure it was real.

Marlowe, S.

The eggs were hers.

"You okay?"

Sadie shook her head. She could barely feel her feet on the floor. She was suspended in the thick, cold air. Choking.

Jessica squeezed her hand and pulled. "Let's go."

Sadie let Jessica pull her along toward the door. Her head was a mess, all of her thoughts half-baked and intertwined. She shook her head and pressed her eyes shut, but nothing came loose. She needed to get home to think.

"Jess, hurry. I need to get out of here."

Jessica stood in front of the double doors, her back to Sadie. "I know, but—"

"But what?"

Jessica turned around, and Sadie could see panic in her eyes. "It's locked. Maybe it was on a timer or some—"

Then the lights went out, and they were in total darkness.

Chapter 25

Even before the chopper blades started up, she knew where they were going. Back to Keating, back to the tower, where they would figure out what to do with her. She wondered if her mom had taken this trip after they found out she wasn't of any use to them. She wondered if Anna had.

She thought about what the nurse had said about her mom. "Swimming. Got too close to the rocks." At the time, she had pictured her laughing and splashing around with friends on the beach, carelessly drifting toward the rocks. Now she only wondered who had pushed her, and how she had managed to survive the fall.

She could feel herself slipping in and out of consciousness. They had given her something that made her feel flat and plastic, like she was all body and no brain.

She thought about Jess. After the lights went out, Sadie knew it was over. There was no use fighting them, not like that. Wordlessly, she had pushed Jessica into the storage closet and placed a hand over her mouth. She had tried to protest, but Sadie had shut the door in her face. She had to do this part alone.

It was only seconds before they had swarmed in and taken her. She had felt the hood slip over her head, the now-familiar pricking sensation in her arm, and then she had gone under. He had whispered in her ear one last time before things had gone black: "It'll all be over soon."

❧

When she woke up, she was in the tower. She could hear the wind roaring outside the stone walls and the rumble of the waves as they launched their nightly assault. She was stretched out on a couch, and her legs were freezing. She was in the boring black cocktail dress she had borrowed from Jess, and it occurred to her that she was already ready for her funeral. When they found her body, at least for once she would be properly dressed. The thought made her want to laugh out loud, but she couldn't.

She looked around the room, and even though it was dark, she knew exactly where she was. Across from her was the large desk and high-backed leather chair. Nothing moved.

She tugged down the hem of her dress and tried to sit up.

"I wouldn't do that." She felt a cold jolt of fear travel up her spine and settle at the base of her neck. She knew that voice. "I've been pretty fucking charitable, I think. Not tying you down." He sounded so casual she wanted to scream. "You probably would have liked that, anyway. But I will, if I have to."

Something was off. The voice sounded harsher somehow. The Southern drawl had melted away, leaving only cold metal. Things had changed.

"Leave me alone. Let me go—" She tried to yell the words, but they came out slow and clumsy, sticking on her tongue like lumps of peanut butter. All of her limbs felt heavy. "What did you do to me?"

A match struck, and she heard the hiss of a wick catching flame. She saw the glow glinting off the desk's lacquered surface. Another candle lit, and the light slowly spread to the corners of the room.

The familiar jawline was there, but the face was smooth and unwrinkled, and in that moment, her last bit of hope fizzled and snuffed itself out. Not Finn. Anyone but Finn.

He sat behind the desk, hands folded. His face was hollow in the shifting candlelight, all brittle bone and sinew. She could see a deep purple bruise under one eye. Jeremy.

"You should really be asking what you did to me. You and your whole, fucked-up family." He stood up and walked around the side of the desk, pointing to his eye. "Not to mention your boyfriend."

Her body recoiled as he came closer, and she pressed herself back into the cold leather of the couch. He stopped and sank into an armchair.

"I've got to know, though. Could you seriously not have just minded your own business for like ten minutes?" He pulled out a long, thick cigar from the breast pocket of his jacket. He held up a lighter and lit it, spinning it in his mouth and letting out small puffs of smoke as it turned. "Once they had what they wanted, they would have let you crawl back to bumblefuck wherever as long as you kept your mouth shut. But clearly you would have become a problem."

He took a long draw and blew the smoke into the air.

"And now we have to waste time dealing with this when we have way more important shit to handle. Do you know why?"

He leaned toward her, one elbow on his knee, and let out another cloud of smoke. "Because you're a stupid whore. Just like all the other Ralleighs."

She felt like she had been punched in the chest. She couldn't breathe, and the words echoed around the room and closed back in on her like a vise.

"Fuck you."

He laughed.

She looked around. There were no windows, and the door was behind her, simultaneously just a few steps and millions of miles away.

"Like my office?" he said, waving the cigar in a slow circle.

"You mean your grandfather's?" she said, through gritted teeth. "You're no one."

He breathed out a stream of smoke and grinned. "Not for long."

He looked so smug that suddenly it was all perfectly clear. Even after everything, she was stunned.

"This is all about your family. The whole grand scheme to save the world. You don't care about diseases or education or any of that. This is about control."

He grinned wider.

"You're building a dynasty."

He looked thoughtful. "I wouldn't call it a dynasty so much as . . . a new strategy. Clearly the system is broken. We're fixing it. No government lasts forever, not even Rome's. It's time for our next phase."

He leaned forward, resting his elbows on his knees. "Look, there are two types of people in this world, and it's time to stop pretending that isn't true. We need some separation between the people who can and the people who can't. Think, vote, decide, lead. But it's not as simple as just drawing a line in the sand. We built a new ruling class from scratch. It may have taken forty years, but it was worth it."

He sat back in his chair. "Leadership is initiative. Men take the things they need, and history rewards them for it."

She couldn't even believe what she was hearing. Everything he was saying was just meaningless propaganda. He was like a dutiful cult member delivering his lines. She wanted to shake him.

"Finn, listen to me. Your family is brainwashing you, just like everyone else. But you're wrong. That's not how the world works. You don't take power—you earn it."

He took another draw on his cigar, and let it out in a series of lazy smoke rings. "That's what weak people always say."

He loosened his tie and pulled it off. When he started unbuttoning his collar, she thought about Olivia and gagged. Even that felt weak and slow.

He snickered. "In another few weeks you would have been begging for it, but I'm not interested." He leered at her anyway, his eyes running over her bare legs. "You're unsuitable. You all are."

She paused. There was something there. She could feel it. She didn't let herself hope, though. Not yet.

"That's not true, Finn," she said slowly. "I passed."

He shrugged her off, now rolling up his sleeves. "That's what they told you so you would cooperate, but it's in your blood. The only reason you're even here is because they couldn't pass up your fortune."

Before she could stop herself, she let out an exaggerated groan.

"Nothing you're saying is even making sense. I don't have a fortune—I don't even have a car. Let me go, and I swear none of you will ever see me again. I'll go back to Portland and never come back."

"Do you really think I'm that stupid? You're the last heir. You may not have the money yet, but you will."

Sadie flashed back to the night of her initiation, when Thayer had told her about the Ralleighs. There's no one left.

The room around her was starting to blur, and she blinked until he came back into focus. His edges were muddled now, like his body wanted to spread out beyond its borders.

He grinned. "Feeling the buzz?"

She shook her head, but as she did she had to put out a hand to steady herself on the armrest.

"Look, members of the Order are recruited for two reasons. Some are here to improve the bloodline and keep it pure. Others are here to provide capital. Ideally, most members fall into both of those categories, but you're not so lucky. Even if you had stayed, you wouldn't have been allowed to reproduce—at least not in the traditional way."

Sadie closed her eyes. "That's what the eggs are for."

He smiled. "The technology isn't quite there yet, but we're working on it. Soon we'll be able to clean them all—create a stock of perfect eggs to use for future generations. That's why all female members are required to make regular donations. They need a constant supply."

He picked her phone up off of the coffee table and smirked. "Have you had this since, like, second grade? I didn't know they still made these." He flipped it open.

"Now, let's say you were going to kill yourself. Which you are, by the way. What would you say to your dad?"

"Finn, please. You can still stop this."

He waved his hand. "We'll go with the tried and true, 'goodbye' then. You would be boring like that. Plus, with your family history, they won't need much to connect the dots."

He hit a button and snapped the phone shut. "No points for creativity, but I think it gets the job done. I would send one to your mother too, but we both know she pulled a similarly uninspired goodbye-cruel-world years ago."

Sadie shut her eyes, willing him to stop talking.

"What happened to my mom?"

Finn shrugged. "Who knows. She was crazy and drugged out. She ran away." He held up his hands defensively. "That one's not on us, promise."

"Bullshit. Someone hurt her when she was here . . . she almost died on the rocks below the tower."

Finn looked almost sympathetic. "Dude, your mom was trash. My mom told me all about her. It's not our fault she couldn't handle everything that was going on. Some people can't. Anyway, we need to get going. Any last questions?"

Sadie floundered. His mom? She needed to keep him talking—by now Jessica and the others would be looking for her. "What happened to Anna?"

Something flickered across Finn's face. His features flinched just slightly, and Sadie's heart beat faster. Now hope flared, white and hot and fast.

"He killed her, didn't he? Just like he tried to kill my mom." Her limbs were starting to tingle, and she had the urge to stand, but she forced herself to stay still.

Finn's lip curled. "You don't know what you're talking about."

"You guys dated, didn't you? Before you started pretending to like Thayer again. What happened to her, Finn? Did she find out about your stupid eugenics plan and tell you to kick rocks?" She stood up. Her body was light, humming with raw energy. She felt the urge to go higher. She wanted to be free.

"We both know you don't handle rejection well. Did Daddy have to step in?"

A tremor passed through him, and for a moment she could see every vein in his neck. "Anna was trash, just like your mom. I couldn't see it at first, but she was threatening everything. It's time for you to go now."

He was close. She needed more time. "Did she—"

"You still don't get it. It's already over, Sadie. You're dying already, but you're going to jump first. It's more convincing that way."

He stood up then. She was out of time.

He jerked his head toward the door. "Go. It's unlocked."

She just stared, confused, until the corners of his lips turned up in a cold smile.

"We're giving you a head start. Sportsmanship."

Her mouth dropped open, and she almost laughed at how twisted it all was. He wanted her to run. He wanted her to try to get away, just so he could catch her and have the satisfaction of watching her die. But she wasn't done. She wanted to be closer to the sky first. She wanted to fly.

At the door, she turned and made her last move.

"It was you, wasn't it? You killed Anna."

His face stayed frozen in that smile, but one hand—one finger really—started to shake. He was breaking.

"She was unsuitable. She tricked me."

Sadie took a step back toward him and shook her head. "No Finn, she wasn't. I saw her results. She passed."

"You're lying." His voice was low and flat, but she kept pushing.

"Whoever told you that is the one that lied. Who was it—your dad? He made you kill her for nothing."

He looked at her with such hatred in his eyes, she felt a new, cold lick of fear spread down her spine. He lunged around the desk and came toward her.

Then she was running. She stumbled down the hallway, trying not to listen to Finn's voice as it echoed around her. She just knew she had to go up. Thayer's voice rang in her head: *It's not like there's a fire escape.* She kept going, anyway.

Finally she found the stairs and climbed. Each time she lifted a foot it felt like it was stuck in quicksand. Her chest burned, and she gasped in air until the edges of her vision went black, but she kept going. She thought about the running test at the beginning of the year, and she almost laughed. She clenched her fists and pressed on.

The stairway spiraled upward for what felt like miles, and by the time she reached the top she was dragging herself up with her arms, one step at a time. If she could only make it to the top, she could fly away.

At last she saw a door. She swung it open wide, and the rush of air that met her was so bitterly cold she had to fight to stay standing. She struggled forward, feeling the icy stones burning her skin.

When she got to the ledge, she looked out over the wall. It was all darkness, but she knew what was beneath her. Rocks and waves. Freedom.

She placed one foot on the ledge and hoisted herself up so that she stood with her back to the door. She knew he would be there soon.

She watched a single snowflake as it floated past her. A cold wind hit her bare legs, and she shivered, but she kept her head high. She was numb already anyway.

Muffled footsteps fell on the stairs, and the door behind her opened. She heard him pause to catch his breath. She didn't turn around, but she knew he was watching. She lifted her chin and squared her shoulders. She couldn't let him win that easily, even though everything inside of her was whispering to jump.

"Just tell me why they tried to kill my mother. Then it'll all be over." She shouted the words out into the abyss. She didn't want his face to be the last thing she saw.

Silence.

"Anna, then. I have to know what happened to them." The wind whistled around her, muffling her words.

Finally someone spoke. "It's simple, really. They didn't belong."

Sadie whirled around, one foot skidding beneath her on the icy stones. The woman had short blonde hair and a long black coat wrapped tight against the cold. Something about her face triggered a memory, but it was all wrong—like it had wilted and hardened into something Sadie didn't recognize.

The woman took a step forward. "They were unsuitable. They were a threat to our plans. And now so are you. Jump, please."

Sadie shook her head. One of her feet slid a few more inches on the slick stone, but she caught herself. "Not until you tell me the details."

Another step forward. "Your mother tried to take something that wasn't hers. Anna did the same."

Sadie wanted to scream. "What does that even mean?"

Moonlight glinted off the woman's face, and something slid into place. Sadie saw the woman decades earlier—younger and happier, in a photo with her arm around her best friend.

"It was you, wasn't it? In that photo with my mom."

The woman just stared back at her. "That's not important."

Sadie clenched her fists. "But you did know her. Did they try to kill her because she wanted to leave? You at least owe me that much."

The woman just threw her head back and laughed.

"Honey, your mom didn't want out. She wanted in. But she didn't have what it takes."

"She was unsuitable?"

"As far as the Order is concerned."

Sadie shook her head. "What are you saying?"

"Her test was fixed. Everyone has a price, and she had to go."

Sadie's jaw dropped. "But you were her friend!"

The woman's eyes glittered like black marbles. "And she stabbed me in the back."

She moved closer, and Sadie studied her face. There was something else nagging at the edges of her mind.

The woman took another step forward, and the moonlight glinted off a stone she wore around her neck. Sadie had seen that stone before—green, with a gold C that clutched the gem like a spider.

The weight of the realization almost sent her crashing to the ground.

"It was you." Anger built behind the words.

No reaction.

"You're Pamela Cranston. Teddy was going to choose May instead of you. You were jealous." With the anger came fire, burning away the numbness in her arms and legs and head. Things started to clear. Maybe this was what dying felt like. At least now she knew.

The woman's mouth stretched into a thin line.

"And you're out of time."

"You tried to kill your best friend, for what—a last name? Some creepy, manufactured life that was all planned out ahead of you?" Sadie could hear her voice rising to a shriek. "Did you ever even love him?"

Pamela raised her chin. "They weren't a good match, anyway. A Cranston marrying a Ralleigh . . . what a waste."

The anger bubbled up even higher, warming her from the inside. A gust of wind blew around her legs, and she glanced behind her over the wall but the lightness was gone. She turned back to Pamela with new resolve. Fuck freedom.

She made her voice hard.

"That's bullshit. You wanted Teddy, and you did what you had to do to get him."

The cold smile returned. "We live in a meritocracy. Initiative is rewarded."

Sadie couldn't take it anymore. "But murder isn't."

Anger flashed across Pamela's face.

"Did you kill Anna too?"

Pamela took a step toward Sadie. "I did what had to be done."

"She was a kid. What threat could she possibly have been to you?"

Sadie could have sworn she saw a hint of pain in Pamela's eyes, but it was gone just as quickly as it had come. "Like I said, I did what had to be done. Now we're done talking. Jump."

"Screw you."

Pamela smirked. "See now, Ms. Marlowe. That's why I had to make sure your mother didn't end up with Teddy Cranston, and that's why I had to make sure her niece didn't end up marrying my son. I was not about to let the Cranston family bloodline be polluted by filthy Ralleigh genes."

"Then why did you even bring me here? I didn't even know. I never would have found out." She took a deep breath as the last piece fell into place. "You wanted my family's money. I'm the heir. That's why I'm here."

"Despite your family's unsavory reputation, they've amassed quite a fortune. And once we have it, we'll have enough. More than the U.S. treasury. It'll be the smoothest coup in the history of modern government."

She smiled so wide, her cheekbones looked like they would crack in two.

"That's why you took my eggs."

Pamela rolled her eyes. "After you're gone, we'll spread a story that you ran away. And if in sixteen years, someone shows up claiming to be the long-lost last remaining heir to the Ralleigh fortune, then so be it. We'll even have the DNA to prove it. Now jump. Get on with it."

Sadie lifted her chin. "No."

"Do it now. Fly away, Ms. Marlowe."

She shook her head. "I'm not letting you do this. I'm not trash, and neither was my mother. But you know who is? Your son."

"Jump." Sadie could see the tendons jutting out of Pamela's neck. Her face flushed red.

"He's a drunk, worthless piece of scum who raped Olivia. He should be in jail."

"Shut your mouth, and jump."

"He's a rapist, and I'll tell everyone what he did! You raised a monster. How's that for polluting the Cranston family name?"

Pamela stepped toward her, her face now a deep, angry purple. She clapped her hands over her ears and screamed. "Stop talking and jump!"

Sadie took a deep breath and shouted as loud as she could: "Finn. Cranston. Is a—"

Before she could finish, Pamela lunged. Sadie watched her, frozen, as she came forward. Her blonde hair was blowing back off of her face, and in her eyes was a hatred so pure and concentrated that it took Sadie's breath away.

Everything moved in slow motion. Sadie slid to the side and Pamela's clawed fingers sliced through the air, stiff and contorted, like talons. They held eye contact for a split second as her weight carried her forward, pulling her closer to the edge. Pamela's mouth opened in dull surprise as the low stone wall took her out at the knees, then stretched wider in horror as she pitched forward into the darkness. She flailed, twisting back and reaching for Sadie, her face now a mask of naked fear. In spite of herself, Sadie reached back. It didn't have to end like this. Not with more death.

It was too late.

Sadie's fingers just barely grazed the papery skin at her throat before she fell, and then there was nothing. No sound. No scream. No splash as she hit the water. No cracking as she hit rock.

She was just gone.

For a moment, everything was silent. Then another wave crashed below, and a gust of wind blew Sadie back down off the wall and onto the roof. She collapsed to her knees and looked down into her hand, shivering with cold and fear and fumes of adrenaline.

In her palm was Pamela's monogrammed necklace, the clasp bent open at a grotesque angle, and the green stone glinting up at her in the moonlight like a mythological evil eye.

⌘

It took her seconds to get back down the stairs and onto the third floor. Whatever they had given her to make her want to jump had worn off, all of those suppressed emotions now flooding her body with white-hot energy. In the ceremony room, she wrenched the musket off of its wall mount, sending screws and bits of drywall raining down around her. She jammed it under one arm and took off.

She found Finn still sitting in his father's office. He was sitting at the desk, the Order's logbook open in front of him. He stared at a single page with wide, unblinking eyes.

She leveled the gun at him, but he didn't flinch.

"Give me the key, Finn, or I swear on that old noseless guy I will kill you."

Wordlessly, he reached into his pocket and pulled out the card. He laid it flat on the table.

"Take it."

She edged closer. The book was opened to a page she hadn't seen before.

"You were right, you know."

He motioned to the page, and Sadie leaned forward. On it was a list of all the potential members who had been deemed unsuitable. She saw her mother's name near the top, but Anna's wasn't on it.

"Mother told me she was unsuitable. She said I had to do it to keep the family strong and prove my loyalty. She said Anna was trying to trick me."

His face crumpled, and he put his head in his hands.

Sadie didn't lower the gun. "Pamela was the one who tricked you, Finn." She paused. "It wasn't your fault."

"Take the book," he said, pushing it across the desk toward her. "You'll need it."

When she put a hand on the book, he didn't let go.

"They'll kill you if you're not careful, Sadie. They'll find out where you are, and they'll kill you, too."

She grabbed the book and the key off of the table, and she ran.

Chapter 26

Sadie opened her eyes. Above her was a white ceiling with a single crack running across it. Dull and flat. Institutional. She took a deep breath and smelled the air. Disinfectant.

She tried to sit up but felt a hand on her shoulder. "Try to lie still, dear. You need to rest."

A figure hovered into view over her head, and she blinked until it came into focus. Nurse Brennan.

"You Ralleigh girls sure are accident-prone," the woman said, her forehead wrinkled in concern.

Sadie tried to respond, but all that came out was a low moan.

Nurse Brennan patted her arm and made a clucking sound. "Don't try to talk too much. You must have had quite a night."

She felt panic start to creep up the back of her throat, and she swallowed again. She looked around the room. No cops. No security. It was all wrong.

"Why haven't you called the police? We have to stop them."

The nurse frowned and patted Sadie's hand. "It's normal to be a bit confused, so don't you worry about it. I don't think the police are necessary for a bump on the head, though. You're safe here. Don't you remember anything that happened?"

Sadie shook her head—a lie. A part of her could still feel the icy stones beneath her feet, and she could see every inch of Pamela's face as she went over the edge. But after that—after Finn and the book, it all just faded to black.

"Well, a little short-term memory loss is certainly understandable, considering everything you had in your system."

"How did I get here?"

The woman raised an eyebrow. "Jeremy Wood found you on the beach over by Graff. You were passed out cold in nothing but a cocktail dress." She clucked disapprovingly. "You're lucky you didn't get hypothermia. You don't remember how you ended up out there either?"

Sadie didn't answer.

"Well, there's something else I should tell you, as I was required to report it to the Dean." The woman took a deep breath. "When you first regained consciousness, you were acting very erratically, so we did a tox screen. It looks like you were on some pretty heavy pharmaceutical drugs last night." She laid a hand on Sadie's arm and arranged her features into a look of concerned disappointment. "Mixing drugs and alcohol is very dangerous, dear. You very easily could have died. Should have, maybe."

Sadie's mind raced. So Finn hadn't been bluffing. She looked down at her hands, feigning shame. "I'm sorry."

The woman patted her arm again, then busied herself around the room.

Sadie closed her eyes and laid her head back against the pillow.

"Oh dear, are you tired? I was going to go send your friends in— Jeremy and Jessica Harris have been here all night, would you believe that? But I can tell them to come back."

Sadie shook her head vigorously and waved at her to bring them in.

Jessica and Jeremy both looked like they had been awake for days. Jessica's light brown hair lay flat and lifeless against her forehead, and Jeremy's eyes were puffy and bloodshot. They were both smiling.

Jessica ran immediately to the bedside and hugged Sadie hard. "Forgive me?" she said into her shoulder. "I can't believe I stayed in that closet, I fu—"

"No way, Jess. I'm the one who should be apologizing. I never should have gotten you involved in this. I knew how dangerous they were. I wasn't thinking straight."

Sadie patted her back and looked over her shoulder at Jeremy, who stood a few steps away. He had a sad smile on his face, but it was masking something else that hovered just below the surface. Anger, or maybe guilt. He had an old gray duffel bag draped over his shoulder, and he was still dressed in the gray wool slacks he had worn to the party. Dirty now, the cuffs caked with crusted sand.

"How did you guys find me?"

Jeremy nodded to Jessica. "After they took you, they left the doors unlocked. They must have thought you were alone. Jessica came and found me and told me what you guys had done, and we got a ride back to Graff from the twins' driver. We didn't know if we would catch up with you in time, but we didn't know what else to do. We couldn't call the police—we didn't even know if they would be on our side. We were just outside the tower when we heard you on the roof. You were screaming, and I—"

His voice caught, and he looked away. Sadie grabbed his hand and squeezed.

"I'm okay now."

He met her eyes. "You don't understand. We saw someone fall. We thought you were dead."

Sadie opened her mouth, but before she could speak his arms were around her. She pulled him close, as everything around them fell away.

Finally, Jessica coughed uncomfortably, and they broke away.

"Sorry, Jess." Jeremy grinned, and the heaviness in the room seemed to dissolve. Jessica punched him in the arm.

"It's okay. The image of you guys sucking face might haunt my nightmares for awhile, but I'll get over it."

Sadie raised an eyebrow. "You guys friends now?"

Jessica nodded. "Being two halves of one badass rescue team will do that."

"So how did you, anyway? Rescue me."

"Um . . . " Jessica trailed off, looking to Jeremy for help.

"When we saw someone fall . . . I can't tell you how that felt." His voice was suddenly hoarse. "I wanted to kill all of them. I didn't care. Before we could get inside the tower you burst through the door looking completely insane. You were holding a huge musket, some musty old book, and a broken necklace, and you just collapsed on the ground. All we did was take it from there."

Sadie nodded toward the door. "And the nurse?"

"We lied because we didn't know what else to do," Jessica said. "I mean, someone fell off that ledge, and we had to figure out what you wanted to do before we told anyone. You really don't remember seeing us last night?"

Sadie shook her head. "I remember being glad to be outside of that hellhole, but that's it."

"What about before that? Did you find out anything? Did Teddy admit to killing Anna and your mom?"

She closed her eyes and shuffled through the flashes of memory. "He was behind the eugenics plot, but not the murders . . . at least not directly." She took a deep breath. "It was Pamela Cranston, Finn's mom. She and my mom were best friends in high school, but Pamela was jealous. She faked my mom's blood test so she would get kicked out of the Sullas, and Pamela could marry Teddy instead. Then when Anna came and Finn fell in love with her, Pamela convinced him she was unsuitable, too."

"Holy . . . " Jeremy collapsed into a chair and put his head in his hands. "Finn killed Anna?"

Sadie nodded. "I think they just wanted to make her look crazy, like they did to my mom. I bet they drugged her too, but when she jumped she didn't survive the fall. Whatever they gave me made me feel weightless—like I could fly." She looked down at her hands. "And I wanted to."

Jeremy lifted his head, eyes bright with anger. "I can't believe I didn't see it. I knew Finn was a creep—all those comments he made about you. But I never thought he was capable of doing something like that."

Sadie squeezed his hand. "You saved my life. That's all you should be thinking about."

She traced the crack in the ceiling with her eyes and wondered what the hell they were going to do. She might have killed someone—someone people would miss—and her only defense was so far-fetched she knew no one would ever believe her.

Suddenly she felt an overwhelming sense of déjà vu: the bed, the dingy room, the feeling of dread. It was all familiar. She closed her eyes as the realization washed over her. She was in the exact same position her mom had been in twenty years ago when she had woken up—probably in this exact same room.

She felt Jeremy's hand on hers and opened her eyes. He was still looking down at her, the concern showing plainly on his face. "What's wrong? Do you want me to get the nurse?"

"No, it's okay. I just don't know what I'm going to do." She looked into his eyes. "Pamela Cranston is probably dead, and I'm no one. Why would anyone ever believe my story when they find out I had something to do with it?"

Jeremy's face changed.

She struggled to sit up. "What is it?"

He picked up the duffel bag and placed it carefully on the bed. It was an old lacrosse bag, and Sadie could see his last name written on the side in cracked white letters. He unzipped it slowly and pulled back the flap.

Her eyes widened and she reached out a hand to touch it, just to make sure it was really there. "You kept the book."

"It seemed important, and I knew we would need proof. How did you even get it?"

Sadie saw Finn in her mind, the tortured expression that had flickered across his face when he realized what he had done. "Finn gave it to me after he realized what his mom made him do."

"Seriously?"

She nodded. "She manipulated him—convinced him he was doing the honorable thing for their family. He's so screwed up, you should have seen him when he figured it out."

For a few moments, no one spoke. Then Sadie sighed.

"Also, I had a gun."

Jessica flopped down on the bed next to her. "So what are you going to do with it? Use it to blackmail the Cranstons into turning themselves in? Scan the whole thing and put it online?"

Sadie thought for a moment. The book gave her everything she needed to expose them. She could tell everyone what had happened to her mom and to Anna, and she could take down the Order so no one like the Cranstons could ever take advantage of it again. She thought about the other girls—Lillian, Brett, and Olivia, even Thayer—and felt a pang of regret. They would get dragged through the mud if this went public, and from what she had seen in the hospital basement, they were all victims, too. But staying quiet let the bad guys win. Someone had to turn on the lights.

Sadie took a deep breath. "I'm going to take it to someone who will know what to do." She paused, grim satisfaction spreading over her. "And then I'm going to tell the whole fucking world."

❧

That was the plan, anyway. Before things got complicated. The nurse puttered into the room an hour later with a hot breakfast and shooed them down the hall to the nurses' lounge. There were a few couches and a TV, and Sadie instantly felt better being away from that hospital bed. Jeremy dragged a coffee table close to the couch and set down her tray.

She glanced down at the plate of eggs and bacon, and something deep down in her stomach stirred. She tucked in eagerly, and they both watched in stunned silence as she devoured the whole thing. When she finally set her fork down, they were staring at her, jaws hanging open.

"I guess this means you're going to be okay then?" Jessica said with a grin.

Sadie shrugged. "Guess so." She smiled and glanced at Jeremy, but something about his posture stopped her cold. His entire body was tense, and he was staring, unblinking, toward the door. His shoulders were hunched like he was getting ready to pounce, and he was slowly inching closer toward her on the couch.

She followed his line of sight. Two men were standing in the doorway, both in black suits and dark sunglasses. They stood at attention with their wrists crossed in front of their bodies, and she knew instantly who they were. Secret Service.

One of them spoke. "Senator Cranston would like to speak with you privately, Ms. Marlowe. Please ask your friends to wait in the hall."

She looked at Jeremy, and his eyes narrowed. Jessica just stared toward the door, looking too scared to move.

"No." Sadie sat up straighter on the couch and squared her shoulders. "If he gets to have his muscle with him, then so do I." She spoke loudly, trying to sound confident, but her voice trembled. "We do this on my terms."

The men didn't move, and the five of them sat and stared at each other for a long time. Finally a voice murmured in the hallway, and the men parted. Sumner Cranston walked through the door between them.

When Sadie saw him, her whole body started to vibrate. Jeremy put a hand on her arm to steady her, but she could see the tension in every muscle in his neck and shoulders.

"Come near her, and I'll kill you," Jeremy said.

Sumner nodded toward Sadie. "Sounds like she's the one I should be worried about." He had bags under his eyes, and his posture sagged like he had a million pounds resting on his shoulders. He held up his hands submissively. "But I'm not here to hurt you, Sadie. I know what my family did to you and your mother. I want to help."

Sadie's lip curled. Jeremy started to stand, but she pulled him back down. "Hear him out," she murmured. Some sick part of her wanted to see him try to explain himself.

Sumner walked slowly across the room to face them. He looked older than she remembered from the football reception, and his skin hung in deep wrinkles on what was probably once a handsome face. He was tall, like Teddy, but his gut ballooned like rising dough over the top of a thin black belt, and his forehead was shiny with sweat. It was the almighty "Zeus." Clammy and soft.

"May I sit down?" He motioned toward one of the empty chairs.

"I'd prefer you didn't."

He sat down anyway and set a briefcase on the table between them. "I'll make this quick, since I know you've just been through an awful ordeal. We all have."

She saw Pamela's body pitching forward over the ledge, and her hands started to tremble. She clasped her hands tightly together to keep them from shaking.

"I'm deeply sorry for the trouble my daughter-in-law put you through."

Sadie almost choked. "Trouble?" She felt her voice rising out of her control. "If you knew what they did, and you did nothing, then you're just as much to blame. And don't even get me started on that room in the hospital. You're a sick bastard who's playing God, and I'm going to make sure you pay for that."

Sumner held her gaze. "Our methods are extreme, but so are the problems we're up against. Whether the ends justify the means is a matter of philosophy, and I happen to think that in this case they do. I can see you're of the opposite opinion. It's possible my son has taken the means a bit too far, but when you're a parent you'll realize that our children do not always make us proud. Still, it is our duty to stand by them." He looked her in the eye and spoke slowly. "My daughter-in-law is a sick woman, and it's clear her demons have spread to my grandson. I had my suspicions about what happened to your mother back then, but I wasn't sure until last year when Anna Ralleigh went missing. You're right that I should have stopped them." He spread his hands in an apologetic gesture. "But a man protects his family. At all costs."

Sadie gritted her teeth. "Women do that, too. And my family deserves retribution."

He sighed. "After you've heard what I have to say, you can make your own decision about how you would like to proceed."

Sadie crossed her arms.

"After your mother was deemed unsuitable, she disappeared. Her drug problems started soon after, but we had nothing to do with that. It's my belief that Pamela paid one of our lab technicians to rig the test, but Maylynne's spiral into darkness was an outcome no one could have predicted."

"How did you find me?"

"There are a certain number of American families that hold a large percentage of the nation's wealth, and the goals of the Order are dependent on those families holding together. After Maylynne ran away, and we lost Anna too, we needed someone else from your lineage. You were the only one left. We knew it was a risk, given your mother's complicated history, but we had to give it a chance."

"The scholarship. You rigged the whole thing."

"We sponsored your education, yes. But I like to think that was a mutually beneficial scenario."

"And the eggs?"

He at least had the grace to look uncomfortable. "An insurance policy. In case you were also . . . lost."

"But there were hundreds in that room. Why all the rest?"

"Research, and population control. With such a small gene pool, we need to carefully monitor how we combine them to make sure we maintain sufficient genetic variation. Inbreeding has led to the downfall of some of the world's most powerful dynasties."

Sadie felt sick to her stomach, and she held up a hand. "I don't want to hear anymore."

"I'm telling you all of this because you needed to know the truth. And I need something from you in return."

He spoke the next words slowly and carefully. "You have sensitive information—all of you do—and I'm sure you can understand that it's very important to me, and to many of my associates, that information stays between us."

She narrowed her eyes. Here it comes. Out of the corner of her eye, she saw Jeremy slide the duffel bag out of view behind the couch.

When she didn't respond, Sumner reached forward. He unlocked the briefcase and lifted its lid. Instinctively, the three of them leaned forward and looked inside. At the bottom was a leather portfolio.

"Open it."

She spread it open on her lap. In the left pocket was a thick document printed in small, even type. In the right pocket was a check. She looked up. "What the hell is this?"

"I know you've been through a lot, Sadie. And I don't just mean last night. I know about your family, your financial problems."

That you caused.

"I want to make things right, and I'm willing to make keeping our family secrets worth your while."

A fresh wave of rage coursed through her. "You think you can buy me just because you admit you feel bad about it?" Her voice rose higher, and with effort she brought it back under control. "And I don't need your money, anyway. Apparently I'm the heir to some long-lost great American fortune, which is the only reason I'm even here."

His face hardened. "That's true, but you'll never see a dime of it. It's been tied up in litigation since Anna died, and we have the resources to make sure it stays that way for a very long time. If we have to produce another heir, we will."

Before she could process that, he stood up.

"Think it over. My lawyer will come by tomorrow to pick up the signed confidentiality contract, and after that I'll clear the check." He looked at Jeremy and Jessica. "There are conditions included in the confidentiality agreement that also hold you accountable for your friends' actions. Should either of them choose to breach the contract you will be held personally accountable." He held out a hand for her to shake.

The three of them just stared as his hand hovered motionless a few feet from their faces. No one moved. With a resigned shrug he picked up the empty briefcase and walked toward the door.

"Wait," Sadie said. "What happened to Pamela Cranston? Is she dead?"

Sumner turned back. "It's a big ocean, Ms. Marlowe. I don't think anyone will be hearing from Pamela again. We'll make sure of that."

He walked out of the room, the secret service agents trailing in his wake. Then they were alone.

They sat in silence for a few moments until finally Jessica spoke.

"I can't handle it, Sadie. You have to at least look at the check."

Sadie sighed. "It doesn't matter, Jess. These people have to pay for what they did. And I don't mean with money."

Jessica shrugged. "I know. But it can't hurt to look, right?"

Sadie looked at Jeremy, but he shook his head.

"If you're not going to take it, wouldn't you rather just not know?"

She bit her lip and looked down at her lap. Slowly she reached down and pulled it from the folder. It was just a regular check—light blue paper with watermarks across the back. She flipped it over. Jeremy made a noise that was somewhere between coughing and gagging.

"How much?" Jessica leaned forward. "Come on, you have to tell me now that you both know."

Sadie looked up. "A million dollars." She watched as the color slowly drained from Jessica's face.

"What are you going to do?" Jeremy asked.

She leaned back against the cushions and looked down at the check in her hands. She looked from Jeremy to Jessica and back again.

"I think it's obvious, right?"

⁊

Ten minutes later, she called Charlie Ronson. When she told her she had a story she might want to run, Charlie sounded only mildly interested. But when she explained it had to do with the Cranston family, Graff, and an unsolved murder, the line went silent.

"Sit tight. Don't talk about this to anyone—especially on the phone," Charlie finally said. "I'll be at Keating in less than two hours."

Charlie sat on a plastic folding chair in the infirmary's lounge for four hours that day, while Sadie and Jeremy told her the whole story, from start to finish. She typed notes furiously on her silver laptop and looked up only to ask questions. As they talked, her face started to look pale, and by the time Sadie was finished, she looked like she might be in shock.

By the time she finally left, Jeremy's duffel bag slung carefully over one shoulder, Sadie knew she had officially crossed over. The story was out. No turning back.

Chapter 27

She left Keating the next day. Her dad got on a plane hours after she called, and at 5:30 the next morning, she was packed and ready to meet him at the airport. She didn't sleep, and when she ran out of things to do she sat in her empty half of the room, listening as the twins tossed and turned. After she had told them, Gwen had stayed quiet for a long moment, then hugged her so tight it had been hard to breathe. Trix had made her promise she could play Sadie in the movie whenever she sold the rights.

She heard a knock on the door and stood up. Jeremy was outside with a bag slung over his shoulder, eyes still puffy and red. Charlie had promised to wait a few days to run the story, and in the meantime, Sadie and Jeremy wanted to get as far away from Keating as possible. It was going to be anonymous, but she knew anyone who mattered would know where the story had come from.

Jessica was back in Chicago already, having taken a redeye late last night, and Jeremy was coming to Portland for the week to stay with Sadie and her dad. Charlie had released just enough information to a contact she had at the FBI so that all three of their families would be protected for the foreseeable future.

"You ready to go?" Jeremy raised his eyebrows. Sadie turned and glanced at the twins one last time, then followed him into the hallway and shut the door behind her.

"Just give me one second, okay? There's something I have to do."

Down the hall, Sadie knelt in front of Brett's door and slid the sealed envelope through the crack. She stood and waited, part of her hoping Brett was awake, but there was no sound. She walked back to Jeremy and took his outstretched hand. He pulled her in toward him and wrapped his arms around her.

"What did the letter say?"

She buried her face into his chest and shut her eyes. "Just that I'm sorry."

✧

Outside, day was just beginning to break. A watery, blue haze of early morning sunshine was just starting to gather on the horizon, and the quad was completely still. A taxi idled on the circular drive, its headlights slicing through the darkness and dissipating into the fog. Behind it sat an unmarked black SUV.

As Jeremy loaded their bags into the trunk of the cab, her eyes wandered the quad, taking it in one last time. It looked exactly like it had that first day Sadie's dad had driven them through the doors, but now she could see the flaws. The stone buildings were heavy and staid, and dying brown vines clung to the walls like shriveled tendons. Even the lawn looked black in the dim light, the stone benches scattered across it like crumbling headstones. Across the quad, something caught her eye. Movement, and a flash of white.

"Be right back, okay?"

Jeremy threw the last bag into the trunk, then rubbed his hands together against the cold. "You sure? I can come with you if you want."

She shook her head. "I'll be careful."

She crossed the lawn, watching the figure as it stood in front of Anna's bench, arms full of deep red roses. In the early light, her blonde hair looked almost white.

Sadie stood next to her.

"You don't have to explain anything, Sadie. You did what you had to do. I wish I could say the same thing."

"When did you know?"

"I didn't"—Thayer didn't turn her head—"and I guess I did. Some part of me, anyway. He lied about where he was that night, and I covered for him, but I just didn't want to see it. I guess I couldn't." Thayer took a deep breath. "He's going to turn himself in."

They stood in silence for a moment, until finally Thayer leaned forward and laid the flowers on the bench. She faced Sadie, and for the first time since they had met, Sadie felt like she really saw her. She had no makeup on, and she wore her coat over an old gray shirt stamped with the Keating crest. Her hair was rumpled with sleep, and she had deep bags under her eyes. She really was beautiful.

"How often do you do this? With the flowers."

"Every week." Her eyes welled up with tears, and Sadie took a step forward to hug her, but Thayer backed away.

"So you're going home?" Thayer jerked her chin toward the car and wiped her nose with the back of her hand.

Sadie nodded. "Jeremy's coming, too."

"That's good." She held out a hand and Sadie shook it. "Good luck, Portland."

Before Sadie had taken more than a few steps away, she stopped and turned. "You know, maybe you should, too."

Thayer raised an eyebrow.

"Go home, I mean. Just for a few days. Things might get pretty intense around here."

Sadie saw recognition flicker across her face, and she knew Finn must have told her about the book. She knew what was coming.

As Sadie watched, she took a deep breath and squared her shoulders, and just like that, the old Thayer was back. For the first time though, Sadie could see that the mask she wore wasn't cruelty, or snobbery, or any of the other things Sadie had thought about her since September. It was strength. Thayer was surviving, the only way she knew how.

She smiled then, and Sadie could see the sadness in her eyes.

"I can't leave, honey,"—she spread her arms wide—"I'm already home."

Chapter 28

Sadie got the letter a year later. It was a clean, white envelope with an orange and navy seal in the upper left corner. Her hands shook as she turned it over and slowly slid a finger underneath the flap. She pulled out the single sheet of paper and laid it flat on the table in front of her. She took a deep breath, exhaled, and flipped it over.

"I got in!" she yelled, jumping up and running into the den, the paper held over her head like a standard. Her dad was sitting on the couch, a sandwich poised inches from his mouth.

"I got into UVA!" she cried, thrusting the paper toward him and dancing a little jig in front of the TV.

Her dad frowned. "A letter? What, Coach McHenry couldn't pick up the phone?" He grinned and stood up to give her a hug. "I knew you would, sweetheart. Congratulations. And as long as she comes through with that promise of a full scholarship, you'll actually be able to go." He gave her a sad smile, and she dropped her arms to her sides.

"She will, Dad. Coach Fitz told me it was a done deal as long as I got in." She punched him in the shoulder. "And, this means I can accept that summer internship Charlie offered at the *National*, too. So quit worrying."

"I'm always worrying, Sadie. The idea of you going back there—it scares me. Hell, the idea of you being more than ten yards away at any given time scares me."

She let her head fall to the side. "I'm safe now, Dad. I promise." She gave him another quick hug. When she had told him what had really happened to her mother, he had cried for three days. Sometimes it had seemed like he was grieving all over again, but at others what he was going through had seemed almost like relief. He finally had answers. He could finally let her go.

She ran up the stairs to her room and flopped down on her bed. There was a stack of magazines on her bedside table, and the cover of the one on top showed Trix and Gwen sitting on the pavement outside a bar in London, both their heads thrown back with laughter. They had their legs splayed awkwardly in front of them like a pair of rag dolls, and there was a third girl sitting cross-legged on Gwen's other side. They were holding hands. Every time she saw the photo, she couldn't help but smile.

After Keating was shut down during the investigation, they had both started attending a public school in England. Sadie loved thinking about how Ellen Bennett must have reacted to that news. The tabloids had been breathlessly reporting every second of Gwen's coming out, and now her new relationship with one of her classmates. They all exchanged e-mails often, and Sadie and Jessica had a standing offer to visit both of the twins in London as soon as the FBI decided it was safe for them to travel without a security detail.

Out of habit, Sadie glanced out the window and saw the usual black SUV parked on the street in front of their house. "Real subtle, guys," she muttered.

Ever since Charlie's story ran, the FBI had been a constant presence. Her name had never been released, but until the Cranstons were found and brought to trial, they wanted to make sure Sadie and her dad were protected. By now, she barely even noticed they were there, but she hoped they would back off soon. Dragging two beefy guys in black suits to a bunch of college parties was going to be really embarrassing.

The phone rang.

"Did you get in?" Sadie said, as soon as she picked up the receiver. "Yes! You?"

"Um, duh. Otherwise I so wouldn't have answered." Sadie laughed and she heard Jessica squeal with happiness.

"Oh my god, I can't wait. How's everything in Portland?"

"Pretty good. My dad's still kinda shell-shocked, but at least we've started occasionally talking about other topics."

A pause. "Do the police have any leads on the Cranstons yet?"

Sadie's mood darkened. "Not yet. I promise I'll tell you as soon as I hear anything, though. For a long time, they thought they were both hiding out in Europe or something, but the police there still can't find them." The police had found plenty of evidence to corroborate Sadie's story, but without Teddy and Sumner, there wasn't much they could do about it. The files and computers in the hospital basement had been removed long before the police got there, but the equipment was left, and it had been enough. They had even found Sadie's DNA on the operating table. The closet with the metal canisters was empty, too. They told Sadie chances were good her eggs had been destroyed.

"And Pamela?"

"Nope. Still nothing."

The line went silent.

After the story broke, Sumner and Teddy had both disappeared, and Sadie knew that wherever they were hiding, they would stay there for a very long time. They had left Finn behind, and he was on house arrest in Virginia. She couldn't help but feel a little sorry for him. What he had done was awful, and he needed to pay the consequences, but he had lost his mom, too.

She tried to make her voice light. "Enough about them, though—I'll be happy if I never hear the name Cranston again."

She heard Jessica sigh. "God, me too. Hey, how's Jeremy?"

Sadie smiled into the phone. "Really, really good. He's coming to visit this weekend, and then I'm flying down to San Diego for Christmas with his family."

"That's so awesome, Sadie. Does he know where he's going to be next year yet?"

"No, but I am dying to know what he's going to decide. He already has offers from Maryland and Virginia, though, so either way at least he'll be close."

"Perfect," Jessica said. "I just can't wait for senior year to be over. My mom signed us up for weekly mother-daughter ballet classes. I need to get out of this house."

Sadie laughed. "Me too. It'll be just like old times, except, you know . . . " She trailed off. "Hey speaking of which, you know UVA was founded by Thomas Jefferson, right?"

Jessica groaned. "Oh, god. Don't remind me. I'd really rather not have anything else to do with that guy—ever."

Sadie snickered. "He wasn't so bad. The whole Order thing really wasn't his fault, you know? He just underestimated how terrible people can be. Not everyone can handle having that kind of power without abusing it."

"I guess."

Sadie flipped over so she was lying on her stomach. "So what do you think college will be like?"

"Umm, probably kind of like boarding school was, but with coed dorms and frat guys with STDs?"

Sadie laughed and rolled back onto her side. "You're probably right. But I mean, you know what the real difference is, right? According to my sources, it's the highlight of every good Keating grad's college career . . . "

For a moment, Jessica didn't answer. When she did she sounded horrified. "You're joking, right?"

Sadie laughed into the phone. "Of course, you skank. I wouldn't touch Greek life with a ten-foot pole."

She heard Jessica exhale. "Thank god. I love you to death, Sadie—you know that—but if you ever join a sorority, I will seriously kill you."

Acknowledgments

I wish I could say this book came to be over a month-long retreat in the mountains, flowing from my fingertips while a fire crackled and a bottle of wine decanted. That's how I always pictured the life of a writer: secluded, romantic, and a little drunk.

But alas, *Poor Little Dead Girls'* conception was clumsy and haphazard, written in snippets at coffee shops and kitchen tables, on trains and city buses. Without the help of friends, family, and colleagues, it may never have come to be at all.

I would like to thank my agent, Lauren MacLeod, as well as her wonderful, unbelievably supportive community of authors. Thanks too, to Jacquelyn Mitchard and everyone at Merit Press and Adams Media for taking a chance and bringing this creepy little book to life.

To my husband and family, thank you for supporting me, believing in me, putting up with me, and enabling my delusions of grandeur. And finally to my son, Lincoln, who when this was written was still just a few strands of very redheaded DNA: I can't wait until you're old enough to read it. You're going to be so embarrassed.

About the Author

Lizzie Friend is a Palo Alto native who now lives in Chicago with her husband and son. By day, she's an analyst who writes about things that aren't nearly as much fun as political conspiracies; dark, writhing underbellies; and other important stuff like the prom. *Poor Little Dead Girls* is her first novel.